House on Fire

Charles Foran

House on Fire
a novel

Harper*Flamingo*Canada

Canadian Cataloguing in Publication Data

Foran, Charles, 1960–
House on fire

ISBN 0-00-224551-5

I. Title.

PS8561.O63504H68 2001   C813'.54
C00-932362-7
PR9199.3.F67H68 2001

01 02 03 04 HC 4 3 2 1

Printed and bound in the United States
Set in Melior

to David Bierk

The self is a house on fire.
Get out, quickly.

The Buddha

Just do it.

Nike

Author's Note

I magining Tibet has long been a preoccupation in the West. Though the country I call Gyatso is indeed a mirror of that nation, it is only one reflection. Thus, things in the book don't quite match things in the world. The streets of Bon aren't intended to be superimposed on the streets of Lhasa; the dogs of Tibet, to the best of my knowledge, do not carry the same philosophical weight as the dogs of Gyatso. As for the characters, a few borrowings from headlines aside, they all belong, with the dogs and the streets, in the world of the book.

Contents

Prologue

At first she doesn't understand what he wants.

"Leave it on," he says again.

She reaches behind her neck with both hands to unclasp the chain. "Leave what?" she asks. She sees where his gaze has settled. "Why would I do this?"

"Because it's sexy. Because it's fun. Catholics never have any—"

She pronounces his name in censure.

"I love how you say my name," he sighs.

The silver cross, a confirmation gift from her grandmother, is coiled onto the end table. She joins him in bed.

"And the window?" he tries. "Does it have to be open?"

"I like the heat."

"It's as if—"

"A hair dryer is blowing in your face? Poor you."

They kiss. She likes how he kisses. She likes how he rests a hand, easy and at home, on her hip.

"You know me so well, don't you?"

"Don't tease."

"Then you must know I'm wild about the nape of your neck," he says, kissing her there.

"Even without the cross?"

"Wild about your amah arms. All that floor scrubbing and clothes washing."

She giggles at the brush of his lips over her forearms—she is ticklish in unusual spots; he has found most of them—and runs her fingers through his hair.

"Crazy about your—" He rolls her onto her stomach.

"Moles?" she guesses.

"The map of a landscape. The path to pleasure."

She feels him kissing the moles on her shoulders and back.

"And me," he murmurs. "Is there nothing you're crazy about?"

High forehead and rainy eyes, boyish grin and glossy lips. Long torso and flat tummy. Strong, insistent thighs. "Nothing I can say out loud," she answers, fighting a blush.

"Then I'll talk some more."

To end his talking, she kisses him a certain way.

Afterwards, swimming in the sweat of their bodies, she presses her palm over his chest. His heart pounds in rhythm with hers, another comfort.

"Are you real?" she asks quietly.

He makes a joke. Her need to be reassured confuses him, she recognizes. Her need shames her.

"I am real."

"And the kids?"

"Safe and sound. And cool, lucky them."

"My life?"

"Not a dream," he assures her. "Not a fantasy."

He is suffering, she can tell: face flush, eyes stinging. "Go," she says. "Close the window."

All at once the air is empty of the scents of cooking oil and diesel, the honk of ships in the harbour below and the buzz of cicadas farther up the hill.

"Why *do* you love me?" he asks.

Because you are kind and generous and hope to be better. Because you had the strength of character to let yourself fall for a girl like me. "Because you want to smoke a cigarette right now," she replies. "But you won't."

"Banned, in my own house."

"A disgusting habit."

"Maybe I'll light up on the balcony."

Why does this make her mad? "Men are always dissatisfied," she offers.

"And women aren't?"

"Men always want more than they have, without ever know-ing what they want more of."

"And women?"

"Please promise me," she says, unable to express the senti-ment, the fear, any better.

"Promise you?"

"Please ..."

He promises blindly.

She wants, in effect, to say only this: *We are so blessed.* And she does. She wants him to answer: *I get it. I won't act stupidly. I won't mess up what we have.*

But he can't, can he? Not yet.

She must be patient.

Part I

All Hallow E'en

Chapter One

H e answered the knock. To do so, he had to be somewhere. He had to be in a certain place on a specific date, at an exact time; he had to be awake. Dominic's head was fogged, his thoughts floating, but he still possessed the information. Ten-fifteen in the morning. October 31, 1999. Gyatso. Never mind those plain facts; he was in the lost paradise! The sky kingdom. The one outstanding mystery. The world might be forever shrinking—no country was foreign to any self-respecting corporation—but Gyatso constituted the last frontier. Most of it, of course, remained an abstraction. Most of it, he had decided, flying over the eastern half of the country, *was* an abstraction—an abstract of mountains. How big were the mountains? Higher than the Rockies. More sprawling than the Alps. These, after all, were the Himalayas. This, after all, was the heart of the heart of the continent. On that same flight he had gazed not far below at the incisor peaks and fluted pinnacles, the vertical flood plains of ice, and decided that the mountains never ended. They were eternal. A man or woman attempting to cross the range, in contrast, would exhaust themselves. They would die.

He answered the knock. To do so, he couldn't be in bed fantasizing about a copper-skinned woman, her scent of pine cones. Anyway, what did Dominic know of the mountains of Gyatso? His familiarity was confined to one valley and the city it held. Fog rarely lay in the valley, he had been told, but when it did the surrounding peaks appeared isolated and adrift, islands scattered across a sea. Foothills stretched to the city boundaries. He had almost said they stretched to the city gates. But for the longest time the capital, Bon, hadn't needed a wall to keep its enemies at bay. The Himalayas had done nicely. The Himalayas

3

and the rasping air, the blinding sky. Now, though, town and valley were both occupied. While the invasion hadn't been a cakewalk, in the end flying machines and press-ganged roads, wirelesses and walkie-talkies had bypassed the natural defences and adjusted to the sky, the air. Soon, too, other invaders would barge in. Try slowing *them* down. E-mail and the Web, digital technology and satellite phones. Men with Powerbooks and business cards, vocabularies bragging of telecommunications markets and Internet content providers. Him, for example. Dominic Wilson, President, WilCor Communications, 32A Tower 2, Landmark Building. Central. Hong Kong.

He answered the knock. To do so, he had to rule out being trapped in the cold snows of a daydream. And Bon fed neither fantasy nor nightmare. Bon addled the brain with none of the usual stuff. He couldn't have pictured the city before landing at the airport six days ago. Movies sure hadn't done it justice. Again, he might have guessed this would be the case. For the rest of the world, the capital served more as metaphor than metropolis, some weird airborne palace, Oz at twelve thousand feet. Well, Bon wasn't Oz or a palace, but it definitely was strange.

"Mr. Dominic?"

A man looked down at him. That meant he was seated. On the couch. In the hotel lobby. Silly from the altitude? He hoped so; how else to explain the sensation?

"Mr. Sun," he replied, his voice amplified by fake marble floors and high ceilings, virtually no furniture.

"I knock on your door."

"I heard you."

"In your room," Sun said. "Upstairs. Fourth floor. Three times I knock. You not answer."

"I wasn't there."

"You were here?"

"In the lobby," Dominic agreed. "Smoking a cigarette. Enjoying the hustle and bustle."

The guide's cheek twitched. He glanced around the lobby, in

4

case he had somehow missed the hustle and bustle.

Dominic sat with his left hand in his pocket. The position wasn't comfortable, and struck many as affected—his Cary Grant pose, a friend once called it—but he had no choice. He had to keep his problem secret. He had to stop people from using it against him. He draped his other arm over the couch. "I was kidding. Not a single human being of any race has passed by in the last ten minutes. Just me and the doorman, and I'm pretty sure he is a statue."

Sun Nanping, to his credit, did not check to see if this was true.

"Even the clocks aren't moving," Dominic added, nodding to the display above the counter. "Beijing, New York, Paris, and Moscow, all stuck at noon. Or midnight, take your pick."

"Broken," Sun observed.

"It would seem so."

He should quit messing with the guy. Still, with the job well done, why not amuse himself? He was two hours from the flight back to Chek Lap Kok. He was eight hours from Esther and the kids.

"Speaking of time," Dominic said, standing up, "shouldn't we be high-tailing it out of town?"

"High-tail?"

"The airport—you're driving me, remember?"

"Ah." Mr. Sun nodded. "Complication," he announced.

"Yes?"

"Airplane is, ahem, full today."

"I'm not surprised," he answered, unhappy about the "ahem." "But I'm one of the lucky ones with a seat on that plane, aren't I? You arranged it yourself. You told me it was taken care of."

"Also, airport is, shall we say, closed."

The "shall we say" knotted his stomach. Sun Nanping was the worst liar Dominic had ever met. Every excuse or delay tactic, obfuscation or untruth reduced him to stuttery speech hiccuped with verbal fill. And yet the man headed up Bon

Tourism? Meaning he lied, more or less, for a living?

Dominic had been pondering his keeper for the better part of a week. He couldn't shake the conviction that Sun was decent. Damaged by what he did for a paycheque and complicit in a giant injustice, but decent still. How could he tell? Not by Sun's wardrobe. This morning, the bureau chief wore the same ill-fitting blue cotton jacket and baggy blue pants. Once a sort of revolutionary uniform, in 1999 the outfit worked only as kitschy fashion statement, best accompanied by the famous hat. Trendy taipans and their tai tais got their kicks sporting the costume at balls in Hong Kong's five-star hotels. Staff dutifully smiled at their post-handover cheek; friends laughed and silently regretted their own choices of Michael Jackson or the Monkey King. Worn unironically, however, the clothes amounted to an admission of crushing defeat: by finances, the age, one's own nature. Gym socks and black slippers confirmed that, for Sun Nanping, this was no joke—except, inevitably, of an existential sort.

Other officials in Gyatso boasted fake leather jackets and Nike sneakers. They packed cell phones in hip holsters and dangled Discman headsets from their necks. They smoked Marlboros. But those officials also offered private tours of authentic Gyatsian homes for twenty U.S., cash. They alluded to karaoke bars along the strip in southwest Bon. They let slip about girls from the mainland. Beautiful girls, and fresh—eighteen, some younger. Prices came out: fifty, never overnight. More expensive than Bangkok or Manila, but less than the Russian hookers at the Vacation Inn or anything for sale in Hong Kong or Tokyo.

Sun's face offered no better clues. His features were regular and his expressions were mild. Being near forty, he seemed a bedraggled twenty-five, his false youth propped up by a mop of hair that bounced with every step or emphatic gesture, and a frame strung together with wire. Even his eyes told little. Their one striking quality—glassy pupils that easily went black—could be found in some two billion southeast Asians, most arrestingly in the children.

"The airplane is full and the airport is closed," Dominic said, lighting another cigarette. "That does sound complicated."

"Maybe tomorrow will be better."

"Or the day after?"

"Maybe."

"I'd better check back in."

Sun Nanping skirted around a chair. "Vacation Inn is also, ahem, no vacancy," he said, blocking Dominic's path to the reception. "You cannot stay here."

"No vacancy?" Dominic repeated. He recalled his room. It lay halfway along a corridor. Ten doors per side: twenty rooms total. For the previous several nights, he'd had the wing to himself.

"Manager tells me this," Sun claimed.

"Or you, ahem, tell the manager?"

"Sorry?"

He saw little purpose in keeping the needling up. The decision, he recognized, had been made. Dominic wasn't flying out of Bon today. His stay at the Vacation Inn had ended. He slung his duffel bag off one shoulder and his computer case off the other. He had the adventure look down cold—a quilted parka with more pockets than a magician's coat, khaki pants and hiking boots, a knobby Briefling on the wrist and black Safaris tucked into the shirt collar—and figured such details mattered. The intended effect had been blunt; he was the West. Not some retro hippie in Gyatso to spiritually awaken, nor a human rights crusader armed with the truth that can set you free. Dominic Wilson was the *other* West. The market that refused to crash. The currency that wouldn't deflate.

The part had been fun to shop for, and fun to play. It had even worked, up to a point. What point was that? Now, apparently.

"Am I being arrested, Mr. Sun?" he asked with a stretched smile.

His guide ahemed.

"Are you accusing me of a crime?"

Sun Nanping's cheek twitched again.

"You think I've done something wrong?"

The Bon Tourism boss said nothing.

"Not that I have," Dominic said. "Done anything wrong, I mean." He paused to coax open his saliva glands. The third—fourth?—Scotch in the hotel bar last night had been a bad idea. Getting drunk at high altitude made for a ripping buzz and a ringing hangover.

"And you know who I am, right?" he added, the words inviting more ambiguity than intended. "You know why I am here."

"Yes?"

"I'm a tourist."

"Ah," Sun Nanping said. "In Gyatso to visit Kundun palace and Kata temple. Om monastery and U-Chen market."

"There you go."

"No other business in Bon, Mr. Dominic?"

"None at all. My business is all back in Hong Kong. We discussed what I did, didn't we? We had a long talk about it. This is—was—a vacation."

"Happy holidays," the man offered.

"So there's no reason to arrest me, is there?"

"Not arrest," Sun replied. "Airplane full. Airport closed."

To hide his crumbling poise, Dominic set off for the door. His boots clacked over the floor, a warning shot that jerked the doorman awake from his upright slumber. He hadn't gone far before Sun Nanping caught up.

"We have found you nice place to stay," the guide said. "Special hotel."

"In town?"

"Very close by."

He had cause to ask. The Vacation Inn was one of only two hotels in the capital deemed suitable for foreigners. The other, the notorious Bon Government Facility #1, had been dubbed "the Stink" by his guidebook.

"An authentic Gyatsian guesthouse?"

Sun didn't bother to answer.

"Or is it like the Vacation Inn here—another shining example of Shamo initiative in defiance of local resentment and back-wardness?"

"Shamo?"

Dominic cursed to himself. The term was not for all ears. Gyatsians were Gyatsians, plain and simple. But the Shamos went by a more globally recognized name, as did their behemoth nation. He had been scolded his first day in Bon for referring to them by that moniker. Forget, his scolder had lectured, who was who and where was where and what you thought you knew down there at sea level. Up here, nearly three miles above the good earth, the occupiers were called Shamos, the Gyatsian word for "shame," and they hailed from the bordering country of Shamdenpa, or "disgrace."

"You know what I mean," Dominic said as apology.

"I don't think so."

"It's Halloween, Sun. I have to take my kids trick-or-treating. My wife hates to do it, and I bought these special costumes. My children!" he cried, the uplift in his voice suggesting that Gabriella and Michael were racing across the lobby. "They're expecting me home by dinner."

"Hotel is special," the Shamo said, "because it is owned by army."

That shut him up.

"Army hotel for your service, Mr. Dominic."

Crude words—*screw you*, say—perched on his lips. But Dominic didn't curse; in this respect, if no other, he was his father's son. Sun Nanping, for that matter, had previously evinced zero capacity to gloat. He, too, seemed child to the parents who had reared him. Clearly, everyone was feeling the strain.

At the entrance they waited for the doorman to make ready for battle. This conscript even looked the part. He wore the costume of men from Kashang, a province celebrated for its tall, robust warriors whose laughing eyes and explosive smiles marked them as magnificently Gyatsian. Kashang garb included a fur hat and boots, hair wound in cockscombs of red yarn, a

leg-length sabre. That the doorman was neither tall nor robust—
he wasn't, in fact, Gyatsian—may have contributed to his
twitchiness. The threat of accidentally impaling himself on the
sword had to be weighing on his mind as well. And then there
was the parking lot, and who dwelt there, and whose task it was
to clear a path for guests without the aid of cattle prods or
pepper spray.

Dominic observed the enemy through the glass doors. Close
to the steps stood four hook-horned, broom-tailed yaks. These
animals always struck him as unlikely fixtures outside the
hotel. Central Bon lacked much good grazing, but it was a
savannah compared to the Vacation Inn grounds, a prairie of
asphalt. Though *The Rough Guide to Gyatso* claimed the thin-
air oxen were "sociable," whatever that meant, and went on
about how locals believed the beasts to be philosophers, forever
meditating on some event along the horizon, it also warned visitors to be wary.

About the dogs of Bon, the guidebook was more emphatic:
keep well away. A quick count put the number in the parking
lot at near twenty. Heads twisted to fire murderous glances back
at the entrance. Growls were low and steady, like distant lawn-
mowers.

Finally, Dominic noted the car idling near the gate. The vehicle would have been difficult to miss; it alone prevented the lot
from being deserted. Two men leaned against the hood. One
was Shamo. He hailed from a Triad action flick: toothpick and
mirror shades, gold chains and a stiletto fingernail. The other
was Gyatsian. He looked like who he was.

Sun Nanping spoke to the doorman. The warrior patted his
forehead with a cuff and reached for the handle. As he did,
Dominic made a connection.

"Was that your boy I saw in the park last night?" he asked
Sun Nanping.

A yak lifted its peeled-egg eyes to them. When Sun did not
move to cross the threshold, the doorman glanced in his direction. Shrugging, he released the handle.

"You saw...?" the Shamo replied weakly.

"In the park behind the Kundun. You were playing soccer with a small boy. He was maybe four, and had on a puffy jacket and an army hat. At least, I'm pretty sure it was you."

"You saw my son?"

"You weren't doing anything wrong," Dominic said, remembering the beauty of the image. The twilight had held them both. At first he could distinguish only their outlines, as though the light was being reflected off water instead of sky. But then the father had come forward. He put aside one troubling aspect of the memory—the child's gasps as he chased the ball.

"Gianbao," Sun confessed. "My boy's name is Gianbao."

Dominic could guess what the Shamo hoped to say without actually saying it. Sun Nanping felt responsible for another life; that responsibility mostly imbued him with purpose and joy, but sometimes also shook him the way one is shaken by serious illness. Still, he didn't want to have the discussion. Not here. Not now.

To end what he had started, Dominic indicated to the doorman. The open door welcomed in growls. The doorman saluted with gestures that started off slow and refined, wound up curt and impatient. *Would you please just go!* his expression pleaded. But Sun actually withdrew several steps, as if water was flooding into the lobby from outside.

"You saw me with Gianbao in the park?" he said.

"I must have, right? Unless I'm clairvoyant."

"I knock three times on your door."

"This morning?"

"Three times."

"Only I wasn't there."

"You not there, but you still hear my knocks?"

A quote from "Ocean," Dominic's private rough guide to the country, popped into his head: "The imagination of Gyatso is infinite." But he hadn't been kidding; he didn't possess a mystical bone in his body. So much so, even a week in this carnival of the elusive and bizarre, where all children might be Buddhas and many adults spent years making crawling pilgrimages, where yaks were sagely scatological and dogs were revered as guides through the underworld, and where death, according to the culture's most sacred text, functioned as a three-step dance, with the dead self-aware and generally content, as much observers as participants, as much dancers as dance, and the end simply referred one back to the beginning, a caller's call to step up and begin again, begin again, begin again; even a week in Gyatso had done little to cause him to doubt the firmness of the ground beneath his feet. Worse, the literary reference would go unnoticed, and the conversation was already elliptical enough.

"I'll explain in the car," he said instead.

The Shamo didn't follow.

"The Bon Tourism car in the lot—isn't it waiting, like this doorman and those dogs, for us to exit the hotel? Aren't you in the process of not arresting me for unspecified crimes I didn't commit? Isn't your job to escort your non-prisoner to a special hotel run by the Shamo—oops—army?"

"Yes," Sun said. "I mean, no."

"Okay then."

What did the sentence about Gyatso's imagination mean? For all his rereadings of "Ocean," he still couldn't say. Maybe Bon hadn't produced a tremor, but Tashi Delag's short story had rocked him. The trip here had been the result. To that extent, he hadn't mislead Sun Nanping about his motives. His reasons for flying into Bon had nothing to do with WilCor Communications. His earlier reflection, while waiting on the couch, had been ridiculous. How could he be invading Gyatso? His briefcase lay on his desk in the Landmark Building. He hadn't bothered to pocket his phone. For the last week, Dominic had once again been a journalist, a job he last held more than fifteen years before, and then just for six months as part of his training in the old family business.

Chapter Two

"Keep moving."

"Shit."

"Don't hurry your walk," Sun said. "It shows you are afraid of them."

"But I am."

"Never show this."

Dominic, who rarely cursed, cursed again. He didn't like dogs; dogs, it appeared, didn't care much for him either. Asian mutts were especially nasty, deserving of the death squads rumoured to circulate the major centres after dark hunting strays. Dogs made strolls through Hong Kong's cemeteries and shipyards perilous, but the city was otherwise too congested, and too vertical, for the keeping of such pets. Gyatsians, of course, saw the animals differently.

The dogs had split into squads. Though a few just trotted along, like kids at the rear of a parade, most threw themselves into the menace. One mud-caked beast, ribs raw and eyes mad, kept hard at Dominic's heels. His duffel bag blocked his view, but every time he swung it clear the dog would snap. For a moment he locked gazes with his tormentor. Where its left ear should have been was a wound the pink of salmon sushi.

That dog leapt. Lunging at wrist, it got jacket cuff. Rearing up on its hind legs, the animal swivelled its head. Dominic smacked it on the snout. His palm hit flesh and returned bloody. The mutt sprang back, airborne and yelping, at the pain.

His own aggression startled him. "You're dead, dog," he said. But his outburst had a purpose: to show he could regain control of a situation marking him as a clown. Maybe Sun Nanping could show vulnerability in the lobby. Maybe Dominic could respond with decency—as he had, surely. Out here, however, sensitivity was not an option. He had to aim for the wound. Metaphorically, he now had to move in for the—

A sharp *pop*, not loud, dropped the animal onto its backside. Though it rose once, its legs soon buckled. The mouth settled into a smirk. One jerk, as if from an electric prod, and the dog lay still.

Its comrades scattered.

A sucking noise told Dominic where to look for the shooter. Wu Jing lowered the barrel of a rifle. Bon Tourism's "driver" gave him a smile devoid of well wishes or good dentistry. Cradling the weapon—a pellet-gun imitation of an AK-47, available in toy shops everywhere—the Shamo repositioned the toothpick in his mouth and pushed the shades further up his nose.

"Bagged another troublemaker, Wu?"

Wu Jing bared his fangs.

"Pellet should only stun dog," Sun said, hustling to keep pace. "Make him freeze. He wake up again."

"In time to steer a new soul through death?"

The head of Bon Tourism frowned. "Wake up again," he repeated without conviction.

Dominic, as surprised as anyone by his own remark, reached the car first. "Nice shirt," he told the driver, who now stood before him, jacket unzipped. He had a mind to wipe his bloody hand on Wu's shirt, a guaranteed tension escalator. But he also recognized that his reaction to the shooting lacked consistency. Hadn't he threatened aloud to end a dog's life?

"Do you know what it means?" he said, indicating the letters stencilled across Wu Jing's chest.

Wu kept grinning.

"Super Bowl thirty-three," Dominic read.

"America?" the Shamo answered in his squeaky voice.

"Sorry?"

"My shirt," Wu Jing said, "it say America, right?"

Air tickling the cavity where a tooth had not long ago been pulled collapsed the grin. The wince stretched skin taut over an already skeletal face. Wu had a goofy grin and, when he lifted the shades to scrape grit, protuberant eyes. A shaved head and wannabe gangster attitude granted him some edge, but a young man with a tooth infection and acne traces could only look so tough.

"Right," Dominic replied.

Anatman Sangmo, the bureau's "translator," stripped Dominic of his duffel bag and tossed it in the trunk. When Ant, as the giant was known, reached for the computer, Dominic held on tight. That induced a typical Gyatsian smile, a high-beam of teeth and gums in equal parts heart-warming and disconcerting, given how automatically the electricity went on, how indiscriminate its focus.

"Tashi Delag, Ant?"

"*Tashi delag,* Dominic," the translator answered.

The exchange was an inside joke, though both men knew better than to laugh. Dominic knew better than to assume any informality with Anatman Sangmo. He sensed no respect from the Gyatsian, even on the basis of their shared six-foot-three-inch frames. In turn, he felt scant desire to empathize with the middle-aged Bon Tourism employee whose physical prowess was celebrated around the capital.

"Are you okay about Wu Jing shooting that dog?" Dominic asked.

Ant shrugged.

"I thought Gyatsians were—"

"I do not care what you think."

"Because I'm a tourist?"

"Because you are fool," the translator clarified in his baritone, a perfect instrument for chanting Buddhist liturgy.

Dominic swallowed the jibe with difficulty. "Could you be more specific?"

Anatman Sangmo did not oblige. He also kept up his glare. Of all his qualities, this one unnerved Dominic the most: the Gyatsian's capacity for concentrated, hostile attention.

"Dogs," Sun Nanping warned.

Mutts were moving in on the car with slow, cautious steps.

The men opened their doors. Might Dominic have just blown an opportunity to find out what Bon Tourism had on him? What they knew about his "vacation" in the capital? While it hardly mattered—this was a footnote to the real story, already reported—he couldn't help but be curious.

The vehicle, a beige sedan, literally had no name. Dominic had searched in vain for a logo on the trunk or glove compartment. The cushiony dashboard suggested the 1980s, as did the oversized steering wheel and gearshift with the bulbous grip. The scars of a socialist fire sale were in evidence: the curtained windows and multiple ashtrays, the front-panel flag and portrait-sized stain where a paramount leader had once kept watch. His new friend, and fellow conspirator, Paddy Chan had put the matter succinctly: "If the Russians no longer want a piece of equipment, neither do you."

Next to him in the back seat, Ant unscrewed a thermos. The routine was set. The Gyatsian would pour a serving and extend the lid with the mocking invitation: "Nescafé?" Dominic, his tongue still scalded from his only sip of the heart-attack brew, would decline, producing a rumble of laughter from the translator. That done, Dominic would shake cigarettes into the mouth of a pack. Sun Nanping didn't smoke. Ant usually took one. Wu Jing always went for the entire package, his grin that of a boy determined to act bad.

The driver shifted into reverse. Dominic parted the window curtain. Fifteen feet away, the dog hadn't revived. It blinked its exposed eye, though, and raised a limb, as though to whiz against a lamppost. He went to alert Wu Jing. The manner in which the Shamo slurped air into his mouth suggested he knew exactly where his prey had fallen. First came the yelps of those able to flee. Then came the thud. When Wu braked and changed gears—the body lay pinned under the car—Dominic raised his feet.

A second thud spilt Ant's coffee. Muttering, the translator cuffed the Shamo across the back of the head. Wu apologized, but through the rear-view mirror Dominic saw him curl his lips into a sneer. Sun Nanping, meanwhile, had asserted his authority by saying and doing nothing, his expression, even glimpsed in profile, making clear that he wished with all his heart he could be some place—any place—else.

Dominic recalled a piece of cynical advice in *The Rough Guide to Gyatso*: "In Gyatso, remember to stop for the horses, slow for the yaks, and drive like hell through the dogs."

"Live and let live, Wu?"

"Stupid dogs."

"You kill that animal, tourist," Ant said.

"Pardon me?"

"First you shoot it, then you crush it with wheel."

"What about Wu Jing?"

Ant issued a more mocking laugh. "Wu? Give him Marlboro, he will beat up child. Give him pack, he will kill own—"

The car swerved, sending Dominic into the Gyatsian and the Gyatsian into the window. Ant knocked his head against glass. Dominic knocked his cheek against a blade of bone. Wu Jing hunched over the wheel, his shoulders narrowed in anticipation of another slap. Anatman Sangmo glared into the mirror. When Wu did not acknowledge him, he reached up and ripped the glasses from the driver's face. Unrolling the window, he tossed them out. Only then did he cock his hand a second time. Desperate to widen the gap, Wu voluntarily cracked his forehead against the windshield.

And how had Sun Nanping let his staff know who was in charge? He found his seat belt and buckled it.

"Wu Jing?" Ant said. "Bah! He is Shamo man with no sight. Shamo nation with no soul."

Dominic waited for a complaint about the use of "Shamo." Gyatsians referred to their occupiers in this manner, but rarely, as far as he knew, in their presence.

"How much longer?" he asked.

No one answered.

"This special hotel I'm being taken to, as part of my punishment

17

for the crime of killing the dog that Wu just ran over—is it much farther?"

Wu Jing sniggered.

"Five minutes," Sun Nanping finally replied.

They completed the trip in silence. Dominic tried making sense of the route. Wu had followed the new ring road for about two miles, past the drab apartment blocks, restaurants, and bars that marked the slow progress of Bon—in Shamo eyes, at least— from medieval pigsty to modern city, but then had veered off before crossing the Samsara. Now he blasted along Liberation Boulevard, one of two thoroughfares linking what the same Paddy Chan had dubbed the Shamo Three Quarters with the beleaguered Gyatsian Quarter. They seemed headed straight into deepest, darkest Gyatsian Bon, an unlikely location for a military installation—even just a hotel.

He'd call his wife from the room. Making small talk off the top would be unwise. Not with the phone line crackling, proof that Dominic wasn't enjoying state-of-the-art digital optics at the new airport at Chek Lap Kok. Not with the apologetic tone that even his "Hi, Esther" would convey. "I'm being delayed here," he would begin. "Nothing serious. A misunderstanding. It'll clear up tomorrow, or the next day at the latest. Call Betty at the office. Don't tell Bill Coren if he rings. And, honey, please take the kids trick-or-treating. A dozen floors, a dozen doors— that's all. Their costumes? Shit! I stored them in the cloakroom at the F.C.C. They were going to be a surprise. Sailor Moon for Gabriella and the blue Teletubby for Mike. Speak with Mr. Lee at the club and explain that I have the ticket here in my wallet. The costumes are in a large plastic bag on the top shelf ... Sure Lee will give it to you. He knows who you are."

He doubted she would confront the cloakroom attendant at the Foreign Correspondents Club. He felt certain she would confront him about his lame excuse. "Hokay, Dominhic," she would lilt, her pronunciation of his name a boost to the spirit, "if that is all you can say to you whyfe, who knows you so well." But what else could he say? The army hotel phone would be tapped. More to the point, Esther, who *did* know him so well, didn't know the real reason for his trip to Gyatso. He hadn't been precise. He had told a small lie.

Dominic sketched out a reply. "I can't talk about the delay," he might tell her. "It wouldn't be smart. My *vacation* here in Bon has been great, though, and I'm really glad I took the *time off work.*" Not a chance that would fly. "Why you raise your voice at me?" she would fire back. "You think I am deaf *and* dumb Filipina girl?" He needed to find a middle way between not saying much and assuring her he was being reasonably honest. "Things got complicated," he could try. "Other people became involved. I need to make sure everyone is safe. I need to make sure—" But what other people? If the complication concerned business, she couldn't care less. He knew what she would assume, though. She would assume—

The phone call, a disaster even in the hypothetical, was cut short. Dominic watched as Wu Jing parted a stream of bicycles to turn onto a street barely wide enough for the car. The lane was newly paved and lined with houses. The homes were among the finest he had seen in the city: carved balconies and decorated window frames, fresh coats of paint. But he also noted a curious lifelessness to them. Windows were shuttered and sills supported no plants. Stoops were bereft of children and urns. For the past six days Dominic had wandered up and down the Gyatsian Quarter and, aside from one lane—quite similar to this one, he remarked—the city had teemed. Teemed with merchants. Teemed with kids. Teemed with yaks and dogs and, hardly a surprise, swarms of flies around both. Teemed with incense clouds from stupas. Teemed with other smells as well, not so aromatic: sewage and mud, butter lamps and boiled meat. Gyatsian Bon had teemed, he granted, almost like a movie depiction of Quasimodo's Paris or London during the plague.

The car halted next to a white brick building, the only commercial structure in the lane. Aside from a Shamo flag draped over the entrance, the building kept mute about its function. Credit card decals failed to reassure the traveller. A doorman declined to assist passage from one side to the other. As Dominic climbed out, he took in the lengthy brick wall along the street and an upper floor that extended halfway down.

"Maybe there's a pool," he said to Ant, who handed him his luggage.

"Go swim in river," the Gyatsian replied.

Ant wasn't only wishing him ill. The lane ended ten feet ahead at the rocky banks of the Samsara. Once Bon's southern boundary, the far side pasturage for yaks and farmland for barley, across the river now sat an industrial park. Drab factories, many under construction and others already abandoned, added a touch of urban blight to the landscape. Smokestacks, most basins for birds' nests, smudged the sky. Too spotty and haggard to pose much threat, the buildings struck Dominic as a kind of design model, like the solitary prefabricated house plopped into a farmer's field north of Toronto where, a developer claimed, would soon be a community with roads and sewers, plazas and hockey rinks. In the case of the Bon industrial park, the pitch was for the ROA—Rest of Asia—and Gyatsians were being asked, in effect, to envision a future of belching stacks and spewing pipes, highways ploughed through temples and reserves.

"Looks a bit rough," he said.

Ant smiled. "You get pulled under. Wind up many miles from Bon. Up on glacier, maybe. Lost in mountains."

Wu Jing rested his arms on the car roof.

"Need any more cigarettes, Wu?" Dominic asked. Hardly a subtle bribe, but he had to try.

"You have Marlboro?"

"Come by my room later."

"I see you again, sure," the Shamo said.

Dominic walked around the back of the car. "I might even have an extra pair of sunglasses," he whispered to Wu. "Ray-Bans. All the evil guys in Hong Kong wear them."

What a line. Had he actually spoken it? Was he seriously working the situation, as would an investigative journalist?

Blame the effects of thin air on the brain. Blame the fatigue.

Sun Nanping issued an order to Wu Jing, presumably to keep the engine running while he checked in the foreigner. The head of Bon Tourism held the door open for his ward.

"Have I been down this street before?" Dominic asked.

"Sorry?"

"Did one of your guided tours include the lane?"

"I don't think so."

He studied the houses. The windows and sill pots, the balustrades and doorways: very little of Gyatsian Bon looked so stately. He had been in the lane. He had been—

How scrambled was his brain? "I must be mistaken," he said, nearly pushing the other man into the building.

"Many aristocratic families live on street," Sun offered. "Old Gyatsian families. From before liberation. You know one Gyatsian aristocrat, I think? Young woman?"

Dominic decided he hadn't heard. "Do those sorts of people still live here?"

"No longer. Many of them leave the country for India or even America."

"Because of you?"

"Me, Mr. Dominic?"

"The occupation," he clarified.

He expected the guide to feign puzzlement. He had used the term out of panic, to cover his latest gaffe. Instead, Sun Nanping glanced over his shoulder at the car. "I do not want to occupy any country," he said quietly.

Dominic's heart started to race.

"Gyatsians believe this bad time will end," Sun continued. "They see no signs and expect no good luck, but still they believe."

"And you don't?"

"I believe in my wife. I believe in my son."

"Family is all that really matters."

"Not all that matters," Sun replied. His sad eyes darted from Dominic to the Bon Tourism vehicle. "Not even very much."

Dominic would have challenged the remark—it was, he recognized, in equal parts ferocious and desperate—but he was suddenly thinking about Esther and the children, and how he really ought to be getting home.

Chapter Three

A soldier emerged from behind a wooden screen. His uniform fit him like a father's shirt on a five-year-old boy. Dominic had noticed this design flaw with other military as well. Someone had played a bad joke on the Shamo army and issued a regiment's worth of extra-large khaki pants and pea-green shirts. The trademark hats had to be kept either perched low, hooding the eyes, or else high up on the skull, giving an aw-shucks air.

The soldier greeted Sun Nanping with a nod. He listened to him, turned his visor on the new arrival across the desk, and then delivered a speech made up of staccato bursts, as though Sun was a lowly enlisted man.

Satisfied with his own performance, the receptionist removed a ledger book from a drawer. He found a blank page and scrawled a line of ideograms. While he did, Dominic studied the lobby. The area was more a landing, stuccoed white and kept bright by a staircase and a wide window that gazed onto a courtyard. Besides the desk and screen, the only furniture was two armchairs of the cushiony sort favoured by leaders for meetings with visiting dignitaries. Between the chairs stood a rosewood table, a bowl of hard candies on top. Over the table hung a painting of mountains and waterfalls, trees clinging to slopes. These were not the sky peaks and moonscapes available across the Samsara river. The scene belonged, as did most art in most public buildings in Gyatso, to a region in southern Sham-denpa famous for its gnome hills and checkerboard valleys.

"Dominic?" Sun Nanping asked, finally dropping the Mr. "He wants to know your rank."

"Rank?"

"Guests in this place are army people," Sun said flatly. "He must write down a rank."

"President," Dominic replied, almost adding: *like my father, and his father before him.* "I gave you my card the other time, remember?"

"Please ..."

He had intended to push the joke. These days, he would say, CEOs and company presidents fancy themselves four-star generals. Strategists, first and foremost, at their best in secured war rooms, a cigar in one hand and a Scotch in the other, but also game for the field. A common touch with the grunts. Unafraid of wading through the gore. He had resolved to stop at colonel, on account of his relative youth and come-lateliness to the Asian theatre of operations. But then an authentic rank slipped from his lips. "Major Wilson," he said. "'C' Force, Royal Rifles."

What had made him say it? Why—why on earth—had he issued the title in Charlie Wilson's prideful tone? He watched as his guide translated the information without incredulity and the soldier wrote it down. *You?* he expected the Shamos to sneer. *You may have the wound—obtained slicing lemons for a gin and tonic, no doubt—but you haven't got the balls!* The receptionist, however, simply reversed the ledger and held out a pen for Sun Nanping. He signed the page and then headed for the stairs. Dominic's mouth abruptly tasted more than dry; it tingled, a plea for nicotine or caffeine or some other stimulant.

"Major is high rank, yes?" Sun called from the top.

Dominic climbed before asking him to repeat the question. "I guess it is," he admitted.

"You are not too young for this?"

"Sun!"

"To be major in army, and also president of company, is great accomplishment for man who is one day less than forty."

He understood not to be rattled that the chief of Bon Tourism knew his date of birth. In the last week Sun Nanping had taken every opportunity he could to study his passport. Hardly a surprise he could recall details. *So why do you also need to come to Gyatso and pretend to be a journalist?* Dominic asked himself on Sun's behalf.

"And me?" Sun said. "I have done nothing in my thirty-eight years. No accomplishments. Nothing to make family or country proud."

Dominic had to swallow to let that equally startling confession pass unremarked. Halfway down the hall the men halted before the floor monitor's station. A woman sat at the desk, her face buried in her arms.

"Shh," Dominic said. "You might wake her up."

Sun shook the monitor by the shoulder. She bolted upright and in a single motion grabbed a hat and plunked it on her head. He handed her a slip of paper. She sniffled at the room assignment, first wiping her nose with her fingers and then pinching her nostrils to catch dribble. She rummaged through a pile of keys, rose from her chair, and inserted one into the door immediately beside her.

The Shamo appeared to be introducing him. Twice he heard the English word "major" parachuted into sentences. The monitor digested the information using a series of blinks. Next she turned to Dominic and, straightening her posture, saluted.

Startled, he saluted back. He could do so, thanks to movies and playing war as a kid; thanks as well to a lesson he once received, he seemed to recall, from his father. Now that he thought about it, he remembered the lesson clearly. *Think of your arm as the hand on a clock, Dommie*, he heard Charlie Wilson say, circa 1970. *Show your pride, son. And your respect.*

In the room he dropped his gear on the nearest of two beds. Wasting not a second, he pulled a silver flask from a duffel pocket and unscrewed the lid. The Scotch ran a match flame over his skin. It burned up those foolish memories.

"Care for some?" he asked, extending the flask. The offer, he assumed, would be rejected; Sun Nanping was on duty. Besides, Shamos were famously unable to take hard liquor.

The Bon Tourism chief accepted the canister with an apologetic

25

smile. Standing before a large TV, he delivered a speech at odds with both the fatigue frogging his speech and the object in his grasp. "You are guest in this special hotel," he said to the walls. "Many important military officials stay here. Excellent room with hot water and colour television. Excellent dining hall downstairs. Please eat all meals in hall at eight in morning, noon at lunch, and six o'clock for dinner. Please do not be late. Also, tell security person in lobby if you must leave the building."

He raised the flask and drank. His Adam's apple rose.

"Go easy," Dominic said.

"No," the Shamo replied, his voice scraped by a knife, "*you* go easy. And please say *where* you go."

"What, so you can follow me?"

Sun Nanping nodded, casually confirming a suspicion Dominic had kept secret, almost from himself. He then held the flask to his nose. He flinched at the smell, as though a single malt, aged twelve years, gave off toxic fumes.

"Send it back around," Dominic said, unnerved. He took another slug and inspected the excellent room. Covering the concrete floor was a wine-red rug; adorning the brick walls were more landscapes. Duvets showed burn spots and curtains filtered pencil tips of light. The dull aftertaste of cigarettes lingered, but the room stank mostly of boredom, the air not often stirred by exertion, never mind by lust. All the small Shamo touches were on display: slippers at the foot of each bed, the pads of ghost feet visible in stains; a thermos of hot water and mugs on a tray; packets of herbal teas. Inside the bathroom he bet he would find a kit containing a toothbrush and tube of creamy chalk, a soap bar the heft of a throat lozenge, two napkin-sized towels.

The Scotch was having the desired effect.

"How long do I stay here?" he asked.

"Until ticket is arranged."

"You're sure I'm not under arrest? Shooting a guide *is* a serious crime."

"You are guest in Gyatso," Sun said stiffly, his gaze wandering over to the television. "No arrest."

26

"Then I can leave the country?"

"As soon as plane—"

"Ride a bus?"

"No buses out."

"Hitch a lift with a truck?"

"Foreigners not permitted—"

"Hire a private jet? Saddle up a yak?"

"Do not worry so much," the Shamo advised in a different tone. "You have, um, passport. You have visa for Hong Kong. No big problems, shall we say, for you. OK?"

Dominic refused to answer. Not with the bug in the TV and an "um" and a "shall we say" in the disclaimer. The flask remained in his grasp. He shouldn't—a third shot could prove sleep inducing—but he wanted to, and so, as usual, he did.

Sun Nanping wanted something as well. The way he gnawed his lip suggested he could have tolerated another sup of single malt. Dominic, though, had a notion. He unzipped the case and lifted the Powerbook into his lap.

"You still haven't asked," he said.

"Asked?"

"About my baby finger. Why it's, you know, chopped off," he added, displaying the hand. The finger had been amputated above the second joint.

Sun's cheek twitched once more.

"Most people eventually ask. You can't blame them. But it's nothing. An accident when I was eighteen. Working with heavy machinery, believe it or not. My blue-collar phase. You can hardly notice."

"I hadn't."

"Come on, Sun."

The Shamo's confusion took on an abject quality.

"Forget it," Dominic said quickly.

"Those voices," said Sun with obvious relief. He indicated the computer. "You can maybe put them on?"

Dominic pressed a button. There was a musical byte and the screen jumped twice. First up were some specs, then the

27

manufacturing logo, then that of the software. As the latter faded, to be replaced by a choreography of codes and counter-codes, all programmed to boot him into his account, voices came on instead of synthesized sound washes. "Hello, Daddy!" the children sang in unison. "We love you," Gabriella proclaimed. "Now go to work!" her brother ordered. The audio's finest moment—three seconds of canned kid giggles—induced a final splatter of corporate puffery. Another blink, and the screen turned black, then blue, then black. At the third request for a password he hit the same button, taking a moment to once more bemoan the absence of easy Internet connections in Bon—a seventh day without e-mail.

Only by snapping the notebook closed could Dominic break the spell it held over Sun Nanping. The expression on his guide's face made him uneasy. "It's no big deal," he offered. "You just need a microphone."

"Where you get?"

"In Kowloon. The computer has to be state-of-the-art, natu-rally. That means no older than a week," he said with a grin.

"Expensive to buy?"

"I suppose it would be. This is an office machine."

"Your newspaper give you this?"

He should have let the remark—a partial truth—pass uncon-tested. "What newspaper would that be? I'm an army major and company president. Who has time to also write journalism?"

"Okay."

"And now," Dominic said, rising with an exaggerated stretch, "I think I'll rest before lunch."

At the door the head of Bon Tourism requested his passport.

"Not again!"

"For one minute, please."

Dominic watched while Sun Nanping examined the docu-ment, for maybe the twentieth time. He had long ceased wonder-ing how often the Shamo felt he had to verify a one-week visa to Gyatso. He had stopped puzzling over what could be so interest-ing about the stamp, the third and final in a multiple-entry visa to

Shamdenpa, that he had received on crossing the border. By now he knew where Sun's fingers would carry him. Japan and Taiwan, twice each, Indonesia and Thailand, both for holidays, Vietnam and Malaysia, plus a family trip to visit Esther's grandmother in Manila. Several passages in and out of Canada, along with a page showing an arrival in New York, a departure from Chicago. A set of stamps from Heathrow; another from Schiphol, the result, he had explained before, of a layover in Amsterdam. Yes, he had been to most European countries, at least once, though many of them years ago, when he had roamed the continent using student rail passes. Yes, he knew Italy well, especially Tuscany, where—why had he told this to a stranger?—his mother came from. And had he visited the imperial museum in Taipei? The Uffizi in Florence? The Met in New York?

His work visa, encased in a collage of chops, never failed to give the bureau chief pause, as though there might be some secret he could learn, some advantage he could gain, simply by staring at the rectangular stick-on paper that allowed the named individual to reside and work in the Special Administrative Region of Hong Kong for two years, expiring on January 8, 2000.

This morning Sun focused less on the visas and more on the information page: Wilson, Dominic Gordon, Canadian, 01 Nov/59, male, Toronto, Canada, along with date of issue and expiry, issuing office. The photo caused him to frown and twice glance up at the real-life model, as if the resemblance was at best passing. Sun's own face had shifted. He now wore a look that had Dominic wondering whether the man had decided to imitate a poker-faced immigration official.

"Everything in order?" he heard himself ask. His mouth went dry.

"I would like very much to go to Italy," Sun Nanping answered, returning the passport. "I like Italian movies, and the art of the Renaissance."

"*Erzi? Erzi?*"

A voice entered his dream. Dominic welcomed the intrusion. He could sense himself struggling to wake up. "What are you doing?"

The floor monitor collapsed onto her backside, hat off and hair mussed. "*Erzi!*" she pleaded. Using her hands, she sculpted *hard-suhs* in the air, implying that she had been seeking them under his bed. The creatures appeared to be about three feet tall, thin, and, if he got her gestures, fluffy.

"Children?" he asked. "You're looking for children?"

Her face relaxed, and she issued an imitation of Gabriella and Michael's computer chant: "Nah goo doo wuk!" Clearly pleased by her own pronunciation, she smiled. Her gums reminded him of a horse's.

"No kids here," he replied, standing to retrieve her hat. "And why are you in my room?"

More mime: a bowl held at chest level, chopsticks shovelling food into a mouth.

"Lunch?"

"Yes."

"Fine."

"You come."

"In a minute."

The monitor showed her watch. It read 12:03.

"In a minute," he said again.

Once she left, he retreated into the bathroom with his toiletries kit. Cold water washed away the grog. A bar of Burberry rubbed off the dust. He applied Brylcreem with a comb and splashed Old Spice on his neck—homages, he granted, to his father's conservative grooming. He examined himself. Wilson men aged pretty well, thanks to lanky frames and regular features. Wilson chins were neither weak nor strong; they simply united jawbones, tied up facial lines. Wilson mouths, likewise, went about their business without attracting attention. Lips tended to be thin and smiles cursory, but teeth were movie-star and gazes stayed as firm as the handshakes taught in youth.

If a nose betrayed an ethnic bridge, chalk it up to a bad fracture. If eyes showed anything other than the bonnie blue, murmur about dissolute habits. Foreheads were narrow and high. Hair rarely strayed from rust brown.

Dominic fit the mould, but with a twist. She was Gina Ponti and she was born, as he had informed Sun Nanping, in Italy. Name and country of birth both made her wrong for a Wilson. Not a Webster or a Brown, a MacGregor or a Galt. Not a girl from Branksome Hall or Havergal, and certainly no graduate of Trinity College, University of Toronto—moulders of the nation's instinctive ruling class. Sure enough, the marriage of Charlie Wilson and the Italian girl produced in Dominic and his sister Francesca Mediterranean flushes and Latinate undertones. Franny had won the DNA lottery hands-down, and could pass for a Florentine. At best he resembled a Saxon sporting blush. Her eyes were green, but his had retained the Highlands hue, albeit a washed-out version. His lips also had a natural gloss courtesy of his mother that some women associated—as they apparently did the moist eyes—with a slow-burn sensuality. While he could never be sure of what they were talking about, he did not complain.

A soccer match filled the TV screen with the blaring green of a playing field under stadium lights. He stood before the set, not really watching, summoning the courage to pick up the phone and call Hong Kong. His gaze fell upon an advertisement. Holding the screen for five seconds was a single image. Dominic, along with the rest of the world, recognized the image from a news event a decade before: a young man in the middle of a boulevard, shirt untucked and shopping bag by his side. Here stood the boy David, minus a slingshot. There, in the form of tanks lined up single-file before him, loomed the giant Goliath. Though the street was wide, the tanks lacked the mobility to do much more than advance or retreat. Realizing this, the man blocked the convoy by stepping first one direction and then the other, shooing the lead cannon away.

That image blurred into a woman at a check-out counter. She wore nicely pressed clothes. Her bags were stuffed, the brand names popping over the rims. Slogans were sprightly spoken in Shamo. The logo of a Taiwanese grocery-store chain materialized in the corner.

Lifting the receiver—the phone was a hefty rotary-dial, perfect for clobbering someone—he didn't have to spin the wheel to summon an operator. "*Wei?*" a voice said. He outlined his intention of dialling an international number and gave, in rudimentary Shamo, the sixteen digits. She punched in the numbers. The line flooded beep-beep-beep into his ear until the operator cut back in. "*Meiyou,*" she concluded, meaning busy.

Dominic asked her in English to wait, and he scanned page 39 of the guidebook. Under the brief list of accommodations in Bon was a number for the Stink. He rhymed it off. The operator said "*Ayyaah,*" but patched him through. At the other end a second operator asked a question. Guessing, he answered "*Gee-oh,*" twice. She, too, said "*Ayyaah.*" She, too, patched him through—to room 9, he hoped. His grip on the receiver tightened. *Don't be there, Paddy*, he silently requested. Two rings, and he relaxed his hold. *Be long gone from Bon*, he counselled as the third ring twittered. *On your way back to Belfast. Better still, stopping over in Hong—*

"*Wei*, way, wee?" a voice said.

"Tashi Delag?" he managed.

There was a pause. "The fucker himself, I take it?"

"You're still here?"

"Don't you sound pleased."

"What happened?"

"Hark, is that a Shamo mole I hear scuttling about the phone line?" Paddy Chan said, his accent taking a turn for the thick— to jam those same moles, no doubt. "And isn't such a rodent infestation cause enough not to speak frankly our hearts and minds? Isn't it, my old chappie, my hard man?"

"Cause enough," Dominic replied. Despite the letdown, he couldn't help smiling. It wasn't just the flamboyant speech and burr-infested accent associated planet-wide with poets and terrorists, respectively. It was the owner of that accent, the speaker of those words. Where he came from, what he looked like, who—by far the biggest mystery—he was.

"Can I buy you a beer?" Dominic asked. "Or do you have a plane to catch?"

"Airport is closed. Haven't you heard?"

"Planes are all full, too."

"Imagine it."

"Guess they want to extend our stays as honoured foreign guests. They must really like us."

"Hard to fathom in your case, truth be told," Chan said. "You're just one more tailored suit in town. What could you have been up to that would be so different from the visit by Hans from Hamburg last month, or next month's cold call by Otsu from Osaka?"

Dominic almost went for the bait. Paddy Chan's recklessness—he had said it himself; the moles were listening—irked him. "What suit?" he answered. "What sales pitch? I'm just a tourist, Paddy. Like you."

"Me, McNicky? I am neither one thing nor the other. Totally unique. Totally freak."

"Will we meet in the same place?"

"Give us an hour. It isn't even the half."

Dominic could hear the soccer game in the background. He turned to his own television. Men in black shorts and yellow shirts raced up the field, chasing a ball that seemed to spin counter-clockwise. But his memory kept replaying the commercial. "Did you see an ad? Maybe five minutes ago?"

"Fucking unbelievable."

"What was the slogan?"

"Don't get stuck in line," Chan chirped in pitch-man mode. "Shop where the customer is never in the way."

Dominic kept silent.

"Those grocers are all over Asia now. You lads must own a chunk?"

"Maybe," he lied. WilCor's Pacific Rim investment portfolio

included stock in the chain. "But I can't believe they'd use that footage."

"You can so believe," Chan said. "You'd just rather not."

"In an hour, then?"

"Fine by me. I may try squeezing in a lie-down."

He hoped his relief at the shift in the conversation wasn't obvious. "The Stink was noisy last night?"

"I slept elsewhere."

"Good for you."

"Fuck off, Nicky. Not all of us are horny toads, you know. Point of honour, I spent the evening in the company of two of the three stooges. Curly and Moe made me an offer I couldn't refuse. Puke-crusted floor. Maggoty linen. Jakes with a stench off them that would have had a sewer rat perfuming its hankie."

"You're kidding."

"The Maze is the Vacation Inn by comparison."

"But you're—?"

"Yellow man with a red passport," Chan said, bitterness now souring his banter. "Temporarily overseas. Besides, you know the rule—if there's Shamo in the stew, they can always get to you."

"I'm sorry."

"He's sorry ..."

Dominic was distracted by the sound of a key in the door. It opened and the monitor poked her head in. He shooed her away. "One minute," he said. "*E-ge fen.*"

The woman withdrew so hastily the visor of her hat nicked the frame. She slipped out; her hat didn't.

"One question before I, and my mole friends, sign off," Paddy Chan was saying as Dominic raised the phone back to his ear.

"I'm listening."

The pause was even longer. "All kidding aside. What have you done, Dominic Wilson? What the fuck have you done?"

Dominic found the monitor at her station, head bowed and hands in lap, and returned her hat. Flustered once more, she accepted the hat back with an expression suggesting—improbable though it seemed—sudden concern for Dominic's health. The moment passed, and the woman reassembled her uniform and set off down the hall. From the bottom landing ran a glassed-in walkway connecting the hotel with the restaurant. Beyond the glass lay the courtyard garden he had glimpsed from the lobby. Ahead were double doors beneath a red and gold calligraphy banner. The monitor stopped on the threshold, passing him on to a waitress in a starkly non-military cheongsam, red silk with yellow stitching around the collar, fabric slashed at the knees. She neither smiled nor greeted her customer. Instead, she turned and, assuming he would follow—she had a lithe figure and shapely calves—crossed to a table designed for a dozen, set for one. He dropped into a seat before a spoon and cup, plate and napkin, lacquered chopsticks on a mount. A dish of chicken and another of beef. A bowl of rice and a sweating bottle of beer.

Half the other tables were in use. Seated at each were Shamo officers in full uniform, hats arranged in rows on a shelf near the door. A quick visual raid put the count at thirty-odd men and one woman. She, alone, wasn't staring at him. He filled his glass of beer and raised it in her direction. Several officers scowled. To his delight, the woman acknowledged the gesture with a nod.

He ate the meal, tasting nothing. He glanced around the room, seeing no one. Chan's question had ensured his lunch would lose its flavour and his surroundings their focus, leaving him with an itchy scalp and prickly skin, a periodic need to close his eyes and press his palms on the table to quell the nausea, keep his balance.

What *had* he done?

Chapter Four

Two weeks earlier, he had sat in bed next to Esther leafing through an English edition of contemporary Shamo fiction. The book had been a gift from a business associate at a banquet, a nice change from the usual bottles of *maotai* and baskets of lychees, brocades for the wife and scarves for the mistress. He tried the first three stories. One told of a farmer reunited after a quarter-century with the daughter he had sold to a landowner before the revolution. Another related the life of a professor, shell-shocked from decades of political upheaval, who falls in love with a former student tormentor. The third story, which he quit after three pages, starred an ancient woman with bound feet and no teeth recalling her childhood as a hired playmate for the boy emperor.

Granted, Dominic didn't read much serious fiction. He hardly read fiction at all anymore, except for thrillers, and mostly blamed time, or the lack of it. Up to his eyeballs in on-line reading and e-mail, he also had to ingest a glutton's daily intake of newspapers: hard copies of the *Morning Post* and *Asian Wall Street Journal*, the *Globe and Mail* and *New York Times* on the screen. Plus magazines: *Time* and *Maclean's*, *Far Eastern Economic Review* and *Asiaweek*, *The Economist* and *The Spectator*. He had to keep up. He wanted to keep up. His father would never believe him—to do so would oblige the Vicar to give credit where due—but he still loved the printed word. He was a Wilson, wasn't he? A quality paper at the front door every morning and a smartly written weekly with the mail. Dominic loved the old family business, just not enough to stick with it to the death, paradigm shifts be damned.

Back in Toronto, he would probably have slogged through the

anthology, in part because a book begun should be finished, in part because he couldn't have articulated what frustrated him. Two years in Hong Kong had clarified his impatience. This had to do with time as well. Asia had jumped out ahead of it; Canada and the West had fallen behind. Forget the tedious drum roll for the millennium, still sixty days away. From the vantage point of the Landmark Building in Central, the twenty-first century was already several years old. Most books and writers didn't appreciate this. Their stories were so familiar and their characters so worn. The past, and who is to blame. History, and how it can't be escaped.

Hong Kong appreciated the new century. Hong Kong knew how to get over the past. British rule had faded to memory before the last fireworks illuminated the harbour back in 1997. The Japanese occupation during World War Two survived in the fogged minds of only a few octogenarians. Brits were welcome to stay on and keep making money; the Japanese had begun to reap profits in the colony within a few years of their brutal regime. No wonder every major corporation on the planet paid outrageous amounts to plant its skyscraper in the steel-and-glass forest growing along the slope of a scrubby island.

His reading that night was also waylaid by his wife's mood. Dominic had not suggested anything, assuming practical impediments. Esther had assured him this wasn't the case— she frowned, as though herself surprised—but still admitted being out of sorts. Directly to blame for her mood was the most recent evidence of the cruelty of their current home. Indirectly to blame was her own unwillingness to give Hong Kong a break, to see any good in the place, to be reasonable wherever her passionate heart ruled. She was talking, of course, about how often poor people and immigrants watched their dreams crash to the earth in the world's most vertiginous city. Esther read the two local English newspapers with an avidity her husband admired and an intensity that unnerved him. She knew her current events. She made sure he knew her current events as well.

Admittedly, the day's story was shocking, even by Hong Kong scale. Both the *Morning Post* and the *Standard*, normally content to banish the most grisly of domestic tragedies to the news digest columns, had elevated the tale to page one, complete with photographs. A mainland couple, part of the legion of illegal residents, had left their children alone for an hour in their fifteenth-floor flat in Sham Sui Po. The kids, aged three and two, had somehow opened a window and fallen out. Photographers had captured the afflicted parents in front of the building, barred from entering by police. Later that same afternoon—the twist worthy of a headline splash—husband and wife hanged themselves from a girder in the unfinished high rise where he was employed.

Esther raged, her English haywire. She raged at the parents. She raged at the landlord. As for Hong Kong, with its ethos of dog eat dog and winner take all and exploit the disadvantaged, pamper the rich, she could add little, except those few hundred words she managed. Sisters of Mary, her do-gooding Filipina friends, had visited people like that mainland couple. They'd seen how they lived and heard their sad, moving stories.

He sat through the lecture mostly quiet, entirely quiescent. What a woman Dominic had married. What a marvel was Esther Ramos-Wilson.

He was about to close the book for good on contemporary Shamo fiction when he chanced upon the first line of a story called "Ocean." The sentence grabbed him, as did the author's unusual name: Tashi Delag. He turned to the biographical notes. Tashi Delag was born in 1969 in a mountainous border region. He had worked in theatre on the mainland, both as an actor and a playwright, before turning to fiction—"into fiction," the sentence read, one of many typos—in the early 1990s. In his stories, written, oddly enough, in Shamo, Tashi Delag sought to portray young Gyatsians on the cusp of the new millennium. The author now lived in Bon.

Dominic read "Ocean" three times that night. For the second pass he retreated to the living-room couch, the apartment silent except for stirrings from the family parakeet, Lucien, on the balcony. By the end, he had no idea where he was. He hallucinated drifting on a raft. He heard waves crashing over rocks. All that, from a short story? Improbable though it was, Tashi Delag's fiction spoke to him. Directly. Man to man.

His third reading of "Ocean" followed an hour of tossing and turning in bed. Esther banished him to the maid's cell shortly before dawn. She didn't call the closet by that name, and technically she was right; the Wilsons employed no domestic help. His own title for the room—the amah shrine—remained a badly kept secret. For reasons still largely her own, his wife had chosen to deal with the fact that their apartment came equipped with modest quarters for staff, located, as was the Asian custom, behind the kitchen, by converting the area into a cross between museum and temple. She had insisted on a cot rather than a bed. She had scoured Wan Chai for the cheap linen and wobbly furnishings a miserly Hong Kong clan might bestow upon their lowly maid. Her choices of personal possessions for the phantom amah, moreover, were both accurate and, in his opinion, creepy: a Bible and rosary, Tagalog romances and cassettes of pop music, jars of purple yam jam and sweet jackfruit. Esther even picked up a plastic vase, supplying it weekly with pink roses and sampaguita stems. About all the shrine lacked was incense and an idol.

One feature of the room belonged more to a police station bulletin board than any temple. Dominic's wife not only scoured newspapers every morning for the latest outrage against the city's itinerant residents, she clipped and displayed them. Cursory reports of abuses and suicides, accidents and deportations lined the cream-coloured walls, a gruesome and blinkered vision of the Hong Kong experience that left him mostly speechless with dismay, except to demand a lock on the door, to spare the children their mother's unhealthy obsession.

Dominic never slept well in the cell—the headlines loomed over him, like the crucifix in the chapel at St. Ignatius, his alma mater—and he ended up watching daylight fall across the apartment from the dining-room table, the book open, a cigarette smoked and a second cup of coffee poured. He was preoccupied at breakfast and useless at work and didn't pay much attention to his family that evening. She asked, but he had an excuse: "A rare phone call from the old man. When you're thirty-nine, a scolding from your dad stings."

He was only half-fibbing. His father *had* called that morning, the second time in twenty-two months that Charlie Wilson had contacted his son at work. Usually he rang the apartment when he knew Dominic wouldn't be there and chatted with Esther, whom he adored, and Gaby and Mike, whom he sorely missed. So the call to the office—even the receptionist's Cantonese-inflected greeting: "WilCor Communykayshuns, how may I hep you?" probably bothered him—was a rarity. Not a breakthrough, though; nowhere near the reconciliation Esther claimed had to happen soon between Wilson *père et fils*, estranged now for ten years. After a few minutes of stiff conversation, Dominic finally asked what was on his father's mind. The Vicar shot back: "You tell me?" Dominic was so startled he nearly told him he was thinking of travelling to Gyatso to profile a writer for a magazine. But then his parent explained the call. "I've just received an invitation to my own daughter's wedding," the old man said. "Can someone please explain this to me?" *Sure, Dad,* he could have replied. *Franny and her lover are tying the knot. You know Leonora, don't you, the woman she shares a house with? The bride will be in a fabulous dress. So, for that matter, will the groom.* But he just promised to call Franny and find out.

Finally, at ten o'clock, he poured himself a measure and, sneaking a phone into the amah shrine, dialled a number in Toronto, not his sister's. An assistant at the magazine his family once owned and he once briefly worked for passed him through to another mogul offspring, now the editor-in-chief. Having listened to Dominic's breathless pitch—a basic "climb a mountain and meet a wise man" travel piece, in this case the obscure author of a perplexing story who apparently dwelt in the mythic city of Bon, Gyatso—the editor, an acquaintance of long standing, went silent for a good five seconds. And how was Dominic doing these days? he eventually asked. Hard on forty, like him, eh? Tough age for men. Mid-life crisis. Hitting the proverbial wall. But things were well with his family? His wife and kids? Must be loads of temptations over there. Gorgeous women. Plentiful booze and drugs.

Dominic waited until confirming the ticket to tell her. He didn't mention the assignment, which he'd had no trouble cajoling the editor into giving him; he just said he had a meeting in the capital of Gyatso. Esther raised an already naturally arched brow at the destination, but true to her disinterest in business only asked him to keep the trip short. She began another sentence twice. Although she abandoned the thought, he gathered it had to do with a conversation earlier in the month about male dissatisfaction. Halloween was eight days away, she said instead, and she had a doctor's appointment on the first of November, which also happened to be someone's birthday, when gifts needed to be extra-special. He noticed the purposeful mystery to her words and promised to be back on the thirty-first with hours to spare. He'd buy costumes for the kids and take them trick-or-treating.

Bill Coren in Toronto had to be told something as well. Mentioning the magazine commission to him was equally out of the question; Dominic would hear about it for months, and Coren's derision rankled no less on the phone than in person. Given that his partner—and his father's former associate—considered adventure travel a trip to the Keys from his condo in Palm Beach, playing up the lure of the roof of the world seemed smart. Sure enough, Coren could only huff and puff about Dominic's idea of fun. "Gyatso?" he said, his voice booming across the Pacific. "Does that place even exist? I thought it was just a fucking movie, starring another Hollywood pretty boy and a bunch of bald guys in dresses."

Dominic flew from Chek Lap Kok to a pot-lidded Shamo city in a bordering province, where, for a king's ransom, he purchased a one-person "group tour" of the Gyatsian Autonomous Region departing the next morning. His visa, a slip of paper stapled into his passport, lasted seven days and denied him access to any of the million square miles of the autonomous region outside the capital. At Bon airport two things happened: he watched as a blond Russian who had disembarked without luggage or, apparently, a visa was escorted away by soldiers, and he was himself greeted by a squad from Bon Tourism. At the Vacation Inn the leader, a Mr. Sun Nanping, presented him with an itinerary full of twelve-hour days of touring, all in the company of guide, translator, and driver. Lighting a Marlboro and then sharing the pack, Dominic expressed excitement at the prospect of visiting the Kata temple and Kundun palace, Om monastery and U-Chen market, a television station and radio transmitter, bottling factory and tannery. But first he would rest. Maybe in a few hours the room would have stopped spinning and vomit would no longer be climbing his throat.

Actually, he felt fine. *The Rough Guide to Gyatso* had described altitude sickness in generous detail, and he had simply rhymed off a few symptoms. He waited five minutes before leaving the hotel. His goal for day one was modest: find the compound known as Gyatsian Literature, listed as publisher of the anthology in which "Ocean" had appeared. In Hong Kong he had made some calls. One dissident, from an organization called Friends of Gyatso, proved helpful. He hadn't heard of Tashi Delag—"Is that his real name?" the man had asked—but he did know of two publishing houses in Bon. If Gyatsian Literature existed as a proper work unit, then its employees, including its authors, probably lived right on the premises.

How great an assault were those first hours in Bon? So much so, Dominic had to keep reminding himself that, geographically at least, he was still in Asia. Asia he associated with water. Asia he considered his swim hole. Unlike most Westerners working the region, who insulated themselves from the untreated bathing of Eastern living in the bodysuits of the global economies—the Oriental in Bangkok, the Grand Hyatt in Jakarta—he had taken the plunge. Being married to a woman from the barrios of Manila helped. Being father to children the inky brown of Dalat coffee with unstirred condensed milk made a difference, too. But, if he did say so himself, he had been ready. For the contact, and the immersion. Until the age of thirty-eight, Dominic Wilson had never travelled outside Europe or North America. For all those years, it was now clear, he had been a stranger to himself. His sensual self, more precisely; his sensual self that fed on the salt lick of skin and the brine of pooled sweat, the tonic of warm, teeming rain. Within a week of landing in Hong Kong, after one daytime stroll through Kowloon with the family and one nocturnal prowl of Mongkok on his own, he was soaked.

Neon signs and wine-red shrines. Leaded exhaust and reused cooking oil. Animal flesh exposed to the sun: clotheslines of dried fish. The narcotic of incense. The allure of cheap cigarettes. Skin of vinegar and hair of chalk—or was that straw? Chilies and coriander, basil and mint. Waterways of lily pads and excrement and puddles of urine and tea. Starving cats, furless dogs. Rats climbing canal banks strewn with garbage. Heat so heavy it felt like a wet cloth; humidity unchanged from noon to midnight. Raindrops that buckled tin with the force and clamour of hailstones. Monsoon days where all light stayed blurred, a bulb at the bottom of a pool.

His Asia, the Asia of water. He liked the urgency of it, the assault. He liked the doubleness of experiences and people, nothing and no one simply one thing or the other; nothing and no one simply black or white, light or dark. Dominic knew Bangkok's Hualamphong district in the wee hours. He was familiar with Cholon, the infamous quarter of Saigon, past the curfew that guidebooks recommended. He may have been checked into the Sheraton or the Siam for business, but he roamed widely and sometimes unwisely in these cities, hands in pockets, T-shirt glued to torso. He stopped at holes-in-the-wall for lukewarm bottles of San Miguel and Bintang. He smoked cigarettes named Campanilla and Champion Blue Seal.

What shocked Dominic about Gyatso that afternoon was the aridity. Rain rarely fell in Bon valley, almost never up on the plateaus. Rivers flowed only because snow melted and gravity sent the spill down slopes. As for the air, he couldn't tell if it was too thin, too dry, or just too unpolluted to easily breathe. Not that Bon lacked smells. The city had its oil and dumplings, its carcasses and sewers. Nor were the inhabitants frigid, despite the cold. With their burnished skin and wishbone cheeks, their haughty carriages and frank stares, the women dazzled. With their brawny torsos and smooth faces, more like North American natives than Thais or Vietnamese, the men were pin-ups. And Bon certainly didn't lack for reasons to feel menaced. Rumours of yaks gone berserk were laughable. Dogs could be shot or run over. But how about a capital stiff with military in oversized uniforms, none of them local boys, and plainclothes thugs in mirror shades.

Why, then, hadn't the dread been rolling down his spine? What kept his groin from tingling? Bon felt unnaturally buoyant and non-sexual. Could it be the air? The sun? Or all those smiles, everyone happy, happy, happy, regardless of present misery and future uncertainty? He had no idea. He intuited one truth, though: he was out of the Asia of water; he couldn't swim anymore. This Asia was bone dry. He had to walk.

He found himself in a large plaza in the Gyatsian Quarter. Not any plaza, Dominic recognized at once. This was the public square built to contain the Kata temple, heart of Gyatsian Bon, soul of the nation's faith. The Kata hulked at the far end, its gold domes, as petite and polished as Fabergé eggs, glinting in sunlight so unfiltered it punished gazes accustomed to the usual protectors. In front of the temple, a large stupa the shape of a beehive puffed clouds of scented juniper at the pilgrims who were making their way towards the gate, one full-body prostration at a time. He needed a minute to adjust to the sight of adult bodies sprawled over flagstones, and tried not to stare at the bruised foreheads and callused hands, the clothing torn at the elbows and knees. Other denizens of the square were less arresting. Peddlers sold ceremonial scarves strung along lines and sunglasses pinned to placards. Old men carved prayer stones; a blind teenager seated on a footstool bowed a single-stringed instrument, its sound a toneless squeak. A woman stood on tiptoe to wave turquoise and silver necklaces at him. A girl tugged on his parka to hawk the rings decking her fingers.

Deciding his best asset was the writer's name, Dominic began to whisper "Tashi Delag?" to anyone who returned his attention. How could he be sure he addressed a Gyatsian? Easy: Gyatsians sought his eyes, Shamos did not. His words were actually greeted with replies of "*tashi delag.*" At first he was thrilled. Locals recognized the name! They knew the author! But soon enough it became clear that either the ritual involved repeating a tourist's words back to him, like a tedious comedy routine, or else the name served another function—a coded greeting, a password.

He was still wandering the Kata plaza, ignoring the Shamos wearing earplugs and the surveillance cameras that lined the walls, when he noticed a figure in a doorway. At once, Dominic felt geographically lost. The man wasn't Gyatsian—that much he could tell. But on sensing Dominic's scrutiny, he removed his sunglasses and made direct contact. As if the stare wasn't confusing enough, his eyes were single-lidded and slanted. His face, meanwhile, seemed Asian in features but almost American in character. Shoulders were broad and hips were narrow. Veins corded the arms and neck. His pose against the door jamb, one hand in a pocket and the other pinching a cigarette, and his clothes—jeans and a rolled-up jean jacket, white T-shirt and Doc Marten boots—seemed half James Dean, half Marlboro man. But what about the silver rings climbing the right earlobe and the stud in one nostril? And the hair, brush-cut short and sunflower yellow? Dominic pronounced the writer's name.

"Health and happiness to you too, lad," the doorway dweller

answered in an accent so wrong for his appearance that Dominic briefly decided the lips hadn't been in sync. Taken aback, he explained that he was looking for a Gyatsian named Tashi Delag. The man dragged on his cigarette. "The name is Dim-Fuck-Wit," he said in the same impossible voice. "Mates call me Dim for short."

His name was Patrick Chan, though he preferred Paddy, and if he solved one mystery—*tashi delag* served as "hello" in Gyatsian—he created several others. "Where am I from?" he replied. "What, are you blind? The Lower Antrim Road, Belfast. Up the IRA! Never surrender!"

Dominic gave his home town and present address.

"What about ye, Nicky Wilson?" Chan said.

Though he had intended to keep to himself, Dominic almost immediately volunteered the journalism assignment to a stranger. Why, he couldn't say. Nerves, maybe. Braggadocio, he hoped not. The other man—an Irishman, in effect, though that sure didn't *look* right—took in the plan with a nod, as if Dominic had just informed him that he had indeed come to Gyatso to seek spiritual enlightenment. But then he offered to help with locating the offices of Gyatsian Literature and contacting the author Tashi Delag. Dominic hadn't asked. More to the point, the notion that he required assistance hadn't yet occurred to him. An old joke ran through his head: If a Hong Konger offers you help, you definitely need it. What about an Asiatic Celt?

Paddy Chan listed two conditions for his participation. The first involved renaming a nation and a race. When Dominic mentioned the obvious—that Chan, who talked as though Shamos, as he called them, were the enemy of Gyatsians and him alike, was a member of that very race—he answered: "Fuck all that. Up here they're Shamos, and I wouldn't belong to any family that would call me its prodigal son." The second condition made Dominic wish for a sup of Macallan and a bed. Chan stubbed his cigarette against the heel of his boot. "Ease my troubled mind on one count," he said. "Tell me you're aware this wee project of yours has at least a fifty percent chance of ending in disaster." Dominic pulled a face, and the Irishman grinned. "Because if you weren't aware," he added, "I'd know I was considering working with an eejit or, worse, a Yank."

"I'm Canadian."

"Meaning?"

Holding his gaze, Dominic knew he had to come up with something good. "Meaning even if I was aware of the possibility, I wouldn't tell you, would I?"

He had to slip away between outings with Bon Tourism. Chan claimed he had finagled a two-week tourist visa and had already endured his stooges-guided tours. That left him footloose, with nothing on his hands but time and little else in mind but jamming the Shamos—which Dominic interviewing a Gyatsian author, and then publishing the piece in a magazine, would apparently help to do.

Over the next three days they spoke with a dozen adults and one child about Gyatsian Literature and Tashi Delag. Actually, Paddy Chan spoke with these people, in fluent Shamo and functional Gyatsian, and translated their replies. He appeared content with the role of underling. He appeared to want the record to show that the Westerner was calling the shots, while the oddball local did the work.

Quite the local he was, too. When lively exchanges went untranslated, until Dominic inquired, they would invariably have involved Paddy Chan's dye job and facial jewellery. Had someone set his hair on fire? Gyatsians had all heard stories about interrogations by secret police. Most had a family member or a friend who'd been tortured—and starved, and even worked to death—in a Shamo labour camp. And Chan's earrings and nose stud: were they a protest? For fifty years Gyatsian people, who numbered barely three million, had been inventing sly ways to express their outrage at having been overrun by a nation of a billion, some of them bullies, all of them far from home in the high Himalayas.

Everybody they spoke to offered directions to the publisher. Nobody really had a clue. Locals were just being polite. They were also pretending the city was still theirs. Before the occupation, tiny Bon had hosted an international population of just a few dozen diplomats and adventurers. Now the capital, bloated to a quarter million, was more foreign than familiar, more colonizers than colonized. Beyond the old quarter, Gyatsians couldn't map their own urban landscape. Lanes had disappeared. Row houses had been bulldozed. Too many apartment buildings now piled in confusing clusters, roads laid out in grids that disoriented through their sameness. A Shamo-only sign law was strictly enforced. Police, recruited from the mainland, couldn't be bothered to learn the indigenous gibberish. West of the Kata plaza lay several neighbourhoods that had been declared unfit for habitation. Cleared by decree and boarded up by the army, entire streets of traditional homes now awaited demolition. Beyond a strip of no-man's land called the Zone, and certainly past the Kundun palace, sprawled a city that could have been in Shamdenpa, or Malaysia, for all people knew about it. When Dominic called the capital "divided," Paddy Chan spat back: "Wrong word, laddie. Belfast is divided. Jerusalem is divided. This place was fucking invaded and is now occupied—not the same crack at all."

Those directions that did make sense kept bringing the men to a compound on the far side of the same barren hill that acted as a pedestal for the Kundun. Twin ten-storey towers sat enclosed by a high brick fence at the end of an unpaved road. Antennae on rooftops stretched for sky and satellite dishes turned their faces to the sun. Cameras were evenly spaced. The earth around the perimeter of the compound trembled underfoot and a faint ringing filled the ear. Hot air blasted upwards, though neither Dominic nor Paddy Chan could locate any vents. They waited for employees to approach the gate on foot, or to exit it, in order to pump them for information. But only transport trucks passed through. Once, Dominic stepped into the wake of a vehicle. He saw a shipping dock at the side of the nearest tower and a line of warehouses, railway tracks.

Chan suspected a bomb factory. Thinking of the tracks,

Dominic figured it to be a mine. The compound could have been many things, they agreed—but not a publishing house.

Three separate encounters changed their luck. A Gyatsian boy named Kuno solicited the men in the field of rock and gorse known as the Zone. Kuno wore a soccer shirt and track pants, sandals with brown socks. Clasping his hands together in greeting, he welcomed them to his country in broken Shamo and then asked for twenty American dollars. He needed the money, he explained, to buy medicine for his mother in the underground economy. "Your mother is sick?" Dominic asked through Chan.

"Very," Kuno replied, wiping a waterfalling nose with his sleeve. "The doctors think she will die."

"Even if you buy her medicine?"

"Even then," he agreed. Next, the boy said something that had the two men exchanging astonished glances. "Who can stop a body from dying? Not even a man with a gun pointed to his own head."

How much was that statement worth? Twenty bucks, easily.

Kuno folded the bill into a triangle. Pressing the money between his palms, he raised his fingertips to his forehead three times. Duty done, he turned the tables with a half-dozen rapid questions. Did they like Bon? Had they any Vadra Pani pictures? And Chan's hair: did the dye wash out with soap? Kuno also wondered whether the foreign visitors thought it acceptable that the Shamos had controlled Gyatso for the last four decades. The occupation of a nation that had been sovereign for centuries—surely this could not be okay with the rest of the world? His uncle Thomdup didn't think it was okay. His uncle and some other men, along with the most beautiful woman in the capital, believed the Shamos had to be confronted. The Gyatsian way—patience and long-sightedness, the pursuit of nirvana, where pain and pleasure both were transcended—would not succeed against these invaders.

From those remarks, it was only a small leap to asking the boy about publishers in Bon. That same Uncle Thomdup, Kuno volunteered, had taken him not long before to a building where books were made. A monk with spots over his skull had given him a collection of sutras as a gift.

The building turned out to be in Om monastery, and Dominic found himself being escorted there the next morning. At first he despaired of shaking all three guides. Happily, Wu Jing and Anatman Sangmo chose to stay in the car, leaving just Sun Nanping to deal with. Long legs and a determined climb up a steep staircase did the trick, and soon Dominic wandered alone within the shell of one of Gyatso's four key theological colleges. A monk descending the flagstone knocked into him. He had a chance only to glimpse a shaved head and maroon robe. Recovering, he realized he had felt a tug. In his parka pocket he found a folded piece of paper. "SHAMO OUT OF GYATSO FREEDOM!" it read in elegant script. The monk slipped into a side alley the very moment Sun Nanping's mop of hair appeared over a step below. "Slow down!" the Shamo pleaded between gasps.

In the end, Sun steered him to the printing press. It wasn't Gyatsian Literature, and no one named Tashi Delag lived there, but Om still provided the breakthrough. A susurration of chanting flowed from an open door. Though the prayers were scattered by wind, the tinkling bells that marked the chanting cut through the whistle. Next to the prayer hall stood a flat-roofed brick building. According to the young monk who greeted the visitors, the building was a pretty good replica of the original structure. Just as the press itself was a passable duplicate of the real thing, he said, gesturing to a contraption in a corner that reminded Dominic of a loom, and the manuscripts they were now printing were reasonably okay copies of genuine texts. Just, for that matter, he added—twice, for Dominic, amazed by the man's dexterity in English, demanded that he repeat the sentence—as he himself amounted to a so-so imitation of an authentic printer of sacred works.

Wood shavings powdered the monk's robe and ink stained his fingers. Though the man was still in his twenties, his head already showed melanin speckles, and a front tooth glinted its lead jacket. He demonstrated the procedure. Craftsmen carved the text onto oblong wooden blocks. That required sharp knives and a steady grip, penmanship both pleasing and legible. Next, using ink made of vegetable dye and a hand-lever on the press, blocks were imprinted onto sheets of homemade paper in the same manner, basically, as a footprint into sand. No more permanent than a footprint, either, the man said. The final volumes— he fetched one from a shelf—remained loose-leafed, string glued into the binding for a clasp, the covers of soft wood.

Dominic examined the sample. The box-of-chocolates shape felt perfect for lotus reading, unbound pages ensuring no problems with text folding back on itself. Already the texture of the paper suggested age. Already the script, each word isolated from its neighbour by a dot, implied the remoteness of a culture and a landscape that offered no comfort from extremities of impulse or weather. He would have liked to study the language more closely—he realized he had seen no written Gyatsian in Bon—but another task took precedence. Rubbing one of the pages between his forefinger and thumb, he did the same with the freedom message buried in his parka.

"Tise, the icy mountain known to everyone," the monk said, bringing his hands together in concentration. "Its head covered with snow. This snow stands for the whiteness of the Buddha's doctrine."

"From in here?" Dominic asked, indicating the book.

The man nodded. "My own translation. Very bad!"

Dominic lingered in the room. The scent of wood and ink conjured first a pleasing nostalgia, the way burning candle wax recalled winter mass with his mother and sister, and then, as he admired the equipment and flipped through the volume, a more resolved, less benign memory. A printing press the bulk of an ocean liner engine. Grease stink and a perpetually shuddering shop floor. Men in T-shirts and jeans watching newsprint surging between rollers that ran both vertical and horizontal, the metal spools whirling, the sinuous paper already patterned by columns of print. An alarm, indicating a jam. Abrupt quiet.

Someone—a boy, really—crying out in injury ... Fortunately, the Gyatsian resumed talking. Printing books in this old-fashioned manner couldn't compete with machines, he admitted. Hand-printing was slower and more prone to human error, even simply to human foible. Still, looked at from another vantage point, the procedure could be said to outpace the path to nirvana. Also quicker than a journey across Gyatso on foot.

Even Sun Nanping puzzled over that comment. The monk shrugged, as though he couldn't help playing the aphoristic holy man, and smoothed his skull. A coughing fit forced Sun to step outside. "You have a question for me?" the Gyatsian said to Dominic at once. Dominic asked his question, and the monk nodded. "Yes, of course," he replied. "Very efficient operation. Able to produce hundreds of books per day. But then, Gyatsian Literature uses computers and laser printing. And they have electricity!" He had been given a tour of the facility a few months ago. His guide had offered him a selection of complimentary books, a few in Gyatsian but most in Shamo, a language he knew but did not love. "My present studies keep me from looking at those books for some time," he said. "The year 2003, I hope—in the spring."

The monk thought he might be able to help Dominic organize a tour of his own. The editor of Gyatsian Literature, it so happened, was his second cousin. Lavanya Kamala, of Sikkim Lane, in the Ladakh district. Sixth doorway on the south side of the street. Visitors had to follow a procedure, he added without prompting. If the upper windowsill showed two pots, do not visit. If the sill held five, go ahead and knock. She welcomed those interested in learning more about Gyatso. Outsiders needed to be better informed, to distinguish the real from the fake, the false from the true.

"Lavanya Kamala," he said, "such a beautiful cousin. Famous in Bon for her perfect English. Admired for her spicy noodle soup."

Five pots lined the upper windowsill of the sixth doorway on the south side of Sikkim Lane that evening. Dominic counted, then did as told. A beautiful woman with perfect English and a lilting Indian accent nearly anticipated his summons. She invited him in at once. She immediately closed the door behind them. Inside the house, the woman served barley beer and crackers. She began to speak, her smile pushing her lip up crookedly, her laugh a throaty burst of pleasure, and did not stop until assured that he understood what was fake and believed what was true. He listened to her, watching the lip and delighting in the laugh, and then shocked himself— a little, anyway—by deciding that she might be a risk worth taking. The next morning, she linked her arm in his and together they walked across Bon, a hike of several miles, to a whitewashed building behind another brick fence. This compound had a sign in Shamo announcing it to be the work unit known as Gyatsian Literature.

Lavanya Kamala, whose eyes remained so expressive Dominic could no more keep their gaze than squeeze a hot coal, wore a blue robe narrowed at the waist and a sleeveless wool sweater. She had tied back her hair with a red kerchief. Around her neck dangled yellow and blue beads that drew his attention to the hollow at the base, where no cross dwelt. He noted how skin stretched across her collarbone. He watched the muscles move in her forearms. When, having toured the editorial offices, she directed him to the living quarters behind the main building, a dozen bracelets jangled from her wrist. The gesture breathed the same scent that had set his thoughts reeling the night before: pine cones and oranges. "Knock on the first door of the third hut across that field," she instructed. "Simply say this: *It's me. I know you've been waiting.*"

The occupant of that shed had indeed been waiting for him, though how, or why, he couldn't fathom. Tashi Delag unwrapped a bar of chocolate and spooned instant coffee into two mugs. He opened an English dictionary on his desk. Dominic spent an hour in the room, drinking coffee and eating chocolate. His head, though clearly attached to his neck, felt as light as a beach ball bobbing in surf. The state reminded him of his initial readings of "Ocean" in Hong Kong. Could an author have the same effect on a reader as his work?

Dominic left with ten pages of notes and a mental photograph of a half-Gyatsian, half-Shamo with shaggy hair and a goatee. The man had sunk to one knee to plant a kiss on the muzzle of a brown and white collie who answered to the name Marquez, in honour of the Colombian novelist. "Thanks, Tashi Delag," Dominic said. That earned a lopsided grin from the writer, as though hearing his own name was amusing, and a hello-to-you-too bark from Marquez. "If you see Anitya," Tashi Delag said, referring to a literary character, an invention, "tell her to wait for me by the rock with the painted Buddhas."

He raced back to the Vacation Inn. Sun Nanping and the boys sat fuming in the Bon Tourism car. He knew he had crossed a line this time—how to finesse having stayed out all night?—and assumed he was now under suspicion of engaging in activities not permitted on a tourist visa. Figuring it didn't matter, he presented himself before the passenger window. "Give me an hour to freshen up," he told Sun Nanping, "and I'll be ready to go."

In his room Dominic drew the shades and switched on the computer. He swallowed his last Advil. He poured two fingers of Scotch from the flask. First he transcribed the interview. Then he noted every aspect of his encounter with Tashi Delag; the author's appearance and manner, his living space and pet. Next, rewinding the previous seventy-two hours, he outlined the Gyatsian Literature compound and the home in Sikkim Lane. He described the monk at Om and the note-passing incident on the steps. He wrote a paragraph about the boy Kuno. For good measure, he made quick sketches of Sun Nanping and Wu Jing. He tried to do the same with Ant, but something about the translator eluded him. Finally, he even summoned the energy to draft a lead. It highlighted the "SHAMO OUT OF GYATSO FREEDOM!" note and the tactile congruence of sheets of handmade paper.

Leads, he remembered, were the hardest things to nail down in an article. Once you had a solid opening, the rest of the story would tell itself.

The phone rang three times. One caller, he bet, was Sun Nanping in the lobby downstairs. Paddy Chan over at the Stink may have been the second, wondering what had become of Dominic since their dinner the evening before. About the third call he could only speculate. Esther, maybe, having finally gotten through. Or his sister, Franny, so contrite about sending the wedding invitation to their father that she would track her big brother to one of the most remote places on the planet. Not taking the first two calls didn't bother him. But if he was right about the third, and he'd missed the chance to chat with his wife or sister—his two favourite people, also his best friends— he would kick himself later on.

Chapter Five

"Finish?" a voice said.

Dominic looked up. A woman stood over him. Not the frumpy hall monitor; this Shamo wore a silk cheongsam and a mask of boredom over a gaunt but still lovely face. Impatience now battled tedium for control of her features.

"Finish?" the waitress said again.

He sat in the hotel restaurant. All tables had been cleared, aside from his own. His food dishes were empty, except for residual grease puddles, and his rice bowl had a licked-clean sheen. Three dead soldiers stood at attention. His glass was part full, but the beer tasted tepid. He must have stopped drinking a while ago. Someone else must have poured.

He rose and took several exploratory steps before deciding he could still drive. He wasn't drunk and his thoughts rang clear. So why was he in a funk? To date, he hadn't broken his obscure promise to Esther. Up until now, he had done nothing to further disappoint his dad. Gabriella and Michael were loved and safe. No reason for the faint taste of shame in his mouth, the vague feeling of regret. The cheap ploy of withholding his ticket, the mild intimidation of the army hotel, meant nothing. He needed to get that straight. He needed to straighten Paddy Chan out about it as well.

In the hallway Dominic paused before the courtyard garden. The glass showed a classical design—pond and pavilion, bonzai-like trees and irregular rocks—and manicuring as refined as any property on the Peak. It looked peaceful in there, and serene; it didn't look like Bon—or, for that matter, most of Shamdenpa. Flowers bloomed and trees grew uncrippled. The pond shimmered without ripples, let alone the whitecaps churning up the Samsara river. He looked for a door. The glass ran unbroken. His eyes scanned the other walls enclosing the garden. They offered no entrance, either.

He returned to the room for his computer. Though Chan probably awaited him in the restaurant, Dominic opened the file called Ocean. He had keyed the entire story into the hard drive in Hong Kong. He could have just photocopied the text, but it wouldn't have been the same. Years of working on a computer had left him addicted to the colour monitor. He read better on screen now. He turned pages more easily with a mouse than two fingertips. Determined to know the story inside out, he had reread "Ocean" on both flights and every morning in Bon. The first paragraph he could have recited from memory.

From my father, a cruel man of great import, I learned how to prepare noodles. Over-boiling turns them to mush. Too much spicing spoils the broth. From my mother, a gentle woman of no consequence, I learned how to escape. "In the Kodu mountains," she said, "are sacred valleys where those in distress can find sanctuary. Seekers must be ready to discover these places. Hearts must be pure. Minds must already be on the right path."

A curious opening, he had to admit. "Ocean" was hardly a cautionary tale about the family ties that bind. If asked for a gloss of the story, Dominic would have declared it a guide to *escaping* those ties, to finding your own right path; a sort of pilgrim's progress out of the narrow road of the past into the great wide freeway of the future. But in order to publish, and maybe simply to live, in Gyatso, Tashi Delag had to be clever, operate by indirection. The first paragraph was likely designed to dupe the censors, reassure them the material would be more harmless domestic drama, with a dash of folkloric mysticism tossed in.

He left the Powerbook on the bed, the screen upright but dark. While a snoop might figure out how to turn on the machine, he'd never guess the passwords. Dominic saluted the hall monitor again outside his door. Caught off-guard, the woman giggled, covering her mouth.

"You hokay?" she asked.

"Fine," he replied. Something about the question bothered him. His face probably showed it.

"*Nah goo dew wuk!*" she added as he descended the staircase. Her laugh was high and not far off a horsy neigh. Still, he liked her boldness.

He had similar plans for the receptionist. A better salute, and a bark: *Major Wilson to you, son.* But the lobby was deserted. Dominic helped himself to a candy from the bowl. It had a pleasing melon taste, so he pocketed a fistful.

Of course the lane looked familiar—Lavanya Kamala lived here! The hotel lay a hundred yards south of the house, but he still should have recognized the location before blathering to Sun Nanping. How many streets in the Gyatsian Quarter boasted such homes? The balustrades and balconies, the woodwork and whitewash: in Bon, such elegance—*Haffluence, Dominhic*, he could hear Esther saying. *Rich peepull, they pay big money to haff such good taste*—seemed the exception, scrappiness the rule. Same went for the silence. How many streets were devoid of cars and trucks, bikes and carts, pedestrians and even dogs? Two that he knew of. One, Sikkim Lane, where the second cousin of the monk from Om monastery lived. The other, this very lane, where he now dwelt under genteel house arrest.

He tried not to be rattled. The shared address was unsettling, but not as much as his own muddle-headedness, which he deplored, regardless if it was a natural function of attempting to think on his feet with only a quarter the usual oxygen pumping into his lungs. He passed her house without slowing. The doors were closed and the drapes were drawn. No clothes on the balcony. Fewer than five pots on the sill. At the intersection of Liberation Boulevard he skirted around the dogs sprawled across the lane, their backs to traffic. The other night, he'd assumed the animals were a neighbourhood patrol, sizing up any who dared encroach on their territory. Now, canine body language alerted him to another sobering truth. The dogs weren't gate-keeping Sikkim Lane; they were afraid to venture down it.

The quickest route to the restaurant followed a trail that ran along the east side of the Zone. Dominic dodged the usual clog of vehicles, bikes, and pilgrims to cross the boulevard, then looped around a trio of yaks to regain the path. His route took him past the sports stadium and latest demolition site in the Gyatsian city—a row of traditional houses being levelled by bulldozers. Cutting across the terrain in front of the Stink, an unmarked two-storey bunker with its own parking lot wildlife, he officially entered the Shamo Three Quarters along a narrow street behind the hotel.

Mustang Saman's, a rare standing Gyatsian building on the wrong side of the Zone, advertised itself succinctly above the doorway. "Good Eats, No Dogs" promised a painted sign. The entrance struck Dominic as curious. There was a frame, and a curtain tied back with rope during operating hours, but no door. He had checked twice, in case it had been swung around the inside. Other striking features of the establishment included the absence of a blaring television—in contrast to even the smallest Shamo eatery—packed earth as a floor, a bare bulb as lighting, and a long bar where men stood drinking beer in Hawaiian shirts and wide-rimmed hats. Mounted in a corner was a shrine with an incense pot and a photo of the Vadra Pani. Such a display, he had read, could earn the devout a ten-year prison sentence. A pair of framed posters hung over the bar. The first, of Elvis Presley in the uniform of the United States Army, had been inscribed: "To my good buddy Saman." The second, of Madonna in concert, was just signed.

His guidebook recommended Mustang Saman's over every place in Bon, aside from the outrageously priced Vacation Inn eateries. Five stars, no less. *The Rough Guide* broke its rating down: one star for cold beer, one for yak noodles not too clotted in grease, one for an item on the menu involving a vegetable, one for mostly fly- and butt-free servings, and a final star for ... the Elvis poster. Foreigners in Gyatso speculated about it endlessly, even those who didn't think the King was alive and well in the lost paradise.

The restaurant had a half-dozen tables. All but one were empty, aside from a dog curled underneath a chair. It flicked a bloodshot eye at Dominic as warning. Paddy Chan sat hunched over a clean plate. Empty mugs, their insides stained like toilet bowls, waited next to a steaming Nescafé.

"Go easy on that stuff," Dominic said.

"I'm pumped all right," Chan answered, his right leg a piston. "And you, fuck wit, are late."

"Sorry."

"As ever."

The owner, a giant the equal of the translator Anatman Sangmo, hobbled over. The book issued precise instructions for dealing with the restaurateur called Saman; ask no questions about the sign or shrine or, for sure, the posters. Saman had shoulders so broad they seemed a burden, a yoke worn in punishment. His eyelids drooped and his stare also rivalled Ant's in its innate contempt. While not far off sixty and bothered by a limp, he still exuded the physical vigour of the Kashang warrior, especially in the arms and hands, one of which was notable—to absolutely everyone—for two missing fingers. They had been amputated near their base, without the aid of a surgeon.

"You eat again?" Saman asked.

"No food, thanks."

"You eat good in Bon this day, yes? More delicious than my noodles?"

"I love your noodles, Saman," Dominic replied. Amazingly, the connection with "Ocean"—a coincidence, he assumed—occurred to him only then. "They could be even more spicy for my taste. Just a beer, though. Please."

"Nescafé better," the owner advised. "Clear your head. Make you smarter. Make you do job not so fucked."

Saman knew what he'd had for lunch at the hotel? "Beer, please," he repeated in a voice boasting an ease he did not feel.

Shrugging, the man walked away.

"Who is Saman when he's at home?" Paddy Chan said. "And why does he know all that he seems to know?"

"You noticed it as well?"

"Notice it? I show up here an hour ago—at the agreed-upon time, I might add—and your one informs me I'm a lucky Shamo pig boy not to be chained to the wall in some cell. He says I deserve as much. He says 'they' went easy on me!"

"I'm lost ..."

"Ta, love," Chan answered, his accent suddenly inner-city London. His gaze ordered silence.

Yet another strapping Gyatsian, his shaven head showing off a nasty scar zigzagging his skull, dropped a beer onto the table from such a height that foam shot back up the spout. Running a finger over the bottle's jagged mouth, Dominic decided he could live without a glass.

Chan helped himself to a Marlboro from Dominic's pack. He struck match to flint with studied style. The way he extinguished the flame—three vigorous shakes, two of them superfluous—was equally posed. "Hate to say it," he began, "but Captain Bligh has a point about the boozing. You need your eyes settled in their sockets this afternoon, McNicky."

"I want to talk to you about that. I'm not so sure we should do anything."

"What, you have your story?"

"Kind of."

"Just doing your job? Never mind the consequences, or the casualties?"

"Don't put words—"

"Let me tell you a story that *is* part of your story, whether you know it or not," Chan said. "Matter of fact, stories that are 'yours,' in so far as you birthed them, are happening all over this town, even as we speak. Why, your Tashi Delag tale was simply the top rock in a landslide, now an avalanche. Houses are being crushed and children getting bonked with stones thanks to you. Bon is shake, rattle, and rolling, boyo—can't you feel the beat?"

Dominic glanced across at the man's fevered eyes, checked down at the mug in his grasp, and decided that, while he still thought it best to do nothing, and he certainly didn't think he merited this anger, he had better listen to Paddy Chan's story. Chan shifted so his back showed to the bar and the other drinkers. That placed Dominic in a constant line of vision with those drinkers, and that bar. He wished they were outside. He wished, not for the first time, he knew more about his accomplice.

"I'm in my room yesterday morning, right after we bid adieu in the lobby, when Bon Tourism rings to say that the departure has been changed from mid-afternoon to early evening. 'Fine by me,' I answer. 'I've no place to be.' They collect me at three, Sun Nanping and this other one, and we drive all the way to the airport, only to learn that the flight, get this, has now been cancelled! So says Mr. Shamo, at any rate, who makes me wait in the car while he pops into the terminal. Back to Bon we go, the car slowing to move around these chunks of rock—boulders, more like it—that have crashed down onto the motorway since we drove out. Sun drops me at the Stink and says he'll ring in the morning. 'So, it isn't settled that I leave tomorrow?' I ask. 'Not settled,' he replies. 'What about my visa?' I say. 'It expires at midnight tonight.' 'You cannot remain in Gyatso without proper visa,' he agrees. 'So ...?' I add, bugging my oriental eyes. 'So, good-night,' he answers. The weasel even hints I should stick close to the hotel. Stick close, and not bother calling up foreigners staying in the brand name kip across town. A Canadian foreigner, say. A Canadian foreigner I've been snooping around with for the past several days. Two reasons why I shouldn't ring you for a chat, Bon Tourism explains. One, my face, if not my passport, tells him I'm not immune from prosecution. Two, I might be—"

Dominic couldn't let the accusation about Sun—a decent person, he firmly believed—go unchallenged. He waited until Saman plunked down more coffee and beer. The Gyatsian left the empties on the table, his version of a tab, and walked over to the shrine. Using a lighter, he fired a thicket of joss sticks and bobbed his head before the framed photo of the fourteenth reincarnation of the living Buddha, an exile of nearly a half-century in a neighbouring country. The dog under the table joined the owner, as if it, too, wished a moment with its spiritual leader. Saman limped back to the bar; the dog sagged to the floor.

"Did Sun actually threaten you?"

"He asked a question."

"Which was...?"

"He wanted to know the name of my parents' ancestral village in Guangdong province. He said there were hundreds of Chan family villages down there—did I know which prefecture?"

"Maybe he was, you know ..."

"Making polite conversation?" Chan pitched his cigarette into an empty bottle. A funnel of smoke coiled up the neck, clouding the glass. "Think that if you'd like. Sun Nanping was making polite conversation and, by the by, letting me know that, if they wanted, they could shred my EU passport, plunk a red-starred cap onto my head, and call me one of theirs, home after a long holiday."

"Okay."

"You've read that fella all wrong."

Dominic kept silent.

"What, because he has a wife and child he's automatically above suspicion? Because he's doing a job he despises, and is probably stuck with, means he isn't responsible for—" Something in Dominic's expression—impatience, most likely—caused him to drop the diatribe. "Mr. Adoring Daddy and Loving Husband," he resumed, his tone almost hurt, "remembers to mention that I might be receiving visitors later on. 'Just for a talk,' the good family man adds. Sure enough, midnight comes a knock at the door. Fuck me if it isn't the other stooges. Luckily, I can't sleep for the howling of dogs in the parking lot. I'm also fully dressed underneath the duvet, on account of the negligible difference between the temperature inside my room and outside it. The lads don't want a cup of tea or polite conversation, either. They want to take me on a wee ride. 'Thanks but no thanks,' I reply. 'I've already seen plenty of the countryside today.' I'm bearing in mind stories of one-way trips in the dead of Belfast nights. The bodies dumped up behind Cave Hill. Single bullet to the head, indications of a pummelling beforehand."

Though Dominic was doing his best to focus, he couldn't completely ignore the Gyatsians at the bar. Not with them pointing to Chan's hair and laughing.

"Turns out the car ride isn't an offer," the Irishman said, starting in on his fresh mug without regard for the steam. "'You want to leave Gyatso?' Wu Jing asks in Shamo. 'You cooperate.' 'Remember who you are,' Ant says in Gyatsian. 'Well do I remember, praise God,' I answer them in English. 'Paddy Chan is the name. Belfast is the ancestral village, Northern Ireland the nation once again. British subject, natch. So, lads,' I conclude, 'go get fucked, if you don't mind.'"

"Nice."

"I'm dragged down the hall, a Shamo squeezing one arm and a Gyatsian bruising the other. Wu Jing is a pathetic wisp, and I could swat him away. Ant, though, has a garda's iron grip. He also keeps doing a trick with his knee, brushing it up against mine, causing me to ... Are you even listening?"

"Sure," Dominic said.

Chan rested both elbows on the table. "Tell you what. I'll finish what I'm saying, and you'll finish listening to me say it. Over my shoulder the carry-on will carry on. A few of the lads may dust it up, add more skid marks to their skulls with smashed beer bottles or those swords they're fond of. Soldiers may storm the bar and arrest Saman for the crime of owning a Vadra Pani shrine but no front door. Maybe Tashi Delag himself will stroll in and order a can of Heineken. Maybe all this will happen, Nicky boy," he added, donning his sunglasses with a flourish, "and you will be witness. But I won't, and I won't be sorry, and I *won't* wish to be kept up on current affairs."

"Got it."

"Good. Off we go then through the streets of Bon. I'm in the back seat with Ant and try marking our course. With those useless twenty-watt bulbs in the street lamps, and half the cars driving blind, it's hopeless. We negotiate the Shamo Three Quarters, that I know, and pass the bomb factory. Trucks going in, naturally, but none coming out. Wu turns up an alley. He cuts the lights and motor and the car glides to a stop outside a building. I say something stupid—'Home, sweet home' I think it was—and Ant barks that I should shut my gob.

"He guides me, his grip murdering my arm, into a room. It has desks with computers, a fax machine on a stand. The reek is the usual—duck fat and cabbage. Likewise the filthy tea mugs and ashtrays choked in butts, floors of poured concrete and walls the colour of dried shite. The walls are bare, except for a couple of posters. One shows the Eiffel Tower. The other, believe it or not, is that castle over in your neck of the woods— Quebec City, right?"

Dominic knew the room. Every detail, including the poster of the Château Frontenac in Quebec. "That's Bon Tourism," he said. "Off the square with the fighter jet at its centre. Sun had to collect something there the other day, and I spent fifteen minutes waiting for him."

"It fucking well is not Bon Tourism."

"Honest."

"Behind the main room is a corridor with four cells. Know many tourism offices with their own holding pens? What, for Germans who don't buy enough fake mandalas? Brits who want a refund on their rip-off visits to peasant homes? This is a lock-up, laddie. The cell I get tossed into is lined floor to ceiling with newspapers and leaflets. There's an old copier with a hand crank, the sort that might have been used to print republican circulars during the Spanish Civil War. A piss pot in the corner. A rag for wiping your busted lip."

Dominic sipped his beer and smoked his Marlboro. Twice his eyes wandered. The first time, he observed Saman and another Gyatsian touch foreheads. That, at least, was what the men appeared to be doing: leaning in so that their brows came into gentle contact. The gesture was open and unashamed. He glanced away again, earning a scowl from Paddy Chan, to watch more customers enter. One Gyatsian made for the counter. The other, a foot shorter, got lost behind bodies.

"The stooges begin by grilling me on your escapades," Chan said. "I find that insulting. 'I haven't just been sitting in my room chanting sutras,' I tell them. 'How do you know I haven't been out fucking up lives on my own, rather than at the behest of the lanky Canuck with the fancy jacket and free fags?' The irony is, Ant and Wu bring *me* up to scratch on your activities. You forgot to call, lover boy. You didn't collect your messages at the reception."

Fucking up lives? Dominic thought to himself. "What did they say I'd been doing?"

"Chat with a monk at Om, which I knew about, and a sleep-over with some Gyatsian bird of aristocratic bearing, about which I surely was not aware. My, my, Mr. Family Man, aren't we—"

"I spent the night on her couch."

"And I scored the winning goal in the World Cup."

"What else?"

"How this bird, Lavanya something or another, took you by the hand—or was it by the mickie?—and walked you across the city, in broad daylight, to the gate of Gyatsian Literature. There, she sent you directly to the door of the very man, the very myth, we'd been seeking. '*Tashi delag*, Tashi Delag,' I assume you said. 'Glad to see you do exist after all.'"

"Something like that."

"Except I wouldn't have your natural eloquence or skills at investigative journalism, would I? Not me, your slanty Ponza, your leering fool. Yez, boss. Very good, Sahib. Mistah Kurtz—he dead. Call me Ishmael."

A flurry of barks spared Dominic having to ask Paddy Chan to explain his outrageous babbling. Even the Irishman glanced over at the dog, which was now up on its feet. Dominic followed the animal's attention to the two people who had recently joined the clutch. Not the grownup; the other one, in plain sight. A Gyatsian boy. Maybe twelve, maybe younger.

"But never mind you and never mind me," Chan continued, "and never mind the writer and never mind the bird. What Ant and Wu are most keen to find out about, Dominic, what the stooges find most arresting, and most worthy of arrest, DOM-EH-FUCKING-NIC—"

"Sorry? You sounded like my wife there," he said absently. *Dominhic*, Esther lovingly intoned, singing the music of his name. The young Gyatsian at the bar, he realized, shaking off the thought: wasn't he—?

"Don't we all look the same."

"I didn't mean—"

"—was the boy."

"What?"

Chan hadn't turned around. He hadn't moved a muscle in several minutes. As for his eyes, they were inscrutable behind glasses.

"That boy Kuno we chatted with?" he said, his forehead furrowing at Dominic's obvious shock. "The one who put us on to the monk? Bon Tourism was keen to get more information about him. 'Dis Gyatsian boy assist you, yes?' Wu Jing whistled through his back-alley dentistry. 'Hep you do illegal things in Bon?' I told them they had it all wrong. How we spoke with Kuno for maybe five minutes. How the conversation was mostly about his mother, and his philosophy of life. And how he was just a boy, just some boy, and anyway, exactly what did they think they were doing grilling a British national, a card-carrying member of the European Union, like he was some freak-haired Shamo enemy of the state?"

But Paddy Chan, Dominic understood, was off the mark about Kuno. He wasn't just some boy. He was *the* boy, the one

standing at the counter. Those eyes. That smile. More important, the way the adolescent carried himself, in this case a
sapling in a forest of conifers—proud and unfazed, an equal.
When the dog trotted over, the boy sank to a knee and, taking
the animal by the snout, nuzzled it with both hands. The
gesture struck a note of familiarity, as though Dominic had
watched Kuno treat another animal with such solicitude.

"Paddy," he said, his gaze flitting from the Gyatsian to
himself reflected in Chan's mirrors, "there's someone at the bar
I think you might want to meet."

"Is it Elvis Aron?"

"I'm serious."

"Madonna Ciccone?"

"Fine."

"Can I please get back to my story?"

"Sorry for interrupting."

"Damn straight," Chan said. He leaned further into his own
narrative, oblivious to the presence of his main character ten
feet away. "Once the lads have copped on that I know nothing,
I'm pitched into a cell. For maybe an hour I lie on the floor,
using light seeping under the door to check out the newspapers
and circulars. It's Shamo propaganda, calling on Gyatsians to
overthrow feudalism and denounce rule by monks, participate
in the Three Rs and the Five Ss, love the army, and grow patriotic rice at fifteen thousand feet instead of subversive barley. I
kid you not. Every inane, vicious Shamo initiative for the last
fifty years was right there, in any-idiot-can-read ideograms. A
brief history of the occupation, under dust."

"In the tourism office?"

"This was not the tourism office!" He stopped. "Are you
messing with my head?"

The thought hadn't crossed Dominic's mind. "I wouldn't
dare," he replied.

"Aye, you would so, I think," Chan said. "I'm lying there
reading this garbage when I hear a scuffle in the corridor. Wu
Jing calls someone a dog. The dog doesn't reply, so Wu sends

him or her to the floor. I'm at dog's level, as it were, and what I
see through the space under the frame is a child's face. A boy
with a swollen cheek and bloody nose. It's the eyes that give
him away. It's Kuno the philosopher."

Dominic hid his hands under the table. Could he trust his
gaze to stay on Chan? "You're positive?"

"Ninety-nine percent."

"And he was beaten up?"

"Smacked around good."

"Did you call to him?"

"I did, naturally. 'Tell me your name!' I shout. Wu orders me
to put a sock in it. He drags the lad to another cell. I keep shouting, asking the boy to identify himself, but Kuno stays quiet.
Finally, Wu and Ant reappear. I have it in mind to bang on a
couple of doors myself, but they escort me arm-in-arm back
through the office. 'Suffer the children, do we, Ant?' I say.
'Finally picking on someone your own size, Wu?' Ant, I can tell,
is nearly out of his head with rage. Wu just keeps sucking air
into his mouth."

"And Kuno," Dominic said. "He was bleeding?" He made a
quick study of the boy at the bar.

"I just said ..."

"And a shiner?"

"Not a shiner. His cheek was bruised."

"And you're *sure* it was Kuno?"

"What the fuck are you getting at?"

Dominic, discerning a commotion over Paddy Chan's shoulder—handshakes and parting words, he feared—stood up so
abruptly he knocked the table with his thigh. A bottle fell and
rolled to the edge. Both men reached for it. Chan caught the
bottle and looked up, puzzled.

"Turn around, Paddy. Right now."

But they were too late. The commotion had indeed been the
departure of all the Gyatsians, large and small, except for
Saman. Even the dog had joined the exodus. Paddy Chan
perched his glasses high on his skull.

Dominic knew what he had to do. "Let's go," he said.

"Where?"

"See if we can track down Kuno."

"I just told you he's in a cell!"

"I have a hunch... Just follow me, okay?"

"Aye, aye, Major Wilson."

And who are you, Paddy Chan?

At the counter Saman counted the bottles and cups with his deformed hand, the limb bobbing in an invisible current. Though Dominic didn't mean to stare at the amputation, he couldn't stop himself. The owner announced a total, declaring it for one plate of not-spicy-enough noodles, along with four coffees and five beers. Chan protested the beer count; Dominic did not.

"They serve a better brand at the hotel," he said. "You should charge a bit more for those." He peeled off a five-hundred-yuan bill. The bill barely came to one hundred, but he told Saman to keep the change.

The Gyatsian studied the bill, which Dominic, by way of apology, held in his left hand. Saman also let his gaze purposefully wander to the pinkie. *You stare at me*, his eyes taunted. *I stare back at you.*

"I'll just leave this on the counter," Dominic managed to reply. He couldn't pocket his hand fast enough.

"Nicky," Paddy Chan said in a different tone. "Will you look at what the cat dragged in."

Dominic didn't need to turn to the door to get that the reference wasn't to Kuno. The scent, and footfall, tipped him off.

"Come for the yak burgers, Ant?"

Anatman Sangmo crossed to the bar. "Visit my brother," he answered, not bothering to look at either of them.

"That would be...?"

"Big brother Saman."

"Of course," Dominic said, the skin stretching tight over his brain. "I see the resemblance, now that you mention it."

Saman served his sibling a Nescafé. Pinching the mug

between fingers, Ant slurped the liquid. Then he, too, examined the five-hundred-yuan note, holding it up to the light as though checking for a forgery. "This tourist visa has run out," he said, indicating Chan without addressing him. "He is no longer allowed in Gyatso. He should stay at hotel, as told, until we get him ticket."

"You mean, until you've finished investigating him," Chan replied.

"Stay at hotel."

"I'm heading back there right now," the Irishman offered, rubbing his palms against his legs. "Going to watch a football match on satellite TV. I've invited along a young sports enthusiast. You might know the boy. You kicked his head in last night, after all."

"We'd better get going, Paddy," Dominic said.

"I'm not done here. And get your hands off me."

"Go to room in Stink instead," Ant advised Dominic, still ignoring Paddy Chan. "Maybe then you not suicide."

The sentence crashed the conversation. Ant repeated the apparent witticism in Gyatsian and the brothers roared.

"Give him army funeral, maybe," Saman said in English. "Bury him with Shamo officer pigs."

Ant howled.

"I'm sorry," Dominic said, "but I don't believe I know what you fellas are talking about."

"Toilet best place for job," Ant concluded. "Maids happy if you not mess up beds." Enjoying another noisy sip of coffee, he turned his back on the foreigners.

Soon the Sangmos were deep in conversation. Paddy Chan looked about to open his mouth again when Dominic, at a loss to communicate, walked out the door. The light ambushed him, and he slipped on his own glasses.

Chapter Six

"Why did you—?"

"We need to talk to Kuno," Dominic said.

"And what do you think I was doing back there? I fully intended to ask Ant where they'd locked the boy up."

"He'd have told you, wouldn't he have? 'Sure, Kuno is still in his cell, nursing the black eye and broken ribs we gave him. It's the cell right next to where we put you. Come on, lad, I'll take you myself.'"

The Irishman frowned at the sarcasm. But Dominic had been made a fool of, and was angry and—if he cared to admit it—hurt.

Chan sighed. "The way you North Americans pronounce the language. *Cum an, laad.*"

"Who's that supposed to be—John Wayne?"

"Aye, or any one of a dozen other American movie stars showing off their miserable brogues."

And what's your excuse? Dominic almost said. He now wondered. Who was Paddy Chan, to use his own colloquialism, when *he* was at home? He wanted to believe he hailed from Belfast. But would an immigrant kid raised in Northern Ireland talk that way? Chan's accent seemed almost too rollicking and profane to be real. Dominic would have expected such a boy to emerge speaking in a manner balanced between belonging to a place and remaining an outsider. A tone more neutral and reserved. Might he be a brilliant trickster? A native of Kowloon or San Francisco playing at a fantasy?

A more sinister possibility presented itself: suppose Paddy Chan was a public security cop gone undercover. Someone working Dominic as a decoy. Using him to flush out local troublemakers. Counting on his condescension, paraded as good will. Counting on his ignorance of the particular, disguised as knowledge of the global. If he had been set up by Chan, and in turn had betrayed those Gyatsians they contacted together, it might prove too much to bear. How could he face Esther again? And his father?

"Where are we going?" Chan asked.

Of course Dominic had had his doubts. From the moment he first approached the Asian Marlboro model in the Kata plaza. Forget the accent. What about the nose stud and earrings, the hair? All over the top. All like a local who, soused on rock videos and teen movies, had attempted a bad approximation of a 1990s Western rebel youth. And Chan's explanation for his presence in Gyatso—a simple vacation? When he spoke, halt- ingly but with obvious fluency, a language only that much less marginal than, say, Dene? How many tourists picked up the obscure lingua franca for a two-week holiday?

"McNicky? Hello...?"

Fear induced bluster in him. "And will you quit calling me that," he said. "Quit with the cracks about my being a global pirateer. As if it's so black and white. As if these countries would really be better off with their old non-economies. As if, for that matter," he added, his words several steps ahead of his thoughts, "*you* aren't Western business in Asia as well. If, that is, you are who, or what, you say you are."

They had halted along the road behind the Stink. The wind, rarely less than a whine, roared into their faces. Paddy Chan squared his shoulders. He had removed his shades in prepa- ration to speak when a figure slid between them without apol- ogy. Chan frowned at the freckles and blond hair, the broad back and military gait. Baring his eyes as well, Dominic blinked.

"I know him," he said. "He flew into Bon the same afternoon I did. He had no luggage and, given how fast he was arrested, no visa either. What's he doing?"

"Let's come back to who he is, and who I am, in a second. First, the small matter of destination. Where are you taking me?"

"The Zone."

"To find Kuno?"

"Right."

"Then tell me this—who's the stranger now? Who's the one not acting the person he says he is?"

"Meaning ...?"

"Was it an hour ago that Dominic Wilson claimed he was in favour of leaving this entire business alone? Now this same Wilson is suggesting we go chat up a lad worked over by the evil powers that be? What next—will we be taking notes and snapping photos to show to Amnesty International?"

"This is different," Dominic answered feebly. How else could he reply: that he was guiding Chan to the proof of his deception?

"Is it? And will we move on from the boy to find out what's become of Tashi Delag and the Lavanya woman? And the monk at Om?"

"Why would we do all that?"

"You still don't get the fucking picture?" Paddy Chan asked. "They're on to us! Everyone we've spoken to, right down, I bet, to the old ones on the street, have been subsequently visited by the stooges, or stooges like them."

"It can't be that bad."

"No, it can be worse."

"This is about a kid," Dominic said, blustering hard. "Even if what you say is true, those other people are grownups. They knew the risks. They accepted that talking to us could have consequences. Half the time they sought us out, remember? But Kuno is a child. He can't know better. He shouldn't have to."

"And why not?"

"Paddy!"

"In exactly what Disneyland, Dominic, what fairy kingdom, are children able to enjoy childhoods not being forever clipped by their having to pay premature witness to, and even bear the brunt of, the fucked-up methods and means of their parents and neighbours, mentors and protectors? Tell me that. Is this place beyond those mountains? Just the far side of Bon valley, maybe?"

Dominic had no reply. All Paddy Chan had done was say aloud what he had been thinking to himself: *They are on to us.*

"Ah, right, the subject is me, and your sudden conviction that I am the enemy," the Irishman said. "In some respects I'm flattered. But in others I'm not, and suspect I ought to punch your lights out."

Again Dominic had no response, even to a threat. Though he could not begin to understand why—the situation was complex, but hardly hopeless—he battled feelings of desolation, like a man who realizes his life is behind him.

"A test of loyalty, is it? Swear allegiance to king and empire? Prove I'm not some fifth columnist, likely to slit the governor's throat one night? Right then. Let's find Kuno."

From the Shamo side, the Zone sloped down towards the Gyatsian Quarter. In the distance shimmered the Kata domes. Beyond the city, foothills of juniper glades and ghostly streams moved in and out of cover. Beyond them again, the mountains loomed above the valley weather. As usual, the adamantine air gave ridges and crowns a hundred miles to the east the appearance of being a few easy hours' walk away. As always, too, the sky itself, was in no sense sheltering. Socked-in skies, whether by pollution or monsoons, were unknown in Gyatso. Light rarely got diffused, and so assailed unremittingly.

The Zone now buzzed with activity. Groups of soldiers sauntered in packs, hats perched high and pant legs flapping. Kids kicked soccer balls. Across from where Dominic and Chan entered, bulldozers snarled and snapped at the row of buildings being demolished. Farther along, a crew with paint rollers whitewashed the sports stadium wall.

They pushed through a crowd gathered outside the Stink. The people were mostly military, along with another work crew in straw hats and slippers. At the centre was a girl performing a dance. She looked ten or eleven. Her features were Gyatsian. Her braided hair could also have been local, though the style reminded Dominic of the cornrows worn by African-Canadians. She had glossed her lips cherry, some of it smeared to slatternly effect, and wore a black body suit and boots with silver buckles. For music, the girl favoured a wordless drums 'n bass, its pulse as flat-lined as the thoughts of an addict letting the drugs kick in.

Her assistant, perhaps her younger brother, squatted beside a boombox. He had on a rain poncho and pants so flimsy they could have been pyjamas. The whites of his eyes startled against his filthy skin.

The dancer's style was hiphop, mimicked from videos. Legs spread and hands on knees, she first swivelled her backside and then commenced shifting foot to foot, punching the air with her fists. The movements were mechanical, as if choreographed out of rage, the cornrows flying over her skull and banging into her forehead. Her expression went vacant and her eyes never lit. Had Dominic been alone, he would have silenced the music and wrapped her in his jacket. He would have offered her American dollars to quit and hailed a cab to return her to her parents.

He dragged Paddy Chan back through the scrum.

"She's fucking brilliant," Chan said.

"Think so?"

"The girl could dance on an MTV video, she could. MTV Asia, I mean, out of Singapore, or Channel V from Taipei."

"I'm sure."

"Do you let your own kids watch those video programs, Nicky?"

The Irishman had asked the question before. As he had the last time, Dominic shook his head.

"But you aren't so fussy about others having access, are you? Bon, after all, is pathetically under-wired—if you do say so yourself. Plenty of satellite dishes and video shops in the Shamo areas, one man one television, one woman one camcorder, but hardly any democracy being practised over in the Gyatsian part of town. You and the lads would soon see to that, of course. Sound business opportunities. A market in dire need of development."

Once more, Dominic couldn't think of an answer. Much of what he had said to the younger man in the past several days had come out wrong. Paddy Chan made him nervous. He also left him self-conscious about certain of his own habits and attitudes. Conversation around personal lives had been halting at best. This despite Dominic's own willingness to share details about his wife and kids, his upbringing in Toronto, even his relationships with his parents. In return Chan had divulged almost nothing: one anecdote, one glimpse.

As for Dominic's banter during their walks around Bon, that was idle chat. How people broke the ice. At luncheons and meetings, on airplanes and in hotels. Shooting the breeze about satellite contracts and software wars, real-time financial services—still WilCor's bread and butter—and e-commerce. Nothing more than the bland, faintly dispiriting filling of dead air during one more departure delay and still another banquet.

Chan was probably further deflecting attention from himself. Even so, and even though he scarcely needed to mount a defence, Dominic had to ask. "What do my comments about the lack of TVs and computers in Gyatsian houses have to do with how that girl danced for us?"

"What do you think?"

"Knock it off, Paddy."

"Then knock off playing the thick git."

They crossed the Zone and wandered down to the stadium, where some kids had gathered. Another yak blocked the path. This hairy ox boasted the usual dripping nostrils and halo of flies, the cologne of week-old meat. But it also possessed a black coat that seemed freshly shampooed and brushed. Claiming he'd read that the animals were mostly bluff, Paddy Chan decided to give the yak's horns a yank. He was serious, and had to be dissuaded.

"This is fucking boffo," Chan said. "Assuming Kuno is even at large again, the chances of finding him are virtually nil."

"There he is," Dominic replied.

Improbable but true: fifteen yards away, the boy from Mustang Saman's squatted in the Asian manner—buttocks on heels, arms over knees—with his friends. Dominic called his name. Kuno turned and squinted. He hadn't thought of it earlier, but the adolescent who had made such an impression on them originally had been far scruffier than the one in the restaurant. Hard to imagine today's Kuno, attired in a collared shirt and jacket, jeans with the tag still showing on a back pocket, begging money. Not with his hair cleaned and combed, as though for church, and his cheeks so shiny he almost appeared made-up, like the dancer. Only the squint was the same. The squint, and the intelligence of his gaze.

Paddy Chan frowned at the boy standing arms-crossed before them. He spoke to him.

"He looks fine, doesn't he?" Dominic interjected.

Chan didn't answer.

"You asked about last night?"

"He claims not to know what I'm talking about." Chan switched languages again. Whatever he said merited only a shrug from Kuno. The Irishman began to berate the young Gyatsian.

"He's a wee liar, he is," he summarized.

"*He* is?"

"That's what I just—" Chan turned to Dominic. "Are you suggesting I made the story up?"

"Someone is inventing things, Paddy."

Chan wheeled and walked away.

"Wait!" Dominic shouted, alarmed by Paddy Chan's response. "I didn't mean to call you a liar. I just can't figure—"

"You surely did mean to. You've been meaning to call me that for the last hour."

"Could you ask him about his mother?"

"Why should I?"

"Let's straighten this out, please?"

He retraced his steps. "You can be a prick, Nicky," he said quietly, before returning to Kuno. This time, the boy's answer had him cursing in disbelief. "He says his mother is in the peak of health."

"No need for medicine?"

Chan translated.

As Kuno spoke, his body language drew as tense as a bow. When his expression snapped, as though the arrow had been dispatched, the release left him openly pained, almost aggrieved.

"He says the state provides medicine for all people. He says Gyatsians live long and happy lives thanks to the guidance of the Shamos."

"His face hardly agrees with his words, does it?"

"What have they done to the lad?"

Paddy Chan extended a hand, apparently to touch Kuno's face. The boy ducked.

Dominic sensed the encounter was nearing its end. "Tell him I'm glad his mother isn't sick and doesn't need black market medicine, as he thought she did. But *he* needs glasses, right? He's nearsighted. He must have trouble reading. Tell him I want him to go buy prescription glasses." He removed another five-hundred-yuan bill from his wallet. "Not tough-guy shades, either. Real glasses, so he can study harder and read more books without ending up blind by forty."

Chan did as told. Sped up, his Shamo sounded gruff and accusatory.

"Watch his eyes, Paddy."

The Irishman did more than watch. Having wet a finger, he took another swipe at the boy's cheek. Kuno snatched the money and fell to his knees, wincing not at the pain to his kneecaps but, given how he held his stomach, a wound to the midsection. His head stayed lowered.

"Make-up," Chan said, displaying a smudged tip. "To hide the bruises."

"See how he winced?"

"I'll wager they cracked a rib."

There was a shout from behind. Kuno's friends had been

taunting a smaller group of Shamo kids. Now they were whooping at the enemy and tossing stones. Once again, Dominic had no trouble distinguishing the sides. The Shamo boys, retreating from the assault, looked in equal parts stunned and sleepy, as though even being attacked was a boring routine. The locals, in contrast, were in the usual high spirits.

Kuno himself managed a smile as he raced off, still clutching his gut. His grin held at the emergence of an escort of dogs, who seemed to materialize, as always, from thin air. They tore after him down the east side of the Zone. All parties made for Liberation Boulevard.

Paddy Chan joined the pursuit, followed by two more mutts. When Dominic finally broke into a reluctant jog, he, too, had a companion. His dog was especially pathetic, a stunted hop-along with three scrawny legs.

By the time the initial wave reached the street, it was far from clear who were the chasers and who the chased. First the Shamo kids, and then the Gyatsians, and the original pack of dogs, and then Paddy Chan with his new friends; all ploughed into the bicycle, vehicular, and pilgrim traffic choking the boulevard. A few boys skirted objects on the road. Chan hurtled a toppled bike.

Dominic had less luck. He had planned to wade carefully through the traffic. But the three-legged beast kept hard on him. Fearing less the bite than the subsequent rabies shot, he roared through the near lane and shifted his shoulders to slide between the back cabin of a truck and a bumper. A yelp—of tire over paw, he hoped—proved too tempting, and he glanced back. The mistake sent him sprawling over a Gyatsian already prostrate on the asphalt. He got up and apologized.

"*Tashi delag,*" the pilgrim answered, his grin toothless.

Dominic assumed he had lost the crippled dog in the melee. Dismay at sighting the animal waiting on the far shoulder drained him of any lingering enthusiasm for this chase. He needed the flask of Scotch. He needed a cigarette.

An end-around worked no better. The barking animal moved

laterally with unnatural ease, given its infirmity. Dominic scoured the ground for something to throw. As he bent to pick up a Pepsi can, a car parked farther along the street came into view. A man leaned against the roof, his elbows splayed like a tripod. In his hands rested a telescope. Only it wasn't a telescope; it was a—

He flinched at a second report of rifle shots in the past six hours. The sound was louder than before: *POP-POP-POP!* Sure enough, the dog yelped and flopped. It rose at once and hobbled away, pellets ricocheting off the terrain. Another hit, a dull percussion, and the animal collapsed for good.

Wu Jing circled around the Bon Tourism vehicle with the AK-47 riding off his hip. The driver was still firing, squeezing the trigger in three-pellet flurries. Dominic had extended both hands, palms out, to act as shield, when the shooter roared past him. Farther down the Zone, Paddy Chan was in trouble. He had foolishly swung his jacket at the dogs, allowing one to seize a sleeve in its jaws. With a yank the animal had dropped him to his knees. The rest of the pack was closing in for the kill when metal sprayed the earth. Dogs and kids alike scattered.

Chan sprinted over. "Christ in heaven," he said, examining the tear in his sleeve, "spare us from the gunmen."

A taxi had slowed on Liberation Boulevard at the sight of a westerner. The men climbed in opposite doors.

"Where to?" Chan asked.

The presence of Wu Jing, the fact that the Bon Tourism driver had indeed caught them chatting with the same boy he and Ant had roughed up the night before, and then blackmailed—these hardly were positive developments. Dominic's chances of seeing his family anytime soon would be enhanced if he returned at once to his monitored dining hall and bugged hotel room, and there sat tight until the authorities grew so tired of his cowardly compliance, his mealy-mouthed assurances of meaning no harm, having no agenda, that they sent him home. The most prudent instruction he could give the cabbie? The one someone like him could be safely *counted* on giving? "Om monastery," he said.

Paddy Chan blew air from his cheeks.

"Tell him," Dominic insisted.

"You're sure?"

"Of course I'm not sure."

The Irishman studied him for a moment, then translated the request.

The driver glanced into his rear-view mirror. Shaking his head, he mumbled a reply.

"Om is off-limits to foreigners, except with an official guide," Chan said. "If he drove us there, he could lose his licence."

Dominic checked out his window. Wu Jing was sauntering towards the taxi, the AK-47 now tucked into his shoulder, the barrel aimed downwards.

"Offer him an extra fifty yuan."

The cabbie still refused. Wu was now so close they could hear him sucking air into his abscessed cavity. He was five paces away. Four. Three.

"Make it a hundred."

The taxi pulled out into traffic.

Chapter Seven

Each man kept to himself for a few minutes. Dominic focused on pulling back from the chasm he had briefly peered over. He could fix this. He could undo what he had done. Though spotty on the big issues—a failed first marriage, a wandering eye, the schism with his father, to name a few—he rarely fell down at specific tasks. And once he had made matters right here and was where he belonged, confessing to his wife and being largely forgiven, loving his children and being unconditionally loved in return, he would smarten up. No more nocturnal walk-abouts. No more indulgent whims. In a few hours he would be celebrating a serious birthday. Time to show he could be wise. Time to act coherently.

Why not still do the magazine piece? The material couldn't be better. As for this ongoing footnote, he now doubted he could leave it out entirely. The personal was what editors wanted, and readers craved. Teller and tale, not so separate. The writer reporting on events he had both witnessed and participated in; the writer involved in the twists and turns that made an article jump off the magazine page and into the hardcover bestseller list. The old man might grumble—no surprise, Charlie Wilson belonged to the "Just the facts, ma'am" school of journalism—but he would read the piece, and have to admire it.

"So...?" Paddy Chan said.

"Paddy," he answered absently.

"Flattered you recall my name. And how about my character? Look into my eyes once more. Windows onto the soul, right? So, old man, am I Allied or Axis? Barbarian Han or fraternal Caucasian?" Chan maintained his gaze, despite the bumpy ride.

"I apologize," Dominic said. "For doubting you about Kuno, and for getting you involved."

"Apology accepted for the doubt. No need to—"

"This is my business," he interrupted, formulating another new rule. "Not yours. You should bail right now. Call us next time you're in Hong Kong. Come by for dinner. Bring presents for the kids."

Paddy Chan threw himself back in his seat in a huff. "Fuck you, Nicky," he said.

"Okay ..."

"You need me. You need the help."

"I'm not saying I don't."

"Why, you can't even coax a cabbie to get you to Om without my translation."

"All right, Paddy."

The cab bounced over a potholed road winding along the lower face of a slope. Though the monastery lay within the city limits, only a few granite-block houses clung to rare stretches of flat land. Dominic recalled the highway from his last trip to Om, with the Bon Tourism squad. The shock then had been the swiftness of the transition from city to country, and how easily the capital had given up attempting to encroach on the valley, itself a buffer between the horizontal and vertical, the known and unknown. Humans and their affairs mattered little to this colossal landscape; Gyatsian lives were of no longer duration, or greater consequence, than the caw-caw of the choughs that had reeled over the car.

Today, filaments of cloud crept along the pavement. Whenever the driver, an older man with chin bristle and a cigarette tucked behind an ear, blasted through a patch, as blind as a pilot in heavy weather, his grip on the wheel would tighten.

"Think Wu Jing is following us?" Dominic asked.

"Aye. Or else he went to collect the other stooges. They can sit by the phone until this fella, having pocketed our juice money, rings Bon Tourism to confess that he dropped some strangers at Om."

"You're sure he'd do that?"

"He's Shamo, isn't he?"

The car felt attached to its suspension with elastic bands. The interior, formerly avocado, was the glossless grey of an ancient turtle. Cigarette scars dotted the vinyl.

Noticing the cabbie give him a once-over in the mirror, Dominic smiled. A crucifix, the first he had seen in Gyatso, swung from the mirror like a forgotten victim on the gallows. His mind wandered to his wife's silver confirmation cross, and their final bout of lovemaking before his departure. Definitely not one of his more coherent impulses.

The driver steadied the crucifix, keeping it from further nicking the windshield.

"The stench!" Paddy Chan finally complained. "What's the guy smoking—yak turds in wrapping paper?"

After a few words with the Gyatsian, Chan traded his Marlboros for a yellow pack with a drawing of a farm tractor and an English name. He handed the offending object to Dominic.

"Seven Agricultural Products," he read. "Spelt a-g-r-i-k-u-l-t-r-a-l."

Mercifully, the cabbie stubbed his cigarette and lit a Marlboro instead.

"So this man is automatically a snitch?"

"He is who he is."

"Is that an answer?"

"Your average Shamo, Dominic, lives in a permanent state of slow-burn desperation. Not only is he going to rat you out to save his neck, he may do the same to his mate. Worst-case scenario, the poor lad might be forced to turn in his parents. 'Humiliation' is his christian name, 'Shame'—as Gyatsians so correctly get—his clan moniker. And, despite being a mystical yellow Asian, with their fabulous temples and funky gods, the Shamo actually believes in fuck-all. At the end of the day. When all is not said and, ideally, not done. Just food, shelter, and sex—so long as no babies get made."

"Phew."

"You have no idea."

Then I guess I was right to suspect you, wasn't I? "Probably not," he said. "But you're still being too hard on him. I bet he's written off a big chunk of his life in the hope of coming away with something for his family."

"He is aiding and abetting the occupation of a sovereign nation. He is contributing to the systematic annihilation of a culture, and possibly a race, for no better reason than a hunger for real estate and a few quid in his pocket."

"It's that simple?"

"Categorical."

"And only two categories of residents—occupiers and occupied?"

"Two categories, aye."

"No room for those caught in the middle?"

"No need to get caught there, if you know what's good for you."

Peddlers were already decking themselves by their stalls inside the monastery gate. The cab's arrival had been noted as well by a group of soldiers huddled at the curb, hats secured with free hands, uniforms pinned to frames by wind. The driver stopped in the middle of the parking lot, and Dominic paid the negotiated fee. They were barely out of the car before a dozen adults tried squeezing into it. Dominic counted five in the rear and three more up front. Chan swore a sixth body had climbed into the back. A now hatless head stuck out one window, a booted foot another. As the taxi crawled from the lot, an object was pitched from a window.

"Scant cab trade, is there," Chan said. "Fancy a ten-kilometre walk into Bon in the dark? Hope so."

Om monastery, a ghost town with a restored block for tourists, dwelt half in, half out of cloud. When not rolling down rooftops, slippery as silk over marble, the mist was steadily lifting, a stage curtain raised to tantalize the audience. Given that Om had been built into a sheer slope, a vertical climb of several hundred feet from bottom to top, and not so long ago housed five thousand monks in nearly one thousand buildings, the set, even in its current state, *was* astonishing—closer to theatrical illusion than to any reality Dominic recognized.

Wisps of cloud scurried away as they passed through the gate into a courtyard. As usual, the Westerner was the primary target of the peddlers. Dominic fended off entreaties of "lookie, lookie" and "cheap for you." He got called "handsome man" and had his arm squeezed, fingers run through his hair. No point denying it: he enjoyed Gyatsian women. Their virtually pupil-less eyes and flattened noses, butter tea fragrances and Hollywood smiles. Their physicality and humour.

"Quit the flirting, lover boy," Chan said, hauling Dominic through the throng.

"I was just being polite."

"Some of those women are sixty years old. What, you want to bed your own ma too?"

He wouldn't dignify that with a reply. Paddy Chan's views on the way men and women related were curious. Suspiciously chivalric. Notably lacking in raw attraction, the stuff of, if not catcalls, then admiring glances, admissions of constant simmering—and yes, faintly ludicrous—arousal.

The staircase, more a stone ladder, was so severe he used both hands to pull himself up, as he had before with Sun Nanping in breathless pursuit. Where the steps narrowed, overhanging wooden eaves, their cornices carved as dragons, served as ceiling. Then the gap would widen and a high, punitive sky would emerge, birds looping and clouds funnelling in the expanse. Earth seemed to tilt, turn topsy-turvy, and he had no choice but to hang on for dear life.

Standing on a platform, Dominic tugged his jacket cuffs over his wrists. The platform marked the extent of Om's restorations. To the east lay the bulk of the functioning parts. Farther up, beyond a barrier of bricks, the staircase disintegrated into ruins that resembled, especially at twilight, photos of Dresden after the fire bombings. All that had survived of most buildings was their foundations. In the extreme regions, only intermittently visible, even those markings had dissolved. Carrion-birds and dogs inhabited upper Om, he had been informed. Monks ventured there in daylight, to erect cairns and string prayer flags, but hurried back down before sunset.

From above, he observed a near repeat of his own encounter with the Gyatsian resistance movement on the stairs. Paddy Chan had stepped into a side-alley, probably to urinate. A monk timed his own emergence from a door so he would knock into the Irishman. Already winded, Chan nearly lost his footing. His expression softened when he registered the robe. This monk, deducing in a split second that the visitor wasn't a mainland Shamo, simply offered him a piece of paper. His brazenness had Dominic checking to make sure the exchange had gone unwitnessed.

"Will you look at that," Paddy Chan said on reaching the platform.

"Is it about the occupation?"

"An advert for a new tourist promotion. A day trip to an authentic Gyatsian village outside Bon. Fifty dollars American per person, including lunch with a village family and a ride on a yak."

"No way."

Passing him the flier, Chan dropped his hands to his knees, gulping air as if streams of it were spraying upwards from a fountain. "Lovely printing," he managed to add. "Pity about the spelling."

The main prayer hall and press were built on a shelf that afforded a spectacular view of Bon valley. The valley, claimed a Gyatsian saying, was water in the palm of the Buddha's hand. The Enlightened One had good bones, especially the ranges to the south and east, and at least one eternal lifeline—the Samsara river. Though it was barely five o'clock, the sun perched on the horizon. City lights had already begun to twinkle, like grounded stars, to the west. Noting the silence from the hall, Dominic hurried to the building adjacent to it, all of a sudden concerned in the pit of his stomach for Lavanya Kamala's second cousin. As he ducked through the entrance, his eyes fixed right away on a change to the interior. On a desk covered seventy-two hours before in unbound texts there now stood a computer monitor and keyboard. In a chair before the darkened screen sat a monk whose broad shoulders and imposing skull—his haircut was military rather than religious—prepared Dominic for an unfamiliar face. This monk showed no alarm at the visitors. Rather than bowing, he shook their hands. On his wrist was a silver watch. On his feet were Adidas.

"They have electricity today?" Dominic asked no one in particular.

"*Tashi delag,*" the monk replied with a ritually polite smile. He spoke Shamo, Chan mentioned in an aside, without accent. Tashi Delag himself, Dominic remembered, had been born to a Shamo mother and Gyatsian father and raised in a border region where Gyatsian was banned from not only schools but public squares and restaurants. Maybe this man was also a hybrid.

Paddy Chan asked a question, then translated the answer. "He says they'll have electricity by the end of November. The computer is just for show."

The monk said more, his expression flat, almost bored. When he crossed his arms the sleeves of his robe—cut for a slighter frame—withdrew almost to the elbows.

"But they'll need electrical outlets soon," Chan resumed, "in order to meet contract deadlines. The press has already begun doing layout and graphics on a computer in Bon. This is a business, after all."

"Did you ask about the other monk?"

"You still want me to?"

The man followed their exchange with his gaze. He seemed to find the sight of two foreigners speaking English at once repellent and amusing.

"He is a—" Chan began to say.

"Please ask him."

"I want to get out of here. Don't you?"

Dominic's legs buckled. He leaned against the wall, bending

a knee to badly affect the pose of someone at ease with his situation. "You will get out," he said. To that prediction, he absurdly added: "I promise."

Paddy Chan, too distressed to mock such a heroic vow, relayed the question. The Gyatsian had been expecting the it. Focusing squarely on Dominic, he answered at length, stopping every few sentences, like a veteran politician, to let the translator perform his task.

"He says they had a meeting last evening and that Brother Dawa—the monk who was, and I quote, your friend—resigned his position. Dawa disagreed with the decision, otherwise unanimous among committee members, to stop printing religious texts and focus on commercial enterprises. Circulars and fliers, ads for businesses in Bon. Like this one," Chan said, passing along a sample.

Dominic glanced at the village visit promotion. "Is my 'friend' Brother Dawa still at Om?" he asked. "If I walk over to the prayer hall, will I find him?"

Chan declined to translate this. Unfazed, the monk began a reply to a query he presumably had not understood.

"He says that the brother had been working too hard and needed a rest. He left today for a monastery in eastern Gyatso."

"Left or was sent?"

"He cannot be contacted at this monastery. Not by you, not by members of... some group, or fella, he apparently knows... nor even by members of his—'aristocratic' is the word he used— family. Aristocratic, Nicky! Brother Dawa requested this himself. He wishes to be alone with his thoughts. For meditation. For... I musn't have heard him right ..."

The man repeated the word.

"Purification," Paddy Chan said. His eyebrows flared.

"Purification? And why is he nodding when we talk to each other?"

"I am getting a bad fucking feeling off this one."

The monk spoke again, his tone different. Even Dominic picked up the officialdom in the voice.

"He's asking if you've had any contact with some group in Bon... No, some guy named... No, that can't be right."

"Please explain that I may have accidentally implicated Brother Dawa in a matter he knew nothing about. That, while he may well want some time off to think and reflect and even purify, he has done nothing wrong."

The man added another thought.

"He's still asking about this group."

"Forget some group. What group?" Dominic said, declining to ponder the snippet of dialogue—concerning Kuno's uncle and his uncle's friends and the most beautiful woman in the capital—that kept replaying itself in his head. "Dawa ran the press by himself. You could tell by the ink on his fingers and the bags under his eyes. And he was completely innocent. He was just kind enough to send me to—"

"This monk, of all people, is *not* your confessor."

"Of course he's my confessor," Dominic answered. "He's a priest, isn't he? A Jesuit, maybe."

"A Jesuit with a fancy watch, sure."

"Rolex," the Gyatsian said in English.

"Copy?" Dominic asked numbly.

The man smiled. "I make little money," he continued in their language. "Not Hong Kong tycoon, like you." He turned to Paddy Chan. "And why you want to get out of Gyatso? You don't enjoy my country?"

"That's it," Chan said. "I'm gone."

"Nice to talk to you. Nice to look at your hair."

Dominic was nearly through the door when the man grabbed his arm.

"Wait, please," he ordered in the same tone. Up close, the monk emitted an odour. Not of cigarettes or alcohol; of incense, seemingly, and the assault of spilt gasoline. "This computer," he said. "I worry maybe it is poor machine. You can tell me if it will work?"

"What do you care?"

"My job," he replied. "We must design better products and increase production."

"Aren't you secret police?"

The Gyatsian slowly raised his head. In his eyes was mild confusion but stronger curiosity. Neither emotion fit a thug's repertoire. Both were more typical, Dominic had to admit, of a humble, nearsighted Buddhist.

"You said so yourself," he answered. "The computer won't work without electricity."

"Electricity will make machine okay?"

Dominic looked past him. The monitor was fourteen-inch, probably VGA, but still functional. The keyboard was a keyboard, the mouse a mouse. As for the tower... He checked below the screen and under the table, then made a hasty search of the room. There was no tower; practically speaking, there was no computer. Just some two-generation-old detritus, free for the taking out of trash bins in cities around the world. "Plug in the adaptor," he said, "and it should be fine."

"Excellent!"

Now thoroughly undone, Dominic retreated onto the path. A quarter-moon helped, but he still had to use a wall as guide. He whispered Chan's name. He cast around for a familiar outline: Sun Nanping or Anatman Sangmo, come to escort him to his hotel room. A parade of saffron robes unfurling from the prayer hall further blurred his vision. He could have hugged these priests. He could have cried, "I'll shave my head and renounce my ways, chant sutras night and day, if you will rescue me from Om!" His thoughts shifted unexpectedly to "Ocean," and a plot twist late in the story; the author's decision to save his characters from the fates he had imagined for them. What could that be about? Why, more pressingly, think of it now? Shaking off the notion, Dominic surfed the procession's wake. Gazes stayed lowered and arms, some carrying beads, others bells, dangled. Sandals padded as soft as a cat's paws over the flagstones. For the most part, he couldn't distinguish features or guess ages. Nuns could have walked among the devout, for all he could tell.

He envied that anonymity, everyone the same, everyone—he presumed—no one, nothing.

Paddy Chan waited on the platform. Together, they watched the monks descend the stairs. Only once the final robe had vanished did the Irishman, a cigarette between his lips, speak. In the silence his voice rang through the ruins.

"This is way over my head, Nicky. Yours too, I'd say."

That observation also reminded him of Tashi Delag's fiction. "I wish you'd taken a closer look at 'Ocean,'" he said, recalling Chan's lack of interest in more than glancing at the computer screen before. "I didn't realize it in Hong Kong, but it captures this place pretty well."

As expected, Chan pulled a face. "I got the impression from you the story was some sort of manual for doing global business. How could that possibly be like Om?"

"It's about a couple who set off on a journey. She's seeking to escape reality. He's anxious to embrace the world. The narrator is also the author, which is pretty weird. He winds up deciding he's done his characters wrong, and needs to rescue them from the story."

"Beg pardon?"

"He understands they're making bad choices and are stuck in tired old patterns of thought and action. He wants to prepare them for the twenty-first century." "Ocean" was much more than that, he knew, but short of quoting passages—short, maybe, of forcing Chan to sit and listen while he read the text out loud—he was hopeless at explaining its appeal, let alone the hold it had over him.

"And that stuff reminds you of here?"

Dominic, who never bit his lip, did so. Just like Esther. And Mike.

"Sounds like rubbish to me," Chan offered. "Worse than rubbish—sycophantic bilge, written to please the Shamo master."

"I'm not—"

"A genuine Gyatsian writer would hardly be singing for his

supper by blah-blahing about some brighter day ahead. The subject, the *only* one, would need be the past, and its ongoing eradication."

Sensing that he would not bring Chan around on this, Dominic silently begged for a change of subject. Paddy Chan obliged by proposing an alternative tale.

"A wee Belfast yarn," he said. "No narrative intrusions. Plenty of eradication. Are you interested?"

"Can you talk while we climb down to the parking lot?"

"I'd prefer to sit."

"You're not frozen?"

"To the bone," Chan granted, squatting on the top step. "Keep an eye out for dogs storming those steps." He indicated where the staircase resumed on the far side of the bricks. "I bet the upper tiers are crawling with them."

"Maybe they're the guides."

"Who?"

"The dogs of Om—maybe they're the ones who guide the souls of the departed through the Gyatsian underworld. Isn't that what people believe?"

"How would you know?"

"I read it in my book."

"Exactly," Paddy Chan said. "You read about the belief and, maybe half-understanding it, think, 'Wow, neat. How weird and woolly and Asian.' They believe it and live and die accordingly. Dogs for Gyatsians might well be a cross between Saint Paul and the Grim Reaper. Dogs for you and me, boyo, are sharp fucking teeth and nasty infections. Nothing less, nothing more."

Though moonlight bathed the platform, it failed to penetrate the staircase above where they sat. Guessing that the beasts, rushing barkless out of the shadows, would be ripping into their flesh before they could react, Dominic kept his back to upper Om.

"I'm in the local one night," Chan began, "in the year of our Lord 1989. The pub, called the United Irishman, of all things, is a block up from our chipper on the Antrim Road. Most of the crowd spill out after last call for a Chinky, and half of them are mates from school or their fathers. One minute I'm drinking alongside the lads, the next I'm just another slant-eyes serving their cod 'n' chips and sausage 'n' chips, spice burgers and Cokes. Most of the pubs along the road have shut down years before, on account of being blown up or shot up or else just bankrupted by the Troubles. But the United, as we call it, won't quit, even after dozens of phone scares—*Ye taig pigs are all fucking dead, ye are*—and two bombs. One comes through the front window, breaking glass but never exploding, and the other, a car job that would have lifted the pub sky high, gets parked on the wrong side of the street."

Already Dominic had questions. He knew better than to ask, though; he had to take what the Irishman gave him.

"That night," Chan said, frowning at his own cigarette, "the last Saturday before Christmas, the United is bursting. We're all jarred. The crack is brilliant. Everyone knows everyone else in Belfast pubs, you see, or at least in those outside the centre of town, in the enclaves, the ghettos. They're people you run into at St. Comgall's on Sunday morning. *Good morning, Missus O'Hara,* and *How is Mister Moore today? Well, are you? That's grand, it is.*"

He smiled once more at Paddy Chan's facility with accents. A marbly Scottish inflection for the caller issuing the bomb threat. A steady cadence for the people outside the church. The beginnings of a vision, based on the childhood anecdote Chan had previously shared, materialized: a boy doing his homework at the counter in a take-out restaurant every evening; the child observing customers, copying their mannerisms and mimicking their speech.

"Have you an extra?" Chan asked.

"Sorry?"

"A fag. I can't possibly stick another of the cabbie's yak turd numbers."

Dominic tossed him the Marlboros.

"Just as Mick Handy, who ran the place for an uncle in

Canada, is shouting, 'Last call, ladies and gents,' the door swings open. No more front windows, naturally—the pub had to brick them up—so there's only one way in, one way out. I'm at the bar, maybe five paces away, and notice a couple of things. Mick's son, Cathal, whose job is to size up prospective customers, isn't giving the usual nod to his da at the bar regarding the new arrival. Cathal, in fact, is lying on the sidewalk, his head smashed in by a tire iron. As well, an arm has deposited a small bag in the doorway. A bag about the size... about the size, what do you know, of your computer case. Where is it, by the by?"

"My computer?"

Chan waited.

"I left it in the hotel room," Dominic said, taken aback by the reference. "I figured no one here would ever guess the passwords."

"Let's have a go. E-S-T-H-E-R for the first?"

He nodded.

"And the second... Gabriella and Michael are both too obvious?" Paddy Chan grinned at Dominic's tight shrug. "What was your other wife's name?"

"Catherine."

"C-A-T— Wait! That's not it. I bet it's your ma. Key in her name, and I'm in like the postman?"

"Wrong," he said. But he nearly barked the word, and Chan saw right through him.

"Well, then," he concluded, firing a match, "your secrets are fully protected."

Dominic stood. "You'll have to finish your story on the move."

Paddy Chan was about to object when low growls separated themselves from wind whistle. Dominic scanned the shadows. Chan pitched his cigarette across the landing.

Even descending Om robbed the Irishman of his equilibrium. He finished his tale between gasps and several pauses to hold on to brick. If they hadn't been negotiating a staircase in the most miserly air on the planet, Dominic might have suggested that he smoke less and exercise more.

"Soon as the mystery arm withdraws, leaving the computer case inside the United Irishman, I understand that I—we, the lot of us—have ten seconds, maybe, to go to pieces. 'Mick!' I shout, indicating the bomb with my eyes. Mick Handy is wiping a glass. 'Ah Jesus,' he answers. 'Bomb!' I announce, vaulting over the counter. Mick, believe it or not, uses his final moments to return the glass to the shelf. 'Will you forget about the—' I begin to say. But then there's a shudder and a giant vacuum sucks away all air—*whump!* The wall behind me appears to fall forward, though in reality it's just every bottle of booze and pint glass crashing down. I get cut good, and still have scars over my shoulders and arms. But otherwise I'm fine. Once I figure this out—at first, you're not sure if you're dead and dreaming or alive and stunned—I get up. It's gone silent, the pub, totally fucking silent, and the dust is so thick I can't see my own hand. Clearly I'm alive and stunned—the explosion left me briefly deaf—for the first thing I do is check my watch for the hour. The face, however, is smashed. No time left to tell."

"What about your friends—were they okay?"

"Excuse me?"

"Did the friends you were drinking with jump behind the bar as well?"

Chan visibly bristled. "What, I should have raced to the door, picked up the bomb, and run out into the road?"

Dominic opened his mouth.

"Or better yet, simply thrown myself onto the thing, absorbed its full impact, and so saved everyone?"

"I wasn't thinking anything like that."

Paddy Chan stormed the final steps to where the merchant stalls now stood boarded.

"The reason I'm sharing this Belfast moment, McNicky," he said once Dominic caught up, his words more spat then spoken, "has nothing to do with my part in it, or with the fate of my friends, or even with the dismal regularity of this sort of atrocity, this garden variety of carnage, during the Troubles. Okay?"

Dominic nodded.

"The point of the anecdote is as follows. The United Irishman has finally returned to life, or, better, I've got my hearing back. There are screams and moans, people calling out names, shouting for ambulances. I'm stepping over the counter, thinking I should mind those hurt, when I come upon this old fella who'd been up on a stool next to me. Dermot Heatley is his name. A cod 'n' chip man, every Friday and Saturday midnight, regular as rain. There Dermot is, on the same stool, sipping the same pint. The only difference is that he's now missing the lower half of his leg. From just below the knee. Only tatters of his trousers and some dangling bits. 'You're hurt, Dermot,' I tell him. 'Aye,' Dermot answers. 'Hurt bad, by the feel of it.' 'Hadn't we better get you—?' I start. 'But the foot is gone,' he interrupts. 'Foot and ankle both. Nothing to be done there. This pint, now...'"

Finally, Dominic had to ask. "Is that," he said with careful solicitousness, "your, you know, point?"

"That, and nothing else."

"Okay."

"Have you got it?"

"I suppose."

"A cab," Chan announced, striding ahead once again. "My kingdom for a cab!"

A single light illuminated the gate. As they stepped into its circumference, their shadows stretched into the parking lot. Then the light abruptly died, and the strength of the darkness beyond it became apparent. So did the truth of a lot empty of taxis or cars. Worse, the temperature seemed to drop a couple more degrees as the men stood before what Dominic privately fancied the edge of the medieval world, the fires of hell below. The wind rallied.

Deepest Gyatsian night briefly drowned their senses. Above them, in contrast, was a blazing sky. A faint smudge before, the Milky Way had clarified into a pink mist. Mars glowed orange-brown in the northeast, while Orion and both Dippers showed their entire configurations to the south, every dot connectable.

"We're fucked," Paddy Chan said.

Dominic replied with a bland reassurance. Chan had no reason to believe him, but he meant it. He wasn't thinking of the heavens. Something was about to happen on the earth, at Om, to him. He knew this for certain. He knew, too, how he would handle the situation, without quite knowing what the situation would be. If that sounded mystical, so be it; maybe Gyatso was finally having an effect on his stolid self.

"I'd sacrifice my first-born to be back in Mustang Saman's right now," the Irishman said. "Plates of yak noodles and a tabletop of beers. Ghosts of Gyatsian boys in make-up, even. This isn't how the night should unfold, Nicky. Not out here. It's All Hallow E'en, are you aware?"

He was well aware. At that moment Gaby and Mike, attired most likely in costumes other than the ones Dominic had left in the F.C.C. cloakroom, would be riding the elevator to selected floors and ringing the bells of selected doors. "Trick or treat!" the kids would be shouting, grins as glittering as any star. Their reluctant escort would be frowning in anticipation of the all-candy bedtime snack and all-morning tummy ache. Hands on her narrow hips. Chewing on her delicious lips.

Headlights cut through the dark. A car roared into the parking lot and executed a loop.

"Thanks again for helping," Dominic said quickly.

The car braked. The passenger window came down and Sun Nanping made purposeful eye contact with him. "Please come with us," he said.

Ant punched open the rear door. As Dominic went to climb in, a glint in the dirt beside the wheel captured his notice. Feigning an untied shoe, he dropped to one knee and swept the ground with his palm. He found what he had suspected was there: the cabbie's crucifix, tossed out by a soldier. He pocketed it.

"Just Ant in the back?" he asked, ducking under the frame. "That leaves plenty of room for my friend."

The translator reached across and slammed the door shut.

"Hey, Wu," Dominic said, "would ten American dollars be enough for the extra passenger?"

"Sorry," Sun replied.

"Ten dollar?" the driver asked.

His boss spoke to him in Shamo. Outside, Dominic heard Paddy Chan laugh mockingly.

"Maybe twenty is a fairer price?"

The head of Bon Tourism turned in his seat. "Not possible, Dominic," he said firmly. Then, noticing that the car still hadn't budged, Sun Nanping smacked Wu Jing across the side of the head. Ant roared in delight. The driver, no less stunned, hunched his shoulders and tried shoving the gas pedal through the floor.

Dominic had a split second to look out the window. If he expected Chan to accuse—or forgive—him with his gaze, he was disappointed. The Irishman's attention lay with the Bon Tourism squad. By calmly striking a match, revealing relaxed body language and a languid expression, Chan apparently fulfilled a greater need than communicating with Dominic. The prodigal son was showing his family that he wasn't flustered, never mind scared out of his wits, at being abandoned once again; that Paddy Chan would do just fine on his own, utterly alone, this All Hallow E'en.

Chapter Eight

The drive back into the city was uneventful. The car stopped once, at Sun Nanping's instruction, outside a shop along Liberation Boulevard. When Dominic asked why, the head of Bon Tourism informed him that he—the foreigner, the visitor—wanted to buy alcohol.

"I do?"

"I think so."

"What about the flask?"

"Not so much left," Sun remarked.

Wu Jing accompanied him. The woman behind the counter started in recognition and fear. Wu grinned at her, his mirror glasses a ludicrous nocturnal accessory, and helped himself to a toothpick from a box on the counter. Dominic chose two liquor bottles from a shelf, then watched as the Shamo added six packs of cigarettes to the tab.

"Three pack for me," Wu said, slurping air into his mouth. "Three for you, to give me as bribe."

In the doorway the driver, having already transferred the cigarettes to his jacket pocket, tried lowering his voice to a whisper. He could get Dominic a girl for the night. One phone call, half-hour wait. "Forty dollar only," he said. "Special price. Make you want to stay in room for breakfast!" Then, as Dominic debated asking him whether he had whacked any children around lately, Wu changed topics. His voice drifted back up. His pasty skin flushed. "My boss," he said, rubbing his temple. "He crazy man. Watch out."

His crazy boss issued a final order outside the hotel. The command displeased his crew. Ant mumbled, but for once Sun

Nanping's tone was authorative. Wu executed a petulant three-point turn.

"I tell them go find Paddy Chan," Sun said. "Not safe for him on roads tonight."

"Dogs?"

"Drivers."

The army receptionist had resumed his post in the lobby, hat low, eyes visored. He complained loudly to the head of Bon Tourism, and Sun Nanping dutifully translated. Major Wilson had departed that afternoon without permission. He had failed to leave an itinerary. He was seventy-three minutes late for dinner.

The same waitress waited below the calligraphy banner. She still wore her cheongsam and high heels. Anger now recast her features, inking her pupils and drawing skin even tighter over her cheekbones. Again, Sun Nanping rendered sour words into English. The kitchen had closed an hour ago. All the other staff had gone home. She was tired.

"Let's eat," Major Wilson said. "I'm starved."

His guide said he would wait in the lobby.

"Join me."

"Dining room is for military only."

"Come on, Sun. You're my guest. Besides," he added, "aren't you supposed to get me drunk tonight?"

"Not you drunk, Dominic. Me."

"You?"

Sun smiled in apology.

He turned to the woman. "This gentleman is joining me for dinner."

She scowled at the suggestion that the remark would be intelligible. Sun Nanping translated once more. Her reply took the form of still another scowl. The restaurant lay in gloom, but the waitress did not turn on a light; the table had been set for only one, but she made no attempt to find another serving. She filled her client's glass and pushed his plate closer to him, then withdrew, duties complete. Dominic stole a glass from a neighbouring table and poured another beer.

"She doesn't seem pleased to see me again," he said.

"Maybe she is not pleased with many things," Sun answered. "You and me are only two of them."

Dominic digested the remark along with the dinner. Though Sun Nanping claimed to have already eaten, he watched Dominic inhale with hungry eyes.

"She has a small daughter," the Shamo offered. "I notice them in Kundun park sometimes. Beautiful child. Always happy. Always smiling. Still, the waitress and her husband are probably disappointed."

"Why?"

"Most likely they wanted a boy for their one child," Sun said. "Most likely they—"

Shouts from outside the restaurant kept him from explaining further. Sun Nanping rose from the table without a word. Guessing the food would be gone when he returned, Dominic held the rice bowl under his chin and shovelled. He caught up to his guide on the back stairs. At the top, the monitor blocked them. Gone were her cheerfully cocked hat and gummy smile.

"Wait in lobby," she ordered in English. "Floor closed."

Glancing past her, Dominic decided his room was being ransacked. A half-dozen uniforms stood smoking outside it. He thought of the Powerbook. He thought, oddly, of a gift he had received from Lavanya Kamala, a ceremonial scarf he had folded inside the duffel bag. But then he noticed an open door across from his own.

"What's going on?" he asked on the way back down.

"Maybe another... I am not, ahem, sure," Sun said.

Three white-jacketed medics, one carrying a wooden stretcher, entered the lobby. The receptionist, in conversation with the waitress, barked a number without looking up, and the paramedics climbed the stairs at a pace more suitable for a funeral than an emergency. When the soldier followed them and the waitress departed, walking past her former clients as though they were invisible, Dominic indicated that he, too, was making a move.

The medics, receptionist, and monitor were all filing through the door, with the smokers already inside the room. Pressing a finger to his lips, he handed Sun Nanping the liquor bottles and strode ahead, leaning over the desk. He inserted the key into the lock and rehung it on its hook. The computer sat on his bed, screen upright; the scarf was where he had stashed it.

"So?" he said.

"Officer in room across from here," Sun replied, removing the bottles from the netting. "He has an accident."

"Died in his sleep?"

"In bathroom."

Dominic remembered the taunts of Ant and his brother about the army hotel and military suicides. "Drowned in the tub, by any chance?"

Sun inspected the mugs from the tea set. Satisfied they were clean, he twisted the cap off a bottle. He poured hefty measures, leaving one on the end table and easing himself onto the second bed. The man hadn't been kidding; he had come here to drink, probably until he passed out. In and of itself, the proposition astonished Dominic. Reading grief in the floor monitor's expression had reminded him of what he found so exceptional about Sun Nanping. Most Shamo smiles failed to light the whole face. Generally left dark, he had observed in Hong Kong—where Shamos accounted for ninety-eight percent of the population, including his office staff—were the eyes. Not so with the monitor's amiable grin or Sun's hopeful smile, which spread like a lit fuse across his features to explode his pupils.

He seemed, in short, like someone Dominic would enjoy getting into the cups with, to *ganbei* until they both stumbled. This seemed as well an opportunity to do better than he had with Paddy Chan; to listen to another man's sodden, silly rants; to wax and wane a little himself. But he also had to keep his head clear. He had a task, one Sun could not be privy to, let alone impede. To warn Lavanya. To track down Tashi and tell him to be careful. Dominic even wanted to find out where Kuno lived and have a word with his parents. Be certain the money got spent on glasses. Give them more—all he had in cash—to help the boy.

"Does this happen a lot?" he asked, stalling.

"Officers from mainland are punished for bad job or incorrect political attitude with assignment in Gyatso. Two years are possible. Five years, not possible. The man across the hall, he was assigned to base in western Gyatso for full term. The base is high in mountains. No towns nearby. No real roads. He cannot accept this. He, ahem, declines."

"Does he ever," Dominic said. He switched on the bathroom light. The face in the mirror gave him a fright. The matted hair and salt-and-pepper chin, the frayed shirt collar and filthy cuffs; a few days more up here, especially with the sun steadily basting his skin, until he finally did end up more Ponti than Wilson, and he would be able to pass for a local. Pass for a local, and no longer be synonymous with an economy that couldn't collapse, a currency that would never deflate.

"I need a shower," he said, "and a shave."

He wet a towel and scrubbed. Rubbing his eyes soothed the retina burn, probably acquired during his few minutes that afternoon without protection. The towel came back smeared ochre.

"Clerk in lobby tells me that officer who is dead had not left his room for three days," Sun said. He held his mug in both hands, as if that much strength were required to lift it. "Only monitor, Private Cheung, saw him. She brought him noodles. She keep him company."

"The woman at the desk?"

"Private Cheung," he repeated. "Friend to many officers who, shall we say, cannot accept assignments."

Dominic took up his tea mug. The smell flared his nostrils. Bouquet of dandelion and vinegar.

"*Ganbei*," the Shamo said.

He could hardly refuse. They clinked china.

"Christ," Dominic managed.

Sun Nanping stared down at the liquor.

"What is it?"

"Bottle says *maotai*," Sun answered. "Maybe very old. Maybe very new." He swallowed another mouthful. Then, wincing again, as though the taste hurt, his eyes settled on Dominic. "My son, Gianbao. He is sick."

"Yes?"

"You wish me good health? Not my health is bad. Not me, foolish, useless thirty-eight-year man. My son. My boy. Four years alive and already *He* is sick? *He* cannot make lungs work? I do not understand," he added, draining the cup. "Why things happen or don't happen. Why I act sometimes and sometimes things get acted—can I say this?—on me. How sad, to be near death maybe and not know much about your own life."

Drawing a line on the acceptable level of intimacy wasn't hard, Dominic reflected, when the other person starts picking up on a conversation you've been having in the privacy of your own skull. Better send a clear message. Keep the banter light. A couple of drinks and then call it a night. "I'm not following." he said instead.

"You understand your life?"

"Of course. I mean, I've never actually thought about it—as a life. Something with a beginning, middle, and end. Which makes sense, because it hasn't got those things. Not yet, anyway."

"I understand."

"Really?"

"Not really," Sun admitted.

"I need a proper drink. I need—"

"A shower and a shave?" Sun giggled, for the first time in Dominic's presence. He would have remembered such a high, boyish laugh.

"That, too, I guess."

"*Ganbei?*"

He hesitated.

"You not like this liquor?"

"You do?"

"Smells like used diaper. Tastes like..." Sun swished some in his mouth. "Used diaper."

"But you're going to empty the bottle?"

"Both bottles."

"Because you don't understand your life?"

The grin faded. "Because my son is sick," he said again. "Tell me, you think he will die?"

Dominic got up.

"I think he will die before his father."

"Sun..."

"Could anything more horrible happen to a person?"

"No... definitely not... Christ," Dominic said. "I'm too wrecked for this."

The men went quiet as what sounded like a herd of yak exited the room across the corridor. The beasts drove headlong down the stairs. Silence fell heavily once the last animal had gone, amplifying a sound neither of them wished to hear—a woman sobbing, probably into her hat.

Dominic resolved to share one more glass with Sun Nanping and then send him on his way. "I should explain a couple of things," he said.

He should? He parted the window curtains. Below, in the sea of feeble street lamps that left nocturnal Bon a blur, the Kundun loomed from shadow. By law the palace, former residence of the Vadra Pani and his predecessors, all of whom, according to Gyatsian faith, were reincarnations of the same divinity, could not be lit after dark. Strobes planted at the base were obviously forbidden. But even a lamp, in just one of the hundreds of window frames on the nearly two dozen floors, was a violation. Studying the outline, its contours apparent only because the eye, familiar with the famous design, extracted them from the murkiness, Dominic thought he understood why the Shamos would insist on a blackout. Strobes, the lesser threat, would render the palace more awesome than in daylight but still show the building to be an empty hull, a museum for tourists. A solitary candle or lonely lamp at the front of the Kundun, on the other hand, would be visible from every alley in Gyatsian Bon. What did a lit window signify? That a house was occupied. That the owners were at home. That visitors were welcome.

"So here's the deal," he said. "I'm *not* a journalist, but I did come to Gyatso for a magazine. The article isn't an exposé of what your country is doing to this one. To be honest, I still don't have an opinion on that. Things are complicated, aren't they? Reality is never as simple as some people need it to be... The piece is about—or is going to be about, once I get to work—a writer who published a story that had an incredible impact on me. At least, that's what I thought happened." The chat with Paddy Chan at Om clanged in his memory. "I wanted to meet him," he resumed. "Tashi Delag, I mean, figuring he had to be an amazing person. Self-possessed. Certain of who he is and what he believes. Tell the truth now, Sun—you have read 'Ocean,' haven't you?"

Sun Nanping treated the question as though he could tell it was being addressed to him only by the upturn in the speaker's voice. He smiled and sipped from his cup.

"*Have* you read Tashi Delag?"

"Health and happiness," the Shamo finally replied. "Gyatsians wish everyone this, including us. They are strange people. Easy to like. Impossible to call friend or enemy."

"Did you arrest—I mean, have you talked to him?"

"Who?"

"Tashi Delag!"

"You, like me, but not like my boy, my boy Gianbao, seem to have good health. Not even being up on roof of world is making you so sick you must stay in bed, as with other journalists. Sometimes we wait days in our car, watching Vacation Inn, in hope that foreigners will go cause trouble. I even order Wu Jing to drive them to medicine store. Once, French TV crew stayed sick for entire visa. Anatman Sangmo gets so bored he offers to bring Gyatsians to hotel room for illegal filming!" He polished off a third helping of the liquor. "Happiness is different thing," Sun said. "All Gyatsians are happy. No other people are. They know this place. They know how to live here. My wife, who is happiest non-Gyatsian person in Bon, she says it is tea they drink and incense they burn."

Dominic flopped back on his bed. Sun Nanping, he was now one hundred percent certain, had never heard of "Ocean," or the author Tashi Delag. Should he mention one more contact they might share in common? He was under no obligation to come clean. He couldn't, point of fact, understand *why* he felt so compelled to talk. Sun's wan smile and lit eyes? The bottle of rot? "What about other people I've met," he said anyway. "A woman, for instance, who lives near this hotel."

"Lavanya Kamala? We are aware of her, of course. You should not mix up with Gyatsians like her and Thomdup. You put us in bad position. Put *me* in bad position. Talking to some writer is okay. I can say to bosses, 'Just some article, who cares? Article published in New York or London. No big deal.' But talking to people like them, I cannot allow."

"What people—book editors? And who's Thomdup?"

"No more!" Sun declared. He poured himself another, refilling Dominic's mug as well. "No more about Gyatso. Too strange. Too saddening."

"I have to make a phone call," Dominic said abruptly.

"You have cigarettes?"

"You don't smoke."

"Now I do." He went through Dominic's bag. "Even better," he said, pulling out a case of slim cigars. He read aloud the Dutch name and the government warning that smoking can cause lung disease. "These will make me sick?"

"At this altitude, they may kill you." Dominic struck a match. "Try not to inhale," he said. "Just enjoy the flavour."

Sun Nanping inhaled. He coughed violently and hacked into his fist, wiping his palm on his sock.

Dominic issued instructions to the operator. Her reply being incomprehensible, he held the receiver out to Sun, who now sat beside him, staring at the dark computer screen. The chief of Bon Tourism listened, then barked into the phone. He grinned at his own bluster. He puffed his cigar.

Two short rings, a pause, two short rings, a pause: the Hong Kong sequence. Dominic's pulse quickened.

"Hello?"

"Esther!" he said, beaming unashamedly.

"Hello?"

"Esther, it's me."

"Anybody there?"

"It's Dominic! Can't you hear me?"

Her tone changed. "Who is this, please? Who is—?"

Click, click went the wiretap.

"Esther!" he shouted. "There's something wrong with the line." Then he heard other voices. Kids singing in the background. Kids with treats in their mouths.

"Gabriella?" he said, his heart crashing around inside his chest. "It's Daddy. Michael, is that you?"

Click, click again. He tried to break through. She did as well. "Quiet, children," he heard her command. "Your mother is—"

The line went dead.

How many times did he shout "Hello? Hello?" into the void? How hard did he pound the receiver on the end table?

"What a dump this is," he finally said. "To wire Gyatso properly, you'd need to blow it up and start from scratch."

There was a knock. Worried he might punch a wall, Dominic chugged his mug of dandelion vinegar. He had no choice but to recline on the bed. He heard Sun cross the room and speak with the hall monitor.

"Is she okay?" he thought to ask.

The Shamo couldn't disguise the pleasant surprise in his reply. "Okay, I think," he said. "Not in trouble."

"Good. Now tell me about your son, Sun. Tell me all about the life you do not understand."

"Maybe you don't—"

"Maybe I do."

Sun Nanping spoke for thirty minutes, pausing only to smoke and drink and speculate as to why his head felt as though it were being squeezed in a vise. His English smoothed during the monologue. The urgency of his narrative may have fuelled the fluency; more likely, alcohol regularized his grammar. For his part, Dominic remained on his back. He kept a forearm across his eyes and drank no more booze. While he may have appeared lost in self-pity, he took in the words. All this, while his heart continued to careen and his own kids fought with Sun's composite family for top billing in his image reel: Gaby slinky as Sailor Moon, Mike dopey as the blue Teletubby. Esther by the phone. Her mouth puckering as, giving up on the call, she didn't even think to add: *Dominhic? Is that you? Is that you somewhere out there, calling your whyfe and chillderen to tell us you luvh us very much but still won't come home?*

Sun was born in the capital. His father trained as a doctor, his mother as a nurse. As eldest son, he tried to esteem his father by following in Dr. Sun's footsteps. Politics intruded, however, and Nanping was denied entry into medical school on account of poor class background. He studied at the Second Foreign Languages University instead, also known as the College of Tourism, and on graduating was hired to teach there. That was fine, but he and his new wife had plans to study abroad, perhaps to emigrate. For his wife—his best and probably only friend—emigration was the ultimate goal. She wanted a career. She wanted more than a single child. Sun Nanping wanted what would make her happy, and was equally committed to improving his language skills, broadening his mind.

His problems were nothing compared to those of his little brother, Sun Gianbao. Gianbao had dropped out of university and joined the army. In 1989, both brothers became embroiled in a protest movement in the capital. The elder Sun marched with his colleagues and students and, on a terrible June night that he declined to describe in detail—Dominic knew all about the night, needless to say: it had been front-page world news, a shock and an outrage, for about a week—pitched rocks at passing convoys. The younger Sun, sent into the city with his regiment to quell the disturbance, deserted his post. An old woman snitched and he was sentenced to a military labour camp. Sun

Nanping suffered less: twelve months of re-education, and a rejected passport application that cost him a scholarship in Arizona. Efforts at obtaining a passport would fail several more times and, to this day, he had no way of legally leaving his own country, never mind of gaining entry, or permission to reside, in another.

In 1994, Dr. Sun helped launch a program to bring modern surgical techniques into the countryside, where nearly a billion people lived in starkly different conditions from those in the urban centres. Borrowing an old idea, a team of doctors outfitted a train car as an operating theatre. To be effective, the team would perform just two procedures: cataracts and cleft palates, from which untold numbers of children and young adults—the only requests that could be realistically entertained—suffered. Newspapers bestowed official approval on the project. The mayor made a speech on the eve of the first voyage. Included on board the train was Dr. Sun, naturally, but also his boys. Nanping, on leave from the college, translated for a curious international press. Gianbao, recently released and discharged, found work as a security guard.

The team performed forty-two cataract operations in six days. One was done on an eleven-year-old girl, blind since birth, who had previously spent her waking hours strapped to a water buffalo. Another procedure permitted a village beggar to see his son's face for the first time. The doctors also repaired, with varying degrees of success, the upper palates of three dozen children, relieving existences that had been brutal, given the culture's deep-seated associations of mouth deformities with mental retardation. In one week, in one small province, six hundred further requests were made for the cataract operation, with still more inquiring about the cleft palate procedure. Demands from the larger provinces were staggering.

Dominic listened to all this. He thought of his relationship with his father. He thought—inappropriately, he knew—of his fingertip. But those congruences paled beside a connection so striking he decided he must have made it up, by way of asserting a wished-for link with Sun Nanping. A month earlier, he had met a fundraiser involved with an intriguing project. Two surgery trains had recently begun performing medical procedures in remote areas of the mainland, as certain Hong Kongers still called the country they were now officially part of. One of the trains had been outfitted years ago; a group had tried this already, without success. Now that train, and a brand-new one, possessed state-of-the-art equipment and keen doctors and a growing network of supporters. Something about the project touched Dominic, and he exchanged cards with the man. Next day—not until the afternoon, a soft sell by local standards—the fundraiser called WilCor for a donation. Dominic had already consulted Esther, his oracle on charities and good deeds, and, as was their custom, they co-signed a cheque.

The same project, surely. The same surgery car. Meaning that he could predict how this part of Sun Nanping's story would end—in general, at least. Meaning their lives *had* intersected before they met.

On the third trip out, Sun continued, disaster struck. Though Nanping had returned to his teaching job, Gianbao still worked as security. The younger brother got caught stealing morphine to feed an addiction he had acquired in the labour camp. Gianbao was sent home to await another arrest; Dr. Sun had no choice but to resign. Some official panicked and ordered the train turned around, cancelling two weeks of scheduled surgery. An old photo of Gianbao, head shaven and prison bound, appeared on the front pages of newspapers. Dr. Sun's career came under scrutiny once again. Worse of all, the project was scuttled. No further operations were performed.

On July 3, 1995, Sun Gianbao threw himself out the living-room window of his parents' seventh-floor flat. He lingered for three days in a hospital where the nurses, on instructions, shunned him, in a room that his parents had to pay for, even though Dr. Sun worked there. For the final twenty-four hours, it was also a room two flights above a ward where his big brother's wife lay with a newborn—swaddled by those same nurses—in her arms. The couple named the boy after his uncle, a gesture of hope.

Baby Gianbao was diagnosed with asthma shortly before his second birthday. On his father's advice, Nanping took action to protect the child against the notorious air in the capital. His wife quit her job. Dr. Sun designed a crude oxygen tent that covered half their floor space. Dr. Sun also "borrowed" inhalers from the hospital where, two demotions later, he was still employed, and stole supplies of steroids. He knew better than most the severity of the situation; young children died every week from respiratory ailments aggravated by coal dust and carbon monoxide. At the age of three Gianbao remained confined in the tent for a month while a toxic cloud, socked in by a weather system, smothered the city. After that, the family resolved to relocate. Sun Nanping pored over a map of the country, along with a list of air quality indexes clipped from an international newspaper. None of the major centres were any better; several, almost unimaginably, were worse. But two of the prospects he learned about through the college's tourism industry association merited a closer look. Both were for bureau chiefs in remote offices. One job was in a city near the border with Russia, the other in Bon, Gyatso.

For Sun, even living near an international boundary would be cheering. He could gaze across a river at another country. He could lobby for being granted a passport and visa—his double disgrace notwithstanding—in order to improve contacts inside Siberia, foster cross-border relations. He failed to get an interview for that position.

Gyatso, in contrast, had to be his worst nightmare. A step *away* from the world. A mountainscape so vast and remote its inhabitants were, by any standard, already in prison. As for heading up Bon Tourism, what a joke. For every week the Gyatsian Autonomous Region opened its doors for restricted, heavily monitored tourist business, for another month it had to be closed. Official reasons dissembled, but everyone heard the rumours: local unrest and determined insurrection, blood on the streets and in the temples where Sun Nanping would be expected to escort Americans and Germans. For all that, the city's elevation rendered it only a marginal improvement over low-lying smear. Gianbao could inhale fresh air, but it would be a strained version—another shock to his lungs.

Nonetheless, Dr. Sun advised his son to accept the job. The boy's chances were better in Bon than in just about any other likely destination. In five years, the length of the contract Sun Nanping had to sign, the child would be beyond the critical stage with the ailment.

Sun and his wife had arrived eight months before. He was indifferent to foreigners using a visit to Bon to denounce the occupation. What occupation? What country? Like holding smoke in your hands, he explained to Dominic. He certainly wasn't cut out to order around men such as Wu Jing and Anatman Sangmo. Not that he did order them, exactly. But technically he was their superior, responsible for all that went on, all they were up to. Not, again, that Sun Nanping always knew what his staff were up to, or cared to know. Did that mean he was biding his time here? Hardly. He was actively hating every moment of it. He kept a calendar in the office. Each morning Sun put a stroke through the date to pre-cancel another menacing day in inner-exile. Each evening he spared a few moments to dream about a future in earthly paradise, a healthy child and contented wife, a new life somewhere, anywhere but Bon.

"All about my son," the Shamo concluded, shaking his head in genuine astonishment. "All about my life."

Dominic sat up. He resolved to sponsor Sun and his family to emigrate to Canada. He decided to toss in an invitation to have dinner with him, Esther, and the kids should the Suns pass through Hong Kong on their way across the Pacific. As he was formulating the offer, Sun Nanping added a footnote. On the surgery train's second outing, he said, they travelled far south to the Pearl River delta. Many of the villages they stopped near belonged to the Chan family clan. That is why he had asked Paddy Chan about his ancestors. He realized the Irishman had taken the question wrong. He had assumed that Sun was threatening him. Sun wouldn't do that; Ant and Wu would.

But Dominic found he had something more urgent to say. "We must run straight into the arms of love. Nothing else really matters, does it? Why a man should have to be forty, or thirty-eight, to figure this out is nuts. But it's the truth. Those who love you. Those who need you. Those who'll *put up* with you, more to the point. Run to them, Sun. Run fast!"

Sun swung his legs around and stood.

"Where are you going?"

"I am running into the arms of love."

"You are?"

"The second bottle," the Shamo said, permitting himself a smile. He fetched the other bottle of liquor. Dominic slid to the floor at the foot of his bed, bringing along his mug. Sun had opened the latest offering and now held it out for inspection. Dominic tried not to gag.

"Old boot," he said.

The Bon Tourism chief sniffed. "Rotten mushroom."

They clinked china again. Both winced at the new awful taste. Sun Nanping examined first the cigar case and then the matchbox. The box was virtually an objet d'art. On both faces were reproductions of traditional paintings. One showed a blue hill jutting from an amniotic sea of gold. Cherry trees blossomed along its slopes; a temple clung to a precipice. On the other face, a river ran banked by high canyon walls and misted in pink cloud. Figures the size of pinheads skirted along paths.

Sun flipped back and forth between the images. "Island-Shangri-la," he eventually said, reading the side of the box.

"A Hong Kong hotel. Five-star."

"Very special place, I'm sure. Everybody wants to go there."

"Canada," Dominic said aloud, "is from a Native word for village."

The Shamo smiled.

"Refill, please," he was quick to add.

"My wife, she told me we should have second child," Sun

offered. "In capital this is not allowed. Up here, no one cares. One more baby, one less—of no importance."

"Have a second baby."

"Taken care of."

"Already?"

"A parent must not live past his child," the guide said with deep feeling.

"I love my children."

"I love them also."

"They are so small."

"My son is tiny."

"Tiny and small and dressed, maybe, like a Japanese valley girl and a blue eggplant."

To this, the Shamo could offer no reply. "More old boot and rotten mushroom for me. Also, another cigar."

"Be careful."

"Know how small Gianbao is?" Sun asked, lying on his side. He held his hand maybe twelve inches off the floor.

Dominic pressed his cheek to the rug to measure. "That's pretty small," he said. A notion staggered into his consciousness. Back up on his knees, he crawled to his duffel bag and pulled out a pink pig. The stuffed animal had a nose and both ears but only a single brown Smartie eye.

"See this? When I told my daughter I was going away for a week she burst into tears. She went into her room and brought out Pink Pig, her favourite." He gazed at the pig. "Okay, her second favourite, after Miss Juice, who she can't be without for more than five minutes. Gabriella told me to bring him to Gyatso. That way, my six-year-old said, I know you'll have to come back to us."

He thought the man was going to cry. More distressing, he thought *he* might. To break the tension he tossed Pink Pig at the television. It missed, knocking over a lamp. When Sun's pupils suddenly went black and an upward rippling motion bulged his throat, Dominic braced himself for a voiding. A sob, perhaps; emotions released, a connection made.

The vomit splattered the rug. Sun lurched into the bathroom, failing to stop the flow. He made it as far as the sink.

"Sorry," he said after the last heave.

"Must have been the mushroom. Must have been the boot."

"My clothes..."

"I can help with that." Dominic found a shirt, pants, and sweater in his bag. Rising with a teeter, he carried the clothes into the washroom, leaving them beside the basin. Sun Nanping had bent at the waist, arms splayed, head in the sink. Dominic tottered at the stench, not only of vomit but the Asian body odour of cooking rice. How did he smell to them? Not like money. More like sour milk. He wanted to say something. Wisely not trusting words, he laid a hand on a clammy back. When Sun raised his gaze the limb slipped off, coming to rest on the basin rim. The Shamo's eyes fell squarely upon the fifth finger on Dominic's left hand. He was about to pull away when his drinking partner twisted his head farther to make sidelong contact.

"Poor you," he said, attempting a smile.

"Poor me," Dominic agreed.

Chapter Nine

They stepped into the night. Still groggy from alcohol and a nap, Dominic stumbled down the step into the lane. Sun squinted at the sight, though his face may also have been pinched from crunching candies. The Shamo, baggy but clean in a taller man's clothes, had driven a hand into the bowl in the deserted lobby. Obviously famished, he had started to peel and pop two at a time. Dominic wondered if this was smart, but could offer no snack alternatives. The men wobbled up Sikkim Lane in silence. One intended to return home to his family. The other, anxious not to be out on Halloween—better to wait until morning to find Lavanya and Tashi Delag, he vaguely reasoned—wished to clear his head. A stroll the length of the lane. Then to his fetid room and rumpled bed.

What a dream he had squeezed into a ten-minute rest. A doorbell had rung three times and a parakeet—Lucien, presumably, from his balcony cage at 21 Old Peak Road, Hong Kong—intoned, "Stop it! Stop it! Stop it!" Figures flitted past, human and canine, none recognizable until her. Gina Wilson, aged about forty, making Dominic sixteen and Francesca twelve. Gina in the company of a man not her husband or his father but *a* father, a priest. Previously, she had come to him alone. Smiling at her son. Extending her arm. But tonight she appeared in an evening dress and pearl necklace, a party mask across her eyes. Behind her floated a ballroom decorated in pink and lavender. Next to her, the priest's soutane passed as tuxedo. She stared at her child and in the centre of her pupils—all Dominic could see because of the mask—was a reflection that had to be his own face. His face at sixteen or, likewise, at forty? He couldn't make himself out. Even now, walking in Sikkim

Lane, his hands shook from the dream. His hands shook and his breath caught. The vibrato in her voice, soft and sensual, as much lover as parent, had him failing to put one foot before the other. *If I give you this,* Gina had said, *then you'll have to come back to me.*

Only she gave nothing. Or else Sun Nanping, having finished in the washroom, had chosen that moment to wake him up.

Halfway to the intersection, Dominic began seeking Lavanya Kamala's house. Despite the dark, he found the balcony and windowsill almost at once.

"There it is," he said.

Sun Nanping stopped crunching.

"A light is on upstairs, so I guess you haven't arrested her yet."

"Arrest who?"

"Lavanya."

"Lavanya Kamala does not live in this house."

"Sure she does."

Impulsively, foolishly—he had checked the sill: just two pots—Dominic knocked on the door.

"Why?" Sun went to say.

It cracked a little and a face peered at them.

"Who are you?" an old man said in English.

Sun Nanping introduced himself in Shamo.

"Can we come in?" Dominic asked.

"Not at this hour."

"I was here much later than this two nights ago."

Of course Dominic had been here, he realized the instant he uttered those words; of course the old man had not. Five pots on the sill meant Lavanya stayed in Sikkim Lane. Two pots meant someone else.

"What you say?" the voice demanded.

Sighing at being drawn into one more mess, Sun joined the conversation. When Dominic asked if he could use English, the Shamo summarized his words. "That is what he claims happened."

"Impossible," the man replied. The door started to close.

"You haven't mentioned her name, have you?"

"Mr. Panu does not know—"

"How you know who I am?" the occupant asked Sun Nanping. His tone made clear that he had already sized up both callers, and concluded he need show false respect for neither.

"I recognize you from newspapers," Sun said.

"Can you see me?"

"I recognize you, Mr. Panu."

"Maybe you do, maybe you don't," Mr. Panu answered. "But I do not recognize you. So goodnight."

For a second Dominic feared Sun Nanping would bow once again to intimidation. Part of him hoped that he would, and they could move on, his latest mistake falling harmless. But he also had questions now, some urgent.

Sun steeled his voice. "Official business," he said. "Matter of state security. If you like, I come by your office tomorrow with my assistants. We talk then. Talk of your house being used by—"

"Talk now, okay, okay."

In the front hall Mr. Panu, an elderly gentleman with a polished skull and a soccer-ball paunch, declined to switch on a light or offer his guests a seat. Mindful of the stairwell to the living quarters—in affluent Gyatsian homes, important rooms were situated one floor above live animals and open sewers—Dominic kept his chin tucked to his chest. Cooking scents did not permeate the landing this evening. A woman's perfume failed to electrify the air. Sun Nanping helped himself to a low bench against a wall. The act of sitting expelled a waft of booze and vomit from his body.

"Panu Tshering," Sun said after a pause, "very sorry to interrupt your evening. Very sorry to be intruding with my esteemed guest. I only must be clear about situation. Two nights ago, your house—"

"Who is this guest?"

"Major Wilson," he replied without hesitation. "Staying at Zhao Dai Suo during official visit to Bon."

"Where his uniform?"

"After hours," Dominic interjected. "Civilian clothes."

Panu Tshering grunted. "I fly back from mainland this afternoon," he said, spitting out each sentence, as though impatient at having to express such self-evident truths. "One week my wife and I are away. This woman the foreigner mentions is my distant relation. Her family live here once. Not for many years."

"She was born in this house," Dominic said. "Through that door. She and her brothers and, for that matter, her father and grandfather. All of them were born right here."

"Her family are traitors who run away to India, where they tell lies about Gyatso and work for Vadra Pani. One of her brother, a monk, is killed while making counter-revolution. Other brother, he—"

"Edits a newspaper for exiles in New York. Yes, I know."

The man lifted his head. Dominic still couldn't read his face, but he could feel the rancour of his glare. He could tell as well that this was someone whose cutting glances and stern silences were designed to intimidate. He knew plenty of men, and a couple of women, like that: his business partner Bill Coren, his ex-wife's father, plus Charlie Wilson himself in high Vicar mode. Not him, though. He had more of his mother's sly openness. More of her manipulative charm.

"Why she tells you this?" Mr. Panu said. "Lavanya Kamala and her friends not talk to military. They hate them. What country you say you from? What position in army?"

Dominic repeated the information he had given the hotel receptionist. He wasn't beginning to believe it, exactly—the C Force was a Canadian army unit during World War Two; the Royal Rifles were out of Winnipeg, a city he had never seen; Major Gordon Wilson died in December 1943—but he didn't mind owning up to the title. God knows, his family had paid for it. "Lavanya told me a lot about the house. While we sat upstairs in the room with the painted cupboards and benches, drinking beer she fetched from the kitchen through that door. She explained how her family had lived here for nearly a century. How her grandfather had been a court tutor and her father a minister in the last independent government. Also, how the new government had confiscated the properties of Gyatsians who fled the invasion and awarded them to key collaborators. Tell me something, Mr. Panu," he added, parading a bravado he did not possess, "how did you come to be master of this beautiful home?"

Sun Nanping chose that instance to belch. The Gyatsian grunted again. Guessing they were in trouble, Dominic shook loose a Marlboro and offered it to his host.

"No smoke," the man said. "Not in house."

"Better to be safe," he agreed, feeding one into his mouth. "The whole lane would go up like dry kindling." He struck a match. The flame brought the head of a cathedral gargoyle, eyes ping-pong balls and ears sprung wings, into relief. Dominic felt like an explorer firing matches deep within a tomb. Each strike of the flint illuminated another shock. "You didn't smell something when you returned today? We must have smoked a pack between us."

"She has done this before."

"Done what?"

"Used our house when we are away. Made as though she is owner."

"You knew she stay here?" Sun asked.

"I decide to talk to her tomorrow. Tell her that next time I call police, or you people. She does not like police. She does not like you people, either, Mr. ..."

Sun Nanping did not repeat his name.

"Sun Nanping, right?" Mr. Panu said. "I remember anyhow, ha!" His laugh wasn't as mocking as he had probably hoped.

"You see Lavanya Kamala often?" the head of Bon Tourism wondered.

"I am her boss."

"At Gyatsian Literature?"

"I have many positions," the man replied. A coughing jag, courtesy of Dominic's cigarette, kept him from elaborating. Penu Tshering stood up and then doubled him over, a hand outstretched for the wall. Dominic recognized the cough: a lifelong smoker's bark in an advanced, possibly terminal stage.

"You mean you work for Lavanya?" he asked.

"Work for? *I* am editor-in-chief of Gyatsian Literature. Sun Nanping here, he recognize me from newspapers, he must know this. Know I am editor, but also know that most of business is in control of Hong Xiuquan. He is Shamo, naturally, like you, chief of Bon Tourism. He is not from here, either." The Gyatsian cleared his throat, an amplified version of a match against flint, and spat onto the floor. "Lavanya Kamala, she operated computer for us. She was asked to leave job two weeks ago. I was given order to let her go. Order by officials, like you. Told it is security matter, like you tell me this is security matter. I do as asked as well," he said with disgust, though it was unclear at what, or with whom. "I want no trouble."

Flustered by the information—and, less logically, by a man spitting in his own house—Dominic crushed his cigarette against his heel. Not knowing what to do with the butt, he folded it in his palm. He had to jiggle the hand to keep from burning his own flesh. "She gave me a tour of the publishing house yesterday," he said. "I saw her office and met her assistant. No one questioned her authority. No one named Hong or Sun stepped up to call her a liar and say he was really in charge."

"Gyatsian Literature office closed yesterday. Official workers holiday. This is true, Mr. Official?"

"Maybe," Sun admitted.

The brush of a fleeing ghost would have knocked Dominic over. "She showed me to Tashi Delag's hut out back," he continued lamely. "I chatted with the author for an hour. Are you going to tell me—?"

"That rubbish?" Mr. Panu interrupted, his scorn invigorated by the subject. "I regret publishing the story. Such views not proper for Gyatsian book. Story is full of lazy people who show society no respect. Full of imported ideas and Western irony, not true to our ethnic selves. Bad writing, too. No Tolstoy, ha! No Lu Xun, either. Young people like the mystical stuff, though. Also sex and violence and bad language."

"I'm told Tashi Delag is a popular writer."

"Very popular, if you consider..." He coughed again. Then, without asking, Panu Tshering reached out and pried the Marlboros from Dominic. "You are real major, what you say... Wilson? Real Canadian army? Sound like one more journalist in Bon to report lies."

He kept silent.

"Clever girl, Lavanya. She convince me to publish health and happiness rubbish. She make theatre with her friends for foreigners in Bon. Some, like her boyfriend, are real actor. They act and, sometimes, take real action. They create many problems and fool many fools."

Dominic had no reply to the insult. As though surmising this, Mr. Panu had already turned on Sun Nanping and begun lecturing him in the manner used by leaders who intend to speak for hours and do not expect to be interrupted, let alone told to get to the point. His cigarette puffs lengthened while he droned, until he was smoking in a cloud. Sun nodded, first vigorously, as if exchanging views with a peer, then as one receiving orders from a superior, and finally as a child suffering a scolding.

"There may be a connection," the head of Bon Tourism said at the break, switching back to English. "We are still—"

"She is seen around Gyatsian Literature every day. I go to my office last week and in my chair is that dog! It runs away before I can find gun and shoot it. Now she spends night in my house? I want no more of this."

"Yes, Mr. Panu."

"Who knows who will be next target."

"Yes, Mr. Panu."

Sun Nanping's waning confidence, evidenced by a shoulder sag so obvious Dominic debated whether he should slap him upright, was halted by the dweedle of a cell phone in his jacket pocket. Mr. Panu used the distraction to escort the visitors back to Sikkim Lane, a palm pressed to the small of their backs. Dominic didn't bother with a parting shot. He was still reeling from the revelations about Lavanya. He felt lucky to be getting out of there alive.

The Shamo had pulled several paces ahead of him, the phone to his ear. Dominic hustled to catch up.

"I must go," Sun said. "Return to your hotel, please."

"Is there a problem?"

"My son. Asthma attack. Wife says it is very bad."

"Is she taking him to the hospital?"

"Only one hospital open at night in Bon. No equipment or medicine. Maybe two nurse for all patients."

The notion came to Dominic in a flash. He felt grateful for it. "What happens when a tourist gets sick? Is he brought to the same hospital?"

The dogs had deserted their post. The curbside was empty as well of bicycle repair stands and shoe cobblers. Though Liberation Boulevard tapered into darkness in both directions, Sun Nanping still checked for a cab.

"Not you ill, Dominic. My son Gianbao."

"Please answer the question."

"Special clinic used by army officials and important visitors. Excellent equipment. Doctor and nurse waiting."

"Do you know where it is?"

"I escort many foreigners there," Sun replied, impatience finally registering in his voice. "Mostly for altitude sickness. Also broken ankles from climbing."

"Call your wife and tell her to meet us at this clinic."

"They will not—"

"Tell her to wait outside the door if she gets there first. You'll both be with me."

"They will refuse."

"I have a passport. I'm an army official *and* an important visitor. You are my assistant and friend."

For all his doubts, Shamo could not hide the hope on his face. The phone argument was brief.

"How far?" Dominic asked.

"Three kilometres."

"Can you get hold of Wu Jing?"

"Maybe not good idea."

Both men cast around for alternatives. Dominic spotted one first. "Two old bikes," he said, walking over to where several bicycles leaned against a wall. "Two old guys. What do you think?"

"I think this is long night," Sun Nanping answered, disentangling a set of handlebars.

They ditched the bikes outside a building along a street off the Kata Plaza. All the windows facing the road were black, but around the west side was a glass entrance. Light angled through the glass, casting a parallelogram over the ground. A cab pulled up. Sun Nanping opened a door and carefully removed a bundle. Slippered feet dangled beneath a blanket; a crown of black hair poked out. Whatever lay swaddled was struggling to breathe.

Sun passed the bundle to his wife to pay the fare. Dominic beat him to it, peeling off a bill for a cabbie whose profile, sighted through a partially cracked window, seemed familiar.

Although her distress was apparent, on first inspection Mrs. Sun struck him as aloof, almost indifferent. She certainly ignored his presence. Despite this, he wanted to study her more. As Sun held open the clinic door, he remembered a key point to his plan, formulated during the bicycle ride.

"I'm American," he whispered.

Sun went blank.

"I won't show the passport unless I have to. Forget Major Wilson and all the army stuff. It's better if they think I'm from the United States."

"Why?"

"Just act natural," he added.

A nurse in the same uniform as a street cleaner—blue jacket and trousers, skull cap, and dangling surgeon's mask—had already intercepted. She wrinkled her nose at Mrs. Sun and the partially exposed boy. On seeing the foreigner, her expression changed, her eyeballs floating freely behind coke-bottle lenses. "You are sick?" she asked him.

"I am—translate this—an American businessman in Bon," Dominic replied with a grin as big, he hoped, as Texas. "Mr. Sun Nanping, who was assigned by state officials to assist me, has been unable to perform his duties on account of his son's illness. I need Mr. Sun. I need his full attention. To have this, I need *you* people to see what is bothering his child."

The nurse wrinkled her nose again. "*Boy* is sick?" she said in English. "This is wrong place. They must go to—"

"They must stay right here. The situation has to be resolved. Not tomorrow morning. Not in an hour." The boy, he noticed, had gone quiet. "Mr. Sun," he said, "please inform this woman of my position. Please inform her of the government and military officials I have met in Bon, all of whom agree on the—"

"Maybe we should—"

"Speak with the doctor? Good idea. He can't be too busy—there's no one else here. Nurse, please tell the doctor that I want a word with him."

She hesitated

"Immediately."

Dominic had not raised his voice. He was counting on America to intimidate. He was counting on blue eyes.

The woman crossed the room to a door.

Gianbao, now unwrapped from his shroud, looked sweet and helpless in pyjamas embossed with a velvet kitten. The decal, logo for a Japanese toy company, was beloved by kids in Hong Kong, including Gaby and Mike. *Concentrate*, Dominic ordered himself. *Make sure you don't screw this up as well.*

Focus proved easy, thanks to Sun Nanping's wife. She undid

the pyjama top glued to her son's torso and wiped away the hair matted to his forehead. Dominic smiled at the child again, glanced once more at his mother. He regretted his previous judgement of her. She wasn't a snob. She was—

"I think we should go to regular hospital," Sun interrupted.

"Let me try the doctor first."

The Shamo spoke to the floor. "Maybe I get in lots of trouble for tonight. One more mark goes beside my name. No passport now or in ten more years. No luck for me or my family."

The doctor joined them. He had on a coat far too large and a frown far too studied. By Dominic's reckoning, the man must have entered medical school as a teenager. He couldn't have been twenty-five. He also couldn't have slept in the past seventy-two hours, given his puffy eyes and greased skin.

"Nick Wilson," Dominic announced. "Good to meet you."

"You are not sick?" the doctor said, glancing first at his face, then at his outstretched hand.

"Asthma attack," he answered. "Pretty bad one, I think. And you won't even shake in friendship?"

"Shake?"

"I am offering my hand."

The nurse spoke to the doctor in Shamo.

"Sorry." The young man first brushed his palm against his coat. "I not understand."

"Apology accepted Sun," he called, "we're getting somewhere now. This fella wants a summary of the situation. Could you go over Gianbao's medical history."

"The clinic—"

"Is for foreigners with problems? I'm a foreigner. I've got a problem. Let's get on with it."

On the release of his hand, the doctor massaged his knuckles. The gesture—one set of fingers covering another—reminded Dominic where to keep his left hand, no matter now foppish it appeared.

Avoiding gazes, including that of his nurse, Shamo retreated into the other room. He issued no instructions.

"Mrs. Sun," Dominic said, "the doctor is ready to see your son. Let's bring him in, okay?"

Gianbao had now gone so limp he resembled a stuffed animal draped over the side of a bed. Offered a choice, Dominic would have preferred a child who flailed and moaned to one that suffered in silence. The area between the boy's lip and nose had turned blue and his chest had literally collapsed, a tent with the pegs pulled out. When the nurse blocked the door, Dominic made clear his intent to remove all obstacles between the patient and the examining table. The woman's eyes boggled.

"Lay him down," he said.

Gianbao's desperate hold of his mother nearly caused her to topple onto him.

"What does he need most?"

"Drug for inhaler," the head of Bon Tourism replied. To Dominic's dismay, Sun Nanping still addressed the floor. Not showing his face seemed an apology to the doctor and nurse— to the government and nation—for his troublemaking. "We run out of supplies four days ago. Other doctor says no drugs in Bon right now."

"You mentioned the name of the drug before. What was it? Ventro?"

"Ventolin."

Mrs. Sun examined the child herself. She raised the Hello Kitty top and pressed an ear to his chest. She pulled back the lids to better study his pupils. Next, she cupped his head in her hands, as though to physically command his drifting attention. Her determination to lock on to his eyes struck Dominic as purposeful. She was drawing her boy back to safety, to a warm and protected space. Her gaze would will him to remain conscious, to maintain faith in the fearsome powers of his parents—gods, after all, able to give and take life with impunity. He read her gesture that way, at least, and his own eyes flooded at the magnificence of her ruse.

And her husband? He, like the foreigner, like the doctor and nurse, acted mere witness to the struggle. Sun Nanping wore a puzzled, almost addled smile, as if the drama before him was touching and even affirming, but not his own. His forehead, however, was dappled.

She spoke to Sun without shifting her attention from the boy. Her voice, though low and gentle, was of iron. Dominic recognized the tone from Esther; he recalled it, faintly, from his father's mother, Grandmother Wilson.

"He needs oxygen machine," Sun translated. "In that corner."

"Bring the machine over," Dominic told the nurse.

She did not move.

"Emergency!"

The doctor bowed his head as well. The request, the bow implied, while sensible, remained beyond his capabilities.

"This is crazy. You people are all—"

"Full of shame?" Sun said.

He had an idea. "Tell the doctor to look around the room," he said to Sun Nanping. "Ask him and the nurse if they see any Gyatsians here."

The question was relayed. The Shamo shrugged.

"Exactly. You're all—" He used the universal term for the nation. "All the same blood, the same old hundred names. Shouldn't you stick together?"

Sun Nanping's bark of incredulous laughter, and a seismic twitch of his cheek, shut him up. Dominic brushed the nurse aside and wheeled over a grey metal box that could have been a science project in a Hong Kong high school. A rubber sack hung out the side like an inverted pocket, and a tube sprouted from the top. At the end of the tube dangled a mask. Sun lifted his child's head and strapped the mask around him, muttering to his wife.

Gianbao coughed, fogging the mask. Mrs. Sun cooed to him, chords tugging in her neck, and then began to sing, or maybe to chant, a children's rhyme. Her efforts, along with the oxygen, calmed the boy, and his eyes shifted from his father to his mother to his father again.

"He'll still need Ventolin, won't he?"

"Very soon," Sun answered. "Machine helps him breathe, but it cannot open up his throat, which is choking him."

The doctor and nurse left the examining room. Dominic followed them. His first step wobbled; despite the bike ride, despite the drama, alcohol was still coursing through his system. He suddenly wondered about Sun Nanping. Might his near catatonia be a woozy man's best effort? As expected, the nurse was making a phone call. Resurrecting his Lone Star state grin, Dominic cut the line with his left hand and removed the receiver from her ear with his right.

"Explain to the doctor," he said to Sun Nanping, "that before he makes any calls, we'd like him to consult about this case with the head of surgery at the most important hospital in the country."

"Who?"

A still smiling Dominic, the phone in his control, drew Sun closer. "Do you think there is Ventolin in Bon?"

"Special supplies always."

"Do you think there may be any in this clinic?"

"Probably."

"Well then," he said through gritted teeth. "He thinks he's doing a good turn for a big-shot in the capital. He thinks, or you'll get him to think, that it might help him get out of Gyatso. Look at the guy, Sun," he added, indicating the doctor, who was involved in his own whispered conversation, "he's dying up here."

"But my father is not important."

"He can be, or can pretend to be, if you alert him without too many words. He used to steal for Gianbao from the hospital, right?"

The head of Bon Tourism did not appreciate the mention of this. "It is after midnight," he said. "He will be asleep."

"He won't mind being woken up, will he?"

Would YOU want someone to call your dad in the middle of the night? a voice in his head objected. *Rouse Charlie Wilson from his slumbers with the news that his son was f—ing up*

132

again, and needed his help again, and would, regardless, prob-
ably further sully the family name?

Sun stared at the receiver. If he didn't dial the capital,
Dominic calculated, their scam would be uncovered and Gianbao would be back on the street, minus oxygen or Ventolin, in
fifteen minutes at the most. If he did dial, and Dr. Sun intuited
the situation, the clinic doctor might be cowed and the boy
would get his medication.

Sun Nanping picked up the phone.

As he crossed to the chairs, no less relieved than he had been
after the successful delivery of his own children, Dominic
patted the doctor on the shoulder, to make amends. The man
flinched and stepped back, as if to give himself a fighting
chance to draw his pistol. Though it sounded demented,
Dominic swore the Shamo kept looking at his damaged hand.
But that was ridiculous. A trained professional appalled by a
tiny amputation?

Phone conversations ensued: son to father, mainland doctor
to local doctor, mainland doctor to local nurse. As he observed
them with studied indifference, Dominic allowed his eyes—
and thoughts—to wander. Mrs. Sun stood framed by the doorway into the examining room. She had removed her jacket,
revealing a thin body obscured by flimsy black trousers and a
red blouse. Her face defied categorization. She appeared
neither pure Shamo nor mixed Gyatsian. At first he thought she
might be Mongolian, on account of her skin pigment. Her brow
and cheekbones made him think of a Korean. The brown of her
irises was lighter than the eyes of most Asians, but her small
mouth and purple lips belonged to a Vietnamese. Many Shamo
men, addicted to regular features, might have declared her
unattractive. Dominic thought she was the most striking
woman he had ever met. What elevated her beauty was a
preternatural calm. Outside the cab, he had remarked at once
how distress registered without distorting, or darkening her
face. Now, relief at her son's prospect for recovery and a
cautious happiness were having the same minimal impact.

Even her smile, girlish for someone who had to be thirty, hardly showed.

In his waning drunkenness—or was it delirium?—Dominic envisioned Mrs. Sun as a pensioner. Her brows more arched and her eyes more slanted, her skin brittle but still impossibly smooth. Her own very different mask, in effect, yet holding. To have such a person as a companion would pose a challenge. Her beauty would be available to him whenever he wanted. Some of her elegance might rub off. But her genuine responses and deepest feelings would also forever stay unreadable, leaving him nothing to work with, to manipulate, using strategies of appeasement. Dominic had skills there, quality life skills for someone of strong but inconsistent character. Aware of this, he had fallen for women the shape of whose mouths and stress of brows, the light, languor, and depth of whose gazes would divulge if his bluff seemed in danger of being called; if his genuine need to honour and love and his capacity for loyalty were currently weighing unfavourably against his all too obvious failings. Men like him, if they were smart, found such women.

Sun finally hung up the phone. Without a word, the doctor and his nurse crossed to a supply closet. Working to control his twitching cheek, the head of Bon Tourism called to his wife.

"Everything okay?" Dominic asked.

"They have Ventolin," he answered, not daring a grin. She struggled as well to contain her joy. "Also," Sun said, "they decide, on my father's advice, to keep Gianbao until morning. Give him drug, let him sleep with oxygen."

"And you'll stay?"

"Maybe I'll send Ba Xiaorong home for rest."

"No," she replied in English. "I stay too."

Her laugh was giddy and she covered her mouth with a finger fan. Then she extended a hand. "American greeting," she said. "Very nice to meet you, important visitor!"

She laughed again, this time openly, showing small perfect teeth.

Though he barely squeezed, Dominic felt only bones. Turning her hand over, he watched the fine bones tracing her finger stems to her wrist move under the pressure, like piano keys. He may even have blushed. In his imagination—or at least in a dank corner of it—she wore no clothes.

"Is Gianbao asleep?" he said hastily.

"He rests."

"Then I'll just slip out."

"Please stay!"

At her husband's urging, Mrs. Sun escorted him to the examining table. The nurse had just finished applying a canister of Ventolin, using a plug in the mask. The boy lay quiet, his breathing regular. Dominic bet that he, too, was all bones to squeeze. He bet his hair smelled like rosewater and his skin like talcum.

"Lovely boy," he said.

His own nervousness surprised him. What, he had no right to look upon the child? No right to praise? At last Gianbao settled his glassy eyes on the foreigner. Dominic summoned his most avuncular grin. The boy's forehead knit and his hands clenched. The mask puckered.

Had he been a young Shamo, he would surely have found the sight of an ugly Westerner distressing. Still, Gianbao's rejection devastated Dominic. He had gone too long without the touch of a beloved. He had been aware for ages that any words of comfort he might offer his own children were nothing compared to the uplift that their voices provided him. He needed to be warmed by their embraces and fuelled by their energy, the life that coursed through them. He needed no less desperately to hear Esther say his name and partially absolve him with her smile, her innate moral balance rubbing off—even just a little. Simply to witness her repositioning Gaby's hairpin or retying Mike's shoe would do. All that casual contact and absent-minded love. And when would Dominic be near a phone again? When would a connection with Hong Kong get made?

Dominic turned to Mrs. Sun for a final nod, hoping to hide

his raw state. Her magnificent face showed only gratitude, along with an eagerness to express it, despite the language barrier.

Outside the clinic with Sun Nanping, he zipped his jacket. "You did the right thing," he said. "You fought back."

The Shamo shrugged.

"What—not acting would have been as effective?"

Sun Nanping shrugged again.

"Fine."

"Are you returning to the hotel?"

"Is that what you'd like to hear?"

"Maybe."

"I am returning to the army hotel, Mr. Sun." Dominic asked whether the doctor would charge a service fee.

"I get money back later."

"Do you have enough cash?"

His silence was his answer.

Dominic separated still another five-hundred-yuan bill from the thinning wad in his pocket. He offered his fist, the money within. "Take it," he said.

"Not necessary."

"The staff in there may be looking to get back at you for how we went about this. Don't give them an excuse."

"I pay you tomorrow. On way to airport."

"Sorry?"

"Your ticket out of Bon will be ready by morning. I give you—"

Dominic cut him off. The morning, and what it might bring, seemed conjectural. The night and its obligations, in contrast, felt urgent and unavoidable. "Don't worry about it," he now replied.

"I learned things this evening about my business that I should have known," the Shamo said. "Panu Tshering provided excellent information. Excellent and disturbing. Maybe you also have excellent and disturbing information about my business, Dominic? Things I should know?" Though he had left his jacket

136

inside, Sun Nanping stood motionless, his words crystallizing before him. His voice was equally calm, or maybe flat with fatigue. "There is group in Bon that is setting off bombs in protest. One bomb wrecked Party head office in spring. Another blew up disco at Vacation Inn."

"Were people hurt?"

"Only buildings. Always while empty."

Dominic waited.

"Panu will cause trouble for me now," Sun added. "Him and doctor, and probably nurse as well..." He stopped, as if pondering his own grim future. "And Panu has heard that group will act again tonight."

"Tonight?"

"Big explosion this time. Before sunrise. Before Bon wakes up. He was told that target would be Gyatsian Literature. Because they publish most of their books in my language, not Gyatsian. Because he lives in the house of Lavanya Kamala. Now, Panu thinks that group has changed its mind. A boy was beaten yesterday, and they will take revenge."

Dominic dared not speak. He checked his watch; midnight, and his fortieth birthday, were three minutes away.

"You are aware of this boy?" Sun asked.

"Aren't you?"

"I would not ask..."

Where to begin? He, too, suddenly pondered Sun Nanping's future. Hadn't he told him his wife was pregnant? Or had Sun implied that she *wanted* to have another child? Again, Dominic couldn't quite recall. "Go inside, Sun," he said. "It's freezing out here."

"But I am head of Bon Tourism. I am supposed—"

Ba Xiaorong opened the clinic door. In a respectful voice, her breaths reluctant in the air, she asked her husband to come in from the cold.

Chapter Ten

A bomb? This All Hallow E'en, already spooky and stressful, had to end with an explosion? No disputing Paddy Chan's analysis; Dominic was in over his head. The cab driver had set off from the clinic without instructions but now appeared to be requesting, not unreasonably, a destination. Dominic knew where he wanted to go. He even had a sense of where that place was located. For all his hard-won knowledge, however, he could do no more than indicate a desire to cross the city. The car passed beneath a lamp, lighting the interior. He noticed the burns and paused to enjoy the bounce.

Only when he smiled for the cabbie who had taken him and Paddy to Om did he lock on to the crucifix dangling from the mirror. He searched his parka for the one he had rescued from the monastery parking lot. It had gone missing. Now seriously concerned for his mental health, Dominic dug deeper, his pulse jumping in his neck. At last he felt a slim hardness at the bottom of a pocket. He had to blink from misting up again, and almost thanked God, or his son, out loud. Yet the Christ on the mirror looked identical. The driver was presumably out on the same endless tour of duty. Would the Shamo really carry a back-up Jesus in his glove compartment?

"Working late?"

The man shook his head.

"Twelve hour days, seven days a week, I bet," Dominic said, finding it easier to presume the cabbie's thoughts than fight him for them. "To get your family the hell out of here. I respect that. I respect you. If you informed on Paddy and me, so be it. But I doubt you're that kind of guy."

In the mirror the driver puzzled over the soliloquy. That, or else the directions—Dominic kept pointing to the Kundun, curving a hand around the palace—disturbed him. He cast doubtful glances into the glass before turning, at what he understood to be the customer's request, onto the road leading to the bomb factory/mine. The compound blazed with the same fervour, almost fury, as the Hong Kong skyline. Every window on every floor of both towers throbbed with light; the yards within the walls were flooded. Before Dominic could say a word the electronic gates began to pull in. Cameras dead-eyed the arrivals. Another splash, from a spotlight in the ground, drowned the windshield.

"Not here," he said. "*Meiyoh!*"

The Shamo braked hard, the crucifix kicking first roof and then glass. Still relying on the mirror, he grinned in acknowledgment of the misunderstanding. He also made his own furtive sign of the cross.

Dominic directed his fellow Christian two miles farther west. Once the car stopped, he debated returning the crucifix. Pretending to scour his pockets for cash, he removed his wristwatch instead, passing it up. This time, the eyes in the glass bugged at the form of payment.

The front gate to this work unit failed to draw open for the visitor. Gyatsian Literature used no security cameras or searchlights, aside from the usual bulb encased in metal webbing over an empty guard house. Dominic admired the compound from the road until the car drove off. Then he climbed the gate and dropped to the ground with a grunt. Fifty yards ahead, a half-dozen brick buildings the dimensions of railway cars formed a train across the back rim of the property. Each car, he knew, contained three rooms. Each room housed an author or editor, technician or custodial staff.

He had nearly crossed the field when his worst fear became real: dogs, barking and bounding towards him. With open ground still to cover, Dominic had no choice but to make a stand. He had a stone in each hand and his feet planted when one of the animals stirred his recognition.

"Marquez?"

The dog stopped. Its mates shot past with such disregard Dominic might have been a cardboard cut-out. Next up, he assumed, would be Wu Jing reprising his Rambo role. Seconds passed. The barks faded. Marquez whimpered.

"Is Tashi here? Can you take me to Tashi Delag?"

With a wag of its tail the animal set off back towards the railway cars. Though Dominic still feared dogs, he could relax around Marquez. The collie seemed high born by comparison, a nobleman obliged by outrageous fortune to consort with ruffians.

Rare among work units, Gyatsian Literature had no rear fence. Beyond the staff quarters lay a slope that constituted a preamble to a higher, sharper incline, itself an early rise of the northwest rim of Bon valley. His first visit here, Dominic had shielded his eyes to study the hill, deciding it might serve as an escape route for harassed copy editors or scribblers about to join PEN lists of authors imprisoned for their work. The slope marked an escape, and the mountains beyond—the rest of the country, in effect—a wide-open freedom.

Now, standing outside Tashi Delag's room, scoping on behalf of the writer he may have landed in enough trouble to compel a scramble, he wasn't so sure. He could discern, even in the gloom, even with only a partial moon, rocks strewn over a lunar slope. He bet the incline would be tough climbing, hard on joints, an ankle easily twisted. Up on the ridge he would find another slope, naturally, this one slippery with scree and blasted by wind. Crawling on hands and knees, skin scraped and eyes stinging, his reward would be a panorama of mountain to take the breath away—if, that is, he had any breath left. And would he, the scribe, then be safe? Not from army helicopters or spy satellites. Onwards he would trudge, his reprieve over the next colossal ridge, his liberty the far side of the looming ice field. Passes between escarpments that appeared open from afar would prove waist-deep in snow, and unstable. Peaks distant at sunrise would have drawn no closer by sunset.

Dominic paused outside the door. A shadow brushed past

and started for the slope. How the figure could have snuck up on him, so stealthily Marquez didn't detect a footfall, was a wonder. Blood flooded his temples. His mouth went the sticky dry of a wicked morning-after.

Who could that man be?

He changed his mind. His sense of the night had been wrong. He wasn't responsible. He wasn't obliged. Not with a family awaiting him. Not with a life, a good one—blessed, surely—to resume. Dominic would retrace his steps to the compound gate and walk the five miles to the army hotel. There, he would wait for sunrise, and a dull percussive noise, a *whoosh*, as Paddy Chan had described the Belfast blast, all air sucked from the atmosphere. He would shower and shave and repack his bag. When Sun Nanping arrived with the plane ticket, bleary-eyed from the clinic and a pre-dawn mobile call about another bomb, Dominic would ask: How is Gianbao this morning? Much better, Sun would reply. Thanks to you.

"Is it Dominic?" a voice said from inside. "Come in, please. I've been waiting."

When Lavanya Kamala first opened the door to the house in Sikkim Lane, he had done a double-take. A Mohawk stood before him, one of Catherine's friends from Kanesatake, the reserve outside Montreal where his ex-wife worked as a youth counsellor. Her tar-black hair had been tightly braided, tied with red wool. Her mica pupils had set off the whites of her eyes. Her face had been wide and round and, like many native women, most stunning at rest. Her voice, too, possessed the tones and cadences he associated with Catherine's colleagues and friends, each word spoken as if only after sober reflection. Lavanya embodied such grace, born, in her case, of a meticulousness about every aspect of her appearance and behaviour. Dominic had been a bit surprised, therefore, to find her tattooed. On her forearm, a stag. Around her wrists, which he first mistook for bracelets, a lattice design. She had explained the second tattoo: handcuffs of ink, binding her for eternity to her dead brother.

Lavanya had welcomed him that evening with a smile that pushed her upper lip back in a manner that he—and many other men, he suspected—found roguish. The entire night had been a heady blend of high-minded conversation about Gyatso and Shamdenpa, Gyatso and the West, with bouts of flirting that threatened, or promised, more. They ate crackers and drank barley beer. They shared a bench, and later a blanket once the cold deepened. He asked to see the stag again and traced it with his fingertips. He rested a hand on her arm. She kept shifting away, but also twice complimented his looks and sought control of his eyes. At one point she ran her fingers along his cheek. At another, their lips almost met. Far into the night, Lavanya remarked on his yawns. "Rest," she said, spreading cushions over the bench. "I have something to do downstairs."

When he came to, shortly before dawn, he lay buried in the blanket and stiff from the chill that had enveloped the room. For an hour he waited for her to reappear, or for first morning light. He spent half the hour calling himself names and half wondering whether he would have dared undress her. How she would have felt spooned against him, her spine pressed to his stomach, his face in her hair.

Finally, Dominic had opened every door to every room. She wasn't there. Worse, he couldn't be certain she had stayed over in the house. Feeling in equal parts humiliated and set up, he slipped through the front door fast, relieved to find himself in an alley where residents slept late and dogs didn't patrol. Partway back to the main street he ran into her. She had a story, which he didn't believe: an emergency phone call after he fell asleep, a sick friend. She had not suggested returning to her home for breakfast. Instead, she promised a tour of Gyatsian Literature and coffee and biscuits with Tashi Delag, if he would escort her across Bon.

All that had transpired four days ago. The same voice now

encouraged him to take a stool beside the desk where "Ocean" had been written. With no lamps on, moonlight through a thinly curtained window could only lend a lustre to the dark, as though the air had been polished. Lavanya Kamala sat in the chair used by Tashi Delag to chat with the Canadian journalist. Dominic had studied the author's work space during his original visit and later transferred the details into the Powerbook. He had noted the pewter vases sprouting joss sticks and golden bowl used as an ashtray, the triumvirate of paperweight busts: Karl Marx, the Buddha, and the Goddess of Democracy with both hands on her torch. Stacks of CDs next to a compact stereo. Books, a number in English, piled on the floor.

His itemizing the room had been prudent. What he could discern tonight was what he already knew to be there. What he knew to be there, and also what he knew, from the interview, to be missing. Such as manuscripts on the desk or a printer to issue text. Writing paper. Even a solitary pen or pencil.

Only when she struck a match to fire some incense did he get a good look at her face. Without light, the quality that he had found most delightful—the play of her eyes and mouth, back and forth, from mischief to sadness—would be lost.

"Good to see you, Dominic," she said.

"So to speak."

"Should I open a lamp?"

The error was rare. Her second cousin Dawa at Om hadn't exaggerated: Lavanya Kamala spoke near perfect English. At age ten, she had told him at the house, having been raised by an aunt and schooled under the new regime, the girl possessed fluent Shamo but poor Gyatsian. On learning this, her father ordered her smuggled out of the country to join her parents in northern India. There, he tutored his daughter in both the classical and colloquial versions of her native language. Not until she mastered Gyatsian did he permit her to attend school with other children. Soon enough, she was enjoying more and more of the English offerings available to the exiles, even in a remote mountain enclave. An Indian television station that aired American movies; outdated copies of *Time* magazine and the *International Herald-Tribune;* Elton John and Whitney Houston on short-wave radio. She thrilled to be away from Bon, a city she associated with Shamo cruelty and Gyatsian forbearance, too little rain. She thrilled to be near her parents, despite her mother's fragile health and her father's all-consuming responsibilities with the government-in-exile. Her best friend, also the daughter of a senior official, talked of applying to a university in England. She encouraged Lavanya. They could share a room, share the adventure, the loneliness, and still wider isolation. They could delight in the English mist.

Her father responded to the plan by ordering his daughter smuggled back into Gyatso, where she would complete her final year of high school and then gain acceptance into the best college on the mainland. The country needed young people like her, he said. Youth who spoke the occupiers' language and understood their culture. Gyatsians were too few and too helpless. Armed insurrection always proved futile. International pressure amounted to nothing. Only from within the borders, using intellect rather than heart, cunning rather than violence, could they be rid of their oppressors.

Lavanya obeyed him, of course, and, taking final leave of her mother, who would be dead within twelve months, she crossed back over the southern Himalayas. In Shamdenpa she studied for four years in the language of those occupiers. In their language and among their brightest, and theoretically most open, citizens. Gyatsians at the university were housed separately and fed in a separate cafeteria and forced to study in a separate corner of the library. Feeling the unprocessed hostility of those very same bright and open Shamos, they kept to themselves. They made their own entertainment—songs and stories, plays written, rehearsed, and performed in secret—and courted each other, shyly and properly. Lavanya stayed on to do a graduate degree, in part to counter the perception of her race as primitive, in part to give herself more options. An M.A. in economics: a critique of the International Monetary Fund.

"Better leave the light off," Dominic answered. "I thought I saw someone outside the building. Anyway, Marquez will keep watch." The dog, seated by the door, thumped his tail. "I wouldn't mind a better look at you, though. Just to be sure I didn't invent our time together in my head."

"I could also look at you some more," she said, a familiar scratch of sensuality resurfacing in her voice.

"I look terrible."

"You are cute."

"Hardly. I am a—"

"Distinguished older gentleman."

He smiled at her attempt to revive the tone of the other night. She had set his head spinning in Sikkim Lane with her shifts between banter and lecture, propaganda and flirtation. Her intellect had struck Dominic as formidable at once naive and cynical, sly and earnest, and her attentions had been exciting. Partly, he was flattered. But he also enjoyed the risk such a woman presented.

She retied hair behind her ears. Even that gesture, performed slowly, hinted at frayed nerves. To buy her a moment, he leaned into the incense cloud. It smelled, unexpectedly, like nutmeg. Like Esther. His wife. His only coherent passion.

"You came to see me?"

"I didn't know you lived here," Dominic replied, shaking off the congruence. "I thought you lived in a house in the Gyatsian Quarter. I thought this was Tashi Delag's room."

"I do live in the Gyatsian Quarter. This *is* his room. But..."

"I'm not tired, Lavanya. What do you make of that? After everything that has happened this evening."

"You are stronger than you think."

"Is this where Tashi wrote 'Ocean'?" he said, suddenly not wanting her praise. "I never got that straight. His English was pretty limited, especially for someone with so many books in the language. We wound up using more gestures than words. Funny, he didn't have paper or a pen at his desk. Nor did he seem interested in the computer. Not the way you are, at any rate,"

Dominic added, observing how her gaze kept flitting from him to the monitor, the way some people are with a television.

"I thought perhaps you left Bon today."

"Were you counting on it?"

She did not answer.

An inkling of a theory lodged itself in his brain. "How that night worked," he began, almost seeing puzzle pieces before his eyes, many so small and obscure he could hardly make them out. "I got the impression you wanted to keep me in the house until sunrise. Why, I don't know, except the following night my friend Paddy Chan was picked up by Wu Jing and Anatman Sangmo, whose names I bet you're familiar with, and detained. Do you think any of this might be connected?"

"The imagination of Gyatso is infinite."

"If you believe 'Ocean,' it is." He watched for movement on her face. "The people I contacted," he said, still trying to see the pieces, "they've been disappearing or acting strange. That includes Brother Dawa and a boy named Kuno. I'm pretty sure the Shamos are after you as well and I'm pretty sure you know that. I bet they're looking for Tashi Delag right now."

"He is ready."

"What I'm not sure about is if all the pursuing and being pursued is the result of my meeting a local writer. I *was* sure, until about an hour ago, and found the whole thing kind of horrible and thrilling. Now, though... Well, I'm hoping you'll tell me, Lavanya. I'm hoping you'll set me straight."

"Gyatsian authors are not allowed to speak to foreign journalists without official permission, Dominic," she said, her words crafted, as though from a speech. "Their work is cut by editors without their consent and sometimes changed. Manuscripts are confiscated and computers are broken into. One of my uncles spent eight years in Garang in western Gyatso for a book he published *before* the occupation. A niece on my mother's side, a nun who wrote an open letter to the Vadra Pani, lost her mental balance after decades in a labour camp."

"And your brother," he said quietly.

"Know why the soldiers who put down a 'riot' of twenty unarmed monks at the Kata took my brother aside and beat him to death with their rifles?"

Dominic waited. He watched as Lavanya Kamala joined her wrist tattoos into handcuffs, resting the bound limbs on the desktop.

"Also because of an article. Eight hundred words for my other brother's newsletter in New York. My older brother, who has not lived in Bon since he was a boy. Who has been out too long. Not just out, but out *there*," she said, nodding her head in the direction, seemingly, of the computer. "He no longer quite believes that Gyatso exists. He thinks old rules and old ways are gone because new rulers and new rule keepers have phones and Walkmans and wear clothes with labels. He wants to do good, to help our cause, but he is drunk and happy and confuses appetite with spirit, desire with need. He has forgotten too much. He is careless..." Now Lavanya, whose clipped tone had Dominic shifting on his stool, ran her fingertips down the monitor screen, generating static. "My little brother still must honour his senior, naturally and our family. 'At least use a different name, then,' I tell him. 'Kamala is too known.' Again, he will not. That would be to dishonour family name."

"A clan of writers," he observed.

"I am living in Shamo capital at this time. He sends me the article so I can correct his English. Even this is a risk, for all letters to Gyatsians at the university are opened. Somehow his makes it through. I improve his grammar. I suggest better words and help clarify his simple, sweet thoughts on why Gyatsians should be free to worship. Then I add a sentence at the bottom. *But we have so much to talk about, Tenzin!* I was so angry. Angry and ashamed and proud. I treated my little brother badly, and I shall not forgive myself."

She pushed the power button and the monitor went blank. Dominic knew almost nothing about Gyatsian culture—witness his ignorance about *tashi delag*—but he was aware of the ritual parting exchange between loved ones on the eve of battle or exile. "But we have so much to talk about!" was meant to be answered: "In another life, then." Did Lavanya Kamala's brother have a chance to offer his sister this comforting reply? He guessed not.

"Has Tashi ever been arrested?" he asked, suspecting she would appreciate a change of topics.

"Until now we have been lucky."

"I think I need to speak with him. Tonight. Right away, even. Would that be possible?"

"Maybe not."

"It's important, Lavanya. I had a conversation earlier with another distant relation of yours, a Mr. Panu."

"Yes?"

"He seems to think the group that is setting off bombs in Bon is going to target Gyatsian Literature next, because of him. He thinks something is going to happen before sunrise."

"Panu Tshering is not Gyatsian Literature. *This* is not Gyatsian Literature," she said, referring, he gathered, to the compound.

"And you're not an employee here, never mind the editor?"

"I no longer work for those people in that building, if that is what you mean."

"*Is* someone going to bomb Panu's office?" His instinct was to guard the information about the rumoured change of target. To see if she'd—

"I don't think," Lavanya said, tying her hair back again. "Maybe you *should* talk to Thomdup."

"Thomdup?"

"Tashi, I mean."

The biggest puzzle piece so far found a fit. "Health and happiness to you, too, Lavanya," Dominic offered.

Studying her in the dark was frustrating. He couldn't be sure, but he thought she had smiled, and that it had emerged weak, minus the pushed-up lip.

"The boy Kuno," he said. "He kept talking about an uncle named Thomdup. Now you tell me that Thomdup is Tashi

Delag's real name. Which means Kuno knows Tashi. Which means maybe you know Kuno."

She closed her eyes. From the other night, he knew this was her way of preparing to express a difficult thought. But she kept silent.

He decided to rephrase. "Would it be crazy to think there might be a link between what happened to Kuno and where this group will plant their bomb tonight?"

"Crazy?"

"To think that... Would it be?"

"Not crazy," she finally answered.

There it was. A terrorist. Him, and her as well, most likely. Or did one plant the bombs and the other write the fictions? To his shame, the initial questions her admission posed were trite. Had her interest in him been pure acting? And the magazine article; could he still write it? You couldn't dream up a better twist—the author revealed as revolutionary *and* femme fatale!

More seriously, she had to tell him where to find her boyfriend. To get her to do that, Dominic needed to brighten her mood. Doom had gripped the room; even the air felt weighed down by the conversation. He suddenly remembered digging through his duffel bag for the scarf she had given him before his interview with Tashi Delag. He had thought, drunkenly, to bring it along on his walk with Sun Nanping. Now, like a magician with an unending string of tied rags, he pulled a long white scarf from a pocket inside his parka.

She clicked her tongue in admiration.

"Could you do one thing for me?" he asked.

"What?"

Holding the scarf before him with both hands, Dominic raised it to his forehead, as was the custom. He extended the scarf to her. "I want you to run it over your head and then around your neck a couple of times."

She followed his instructions.

"Now give it back."

She complied, also in the proper manner. Only then did she clear her throat, a question.

"It was losing your scent," he explained. "Pine cones and oranges. I want to keep you in the fabric for as long as possible."

"Isn't that bold!" she said. Her laugh, which he had been longing for, emerged as a chortle. No chance Lavanya Kamala would cover her mouth in modesty.

"You almost kissed me, remember?" he said.

"I did, didn't I?"

The dog thumped his tail again at the upturn in mood.

"I felt a tingle," Dominic added.

"Never have I kissed a white man. Except, possibly, in my dreams. Never have I ever done what we are doing now."

Unable to help himself, he leaned into her. "What are we doing now, Lavanya?"

"Not that, Dominic."

"No?"

But she was meeting him in the middle. He smelled her hair, her breath. "How was it the almost-first-time?"

"Interesting."

"Interesting?"

"Also dangerous."

"Delicious?" he murmured softly, selecting a better word. "That's more like it."

Their lips brushed. He pulled back to find her eyes upon him. Watching his reaction. Studying his act.

"Dangerous because you have all the power," she said. "We have none, of course, and even the Shamos, who make noise and bully us, are poor and overpopulated. But you have everything. You can be brave and generous and come to our rescue. You can kiss the pretty Gyatsian girl and then keep her scarf, full of exotic scents and mysteries, as souvenir."

"I'm sorry it was a mixed experience for you."

"Not so bad." She grinned. "You are cute."

"I don't think so."

"Soft eyes," she said, decidedly cheered. "High forehead and wet lips. Small features, unlike most Westerners."

He had to stop this. "Hair grows out my ears and on the tip of my nose," he said without a trace of false ease. "Skin sags under my chin. Too many cigarettes have yellowed my teeth and nails. Too much alcohol has burst the capillaries beneath my eyes."

They sat in silence for so long the dog whimpered. Dominic reeled from his own recklessness. Her quiet, he suspected, was shock-induced. To his dismay, he still found it in himself to suspend the self-loathing and wonder whether Lavanya could actually be on the Web. The range of allusions in "Ocean" suggested that kind of access to information, but how? Bon, according to what he had read, had only one Internet carrier, a monitored government service. The computer on the desk probably functioned as no more than a word processor. If Lavanya Kamala had gotten wired, her line out had to be telepathic, no less mystical in concept than reincarnation. What was this woman—the high-tech future of the Gyatsian faith?

"Also, I sometimes wonder...," she said, "I wonder how my life would be now if my father had let me go to England with my friend. She married a Scottish man and lives in London. They have a daughter. Strange to think about these things, no? Maybe I would have met you in Toronto. Maybe we would have become husband and wife. Made babies with skin the gold of the Kata domes, eyes that belong part in one world, part in another. Raised those babies in a large house with many rooms and a private garden. Let them watch television all day. Teach them Gyatsian in the evenings..." Lavanya Kamala reached out and, with an angry jab, switched the computer monitor back on. "Maybe, too, my photo would be glued into a Canadian passport, or one from the European Union. My friend has a passport that allows her to travel the globe as a free person. Visas from eleven countries, she told me in a letter, including a holiday in Singapore." A longer pause followed. "That is why I flirted with you in Sikkim Lane. Silly dreams still flood my head sometimes. And then the walk across Bon—a game, to feel what it would be like to walk with a white man. How people would look at me. How they would show respect."

"It's just because of skin," he eventually said. "And money."

"I am fully aware of this. Are you?"

She watched. She studied.

"Obviously not," he answered. He stood up, anxious to escape further scrutiny. "But I'd better go talk to Thomdup."

"How will you find him?"

"You'll tell me where he is," Dominic said. His tone wasn't aggressive. It was, he realized, resigned in a manner he couldn't be sure he'd ever been before.

"Will I?"

"I think so. You'll want me to fix this up, if I can. You'll want me to do whatever is possible."

She stood as well. "He does not like it when I speak this way, either. For him, it is about duty and fate. Our duty to Gyatso and to ourselves. Our fate to die here, probably soon. He told me once that he does not believe in a world beyond Bon valley. No India or England. Not even Shamdenpa, where we met. He used his hands to explain. Cupped them together, as if he was drinking water from a stream." Lavanya demonstrated. "'All rumours,' Thomdup said. 'TV and movies. Books and magazines.'" She spread her hands; the water trickled out.

"Maybe he's right," he said, not thinking so.

"When he drinks he talks, but only as a man drunk on beer. Otherwise, he is as silent as a sky without birds."

She was crying now. He recognized her last sentence and thought he might be able to cheer her. "What's funny about all this," he said, "is that I really did come to Bon to talk to the author of 'Ocean.' It's an amazing story. Maybe I didn't read it right, but I thought it was—"

"Words on a page, Dominic. Without power or purpose."

"Then why did you write it?"

"I?"

"Okay, why did Tashi Delag write it?"

"Tashi Delag believes that Gyatso is less a nation in bondage than a soul enslaved," she replied, looking past him to the door. "Free the soul, the nation will follow. But even this kind of liberation constitutes an act of revolution. Even this process is a violent struggle, especially if the aim is to escape the future."

"I thought 'Ocean' was about *embracing* the future. About how all the old baggage and beliefs had to be—"

"Excellent interpretation."

Was she also mocking him? Nobody seemed to think much of Dominic's interpretive skills. Paddy Chan, his severest critic, hadn't read the story. Lavanya Kamala, in contrast, appeared to have written it.

"Tashi Delag," she resumed, "he envisions his life's work to be a trilogy of fictions, of which 'Ocean,' a glib and amateurish effort, will not form part. She envisions writing these works in one of the two places where an author from a troubled country can find extended peace and quiet, enough to order his chaotic, conflicting thoughts, and make creativity possible. Until Tashi..." Despite her best efforts, drawing in a breath set off a full-body shudder. She sponged her eyes with her sweater cuffs. "Until she can situate herself in either of these circumstances, she can only jot down rambling notes, like the story you adore, and play silly games with tourists, and go quietly, quietly mad..."

"Let me guess the two places—Shambala or Dorondo?"

"Exile or prison," she corrected. She opened the door. "Marquez will take you to him."

"The dog?"

"Also, we have a plan, in case of problem. Tomorrow morning, nine o'clock, inside the Kata. Look for this over a doorway," she said, using the moonlight to model her stag tattoo for him again. "Careful not to get lost. There are many chambers located beneath the temple. Some contain the stupas of lamas from centuries ago. Few are visited, even by monks."

He nodded.

"I trust you."

Haven't you heard a word I said? he thought. "I hope I'll prove myself worthy," he replied, a line from a movie, with him badly mis-cast as the white knight.

"*Markez*," she said. "*Thomdup, ok-kar-key-ko-kay. Zozo!*"

The dog took off.

"Could you translate, in case we get separated?"

"She will take you to OK-Karaoke bar. Thomdup should be there."

"Marquez is a female?"

"Bar is not far."

She had already retreated into the room before he could explain his ludicrous question about the dog.

Chapter Eleven

"Stay, Marquez," he ordered. Man and animal stood outside another door. The collie had led him to the only establishment along the bar strip still showing signs of life. Not that OK-Karaoke exactly busked for trade; the building had no windows facing the road and relied on a helmeted streetlight to direct customers. Over the doorway, in blinking red neon, ran the letters O K. On the wall, decals welcomed VISA and American Express. When the dog relaxed onto her stomach, indicating both that her shepherding was done and that she had observed many a sunrise from this spot, Dominic steeled himself by lighting a cigarette.

The room was long and narrow, like a bowling alley, with a bar at the far end and a stage near the door. On the stage sat a karaoke machine, its microphone dangling. Next to it, a music stand sagged under a binder as thick as the Hong Kong phone directory. Behind the equipment was an ancestor shrine on a wooden platform. Joss sticks fronted a small bronze Buddha. A Hershey's bar shared space with a pack of Marlboros and a jar of Nescafé. Propped against the statue's belly was a black-and-white photo, hardly larger than a passport snap.

Three of the tables were occupied. Not knowing what else to do, Dominic headed for the bar, ducking party streamers dangling from fluorescent tubes. The noise and smoke were dense. A squad of Shamos with ruddy faces and bowl haircuts were engaged in a drinking game. "*San, si, wu, ecch!*" the men shouted, counting off the fingers on their right hands. On spotting the newcomer they halted to train their sleepy stares. Dominic met the attention with his left hand so deep in his pocket it affected his stride. The second table propped up two women in red dresses. Their cheeks showed crevices where the dried earth of their make-up had cracked. One of them was knitting.

At the third table Gyatsian men sat with arms identically crossed and feet exactly tucked under chairs. Their wide shoulders were set the same, their heads thrown back in an uncanny imitation of each other. The men shared a bottle of beer and traded drags on a cigarette.

"You not suicide yet?" one of the Sangmos asked.

"What a surprise," he said to the brothers.

"I hear of dead body at Shamo army hotel," Ant said. "For sure, it must be foreigner feeling bad for all problems he causes."

"Sit, dead man," his older sibling ordered.

"Thanks, but I'm waiting—"

The Gyatsians narrowed their gazes in a synchronized motion.

"To buy you a drink," Dominic said hastily, stepping into their lair. For the first time, he regretted not having Paddy Chan along. Sparing him further involvement had been the right decision. Chan, he had come too late to realize, was more vulnerable to suggestion than his manner let on. Some part of him wanted to be assigned a mission, to be told what to do. Still, that left Dominic in a karaoke bar in the middle of the night with imposing, probably well-oiled men who despised him. And why else would the Sangmos be here, except to also run into Tashi Delag, better known as Thomdup? He knew why he wanted to speak with Lavanya's boyfriend. What about them?

"Beers," he called to a woman at the bar, "and cigarettes, please."

"You break curfew again tonight?" Ant asked.

"You beat up a boy last night?"

From the moment he had spotted the translator, he knew he held an ace with Kuno. He had vowed to guard the boy carefully, so to speak, raise the matter only if it came to that point. Instead, he'd blurted it out in the first ninety seconds. He was pondering this error when Ant seized the collar of his parka. The Gyatsian pulled him closer and cocked a fist. Dominic decided to don a blindfold. He locked his jaw to absorb the blow and mentally plotted how to slide off the table and crash to the floor.

Time passed. His extremities registered no impact. Finally, he opened his eyes. A grandmotherly voice had ordered Ant to release him. An elderly woman in a traditional dress, including kerchief and apron, served three bottles of Heineken and three packs of Marlboros. Her apparel seemed incongruous with the surroundings, especially the white scarves around her neck, which kept getting tangled in the bottles. Her face, meanwhile, displayed such serenity—he would have used the word *exhaustion* of just about any other woman in any other country—she could have been lost in a temple reverie. Dominic paid her, including a generous tip for saving him a concussion. The waitress smiled at the new customer, her eyes so distended and watery he thought of soap bubbles, and then she turned to Saman Sangmo. He sat, she stood; together, they touched foreheads. Lids lowered and expressions mild. Exchanges entirely non-verbal. The couple stayed together several seconds. Dominic could hear Saman wheeze. He could smell smoke in her dress.

On separating from the older brother, the woman ran her fingers along Ant's cheek and collected her tray. The translator poured servings of beer. His sibling emptied his glass in a gulp and then stood, weaving around tables with only a faint limp. Dominic stiffened at the prospect of being alone with Ant, but the man now ignored him. Saman seemed to linger at the larger table, lean his bulk into the revellers, his grin as reassuring as the accidental smile of a junkyard dog. The Shamos watched him pass with due wariness.

He climbed onto the stage.

"Is he going to sing?" Dominic asked.

"She request. As memory. For OK."

"Who, the waitress?"

"Mrs. OK." Ant said, glowering at him again.

On the platform, Saman Sangmo flipped pages in the song-book and fiddled with the machine.

"Behind your brother," Dominic said, trying another tack. "It looks like some kind of a shrine. Did a friend die?"

"I say that already!"

"You did?"

"Saman sing for OK. Old songs from old days. You be quiet and listen."

An electric piano introduced a melody. The tune was famil-iar—even a title suggested itself—confirming just how many synapses Dominic had fried in the past twenty-four hours. But then, at the count of five, the Gyatsian started to sing about asking someone to love him with tenderness and with truth.

Feeling a smile hurry to his lips, Dominic dragged so intensely on his cigarette that he nearly swallowed it. Sensing Ant's heat back on him, he focused on the stage. Saman was building towards the chorus. His voice was rich and smooth and he kept the melody. His style, though, had a tic: a drone that flattened high notes and rounded low ones. Saman Sangmo was performing Elvis Presley as would a monk more accus-tomed to chanting *ommm*.

As the track slowed for the finale, the Gyatsian sank to his knees before the shrine. He whispered to his darling, his breath splattering the speakers, that he would indeed love her tenderly and truly, forever.

Dominic's hands had come together twice before he absorbed the silence. His third clap was apologetic.

"Pigs," Ant said, glaring at the table of Shamos.

Saman, his limp suddenly a peg leg, walked past them. He touched foreheads with the waitress a final time. She proffered him a scarf.

"This man called OK," Dominic said. "He was a good friend?"

"Pig Shamos not even show respect for Saman's song," Ant answered, a knot working to draw his eyes closer together.

"Also for owner of this bar who sell them cheap beer and put their shit songs on machine."

"I glanced at the photo on my way in. He looked—"

"Let their prostitute women sit every night without buy anything. Use toilet to fuck so wives never find out. Wipe themselves in sink that Mrs. OK must clean up. Fill garbage with... with *tao-zi*...," the translator added, clothing an erect finger in a wrap.

Clearly, not all Bon Tourism employees sought extra income as pimps. "At least the prostitutes aren't Russians," Dominic said for no obvious reason.

"Russians at Vacation Inn only. For tourists."

He wisely did not ask, *What tourists?*

"Fill garbage with *tao-zi*," Ant repeated. He stood, toppling his chair. "And even with unborn baby they make..." He had covered half the distance to the Shamo table—the cigarettes of the finger counters had gone limp between their lips—before his brother caught up. Saman Sangmo placed Ant in an affectionate arm lock.

The older sibling poured this round, including the foreigner in the serving. He tapped out Marlboros for all.

"Nice singing," Dominic said in a voice drained of energy but not without anxiety or fear. He needed toast and tea, just fifteen minutes of shut-eye. He didn't need more beer and smokes.

"To the king!" Saman said.

They clinked glasses for Elvis.

"What happened to your friend?" Dominic decided to ask.

"OK?" Saman replied, pronouncing the name *Hokay*. He held his cigarette aloft. "These." He indicated his glass. "And this, too."

His brother humphed in displeasure.

Dominic rested his head on the table. He bet the surface would be cool. He hoped no one would notice.

"You die here?" Ant asked with mild curiosity.

The question, he decided, was odd but not outrageous. "I don't suppose either of you has an aspirin?"

The brothers discussed the request, a flinty exchange. While-Dominic wouldn't have minded watching, the tabletop contact was easing the throb. A singular sound—pills in a plastic bottle—proved too hard to resist.

"Take two only," Saman said of the unlabelled container.

"Are they strong?"

"Constant pain in the hand and leg. More than twenty years like this. You are also in such hurt?"

"Me?"

"Your hand," the Gyatsian asked. "It gives you pain a little during the day, a lot during the night?"

"Not exactly."

"Show."

"What?"

"Put hand on table."

Dominic hesitated.

"Show!"

He spread his hand out, palm down. Saman Sangmo lowered his head to study the specimen, his prison eyes wide with interest. Then he laid his own much larger, genuinely mangled hand next to it.

"Your skin heal good," he said. "Mine not so good. Bleed at night for months. Get disease that turns fingers green."

"Gangrene?" Dominic asked. His stomach did a somersault. "Not much pain," he admitted. "And no complications afterwards. I got lucky, I guess."

The older brother removed the bottle cap and shook out four pills. Keeping two for himself, he slid the others across. Dominic observed him pop the pills and chase them with beer. He did the same.

"For half that period," Saman resumed, folding his wounded hand into his good one, "I am in prison and receive no medicine. Almost die. Me and OK, both bad. His arm never work again."

Ant barked an objection.

"Bah," his brother said. "Cigarettes, beer, chocolate. Fight with wife. Talk about old days. OK, he even try monastery for a while. Four month he stay there. Then monks say, 'OK, nice man. Go home. Smoke and drink and sing songs. Maybe next life will be better.'"

The early warning signals of a migraine, the fatigue-induced nausea, even the creeping despair—all were receding. Dominic had swallowed his share of pharmaceuticals over the years, and could have sworn the pills combined codeine with amphetamines with whatever chemical mash made up antidepressants. "Incredible," he said, examining the bottle.

"Two pill and I feel good all day," Saman agreed. "More in winter, with cold air."

"Can you buy them in shops?"

"Why you want to know?" Ant said.

"I wouldn't mind some..."

"They have no medicine in Hong Kong?"

"Of course. I meant—"

"So many rich foreigner in that place. Take pills like candy, right? Not for pain or sickness, but pleasure? Because they are foolish people?"

He figured the translator must be confusing Hong Kong with some druggy city—Marrakech of the hippie era, Amsterdam any time—but didn't challenge him.

"These pills made by army," Saman said, and showed unexpected ease with business terms. "Joint venture with international company. Not legal to buy in Gyatso. Some shops use connections to get supply. If shop owned by Shamo, ask for army-style medicine. Maybe they sell you, maybe not."

A brief trip to a washroom whose stench announced which door it lay behind from ten feet allowed Dominic to calm his thoughts. Though technically inside, the chamber had windows without glass and a roof missing shingles. A drain running the length of a wall served as urinal, a hole with stirrups as squat toilet. Stalls had partitions but no doors. Despite himself, he conjured one of the prostitutes servicing a client there, on her knees in the muck, or with her back pressed to the wall.

He had glanced at Ant's watch: two in the morning. Sunrise was still more than four hours off. Sunrise and an explosion, courtesy of Tashi/Thomdup, with Lavanya's resigned support. Suppose Tashi showed up and the Sangmos pounced on him before Dominic got close? Could he prevent that from happening? Strange, the brothers weren't acting like secret police on the job. If anything, they were carrying on like older men committed to drinking themselves into a stupor as homage to a dead friend. And yet neither Sangmo had so far shown the slightest sign of inebriation. Their sobriety abruptly sobered him. Of all the battles to fight tonight, Dominic reasoned, a drinking skirmish was one certain to end in defeat.

Saman gave him such a warm welcome that he nearly checked over his shoulder to make sure the Gyatsian was, indeed, extending a fraternal arm his direction.

"OK and me," Saman Sangmo said, "we are friends since war with Shamos. Gyatsian freedom fighters, Kashang brigade. OK, he even go to Texas for training. Little brother also. You tell this American about trip to—?"

Ant spoke in his own language.

"Bah," his sibling repeated. "Too late for secrets, Anatman. Too late for you and me!"

Ant slumped in his seat, arms dead between his thighs, eyes locked onto the tabletop. Dominic had hardly imagined the translator capable of feeling, let alone of feeling blue.

"We have attacked army base and truck convoy and are going back to Kashang until spring. Shamos are afraid of high mountains, afraid of snow and cold, bear and leopards. We know this land. It is where we train and make plan. Where Americans drop boxes with guns and grenades, clothes and coffee, short-wave radio so we can hear Elvis Presley on armed forces from Saigon. If we can reach Khemo pass, Shamos will not follow. Even airplanes cannot go there. But we are tired and hungry and have left men dead in valley. Horses have fallen through snow and yaks have been eaten. My leg is broken and OK has a bullet in shoulder and another in neck.

Anatman is not hurt, so he must carry wounded men. Not me, though—I walk whole way, never complain. Every step does this to bone." Using a cigarette ripped in half, he ground the stubs together, tobacco pieces further shredding. The act seemed rehearsed, right down to his pause to let the shreds flutter to the table. "I walk and OK walks also. Ant carries our father, who is shot in stomach by Shamo soldier. I kill this soldier with knife in back and then turn him over. He is boy, younger than baby brother here."

Ant interjected in Gyatsian again. He did not raise his gaze.

"No, it not matter how old," Saman replied. "Father tell us to leave him by side of path. He say he will die anyway and wants fast start on next..."

"Reincarnation?"

"This is right English?"

With a nod, Dominic leaned closer over the table, as though to inhale every word. The flight of the men into the Gyatsian countryside summoned surprisingly clear images and sensations—odd, given that he'd never stepped foot outside Bon. Besides, he hoped Saman Sangmo's voice might drown a karaoke performance. The non-knitting prostitute was butchering "Don't Cry for Me, Argentina."

"Ant throws Father over shoulder like sack of barley and carries him one whole day and half of one night. We walk through storm into mountains. Shamos stay close behind and shoot any who fall back. When sky clears, army planes make ground jump with bullets. We hide behind rocks, in caves that local people know about. 'Leave me be,' Father asks us. 'You keep me from passage through death. You bad sons!' Ant is only eighteen, strong as horse and worse temper than yak. It is okay for second son to be quiet, but not first. I must explain to Father. What I can say? He is man I want to be. Man of strength and courage. Good to family. Show his friends honour. Until Shamos come, he is village leader. Under Shamos he is—"

Ant hurled more bitter words at his brother. He obviously despised him sharing their tale. He just as obviously wanted to punch someone. But he was also the number-two son in the family. Deference appeared his duty.

"'Yes, Father,' I answer, 'we leave you to be shot by Shamo boy soldier or maybe watch bird eat your stomach while you still living. Yes, Father, we abandon you in snow like dog. Not like dog—dog is treated better than Gyatsian fighting for his country!' I say this for another day and night. Make excuse. Think of anything. Father is weak, more of his blood on Ant's coat than in his own body. Bad smell brings birds to camp. I try killing them with rocks. One morning we decide it is safe to boil water for coffee. Coffee, ah!" the Gyatsian said, the mere word a caffeine jolt. "Fighters drink only sweet Nescafé. Father drinks more than most, and he asks for cup. 'No coffee for you,' I answer. 'Not good for—' But he say if I am respectful son I let him have drink. 'Why not?' Ant and others ask. 'Okay. One cup.' We have tied his stomach with shirt, but his insides still hang out." He demonstrated by pulling his shirt-tail from his pants. Dominic watched, transfixed, as Saman yanked twice, one finger struggling to do the job of three, until the tail emerged.

"No way coffee is good for stomach wound. Father drink it, though, fast, never mind burn to mouth and throat. We all drink like that. His face show nothing. 'Another cup, please,' he say. 'Father—' I say. 'No hurt,' he answer. 'Taste good.' Someone make him more Nescafé and he drink it also, like I drink this beer. Most of it stay down, but then he cough and—"

Ant pounded the table with his fist. Beer bottles careened. A cigarette in the ashtray flipped out. The translator stormed over to the bar and the solace, presumably, of Mrs. OK. Saman watched his brother depart with an expression both amused and rueful.

"But Father still seem okay. Ant put him back over shoulder and we set off. Snow is blowing now and hiking is hard. Anatman say twice, 'You all right, Father?' Finally he lay him in snow. His face is peaceful. Eyes open to show us he died content. Little brother unwraps stomach bandage. Know what comes from his wounds?"

Dominic knew.

"Nescafé," Saman Sangmo said. "Coffee, pouring out his body!" He glared, as if to say: *See how much we can endure!* He also gripped his deformed hand again, pulling so hard that Dominic winced.

Ant reappeared, a scarf around his neck and three glasses of coffee in his grasp.

"Ah," his brother said.

The men pinched their glasses the same—between fingers, only the rims cool enough to hold—and took similar slurps. They even flinched in unison at the burn.

"You not want?" Ant asked.

"No, thanks," Dominic replied.

Shrugging, the translator drew the extra glass to him before someone more senior demanded it.

"Go home, Canadian," Saman advised.

While I still can? Dominic said to himself.

"You have wife?"

"Yes."

"Children?"

"Two."

"Nine of us alive after march into Kashang," the Gyatsian continued. His eyes were once more incarcerated, a splinter of light at the centre of each pupil. "Next spring, resistance war ends and we are arrested. I am sent to prison for fifteen years. Come out age thirty-nine, useless old man. OK, he gone almost as long," he added, checking that the waitress was beyond earshot. "He is lucky to find woman. They have babies, but all die of disease. Most of time, though, OK cannot even be man with his—"

"Eleven years I am in jail," Ant interrupted. "One hundred Gyatsians enter prison, seventeen exit. Mean ones survive. Mean, like me. Problem is, I am so much this way no woman wants me. No woman, no children. Right, big brother?"

"I'm sorry," Dominic said.

"You go home fast," Saman said again.

He didn't mind being dismissed. Tashi Delag clearly wasn't coming; Lavanya had probably steered him wrong on purpose, in which case it might already be too late. Besides, while the horse pills had worked a miracle, drinking with the Sangmos was otherwise dispiriting—like conversing with prisoners awaiting a dawn firing squad.

"Did you and Wu Jing bring Paddy Chan back to the Stink?" he remembered to ask.

Ant shook his head.

"You couldn't find him?"

"We not look."

"But Sun Nanping asked—"

"I not care what Sun asked," the translator said, already onto his second Nescafé. "Why should I waste my time looking for stupid man with silly hair and metal in nose? I have seen Shamos from other countries like him. He knows nothing to help us."

"Did Wu Jing also disobey the order?"

"Order?" Ant looked momentarily puzzled. "Wu Jing is pig. What he does is not my business. You are not business right now, either. Leave, please."

Dominic watched them slurp their coffees. He counted to ten. "Maybe I do know something that is your business," he finally said. "About a bomb?"

The slurps ceased.

"A bomb that might go off tonight? Or what's left of tonight." He touched his empty wrist.

"Bomb Shamo building?" Ant asked.

"Isn't that what this group has been doing?"

He shrugged. "Okay by me."

"But you work for them..."

"I am translator," Ant said. "Look after foreign visitor. Make sure they not cause trouble. Gyatsians cause trouble, no problem. Gyatsians blow up every building in Bon, no problem. I am happy to watch. Watch Shamo prisons go on fire. Watch this city burn down."

"Then you aren't searching for the people who are planting the bombs?"

"Why I would—?"

"You didn't have the monk at Om arrested? You didn't rough up the boy Kuno at the back of Bon Tourism?"

Ant's face registered confusion and even—was it possible?—hurt. "Why you insult me so? You think they let me do this business? Me, Gyatsian, former prisoner? Talk to Wu Jing. I do not know these things..."

Dominic was stunned. "I'm not insulting you," he said with genuine humility. "At least, I don't mean to. I'm just trying to understand what is happening." A simple, purposeful question begged asking. "*Are* you two waiting for someone?"

"Waiting for OK to come back in better life," Saman answered.

"Waiting to get so drunk we sleep without dream," his brother added.

"No plans to arrest Thomdup?"

"Thomdup Norbu?" Ant said right away. "He is in OK-Karaoke?"

"Seemingly not."

"You are meeting—?"

A voice from the stage cut the translator off. Smoke-filtered lighting and dangling streamers made identifying the aspiring karaoke artist difficult. The shaved head and shabby blue parka were typical of a monk. The bottle of beer and fuming cigarette, the belch into the microphone, belonged more to a hoodlum.

"This song for Anitya and Songsten and all my friends in WanSee," the man announced over a synthesizer intro. Again, Dominic thought he recognized the tune, and dismissed his guess as wild. Again, he was right, and therefore wrong.

The monk sang about being kissed by boys, which he said was boss, but if they don't have money they'd better get lost.

He spewed the lyrics, jabbing at the air with his free hand. Though Ant kept pace with Dominic across the room, his focus was being diverted by activity at the Shamo table. Two men, both seeking the toilet stall services of one of the prostitutes, had resolved to tear her in half. Each had hold of an arm. The woman had planted her high heels and spread her legs, all the while maintaining the same bored expression on her face. The other hooker knitted away, a tongue of scarf trailing to the floor.

The singer waved, confirming his identity. The knot on Ant's forehead showed that he, too, recognized Tashi Delag and wished a word. But the translator was also drawn to the Shamo feud. Mrs. OK was attempting to broker a peace. When one aspiring john shoved her, sending her scarves into a flutter, Ant changed course. He snatched the tray from his dead friend's wife and clobbered the man over the head. The Shamo dropped to his knees. Ant delivered a follow-up blow across the face. Blood splattered the tray. A skull smacked concrete.

The prostitute, meanwhile, had crashed onto the second table, taking her second client with her. Bottles and ashtrays went flying, forcing the knitter to stop. Man and woman now lay on the floor, one writhing in discomfort, the other compounding his pain with her fists. Anatman Sangmo surveyed the wreckage with a smile.

On the platform, Tashi Delag was shouting to the effect that he was a certain kind of girl prospering in a certain kind of world.

Dominic climbed onto the stage. "You'd better go," he said quietly.

The Gyatsian had shaved off all facial hair, including the brows, leaving him with a peeled brown egg for a head. The shearing had brought his features into undistinguished relief. In the space of forty-eight hours a rakish Gyatsian writer named Tashi Delag had been transformed into an anonymous Asian worker called Thomdup.

"How was song?" he asked Dominic.

"You'd better go."

"Poor OK," he said, bowing three times to the shrine. "Now maybe they call this place Not-OK-Karaoke. What you think?"

"I think we should talk. Any chance of that?"

"Why not. Follow me. Follow Marquez."

Tashi Delag carried a plastic shopping bag. En route to the door he stopped and faced the room, an actor suddenly realizing he has an audience. Stepping first one direction and then the other, he waged silent war on a larger, more powerful opponent. He blocked his enemy's path. He wagged a finger. Dominic didn't require the voice-over—"Shop where the customer is never in the way!"—to think of the commercial he and Paddy Chan had both watched, from their separate hotel rooms, along with the counter-image of the contented grocery shopper, her bags stuffed.

The mime, until that moment an absurdist comedy, took a turn for the tragic. Tashi Delag enacted what Dominic recognized to be the execution of a prisoner. Thumb and finger were jammed into the base of the skull. The third finger slowly squeezed, sending the head lurching forward. The actor even managed to convey a notoriously cruel Shamo practice; billing the family for the cost of the bullet. In this pantomime, the bullet, dug out of the criminal's brain, was inserted into an envelope. He licked the seal. He popped the letter into the mail. At the other end the parents, unaware of their son's fate, calmly opened the envelope. Their horror at the contents manifested itself in blank passivity, all the hope, the spirit, taken from them as well.

The actor bowed. Receiving no applause for his skit, he issued a clown's exaggerated sigh. Ant, who had just decked one Shamo and was now encouraging another to take a shot at him—his older brother had pinned a man under his knee—picked up the departure on his radar.

"Thomdup Norbu!"

Tashi Delag declined to acknowledge the name. Not waiting to hear his own name called—he half-expected Ant to shout "Major Wilson!"—Dominic hurried after him.

The dog proved easier to keep up with than the human. Without saying so, Norbu made it clear they weren't going to be seen wandering the streets together. He had surged ahead on the road and soon widened the gap, aided by a military stride and a series of tacking moves between apartment blocks. The cold slapped Dominic awake but also rekindled his migraine. Twice he lost them. Both times Marquez doubled back for him, her return heralded by the clip of claws over asphalt.

After twenty minutes, with Thomdup Norbu's form faint at the end of a vacant lot, Dominic was befuddled. That emotion changed to disbelief when, noting a throb behind a building like a stadium on game night, he followed the dog up a lane to a patch of open ground. Beyond the ground was a brick wall. North, the wall ran into the slope of a hill. South, a hundred yards away, the same luminous towers of the bomb factory/mine, viewed from another angle, boasted their hydro-electric wastefulness. Even the moon got blurred by the light.

Norbu had climbed at the spot where the wall meshed with rock. Squatting on top, he grinned out at Dominic. A security camera caught the corner of Dominic's eye. An up-market model, the camera pivoted on its metal base. Programmed to sweep south to north, the red-dotted lens was maybe ten yards, or two seconds, from locking on to a prowler. He couldn't retreat. He bet the frame captured all open territory.

"Now," the Gyatsian suggested.

He took off. He moved fast, but not as fast as his heart, which felt as if it were punching a hole in his chest. The mortared brick showed no holds. Pointing back down, Thomdup Norbu charted a climbing sequence. Chiselled grips large enough for hands and feet let Dominic pull himself up. At the top he found a platform littered with shards of upright glass that had been sanded until harmless. Norbu had already leapt. Checking for him below, he saw a void. Checking where he had come from, he spotted Marquez withdrawn into silhouette. He took in the camera, now close by. It had stopped swivelling at the spot where the wall met the mountain. Where, in fact, he now squatted.

An arm and a hip absorbed the brunt of the impact. Dominic's head struck ground and he tasted blood. Rising unsteadily, his pride as bruised as his cheek, he whispered a name, using the only one he could remember: of a non-existent Gyatsian writer, also the local greeting. A voice hissed "shhh" back at him. With his sight not yet adjusted, he followed the figure between high barriers. Norbu stopped where the path met a road, scraping his skull with the palm of his hand. As he had during the original scouting missions with Paddy Chan, Dominic immediately sensed a tremble underfoot, as though from underground engines, and felt blasts of hot air like those from a grate above a subway station. Only there was no grate, and he could not imagine why the operation would hide its turbines—if a mine or a bomb factory needed engines capable of convulsing a square mile of earth—beneath the surface.

Trucks were parked along the far shoulder. Down the centre of the pavement ran the railway tracks he had also glimpsed with Chan. Looking out from behind Thomdup Norbu—given his height, he could have glanced over his host—Dominic observed where the tracks originated at the loading dock. Once again they appeared to vanish into the base of the hill. Granted, he couldn't penetrate far into the dark. But where else could the tracks go?

Warehouses large enough to house aircraft lined their side of the road. Norbu slipped past several buildings. They moved in the shadows the hangars provided, scurrying beneath halos of lamp glow. At the fourth warehouse, the Gyatsian put an ear to a door and then tried the knob. It turned and he ushered Dominic inside. A man lay on a narrow bed in a glassed-in office. The sleeper wore the uniform of a security guard, including the hat, cantilevered but still perched on his skull. Next to him curled a doll in stretch pants. The doll stirred, and Dominic waited for his eyes to adjust again.

Two monitors on the desk drew him away. They televised in black and white a brick wall and a diminishing patch of open ground. Though the captured images weren't frozen, neither did they show movement, aside from the flutter of a moth near an off-camera light. Sectors of the screen were blotted in glare. In the upper left corner loomed a semicircle of shade where he faintly discerned the outline of a dog. Dominic watched the camera slide until it came to a halt at a spot along the wall. There, too, he distinguished an outline behind the billion pixils: the ghost of a man falling, not jumping, into the compound.

They crossed the warehouse. The floor was a maze of cartons, many piled so high they tapered into obscurity. Selected boxes were open. On display, as though for prospective wholesalers, were ski jackets and windbreakers, hats and mitts, swimsuits and towels. Dominic narrowed his gaze at piles of CDs and DVDs, CD-ROMs and videos. His eyes widened at stacks of mobile phones, already in their moulded plastic pillows and waxed cardboard. He ran his fingers over gun barrels and sabre tips—a shipment of toys for boys—and rushed past a box brimming with Pooh bears and Piglets, the full rainbow of Teletubbies and Sailor Moon heroines. Thomdup Norbu peeled a layer of tape off one lid to reveal the cranium of a seventeen-inch monitor. Dominic dutifully grinned at the goods, touching what he could, even whispering "Wow" and "Will you look at that," aware that his guide quietly seethed, possibly at him.

Dipping into the final pile of cartons before the rear wall, the Gyatsian finally broke his silence. He punched out a cap and, reaching up, tugged it onto Dominic's head.

"Made in U.S.A.," Norbu said.

Though Dominic dutifully took the hat off for a look, he needn't have; the canvas alone betrayed the brand. A Mao cap, complete with red star.

Now they stood before the door to a tiny trailer parked at the back of the building. "Ocean" had prepared Dominic for what would have otherwise been a surreal sight. He knew the door would be without a handle and the cabin would rock under his weight. He knew the interior would consist of a bunk bed over a table and a mini-bar fridge stocked with six-packs. Twelve-ounce cans of Heineken, crushed with a single blow to the forehead and then plied until they divided, littered the sink. A Vadra Pani shrine, an XT computer with a cracked monitor, and stacks of

Reagan-era *Rolling Stone* magazines completed both the scene in the short story and the setting in the warehouse.

"Here I am," he said, accepting a can. He caught the smell of beer off the other man.

"Why not," Thomdup Norbu agreed. His can went *pssst* and he raised it to his lips before foam could escape. The swig was long and obviously satisfying. Burping, he declined to wipe a trickle from his chin.

"Welcome to 'Ocean,' right?"

The Gyatsian kept silent.

"Has Lavanya ever been here?"

"No women allowed."

"Then you must have helped? I mean, with the trailer in the story. You must have described this to her. So she could, you know, write about it."

Norbu polished off the beer with a second monster chug. His Adam's apple rose and fell; his neck bulged. Dominic watched keenly. How often did a reader get to observe a fictional character in the flesh? But the man known as Songsten in "Ocean" neither drove the can into the flat terrain above his brow nor dismembered it. Instead, he dropped the empty into the sink and ran his hand over his skull again, the sound the rasp of dull razor over a week-old beard.

"Are you disguised as a monk?" Dominic asked.

"Disguised?"

"Dressed up. In costume."

Thomdup Norbu shrugged. "And you?" he said. "You are in disguise?"

"I don't think so."

"I hardly know you at OK-Karaoke. You almost look like different Western visitor and friend of Gyatso. Like one who came last year to expose the occupation. Like one who will come next year to save us."

Dominic hadn't seen a mirror since leaving the army hotel. Twenty-four hours—could that be all?—had passed since his last shower and change of clothes. He bet his hair glistened without Brylcreem and his skin had the sheen of a sun worshipper lathered in oil. Was he Gyatsian enough yet? he thought, the notion growing less crazy by the minute.

Norbu fetched himself another can from the fridge. The fridge, too, served as a prop, or simply as a storage container; the trailer had no electricity. "This place for drivers," he said. "To sleep after one or two week on the road. Sleeping in truck no good for back. Bed is better."

Dominic sipped his beer. A hum in one ear and a throb in the other alerted him to approaching sobriety, and a probable hangover from hell. If ever a situation called for the hair of the dog, this was it. He forced down a swallow.

"I drive from Bon to Shamdenpa for three years," the Gyatsian continued. "I know about sleeping in truck."

"I thought you were an actor."

"Act in what? Shamos only allow plays of Gyatsian legend for tourists. Everything else is trouble. Need permission. Must show script. Person who asks is maybe no longer actor. Theatre is no longer theatre. Turn it into karaoke bar, why not." He chugged another half can.

"But you still perform in the streets?" Dominic asked. "Improvisational. Making it up as you go?"

"I am cleaner at Gyatsian Literature. Sweep stairs and splash dirty water onto floors."

"For a cleaner, you do a pretty good imitation of a short-story writer. A writer who doesn't speak much English, either."

A terse version of the grin he remembered from the interview flitted across Norbu's features. "Lavanya tells me to have no English when I speak to you. She says Tashi Delag must be typical writer—so proud of his language he never learn any other."

"So you speak perfect Gyatsian?"

"Not perfect."

"Your Shamo is better?"

"Where I come from, no Gyatsian allowed. All my school is in Shamo. Even university."

"Then you did—?"

"You are journalist?"

"If I was a real journalist, I'd have asked by now where we are."

"Army storage depot," Thomdup Norbu answered without hesitation. "Most of trucks coming to Bon full of stuff like out there. Army buys supply in mainland, keeps it here."

"That's ridiculous."

"Yes?"

"They store jackets and toys, cell phones and soccer balls, two thousand miles from the nearest market?"

"Drive all the way in, unload, then load again and drive back out."

"But why?"

"Army business." He shrugged again. "*Some* of army business," the Gyatsian corrected himself.

More pieces fit into the puzzle; Kuno's sick mother, for whom he had first demanded twenty dollars to buy medicine, and his uncle Thomdup, whose radical friends the boy worshipped. Dominic asked Thomdup Norbu about his sister. "I heard she was ill."

"You heard?"

"Besides mopping floors and making fools out of people like me," Dominic said, getting more to the point than he had ever thought himself capable, "what else do you do, Thomdup?"

"Drink beer."

"Plant bombs?"

Norbu blinked.

"Do you and Lavanya—?"

"You care about this?" he interrupted, his eyes catching Dominic's for the first time. "You sure this is your business?"

"It's none of my business. Unless people I know—friends—are at risk. Are you planning to bomb Bon Tourism tonight?"

Even a thespian could not mask his shock.

"Can I tell you one thing?"

The Gyatsian dropped his elbows onto the table. "Why not," he said, and issued another belch. Close up, Thomdup Norbu appeared either fresh out of bed after a marathon sleep or else, like Dominic, into his second full day away from a good wash and any kind of rest.

"The Bon Tourism office isn't two floors. The second floor is an apartment. A family live there. A husband, a wife, and their child."

"Yes?"

"You know this?"

"Why would I know?"

"People live upstairs. If someone were to—"

"Gyatsians?"

"People."

"My nephew," Norbu said, "he gets beaten up in this place. Two men kick boy who is twelve, and punch him. One man we know. Other, a Westerner with hair like your friend Paddy Chan, only real, we do not know. Kuno, his rib is broken and his face is all messed."

"I'm sorry about that."

"My nephew is beaten and my sister, she cannot get medical procedure to save her life, and my girlfriend, she is thrown from her house and loses her job and, tell me, *why* do you care about this?"

His gaze now raked him over openly. Its confidence and intensity obliged Dominic to consider that this Asian coolie may well be an individual of some stature. A natural leader. A threat to authorities.

He chose his words with care. "I care about the family who live in the apartment over Bon Tourism. I care that no harm comes to people who didn't beat up your nephew or throw Lavanya out of her house or prevent your sister from receiving proper medical treatment.

"You say Gyatsian family?"

"I say I need a cigarette and a Scotch and two more army aspirin. But I think... I think it shouldn't matter. I think that as a Buddhist, someone with a picture of the Vadra Pani in his trailer, you shouldn't need to know if the family are Gyatsian or

Shamo. They're living beings. The bombs, I've been told, are for buildings."

Thomdup Norbu rubbed his chin. His wrists were covered in the same embroidered tattoo pattern, half of a lovers' handcuff. "Family there right now?"

"Would that be a problem?"

"Maybe."

Dominic was seized by dread. "The man had to take his boy to a doctor earlier tonight," he said, his voice in some kind of echo chamber. "He and his wife are planning to stay at the clinic. They should be away from the apartment until the morning."

The Gyatsian did not stir.

"*Should* be," he added. "I can't say—"

"You say a lot. You know a lot."

"Hardly."

"More than me."

"It might be okay," he said doubtfully.

Norbu stood up. "I go check. Make sure no one get hurt."

Dominic could have hugged him. As though fearing this, Thomdup Norbu scooped up an empty Heineken and crushed it against his forehead. The can went *splat*, moulding itself to the contours of his skull. With an expert twist, he ripped the aluminum into pieces.

The security guard stood outside the office. He had to be seventy. He couldn't have been five feet tall. On seeing Thomdup Norbu, he grinned and stuck out his tongue—the most ancient of Gyatsian greetings. On seeing Dominic he retired the tongue but held the smile. Before addressing them in a diffident voice, the guard removed the hat and held it to his chest.

Norbu listened to the petition. "My friend Doshi has a favour to ask," he said. "His granddaughter practise dancing for contest. If she win, she go to Shamo capital and be on television. She wants to dance for us, for you."

"Now?"

"As favour to Doshi."

"But you have to go check—"

The doll he had glimpsed sleeping next to the guard emerged from the office. Right away he recognized the girl from the Zone. She spoke to Norbu in a sleepy voice, pulling cornrows from her eyes, and her speech included garbled English words. Though he laughed in delight at what she said, Thomdup Norbu's translation was clipped. "She say you are better person to judge her dance. Because you are Michael Jackson and Backstreet Boys. She say you will know for sure if she can win contest."

Having no real choice, he agreed.

Out came the boombox. On came the music. Assuming a spread-legged, stiff-armed stance, the girl—dressed this morning in a tartan miniskirt and yellow tights—drained all expression from her face.

"I bet she'll finish first," Dominic said afterwards. "Everyone in Bon will gather around their television sets to watch her."

Outside, it still wasn't daylight. The sky remained a grey skein, no hint of impending colour. The men retraced their route. In the haze Dominic could see exactly where the train tracks went: into a high metal door carved from the mountain slope.

"Never seen door open," Norbu admitted. "No one has."

"Do people know where it goes?"

"People know little. Drivers who talk about it back in Shamdenpa lose jobs. In Bon they are told to stay inside gates. Must sneak over fence to drink or meet girl. Gyatsians hired to work in warehouses, like Doshi, have to sign papers saying they will not speak. Always, jobs go to men from countryside. Most are old. Many cannot read."

Marquez awaited them in the laneway. The dog wagged her tail and whimpered, especially once her master, with a crooked smile, scratched her muzzle.

"I'd take him for a guide anytime," Dominic said to be friendly.

Norbu, who stroked the animal exactly as had Kuno, shot him a look of annoyance.

"Marquez would make a great guide through the underworld," Dominic elaborated.

"Underworld?"

"Isn't that what Gyatsians think? That dogs—?"

"*You* believe in underworld, maybe. A place where bad things happen. That you must get through, come out safe and saved. Not us."

Dominic suspected he had misunderstood the point, or perhaps simply misread a couple of paragraphs in *The Rough Guide to Gyatso.*

"Dogs help souls with transition between existences," Thomdup Norbu said with the abrupt authority, and English, of a scholar. He continued to pet Marquez, who gazed back with wet, radiant eyes. "Make sure right path is taken and former self gets left behind."

"That is different."

Standing, Norbu shrugged once more. "How you live, how you die, makes no difference to me."

He nodded.

"Now I make sure everything is okay for this family above Bon Tourism," the Gyatsian said. "Then I join monastery."

Chapter Twelve

Room Nine had to be the fifth window along the south side of the Stink. With the lobby door still chained and the night porter not responding, Dominic decided to go directly to Paddy Chan. The dogs followed him, but stopped short at a spectre outside the window. A yak stood facing east, alert to nature's changing of the guard. Of a dozen ground-floor rooms, the animal would choose that one? He cursed his bad luck. But then, encouraged to draw near by the effect the creature had on the mutts—they backed off, barkless—he decided it must be a godsend.

He knocked on the glass. Bars across the hotel's windows were for some reason on the *inside*, between glass and curtain.

"Paddy?"

Two more raps, and the curtain pulled open.

"What the—?"

"Can you let me in?"

"Friend of yours?" Chan asked. He wore a blanket over his head.

"My personal guru."

Paddy Chan squeezed an arm through the bars, flipped a latch, and pushed out the pane.

The action woke the yak from its trance. First it cast Chan a sidelong glance. Then, swivelling its head with the deliberation of a merry-go-round horse, it took in Dominic. In those pickled-egg eyes he glimpsed neither hostility nor curiosity nor even his reflected image; he saw the hues—purple grey, blue green—of the dawn. The animal lumbered on to the next window, rock slides spewing from its anus.

"Wake the porter up to let you out. I'll wait by the gate."

"Do you know what time it is?"

"Hurry!"

At the gate Dominic lit a cigarette. A glaze of frost covered the ground and a wintry snap made him keep his parka zipped to the throat. In the lull his mind, panic-stricken for the past twelve hours, finally settled. The beginnings of an idea for putting WilCor back in the technology game fired his brain. The spark, ironically, had been his ramble through the army warehouse with Thomdup Norbu, an absurd distortion of a sensible idea—on Earth or in cyberspace. The battle to expand Internet bandwidth in Asia, largely carried out by the corporations and now largely won, would soon create lucrative markets for data warehouses, private servers where information could be bought and stored, then sold and shipped back out to those willing to pay. WilCor's first entry into e-commerce had been a crude media version of the concept. Meaning the notion constituted a continuum, a tradition, within the company and naysayers were wrong; the president, though forty, still had what it took.

Chan arrived in a flurry of clumsy kicks aimed at the snarling dogs. He sneezed twice before accepting a cigarette.

"You look like death warmed over," the Irishman offered.

"Thanks."

"Hardly the Western businessman accidently mixed up in local troubles."

"An intrepid journalist caught red-handed," Dominic agreed.

"Fuck."

They smoked in silence.

"Does it hurt?"

"What?"

"The nose stud."

"You got me up at half-six for this?"

"I kept meaning to ask. The ear, too. To do that to yourself... It's a major statement."

"It's no such thing. A few bits of jewellery is all."

"And the hair."

"The hair? Are you—?" Chan shot him a look. "What are we talking about here, Dominic?"

181

"Did Sun Nanping get in touch with you about the ticket?"

"There was a note waiting at the reception desk. I read it after my wee stroll back from Om. Three hours in Canadian cold and Siberian wind. Roving gangs of four-legged bangers. Cars of pole-axed Shamos anxious to run me down if I so much as stuck my thumb out."

"Are you leaving Gyatso today?"

"Aye. And I'm hoping Mr. Bon Tourism sent you the same message, or more likely delivered it in person, since *you* got to ride into town in the comfort and splendour of the bureau car."

"I could leave, couldn't I?" Dominic asked, honestly wanting to know. "I vowed to stay until I cleared up the mess I made. But now it's dawn and things are basically okay. I survived, and so did everyone else. I think I *could* get on that plane in reasonably good conscience."

"Of course you could," Paddy Chan answered in the voice of someone aware that the conversation has taken a turn and he has no idea of the direction. "What in the world would stop you?"

A dull concussion thudded against their chests. The ground shuddered and the air seemed to clench. From a distance, the explosion produced more low shockwave than sharp sound. Striding into the Zone to let his sightline clear the roof of the Stink, Dominic spotted a dust cloud over a neighbourhood near the Kundun.

"What are they demolishing at that end of the city?" Chan said. "I thought all the Gyatsian architecture was—"

"It's okay," he interrupted. "It's only a building."

"I'm sure it is only a building."

"They make certain no one is in them."

The Irishman fell silent.

"Pretty big, wasn't it?" Dominic said, the words slushy in his mouth. "I didn't think we'd feel it way over here."

"Was that a bomb?"

He nodded.

"Where?"

He told him.

"That's six fucking kilometres away!"

He nodded again and licked his lips. Paddy Chan, he gathered, was doing some Belfast math: depth of percussion over volume of noise, distance from site times height of cloud, equals...

"Sweet Jesus," Chan whispered.

"I think I'd like to take a look."

"And see what? Punched-out windows and glitterings of glass? Bits of furniture blasted into the road? Maybe a child's stuffed animal headless in a ditch? Nothing to see, Nicky. Trust me."

But Dominic had already taken off. "I'll explain while we walk," he said.

He sprinted to Liberation Boulevard. Slow to believe his eyes, Chan didn't catch up until the curb. There, he watched in further disbelief as Dominic threw himself into the path of several trucks. One finally halted and the driver agreed to let them ride on his sideboard. The vehicle had already jerked into second gear, with only a single Westerner clinging to the mirror, when Paddy Chan climbed on. They did not speak until Dominic rapped on the window and the driver—disappointed the men weren't committed for the full ten days back to Shamdenpa—pulled over at the bottom of a new city square.

As they angled across the square, Dominic summarized his Halloween adventures. As they moved along a street past buildings with no glass in their windows, he listened as Chan received the summary with a slew of curses. Even if he hadn't known the route, the gathering Shamo crowd, a few bleeding from cuts but still eager to view the disaster, like film extras who wear their blood and gore to the lunch tent, would have guided them to the right lane.

Onlookers, many still in their nightclothes, jostled for a glimpse of Bon Tourism. A man snapped photos in his dressing gown. A woman breast-fed a baby. Thirty feet from the building they paused before a cordon of loose khaki uniforms. Maybe two dozen soldiers stood in a cluster. Dominic assumed they wouldn't be allowed any closer. But even Shamo military seemed to feel it acceptable to let the outsiders through.

The ease with which the cordon snapped would have made him suspicious of a set-up had another explanation not presented itself. He and Paddy were now officially foreign ghosts. Dominic Wilson had been one from the start, naturally, and no level of engagement with the culture could alter his status. But Patrick Chan may have momentarily taken on flesh and blood in Bon, his identity granted an eccentric psychological validity. Not in a moment of crisis, however; not when internal strife led to ugliness and disorder. Then, even a pure-blood who happened to be born and raised in the West became just another phantom.

Maybe one third of the building still stood. All glass had blown out, and the structure had collapsed inward. The bombers had found their target: the offices of the tourism bureau, including its back rooms, were no more. Tiles had scattered like playing cards, but the roof itself had crashed down upon the ceiling below, compressing Bon Tourism into less than a single storey. The explosion had left a chemical smell.

Firemen combed the rubble with shovels. The bomb had been detonated barely twenty minutes before, but crews went about their tasks in a haze, unable to perform without frequent stops for cigarettes, long periods of staring at the mess and scratching themselves. Had they gone deaf from the explosion, like Paddy Chan in his neighbourhood pub? Shouts of "Hurry!" or even "Be careful" would have jarred, the way laughter rankled in a cortège.

"It looks okay," Dominic said. "I mean, I don't see anyone hurt."

"Why the ambulance, then?"

They weren't the only ghosts hovering over the scene. Across the open ruin stood a figure as tall as Dominic. The man was broad-shouldered and muscled, his skin alabaster, his hair like straw. It was him, the Russian from the airport and outside Mustang Saman's. Smoke from a cigarette curled around his head.

"I know that one," Chan said.

"What's he doing here?"

"The fella lives at the Stink. Or so he says. Had a chat with him just last evening. Born in Hanoi, if you can believe it, and represents an Ozzie mining interest—if you'll believe anything."

"I thought he was Russian."

"So he is," Chan replied. "Introduced himself as Ivan or Igor."

Ivan or Igor directed Dominic with his eyes to the stretcher on the ground. The Russian's face stayed as deadpan as cadres caught in a camera scan of a meeting in the old Soviet Union. He was sharing information with another spook, nothing more. A body lay under a sheet. The indifference of the Shamo medics, who stood reading scattered propaganda, convinced Dominic the deceased had to be Thomdup Norbu. Why rush to attend a terrorist? Lucky for Thomdup he hadn't been tossed to the mob—human or animal—for dismemberment.

An unattended corpse did litter the lane. Once Dominic had alerted Paddy Chan to the second victim, he turned to acknowledge Ivan or Igor's tip. The Russian had vapourized.

They squatted before a dog arranged, like some bizare centrepiece, on a bed of broken glass. The tail and hind legs were missing.

"Marquez," Dominic said with a quaver. "Tashi Delag's animal."

"You're sure?"

"Positive."

"And the blood around the body, and up that alley there... You don't have to be a Navajo tracker to realize it doesn't all belong to this wee collie."

Dominic didn't especially want to analyze the blood trail. "I don't get it," he said.

"What's not to get? Someone bleeding a river stopped for a final word with this half-dog and then hobbled off. He's IRA on the lam now," Chan added with the grimace of someone who finds his own conclusions a bitter taste. "A freedom fighter wounded in action."

"But Thomdup didn't hobble off. He's under that—"

He saw the boy. Gianbao clung to a man's chest, his chin nestled into his shoulder, his eyes seemingly fixed squarely on them—the foreign ghosts. The child still sported the pyjama tops but now had no bottoms, his stick legs pink. Father and son stood motionless between the building and the crowd, their composure born, most likely, of shock.

Dominic identified Sun Nanping from behind by the fact that the head of Bon Tourism wore his shirt, on loan from the drinking mishap in the hotel. The cotton, formerly cream-coloured, had a rip down one side, revealing a gash across two outlined ribs.

"Sun," he called quietly. Not wanting to startle him, Dominic laid a hand on his shoulder. Sun reacted anyway, and Gianbao, his arms already tight around his father's neck, locked his legs. The man's skin looked as though it had been shaven by a fish-monger. One eye was the crimson of cooked beets. The other eye pondered him with interest but no real recognition.

"It's Dominic Wilson. Can you hear me?"

He nodded.

"Is Gianbao okay?"

"Okay," he answered, squeezing. The extra pressure called a squeak from the boy's chest. Dominic reached out to rub the exposed legs. Sun pulled away, his gaze now deranged.

"Is there a blanket somewhere?"

"He has no clothes," the Shamo said. "I have nice clothes. Excellent shirt and pants." Clearly, he could not explain the outfit.

"Why aren't you still at the clinic?" Dominic asked. "I thought you were staying there until morning."

"Doctor throws us out right after you leave, Mr. Dominic. Only your threats work. No bossy foreigner, no medicine for Gianbao. He say he know my father is not chief of hospital. He will report us, I think. Maybe I lose my job, get sent to labour camp, like my brother."

Feeding on the mood of his parent—Sun's heart was probably bludgeoning his cheek—the child began first to cough and then to gag. Dominic wished there was someone else to take the boy. Ba Xiaorong, for instance. Her absence was sinking in.

"Inhaler," Sun suddenly said. He rubbed Gianbao's back. "Cannot find inhaler. Workers look for it in there." He indicated the rubble.

"Then you have medicine?"

"Doctor give us one-week supply."

Dominic had waited long enough for her to walk over and offer her sweet smile, her mask unbroken, her stature unassailable. "Where is your wife, Sun?" he finally said.

By way of answer, Sun Nanping scrubbed his face with his free hand. Though he probably hoped to block tears, he worked one cheek hard, moving his palm up and down. When he finally pulled back, the gash left by his wedding band flooded with blood. His eyes, meanwhile, cleared. In them Dominic saw something real and raw and appalled.

His own gaze drifted to the stretcher. Attendants were only now lifting the corpse and sliding it into the back of the cabin. The upward tilt dropped an arm from under the sheet. The limb was slight, the hand composed of piano keys.

An idea came to Dominic again. He hoped he'd get this one right. He hoped it, too, wouldn't end up making things worse. As Sun Nanping watched in a daze, he removed his passport from his pocket and briefly flipped open to the photograph. Satisfied the document was his to give, he stuffed the passport into Sun Nanping's shirt pocket. "Think of how it might be of use to you and the boy," he said. "Ask Ant or his brother. They might know and they might help."

He fled.

187

"What are you saying?" Paddy Chan blustered in the taxi. "That writer fella blew up Bon Tourism because of the boy Kuno? And he accidentally killed Sun Nanping's wife?"

Dominic stared out the window. His insides were on fire. The heat had started in his chest and now was climbing.

"That's what you're saying to me, Nicky Wilson? This Gyatsian literary hero just murdered some poor woman, mother to a sick child? And you knew about it? Knew, and did nothing?"

The burning reached his neck. He sensed muscles tighten in preparation and veins tug in alarm.

"You're as guilty as he is, you gobshite," Chan said, whacking him on the arm. "Guilty as the lot of them. Here or back home. You are... you are... Stop this car!"

"No speak American," the driver said into the mirror.

"Stop the fucking car!"

"Try asking him in his own language," Dominic suggested. "It's your mother tongue, after all."

Chan switched to Shamo and the car halted. They waited while the Irishman poked his head into several shops along a strip and disappeared into one. Back in the cab, some kind of cylinder in a bag between his feet, he issued the cabbie a fresh destination and resumed berating Dominic.

The cab dropped them on the Gyatsian side of the Zone. Paddy Chan took off, leaving him to pay. Dominic did so and decided that, while he would have preferred to be alone, he had better let the younger man complete the humiliation. He found Chan outside the sports stadium, shaking a can of spray paint. A section of the wall served as Bon's public palimpsest. Most nights, despite lights and a security camera, someone brave or foolish or simply Buddhist enough scrawled words over the brick. While the words occasionally denounced the occupation directly, more often they simply listed the names of the disappeared, the dates of raids and arrests, even a line from a sutra, or a traditional song. Every morning, the stadium crew whitewashed the area, whether it required erasure or not.

The crew hadn't been by yet, but the wall was bare of fresh

graffiti. Shadows and outlines of old offerings showed through, some in sprawling Shamo characters, others in tidy Gyatsian script. Chan declared that the protest would benefit from a third language. "TASHI DELAG KILLS," he wrote in black paint. His lettering was expansive, covering the width of the notice board. "KILLS" was underlined, twice.

"There," Chan said. "Hope it gets him arrested. Better still, a lynch mob may find him first."

"Is that how it works in Belfast?"

"In Belfast, old chap, those murals wind up in magazines and books, alongside essays on the guerilla imagination and civil insurrection. The wankers who blight gable walls, spreading their historical disinformation and ideological shite, are rewarded with spreads in the *New York Times*. *That*," he added, unable to suppress a smirk, "is how it works in Belfast."

So saying, he chucked the can over the wall.

Of course, Dominic reflected on the walk back to the hotel, Ba Xiaorong was maybe thirty when she died. Sun Nanping's brother, he recalled from the story, couldn't have been much older than his late twenties when he jumped out that window. And Esther's parents, whom she never knew, neither of them ever saw a fourth decade of life. Come to think of it, on the gravestone of Major Gordon Charles Wilson were the dates 1906–1943. His own grandfather lived only to thirty-seven, his last years in a prisoner-of-war camp? Reaching the age of forty suddenly sounded an accomplishment. Getting much past it must take a miracle.

How strange all this was. Strange for the living. Strange for the dead. "When you are born," he had read somewhere in Bon, "you cry, even though the world is overjoyed. When you die the world weeps, even though you feel great joy."

The way a Gyatsian might view it, needless to say. A man in a sheepskin vest and wide-brimmed hat. A monk. A warrior. A pilgrim.

The army receptionist glared at one arrival and gawked at the other. Darting around his desk, he barred the men from climbing to the rooms. His shirt sleeves, loose enough to hide doves, flapped his disapproval. When the soldier stormed off to consult his superior, Dominic collapsed into one of the lobby chairs, allowing the deep reservoir of cushion to envelop him. Paddy Chan helped himself from the candy bowl.

"Dream journey," he declared, indicating the painting over the chairs. "Contemporary piss-artist copying a Qing dynasty chancer, himself hoping to pass for a master from the Ming. They, to be fair, were themselves looking back to Guo Xi and the man himself—Zhong Bing, the first and most important. Landscapes not about reality but philosophy. Yao and Shun. Yin and yang. Plus the great mother of all Shamo themes," he said, crunching a hard candy with the same starved abandon as had Sun Nanping, "dwelling in a lovely mythic past as consolation for a fucked-up, unlovely present."

Dominic, his thoughts still with Ba Xiaorong and the boy, kept his head in his hands.

"Was I telling you about my thesis the other day?" Chan said. "A PhD in slow progress, courtesy of Trinity College, Dublin, who begged this Belfast homeboy to accept their full scholarship, their posh southern punts. Accept I did, on the condition I be allowed endless visits to the ancestral sod to research my subject. That was grand as well. No problem, son. God bless your tortured ethnic voyages of self-discovery. Looks good on the college."

"The paintings in the take-away?" Dominic offered. "Is that what got you interested in the art?"

Chan reacted as though he'd swallowed a bug.

"Seriously, Paddy. Don't you remember what you said?"

On the walls of the family business in the Antrim Road, Chan had reluctantly explained to him before—a take-away restaurant named the Guilin, after a city in southern Shamdenpa, but known to most as the Gay Chinky—had hung two framed watercolours celebrating the usual bliss. From the age of four through eighteen, young Paddy had done homework and watched television every evening at the counter. He felt lonely in the flat upstairs and wanted to keep his parents company. His English had also leapt ahead of theirs, attuned to the diphthongs and sing-song of Belfast speech, meaning he could translate garbled orders. The boy chatted through a window slot with his mother, who dwelt from noon until midnight in a galley kitchen the size of a water closet. Trapped there like some anchorite, Paddy Chan had lamented—"*some fucking anchorite*" were his precise words—her spirit scarred by fryer grease, her dignity mocked by sausage spit. She would sigh at the paintings and wonder whether such places really existed, whether she would ever see her homeland, which she had left as an infant. His father, too, leaning on the counter next to his son, a hurley stick kept below in case of trouble, would stare at the landscapes, his unspoken meditations filtered through clouds of unfiltered Rothmans. Mr. Chan would sometimes question why the visions were growing more faint, receding into their painted mist.

Though the elder Chan assumed failing eyesight to be the cause, Paddy, barely ten years old, figured out the real problem: the effects of cigarette smoke on cheap watercolours. But even then the child knew to keep the knowledge to himself. His parents liked the story the vanishing landscapes told. The story of Gay Chinky and his wife, another diaspora tale of small, sacrificed lives, with the joyless payoff: the boy with the local accent and scholarship grades, skin so toughened by taunts that a brilliant future awaited him among the planet's multitude of foreign ghosts, one of which he was now on his way to becoming.

"It's nothing to be ashamed of," Dominic said. "Sons are always trying to make good with their dads."

"The cheek," Chan could only reply.

"Do they still run the business?"

"The business?"

"Maybe it isn't too late. Bring your parents over here for a holiday. Show them the real mountains and rice paddies. Show them the Chan ancestral—"

"I am talking about a fucking thesis! Theories of landscape art, for the love of God. Post-colonial tripe. Academic wankery."

Dominic rose abruptly, announcing that he had to stop by his room. "Wait for me here," he said. "Better, let's meet later at Mustang Saman's. In an hour or so, okay?"

Chan tried talking his way up the stairs as well. On being rebuffed, his expression went blank with rage. "But enough about the peasant Chans of the Pearl delta via North Belfast," he said. "How about the noble Wilsons of midtown Toronto? How about lovely, suffocating Gina, dead these ten years but still leading lady in your dreams, wakeful or otherwise? And the Old Man, a.k.a. the Vicar? Pitiful Charlie, who nearly dragged the family empire down. Let's talk about 1989, Nicky, and what you did to console an ailing Ma and save a hapless Pa from the folly of his own values."

Dominic climbed two steps at a time.

In the room, which had been cleaned, towels replaced and tea mugs washed, ashtrays emptied and air freshened, he unplugged the computer and zipped it into its case. Rummaging through the duffel bag, he found nothing he wanted. Rifling among the toiletries, he came to a similar conclusion. The hip flask was half-empty, but also half-full. He had only one pack of cigarettes left, but one pack might be plenty. The pink pig, perched on a pillow by the cleaning staff, fit snugly into a pocket. Lavanya Kamala's scarf, and the cabbie's crucifix, filled another.

He picked up the receiver, then put it down. He had picked it up again, and was again reconsidering, when the operator asked: "*Wei?*" All of a sudden Dominic couldn't remember his numbers in Shamo. He couldn't even be sure of his home number in English. A seven-digit sequence popped into his head. He was about to recite it when he recalled that Hong Kong numbers had eight digits. Whistling "*ayyah*," the operator finally asked, "Same number as before?"

"The same," he answered.

He heard the digital dialling sequence and the ring. The tone was the right one. One ring, two, three—

Click, a line. And a voice.

"This is the Wilson house," he heard himself say. "We can't take your call right now. Leave a message and we'll get back to you."

The beep. Open air.

"Esther?" he began. His spoken voice shocked compared with the one on the message. Its timbre now belonged to an old man: a dropped register and slowed beat, a persistent tremble. "Where are you? What time is it, anyway?... You must be downstairs, seeing the kids onto the school bus. Listen," he said, fighting an overwhelming desire to lie down, "I'm still here in Gyatso. Something has happened. It involves a woman and it's pretty serious... I mean, something has happened to *her*, and now, well, now something has happened to me also. It would, right—it's my birthday!"

Another beep further tightened his chest. Had he programmed the message for one minute only? Part of him hoped so; he felt too tired, too aggrieved, to talk—even, in effect, with himself.

"I know I should explain the woman. There's a child involved too, which is a really long story. Speaking of stories, I have the sinking feeling this is all from 'Ocean.' I'm even wondering if Lavanya made me up as well, so she'd have a new kind of character to work with..." He struggled to hold a thought. He should ask about Halloween. He should ask about her health. Hadn't she mentioned a doctor's appointment? November first, in the morning. Today.

One more beep. Tears now plugged the holes in the microphone. He worried that the water would make him sound more remote and inaccessible. The reverse actually felt true. They, his family, felt remote and inaccessible; they were behind him now. Like his life, which he had squandered. Like his life, which he hardly understood.

"Esther? Are you there? Look, you'll probably get some calls this morning. Franny, for sure, and maybe Catherine. Tell them I'm doing fine, and have just been delayed. Make Franny promise to visit Dad and assure him the wedding invitation was a bad joke. Speaking of which, if Charlie calls, which he probably won't, tell him that this trip wasn't wasted, that I'm onto some amazing stuff up here. I mean, that might not make sense, but it's true. It's true," he added, now barely able to grip the receiver, "and if he knew, if I could explain, my father might even be proud of—"

A fourth beep. He couldn't talk anymore. He had to shut up.

"I guess I keep hoping you'll walk in and interrupt me," he said, a lie. "And here's a tough question, Esther, especially for a Catholic." He thought of one ethical dilemma regarding the taking of a life, asked about another. "Do you think a parent *can* survive the death of a child? You hear stories about men who torch houses to destroy memories, who set themselves on fire to be cleansed of the touch of a lost son or daughter... Of men who never recover... Who wind up leaving their wives, their jobs, their *lives*, really, because of a tragedy."

The beep.

He cut the line.

"I'm sorry," he told the monitor at her desk, waving off her salute.

She squinted.

"I bet you meant a lot to him," he said, indicating the door across the hall. "I'm sure he didn't mean to break your heart." More words came, unbidden. "Who can stop a body from dying?" he asked himself aloud. "Not even the man with the gun held to his own head."

Quoting the boy.

Who got worked over in a room behind the Bon Tourism office.

Sending his uncle Thomdup into a lethal rage.

Making Sun Nanping and his family accidental targets.

Because he, Dominic Wilson, decided to meet some author.

Because he couldn't keep a promise and didn't really know what he wanted—or else just wanted too much.

On the stairs back to the lobby he mulled over the phone number stuck in his short-term recall. The sequence came to him again. Even now, his fingertips sought to compress the keys on a receiver in the correct order. He associated the numbers with North America, with Canada. He associated them with Charles and Gina Wilson, 9 Braley Drive, Toronto, Ontario, M5G 2A7. His phone number from the age she helped him memorize it—1962 or '63—until the house was sold, and the line disconnected, shortly after her death. Dominic had wanted to dial that home. And speak with whom?

He wished he were drunk. Hammered. Stinking. Jarred, as Paddy Chan called it. Scotch would be nicest, Macallan or Dewar's, but boot and mushroom, vinegar and dandelion would do. Instead, he finally felt sober. Sober and wide, wide awake.

His annoyance at finding Chan still waiting in the lobby showed. Nodding to him, Dominic made for the door, driven by irritation and disgust. The Irishman bolted from the seat like a job applicant who has lingered for hours hoping for a word with the boss.

"Think I could pass for a monk, Paddy?" he finally said in the lane. "If I shave my head and borrow some robes?"

The sill of the Kamala house showed two pots; drapes on the upper windows were drawn. For a split second Dominic thought he glimpsed a figure step back from a crack between the drapes, remove herself from the frame. His nostrils flared at an odour, probably traffic out on the boulevard. His legs, motoring of their own accord—he felt as if he were on a moving walkway in an airport—didn't break pace.

"Not for a second," Chan answered. "You're not from here. You're not of here, any which way. This place has *nothing* to do with you. Not its fashions, not its faith. Certainly not its dimensions. Are you clear on how strange Gyatso is? How impossible it would be for someone like you to ever even comprehend it, let alone think of yourself as a part? Are you clear? You want to be, you know."

Dominic, who neither agreed nor disagreed—countries couldn't be strange, he suspected, only people—kept quiet.

"Believe me," Chan added, now nearly pleading, "I know about the strangeness, or at least I know more than you. This place is a cliff, and you are in grave danger of falling off."

They stood at the top of Sikkim Lane. "Look," Dominic said with solicitude but not conviction, "I have to see someone further in the Gyatsian Quarter. Why don't you order food at the restaurant. I'll be along."

Chan took his arm. "Why the computer?"

"Sorry?"

"If you're just going to meet someone, why bring the computer? And why that ridiculous stuffed animal in your pocket?"

"I might do more interviews for the piece. Real terrorists. An exclusive."

Chan let him go. "You're a prick," he said. "Do you know that?"

"It has been made clear to me."

"Wrong, wrong, wrong. Not for what you've done, fool. That's one regret in the scheme of a lifetime. I mean you're a prick, and maybe even a coward, for what you're thinking of—"

"Did I write down our address in Hong Kong the other day? On a yellow sticky?"

Paddy Chan frowned.

"Will you visit?"

Chan gripped the cuffs of his own jacket so tightly the fabric drew as taut as a sail in a tacking breeze. "Am I supposed to have even the faintest notion what is wrong with you?"

"You're supposed to wish me happy birthday."

"Forty, right?"

"An old man," Dominic concurred.

"Fuck you, old man."

The Kata domes shimmered in the gathering light. The temperature had climbed fifteen degrees since dawn. By noon the air would be warm, a sun, hazy but still harsh, the only stable object in a sky otherwise in perpetual upwards flight, a celestial twister, an ascension. Wiping away errant tears—now he could not imagine himself ever *ceasing* to weep—he wove through the streets of the Gyatsian Quarter, certain one of the alleys would open onto the plaza. In the third shop he tried, a woman sold him a bottle of aspirin the match of Saman Sangmo's stash. He flashed her a hundred-yuan bill. She took it, demanded another. Back outside he tore off the cap and inverted the bottle, swallowing four with the help of the flask. The pills went down easy, and the Scotch burned like a rope around his neck. He tightened the noose with another plug. He gulped four more pills.

Over his shoulder, he saw a man using the corner of a building as a shield. Light reflected off his glasses and a small object stuck to his nose. The man withdrew.

Everything in the Kata plaza was exactly as it had been a week before. Pilgrims performed their final prostrations in front of the temple, months or years of journeying now complete, and then rose with expressions at once defeated and victorious, lost and saved, to pass through the gates. So he thought, at any rate; so he interpreted their faces. The giant stupa billowed smoke. Lines of prayer flags flapped. The same blind musician played his instrument and the same men carved their stones. Women in aprons and shawls still chatted beside stalls of fruit flown in from Shamdenpa. The vendor, or one just like her, still approached him, or a man just like him, with her display of necklaces and rings. He noticed the sentries posted outside a building at the south end of the plaza, visors low, hands on weapons. He counted the cameras along the walls. Three undercover cops were discernible, marching the wrong way up the U-Chen, knocking into pedestrians.

Everything outside the plaza was the same. Except for him. He wasn't the same. Not with lives destroyed and loved ones dead and all fault, all responsibility, squarely on his shoulders. Not with the army aspirin coursing calm and forgetfulness, ease at how things must be, through his veins with an authority no booze or reefer could match. Not with the tears in his astonished eyes.

In short, not with his life, squandered and dim, behind him. And a gate into a temple, into the Kata, ahead.

He stepped over the threshold.

Would he be followed? He had read about what happened to Shamo agents who tried penetrating the complex using stealth instead of violence. Throngs of pilgrims would gently raise up the intruders like pallbearers with a bundled corpse and pass them back to the exit. The agents would emerge unharmed but short a cell phone or cattle prod or even a handgun, which would later turn up, minus its firing pin, along the Samsara banks. Westerners caught brandishing their weapons—videocams and cameras, Walkmans with microphones hidden in earplugs to record prayer sessions—found their equipment confiscated as well. This time, the materials were returned. On completing their tour, the apparatus could be claimed on the steps outside, often wrapped in a ceremonial scarf. He wondered fleetingly whether his computer would be taken.

Slowing to a shuffle, he slipped into the stream of pilgrims navigating the rim of the first courtyard. A few wore robes, but most were ordinary Gyatsians in clothes ranging from traditional costumes to socialist apparel to rags revealing patches of bruised and filthy skin. Some carried prayer beads and wheels, others bundles of incense. The scent only partially cloaked their unwashed bodies. After two circuits, with his fellow shufflers displaying outward peace and inward reverence—wrong: surely all they showed was contented vacancy—and paying him scant notice, beyond the usual smiles and requests to touch his pallid cheeks, he further relaxed. Further forgot. Further dissolved. Built into the walls of a walkway behind a wood partition were copper-plated prayer wheels. Pilgrims spun them while chanting, the wheels, constantly in motion, a lulling drone. He completed the circuit twice but declined to perform the ritual. His consciousness was yet too crude and thoughts too encumbered.

Around and around he went, without direction or intent. Two monks now steered in his wake. Jewellery glinted off the face of another pilgrim.

At last he was nudged into an alley running down the side of a building. He understood the push as a courtesy. Sure enough, the lane extended for a hundred feet before coming to an elbow. At the junction stood a door. He also saw, or believed he saw, figures sliding away from the entrance, disappearing deeper into the Kata. As he neared the junction, the stag carved over the frame became apparent, its gold paint fresh. The door had a ring for a knob; droplets of blood covered the handle. He removed the scarf from his pocket and wiped it clean. He draped the scarf around his neck.

A push opened the door partway. What he glimpsed through the crack burned his eyes and caught his breath but left his pulse regular, his heartbeat unperturbed. Lavanya's warning—or had it been an invitation?—to be mindful of the caverns beneath the temple, many home to the stupas of lamas long since reincarnated a dozen, a hundred times more, and long since forgotten as ever having been one man or another, settled in the front of his mind. Still more compelling was the wide window visible on the far side of a stone floor. The window had a frame of heavy beams but no curtains or glass. Beyond the frame loomed the mountains of the central Gyatsian plateau. Bon and its valley had vanished, transporting the viewer directly into a landscape so vast and impenetrable that it remained, to all but a few herdsmen and adventurers, where gods, not mortals, lived.

He exerted a greater force on the handle. With his other hand he checked his pocket for the aspirin and flask. A final look back showed the man with yellow hair and facial adornments standing at the top of the lane. The man did not shy away from being detected again. He stood there, as though wanting to see that he was seeing, to be aware, perhaps even be consoled, that he had a witness.

So noted, he thought. He lowered his head and crossed the frame. His witness claimed this place was a cliff, which an outsider might be in danger of falling off, but he was wrong. This place was a door. A door that was now open. A door that he passed through.

Part II

"Ocean,"
by Tashi Delag

Ocean

From my father, a cruel man of great import, I learned how to prepare noodles. Over-boiling turns them to mush. Too much spicing spoils the broth. From my mother, a gentle woman of no consequence, I learned how to escape. "In the Kodu mountains," she said, "are sacred valleys where those in distress can find sanctuary. Seekers must be ready to discover these places. Hearts must be pure. Minds must already be on the right path."

For my father, I season my broth with beer piss and pepper it with cigarette ash. For my mother, dead these long years, I seek the way.

All writers peddle lies. All Buddhas tell truths for free.

The imagination of Gyatso is infinite.

When I first went to Kodu to greet the living Buddha I found the past becoming the future as quickly as DVDs replaced videos and satellite phones permitted conversations between actors in the Himalayas and their agents in Los Angeles. The post-modern era had arrived in WanSee village. Houses bathed in television glow. Old men did tai chi with Céline Dion in their headphones. I had walked for two weeks to reach WanSee, stuffing the holes in my boots with pages from a bad novel—my own, of course—but along the town's only paved street were Subaru all-terrain vehicles and a limousine with curtains.

In a tavern I drank beer with the man who owned the video store. His name was Du Li Chun Chue—Duli to friends—and he was a talker. Duli rushed in the latest releases by helicopter every Friday; the drive from the capital took two days and customers could not wait. He owned the whirlybird, and the airport, and had recently bid for the contract to install toll roads across Gyatso. "World Bank financed project," he said with evident pride. "Funds for the taking, profits for the bold."

I could offer this groundbreaker no boasts or business tips or even a quality cigarette. I could only show him my trick.

"Watch," I said.

I smashed an empty can of Heineken into my forehead. Gripping either end, I twisted it until the metal tore open like a gutted rabbit.

"I am a busy man," Duli said. "Must run."

"One question, friend. Where are all the children in WanSee village? I see no children on the street."

"In school, fool."

"Learning the new technologies?"

"*Ciao*," he answered, also a linguist.

Ahkeanu, the living Buddha, appeared close to death. He thought he might be forty, but was nearly one hundred. He believed he worked as a noodle maker, specializing in the fatty wheat variety, but in fact he was the twenty-second reincarnation of the lama at Mola monastery. Ah-K, as we called him, was an old family friend and adviser. I had come to Kodu to write an article about him.

"Dried chilies work best," he said when we met. "Fresh ones are too tangy. The tongue on fire soon ceases to register other tastes. Eyes roll back in the head. Consciousness is briefly lost."

"Sagacious," I replied.

"Your father knows best."

"I am not fit to light his cigarette."

"His counsel must be heeded."

"I am not worthy to pour his beer."

"His wisdom is unrivalled."

"I am yak dung beneath his boots."

Ah-K nodded in satisfaction. He pulled a magazine from under his robe. The magazine claimed to be about *Time* and showed a yellow Man of the Year on its cover. "Dorondo," the living Buddha said. "These words speak of the battle for Dorondo. It has begun." He held out a page of *Time*. An advertisement boasted a holiday destination in a city of sky buildings with an upright needle pricking the heavens. The city made a promise: THE GOOD.

"Good versus evil," Ah-K said. "Profit versus loss. Free market versus controlled economy. The struggle, as it ever was."

According to legend a paradise exists on earth. Called Shambala or, apparently, Dorondo, it lies somewhere in the mountains of eastern Gyatso. In movies, Shangri-la is a kingdom enclosed by high ranges and entered through an elusive pass. Many die trying to reach it. Those who survive are greeted by citizens wearing togas and talking BBC.

"My mother told me of a similar paradise," I said. "It is for those who are seeking escape from—"

"Women," Ah-K interrupted.

"I was not fit to braid her hair."

"Nonsense."

"I was not worthy of her loving gaze."

"Be a man!"

"I was an ache in her abdomen."

The lama slapped my cheek. I accepted his criticism through gritted teeth.

"A young couple, very much in love, are searching for Shambala this instant," he said in a failing voice. "Their interests are in global telecommunications and business translation. But they have lost their way and have no noodles to eat or coffee to drink. Help them!"

"Is the woman with child?"

"Children are the future," he answered.

I recognized the tale he was telling me. As far as I knew, I was its author. A short story begun years before but never finished, for the usual reasons: the refusal of my pen to get on with it; my mind's insistence on mulling over ancient history and wallowing in the past. Abandoning the manuscript had left a hole in no publisher's list. Editors had failed to call begging for an ending. Agents had declined to ring with film options. Yet now Ahkeanu was declaring it my duty to intervene once more?

"Cross the Chenla glacier and you will be standing on the forehead of the Lord of the Lotus," he said. "Follow the widest crack, the deepest frown lines. They will lead you to the gate."

"A road map to paradise," I replied. "Like those showing the mansions of the stars in Hollywood."

But his eyes had gone glassy and his hands fell by his side. Next day his body, wrapped in a blue coat and yellow cape, was buried in a stupa in one of the many chambers beneath the monastery. Attendants were ordered to record which stupa in which chamber, but forgot. Ah-K's corpse was soon given up for missing. His consciousness went free, however, to begin its search for another incarnation.

I returned to my trailer in the capital. Stepping through the door, the floor sagged. Ducking into a seat at the table, the trailer shifted again. I unmoored a warm beer from a six-pack in the fridge. With two gulps, and then two vigorous twists, I added more severed heads and tails to the sink. As always, I forgot to bow before the shrine, positioned on top of *Rolling Stone* magazines from the Reagan administrations, to show my respects. But I did remember to flatten my palm over the cracked screen of my XT computer, in order to bond with my cyberfunds manager. I also popped another Heineken and scratched my testicles.

On the table lay a thick folder titled: "Petty Bourgeois Rubbish." A dozen incomplete manuscripts clamoured for attention, like girls in Bangkok brothels. *Choose me*, the stories cried. *Rewrite my tale with a fresh perspective and an eye to the new millennium!* I found the piece of rubbish in question: "Love in the Time of Computer Viruses." This text alone seemed happy as a dead letter. As I reread my slanting scrawl, I began to understand why.

This is their story:

Anitya sighted the figure from the window of her house. She was studying the hieroglyphics of a forgotten language; he was traversing a valley carved between mountains. By nightfall she would have memorized twenty more symbols no longer used by human beings to express love or hate, praise or scorn. By nightfall the man would be passing her door. Anitya shelved her book and spent the day preparing dumplings and flatbreads, yogurt and butter tea. She dusted off a precious can of Coke and arranged the ancestor shrine.

Her father had been gone for years. An actor without a script, he had shoved his wildly painted clay masks—one happy, one sad, one the grinning face of evil—into a sack and informed Anitya and her mother that he could no longer live in such desolation. He needed an audience for his performances and applause for his gift. Anitya was only a child, but he called her grown up, able to manage. He vowed to return for them in the solar new year.

He was not missed. To his wife, he had shown only unfocused rage and insatiable desire. His daughter knew only the back of his hand.

Anita's mother had died sometime between then and now. She took ill in winter and expired before spring. Formerly a scholar, she left her child clothes and jewels, albums and cassettes, along with books on how to learn a dozen languages, some still living but all basically deceased to someone stranded a hundred kilometres from the nearest source of electricity. The girl owned no clock or calendar. Her only neighbour in the valley was a holy man who had vowed never again to speak with a female, as penance for unspecified crimes committed in youth. If the neighbour, whose house lay an hour's walk to the south, knew the date, he wouldn't say.

She calculated such things using her own body. Many years since she had begun to bleed. Some years since hair had started to grow between her legs. Maybe twenty-four full moons since she had last whispered the word "Daddy." Twenty-four hours since she had last wept for her mother. Finally, it had been some time, no time, all the time, since Anitya nightly felt moist in the same spot where the hair grew, and imagined strange men over her, kissing her lips, moving.

At sunset she heard the scrape of feet. Her every muscle tensed, not in fear. The breaths of an exhausted traveller became more pronounced. But then the sound receded, like a tide drawn back out a strand, and with it the scrape. She rushed to the door.

"Please," she called to the figure. "I have prepared food."

He stopped and turned. Light from the house cast itself onto a handsome face beneath a floppy hat. "You live alone?" a husky voice asked.

"With my parents," Anitya answered out of instinct.

"I will eat your food."

Inside, she glanced at his rugged features and slate eyes. The wind had tousled his hair and puttied the lines around his mouth with grime. She offered him a basin of water to wash. He crossed to the shrine.

"Your mother and father?"

She bit her lip.

"We will save food for them, in case we are together later."

The visitor, named Songsten, ate for an hour. The Coke he savoured, declaring it flat and not as good as beer, but still delicious. He ignored her mute queries about her cooking. He paid no attention to her fidgeting. At last he burped and asked if he could sleep on the floor. His snores snapped like ice cracking underfoot.

Anitya stood in the doorframe. Even tonight, with a man in the house, her world remained as silent as a sky without birds. Once again, she had to look to the heavens for conversation. The stars did most of the talking, tales of explosions and implosions and black holes; of the slow self-pleasure of bringing a solar system to its zenith; of the harder, faster thrill of shooting across a celestial dome, delighting at the full round moon; of the afterward melancholy of low cloud cover, earth once more separate from heaven, stars aloof from wishers and dreamers and lovers in the dark.

She went to him. "Open me," she said. He grunted, his breath foul, but did as she asked.

Next morning, Anitya filled a knapsack with her mother's jade necklaces and silver earrings, a thermos and pot, the photographs from the shrine, and her favourite book about her favourite languages, Speech of the New World Indian, *by Dr. T. B. Winchester, M. Phil. She rolled sticks of incense and candles in a blanket. She filled a smaller bag with dried meat and roasted barley, a bar of chocolate the penitent holy man had left on her stoop the previous new year.*

"I am ready," she told Songsten.

He set off, not caring if she followed. For seven days and nights he crossed the plateau, walking with his head stubbornly held high, strides loping. Overhead, choughs sketched figures in the sky, their calls—a cross of chirp-chirp with caw-caw—piercing the air. The wind blasted faces raw. Sere stubble tripped up legs heavy with fatigue. Songsten's jeans were torn and his shirt filthy and his wool vest smelled equally of sheep and sweat. Still, he believed himself a prince. In the evening he would flop to the ground, regardless if the terrain afforded shelter from squalls. Some days Anitya fell kilometres behind and arrived at the camp in despair of ever finding the sacred valley. After they ate he would sing his favourite songs, all written by Lennon-McCartney or John Denver. She would read from her book. "Nican yotlan notlatol," she would say. "This is Nahuatl, Aztec language from Mesoamerica."

"Michael Jordan?" he would reply.

"Who?"

"Stupid girl."

He took her each night. Though tired and sore, the plateau floor as hard as a father's fist, she gave herself happily. Her body liked him. In her eyes—eyes that had never seen more than a few boys—he was a prince.

"Do you have parents?" she asked one morning.

He scowled.

"I miss my mother," she said. "The song of her voice and heat

*of her skin. The way she brushed my eyes with her lips. How I
believed we were one being, one entity, until the day she died.
My father," she added, soaking her sleeve with tears, "I no
longer remember."*

"Families mess you up," Songsten answered. "Beer is better."

"You have no family?"

"I have no past."

"I'm sure that's not true."

"Stupid girl."

To keep track of their journey, Anitya added a white bead
to her hair at dawn every day. She could count fourteen
beads, set in two rows, the afternoon they reached the town.
Immediately Songsten made for the tavern. He instructed her
to come back for him only once she had added a third row of
beads. "A week," he said. "No sooner, unless you want to see
my fist as well."

She felt lost in this noisy place. The roar of Subarus along the
main street startled her. The blare of music from a CD shop
boxed her ears. Above the town she found an unfinished primary
school. A sign promised that the school, a World Monetary Fund
project, would be open in the fall of 1989. The promise confused
Anitya, for she was under the impression that students and
shoppers alike had long gotten over 1989 and advanced into the
new decade, never once looking back. She unrolled her blanket
and read. "Kitsikakomimmo," she practised out loud. To herself
she added: Blackfoot term of endearment.

One day a fat man with a shaved head and ears jutting from
his skull overhead her speaking Quechua. He wore army
fatigues and laced black boots. Around his neck dangled headphones, a cord running to a Discman latched onto his belt.
Under his arms was a laptop computer.

"Lovely lady," the man said. "Tell me what language you are
speaking."

Anitya explained.

"Too bad. I do not think my computer is programmed for the
Inca tongue. It can, however, translate into twenty other*

210

*languages. Let me show you." He dropped to the floor like a
monk into prayer.*

"If you please," she replied.

While he booted up, the man offered his card. Meng Le-Yue.
Translator and Computer Expert. Specializing in Viruses and
Prophesy. Rates Tiered to Minority Group. Meals Served. *"I am
also a chef," he said. "In the noodle restaurant next to the video
shop. Come eat there this evening. I will make your soup extra
spicy!"*

*Meng Le-Yue laughed so lustily his breasts jiggled. Not want-
ing to appear rude, Anitya covered her smile with a hand. He
asked her to speak a sentence in Gyatsian. "Any sentence.
Whatever pleases you most."*

She offered lines of poetry:

> *"Set fire to the wilderness
> Dig holes with sticks
> Sow a handful of seeds
> And leave the rest to fate."*

*"Excellent," the bald man said. He keyed in the words. Then,
pushing Enter, he waited while the screen reconfigured. English
words appeared: "Primitive cut-and-burn agriculture and the
fatalism of downtrodden peasants marked the enduring legacy
of feudalism."*

"I do not think I understand."

"That happens a lot," he said. "Give me another."

*Remembering the lyrics to a tune Songsten loved, she
mouthed in phonetic English that it was the night after a hard
day, and that she should be asleep, like, for some reason, a
piece of wood.*

Meng Le-Yue wrinkled his nose. "This is not Gyatsian."

*"It is English," she said. "Have your machine change the
lyrics into Gyatsian, so I can sing the song more easily."*

*"No, no, no! A computer cannot go backwards. Only out of a
useless local tongue and into a universal language. To head the*

other direction would cause a virus and crash the system. Only a reactionary would wish for that."

Anitya blanched at the violence of his tone. He inquired at once about her health.

"I do not feel well," she said. "All smells, except for incense, make me queasy."

"You must see a doctor."

"I have no money."

"We live in the workers' paradise. Computers in schools and tractors on farms and doctors in every village, all to serve the people. Come with me, lovely lady. If the scoundrel dares ask for a fee," he said, helping her to her feet in a strange manner— one hand on her arm and another on her buttock, "I will pay for you, and you can find some means to thank me later."

A nurse said an appointment cost fifty yuan. Meng Le-Yue gave the woman the money and took his leave. The doctor turned out to be an ancient man who many believed the twenty-first or twenty-second reincarnation of the lama at Mola monastery. Anitya could not resist tracing the lines on his fore-head. They reminded her of the hand of the Lord of the Lotus.

"You are nineteen years old?" the Buddha asked.

"Am I?"

"You have no parents?"

She sobbed.

"Your mother did not mean to betray you by leaving," he said. "Men, though, have only flight, only betrayal, on their minds."

"And beer," she added quietly.

"And one more thing."

He read her pulse.

"Cheer up, girl," the doctor said. "No longer are you alone in this world. Inside your womb a child grows. So long as he is not a reincarnation of a divinity, he will be yours to raise and love and teach to be a better kind of man. He will be your student and protector. He will ease you into old age."

"And if he is a Buddha?"

"Let's not get ahead of ourselves."

Anitya thanked him.

"See my forehead?" the lama asked. "Study it. Those lines are a map across the Chenla glacier to the entrance to Shambala. This life is too harsh for a flower like you. Make the journey over Chenla. You have the goodness, but do you possess the courage? Also this," he said, opening his wallet. "Fifty yuan, the amount Meng Le-Yue paid. Return him the money, or he may cause you harm."

No one had talked to her so kindly—except the stars in the sky. She sobbed loud and long. "I am not worthy."

"Nonsense."

"I miss my mother."

"She was a gentle woman of no consequence."

Outside the office the nurse warned Anitya to steer clear of the restaurant where the fat man worked. "His noodles are over-cooked," she said. "His broth is all fire and no flavour."

She decided to wait until morning to tell Songsten the news. Luckily, she would be adding a seventh bead to her new strand at dawn, meaning their period of separation was ended. That night, Meng Le-Yue found her in the unfinished school and asked to be repaid. Anitya produced five ten-yuan notes. He forced himself on her anyway, his chin wattle flapping over her until she gave up and closed her eyes.

Anitya called in at the tavern as soon as it opened. The bartender knew of Songsten—he pointed to a trash bin of Heinekens—but said that her friend had met some truckers the day before and taken a job hauling long distance. "Did he leave a message for me?" she asked. The man shook his head. He had, however, heard enough of the negotiation to reassure her that her lover would be back in two weeks.

She waited. She read her book on New World languages and thought about her baby. She ate barley gruel and drank clear tea. Finding Meng Le-Yue sprawled over a table in his restaurant one afternoon, she did not think about the risk to her or her child and stole his computer. In a stream outside the town she drowned the laptop, its screen falling forever dark. For days after that she hid in a cave south of the town.

Having lost count of the beads—morning sickness left her dizzy—Anitya returned to the tavern twelve hours later than planned. She learned that Songsten had reappeared but already landed in trouble. The bartender related the tale. Songsten had been drinking with a shaved-skull local. When the fat man boasted of having had his way with a country girl decked in hair beads, Songsten ordered a bottle of Dewar's single malt. The scotch cracked that skull, shattering glass and bone.

At the town jail Anitya asked to see the prisoner called Songsten. The guard refused her request, forcing her to confess her state. "Poor child," the jailer said, "his father a hoodlum and his mother a scrawny girl." She dropped her gaze. "What does it matter if I allow you a visit?" he decided. "The entrepreneur your boyfriend assaulted is in a coma. If he dies, Songsten gets convicted of murder. The state is merciful, and will put a revolver to the back of his head before the next sunrise."

She was allowed five minutes outside his cell. "Songsten," she said, resisting the urge to touch him through the bars. "I have news."

He had welts on both cheeks—from weeping in shame—and swollen lips, from gnawing at them in guilt. "Did he violate you?" he asked.

She did not look at him.

"The fool with the breasts—did he?"

Her silence gave him his answer.

"I hope his hangover lasts for eternity."

"But we are—"

He commanded her to draw nearer. "Outside this dump of a town is a granite rock painted with mandalas. One is of the Buddha, serene and compassionate, the other of a demon with a buffalo head and a human body. Blood pours from the demon's mouth and its claws are spiked with flesh. On top of the rock are five pots brimming with flowers, regardless of the season. No one knows who plants the flowers or how they

214

survive up there. Be at the rock at midnight tonight. Buy supplies without attracting notice. Beef and barley and all the beer you can carry."

"You are going to—?"

"Shh!"

Should she take this moment to tell him about the pregnancy? His eyes warned her to wait.

Anitya stood beneath the pots at the appointed hour, shivering with cold and terrified by the demon. In life a demon represented a mind blackened by bitterness or grief. In death it marked a consciousness refusing to let go, to abandon its attachments to worldly things. Either way, demons were to be feared, even those painted onto rocks. The town lay below her now, a twinkle of lights, and across the plateau, beyond the Kodu mountains, stretched darkness wide enough and deep enough to merit the title of ocean. That way to the sacred valley; that way to enlightenment. Though she peered intently down the path, Songsten came to her via a different route. A winged shadow emerged from the black. The bird veered ninety degrees, like jets landing at Kai Tak airport in Hong Kong, and slowed to a rest on top of the rock. One final flap of wings, and it was still.

"Great one," she said.

She thought she heard the bird beat its wings again. But when she stepped closer, peering into the dark, she saw nothing.

"Come quickly," his voice replied.

Shock rooted her.

"Behind the rock. Hurry, before they send out a search party for us!"

"Songsten?" she asked, opening her arms to embrace him— and make sure his human form was not an apparition. "Is it really you?"

He pulled away. "You have ruined me, Anitya. A bold life was to be mine. After what I saw on the road, I was ready. Opportunities in the transport sector. Import-export schemes. Now I must flee the very people I want to do business with. Instead of widen-

*ing my contacts and establishing relationships, I am fated to act
the role of hooligan and counter-revolutionary."*

*"But we can live in Shambala!" she said, her excitement
bubbling over. "I know how to get there."*

"What?"

*"A doctor, a Buddha, he showed me the map that would
allow us to escape the trap of consciousness, to become more
pure and awakened. He assured me I possessed the goodness.
He begged me, us, to hurry. A paradise for you and me and...
and for our baby," she said quietly.*

He did not speak.

"I am with child, Songsten. We are—"

*"Stupid, stupid girl," he said. He raised a hand. Though she
knew what he intended, Anitya could not believe it. To make
the nightmare end, she closed them again and thought about
her mother...*

The manuscript ends here, with a date: June 1989. According
to a note, I reread the story four years later and scribbled
suggestions to myself: *Spring Songsten from jail using some
other trick; the bird-myth is a bore... Be more specific about the
business proposals, the changes to the transport sector... Is
Anitya too much of a sap? Do I really want to turn Ah-K into a
doctor who overcharges?* Again, in December 1995 I had a look
at the text. My conclusions then were blunt: *Trite and whiny.
Bad commerce, dumb fate, lousy sex. Small mercy for self-
censorship.*

Now I understood. In his dotage, Ah-K had shone light onto
two possible paths for my characters. I had chosen the wrong
one. The era compelled action, not reflection; assertion rather
than desertion; entry instead of escape. Somewhere in the Kodu
mountains wandered a pilgrim couple. Their search for earthly
paradise had floundered. For years—a decade, by most counts—
they had been adrift. To correct my mistake I had to bring
Anitya and Songsten back in. More important, I had to free their

souls from the bondage of history and faith and the silly stories told by peasants still stuck in one place and time.

The literary stakes were high. If my lovers could not be saved, neither could I. If a deeper liberty continued to elude them, I would have no choice but to withdraw into the same ruined monastery, the same burnt-out temple.

I flew to WanSee in a helicopter. There, a man with jiggling breasts and gashes over his skull rented me an all-terrain vehicle. The price—fifty U.S. per day—was steep, but I had no choice. Worse, to close the deal I had to pretend to enjoy a bowl of soggy noodles in a soup that scalded my tongue with spices but lacked any identifiable taste. "Delicious," I lied. The fat man calculated the rental fee on the latest IBM Thinkpad.

In the tavern I enjoyed a few farewell beers. Forgetting where I was, I performed an innocent party trick, smashing each can into my forehead. The bartender leaned across the counter for my jacket cuff. "Tell Songsten he still owes me for the single malt," he said.

"I'll settle his debt."

"Who are you?"

"His therapist."

"A hundred Yankee greenbacks should do the trick."

"For one bottle of Scotch?"

"Aged twelve long years," the bartender replied.

For days I drove across the plateau. Mountains reared up to the south and east, as though the subcontinent was only now crashing into the Asian land mass, buckling the earth the way bone buckled cheap aluminum. Ahead of me loomed Chenla, an ice field so massive some mistook it for a frozen sea, and expected to sight fishing boats stuck until spring thaw. On my third day out I stopped at a deserted village. An old couple lived there. They introduced themselves as the heads of Peoples Commune #8207.

"What commune?" I asked.

"In 1961," the man answered, lisping his words for want of teeth, "the Party asked us to establish a collective. The Chairman willed it. The masses demanded our courage and fortitude. Hundreds of teenage revolutionaries were sent from the mainland. Each arrival was provided a booklet explaining our twin tasks—to grow rice and to engage in steel production. We failed at both. Many of the faithful died. Many more still wandered off onto the glacier."

"In search of Shambala?"

"Television," the woman said. "One member returned years later with a truck. He brought a video machine and forty-nine movies. 'Come again,' that former comrade said to us. '*Still* no electricity? Get with the picture!'"

"Reactionary pig," he said.

"Capitalist running dog," she added.

"I am looking for a young couple," I said hastily, before the radicals found similar faults in my character. "He is proud and angry. She has beads in her—"

"Anitya, Goddess of Mercy," she interrupted, bowing three times to the glacier. "He is her security guard. Songsten, the avatar."

"You know them?"

"They dwelt among us mortals for a period," he said. "Blessed we were, too, by their presence."

"Did Anitya... I mean, was there a baby?"

"The Goddess is heavy with child," the woman said. "But she is waiting to achieve enlightenment before giving birth."

I thanked them. Wanting to leave a gift, I rummaged through the Subaru, finding an old issue of *Popular Mechanics* under the seat. "Maybe it will show how to fix a generator," I said.

"It died in 1972," the man admitted.

From the toe of one of its moraines, Chenla did not resemble a forehead. The ice was mud-grey. Where it had melted, murky puddles stagnated. I saw no prowling leopards and heard no chirping choughs. Spaced every kilometer, in a clear design, were fake bodhi trees—cold-resistant plastic, most likely. They reminded me of Tarkovsky's film *The Sacrifice* and Joni Mitchell's album *Hejira*.

The imagination of Gyatso, I understood then and there, truly was infinite. Despair—and reverence—seized me like menstrual cramps.

Even a 4 × 4 all-terrain vehicle floundered on such a terrain, fish-tailing and churning muck, and I wound up crawling to the lip of a ridge in second gear. I had no complaints about the car, but the radio was picking up strange signals: results from the high dive at the XXIV Olympics in Sydney, the audio track for a *Coronation Street* episode off the Star satellite, and radio exchanges between NATO forces in the third year of their siege of Belgrade. I honked my horn, *beep beep beep*. I stood on the hood and squinted into the sun. In my mind I made Anitya welcome, fixing her a rough bed in the back seat, while Songsten and I drank beer and smoked. Even writers needed companions; why else expend so much energy creating other chattering voices, other annoying selves? I would find the right moment to tell the young man what I thought. "Songsten," I would begin, "forget about this Shangri-La nonsense. Turn yourself in to the police—the fat guy didn't die—serve your time, and come out reformed. There's always room for one more visionary. There's always a child who needs a dad." I imagined him belching with emotion. "We will name the kid after you," he would reply. "If she's a boy."

Our reunion happened in the most awful manner possible. Sensing solid ground under the tires, I shifted into third and then fourth gear. The Subaru leapt forward like a collie released after a day indoors. I was moving at a clip when the earth suddenly fell away. All at once I was sliding down a slope. Directly below me lay a meagre camp: a smoking fire, two spread blankets. On each side of the fire sat figures as motionless as granite bas-reliefs. One of the figures rolled to safety. The other turned her head. My heart sank at the white beads decking her hair, now a night sky so clear the stars did not blink.

The front end nicked her and spun her twice. I continued down the incline with both my feet jammed into the brake pedal, flinging open the door before the vehicle even stopped.

Anitya lay on her back, her hands across her chest. Her pregnancy showed in a bulge the shape of a ruin at Angkor Wat. Songsten squatted next to her, a cigarette between his lips.

"She is dying," he said.

"Master," Anitya said to me. "I have been waiting so long. Instruct me on how to proceed."

My speech, rehearsed for years, got lodged like an animal bone in my throat. "What about...," I said. "What about the baby?"

"Hysterical pregnancy," Songsten interjected. "The stupid girl imagined—"

"Shut it," I said to him.

"The baby lives," she announced mysteriously.

"All my fault," I said. "All my responsibility."

Voices seized the air. They were loud and powerful and could only come from God. Anitya smiled and closed her eyes; Songsten, gripped by the irrational fear and instinctive servitude that marked another legacy of feudalism among peasants, fell to his knees. I recognized the voices—a morning talk show out of a studio in northern Kowloon, blasting from the car radio—but kept silent.

"Master!" she suddenly cried. Her grip on my jacket sleeves weakened. "Please don't leave again!"

"Stupid girl," he said.

This life drained from her. We wrapped her in her blanket and administered an abbreviated, incompletely recalled version of the last rites, as itemized in *The Gyatsian Book of the Dead*, best known text of Gyatsian Buddhism, a faith currently in vogue in certain neighbourhoods in certain coastal American cities. I insisted she be buried with her book of Indian languages, and forced him to listen while I read, clumsily but with feeling, the Cree chant of thanksgiving: "*Nanaskomonan.*"

Songsten pushed his lover into a crevice, its bottom too deep to discern. The body would never be found.

"Those voices," I said as we climbed into the car, "they were not of an angry creator. They were of men, challenging other men to be part of global society."

"Is there beer?"

I felt another pang. I had killed her. I had made him a Heineken drinker, despite my own patriotic preference for Tsingdao. How many other protagonists had I misled in my manuscripts? It was criminal, this writing business. I would kill myself as well if I thought it would make a difference. But a page later another writer would be in my publishing slot. His schemes would be no less incendiary. Her characters could hope for no better results.

"I'll remake you," I said. "Something simple but still cutting edge. Small business opportunity in Web marketing or currency trading. Can you use a laptop? Are you comfortable with a cell phone?"

He gazed at me, handsome but hopelessly dense. I knew I should hit a bump, make his door fling open, and cause him to fly out and smack his head on the ice. It would be a mercy killing, an act of tenderness.

"I like movies," he answered.

I shifted into fifth gear and put the pedal to the floor. My mother, poor woman, would have been dismayed at the direction I was taking. My father, of course, will be pleased. In the mirror I watched the sun rise in the east, as it must.

Translated by Tsa Lhung Gom

Part III

Dead Dog/
Sisters of Mary

Dead Dog

Chapter One

*G*et to Mani, she seemed to whisper. It isn't safe to talk here. Her voice, so subdued I thought of a stone dropped into a pond. Her scent, now blended with gasoline. Get to Mani, the voice repeated. Anyone can tell you where it is. Who is anyone? I asked. I blinked at the darkness where her face should have been, seeing nothing. But I sensed her distress, her grief. We should travel to this Mani together, I continued, gathering spit and swallowing it. Thomdup is hurt, isn't he? I can carry him. I can help.

I waited for her to answer. To emerge from the black, so I could look at her one more time.

Only she didn't. And I finally came to.

Dressed like a Kashang warrior.

Crossing the Samsara, the bridge empty and the guard house unmanned, out of Bon. Out of Bon and into the valley, water in the palm of the Buddha's hand.

Thinking: I am walking along a highway in Bon valley, dressed in a sheepskin vest and belt rope, red cape and rimmed hat. The computer slung from my shoulder. Pink Pig half-stuffed in a pocket. Meaning I must be okay, and must not have done what I'd not exactly been contemplating doing back there, back then.

Thinking: I have something to tell Lavanya and Thomdup. Kids, I would begin, once provided with a glass of water, Listen to me. You can't blame yourselves for what happened. You can get out of here, quickly. Beyond Mani and into the mountains. Along ridge trails and over passes. Across glaciers and through clouds.

To find that kingdom, that door.

Thinking: Forget directing them—how about yourself? I

know where I've come from—a plume of smoke twists over the city, a fire in Sikkim Lane, I'm willing to bet—but do I know where to go?

At which point I am sitting in the back of a clapped-out truck amidst bags of gravel and shovels. The vehicle idles by the road-side, its tailgate down. I am snug on a bag, braced to be bounced and bumped, when I hear the clip-clop of nails on the tarmac. With a lurch the truck starts to move. I stare down at the blur-ring road, watching for him, it. More clip-clops, pants and a grunt, and up it, him, jumps.

Appointed by the office of Gyatsian Buddhism, department of death. At no extra charge. My personal guide.

Not noble Marquez.

Beady eyes coated in pond scum. A foamy mouth and pink gums. Where the right ear should be, a festering wound, blood and pus congealed into paste. Three limbs, each hamhock-sized but tapering into dainty paws. Wounds spotting a filthy coat. Pellets still embedded in flesh.

Dead Dog, I say. Looks like I'm the new assignment.

Meaning I did... Meaning I am...

The news calls for nicotine. I find the pack, locate matches and strike. The flames are all snuffed; the cigarette gets blown away as well.

The old man smoked a pipe. The old man combed with Brylcreem and cologned with Old Spice. His razor weighed heavy in a boy's hand. His brush and bowl, container of black combs, tie rack and dozen dark suits, shoes lined up along the closet floor, laces parallel and horns at attention: such things awed his only son.

Death is real, I am informed in the bed of the truck. It comes unexpectedly. It cannot be escaped.

Fair enough. And who is the dour philosopher? The dog is curled up next to a gravel bag, one leg vertical, snout buried in genitals. I can't help taking a measure. A pink fin of flesh, closer to a labium than a penis. Poor pooch. Can't imagine that equipment drives the girl dogs wild.

He growls, fangs bared into a Halloween dracula. I lick my lips. The thirst is fierce, tongue dry, insides of mouth sticky. Like a hangover. Or an overdose.

Catherine kidded me about my retro fashion sense. "Nineties business ethic, fifties business wardrobe," my ex-wife would say. "Do the math and you're back a child of the seventies." But she also got the serious point, the one I could no more admit I was making than cease attempting to underline. "You're telling your dad that you love him," she said. "You're showing respect for who, and what, he is."

And so here we sit, tramp and mutt, man and best friend, in a truck headed east out of Bon valley. Only this best friend is firing dirty looks my direction. Death is real, I am told again. It comes unexpectedly. It cannot be escaped.

Two questions. First, who is talking here?

Grr.

You?

Flashes of incisors.

Did you have to go to a special school to learn that?

Dilating nostrils, a nice touch.

I skip the second question.

Thunderheads amass near where the valley climbs. The clouds are a phantom parallel range, as though a reflection in a pond, the kind found in photographs advertising splendour in the Rockies. A dissipating screen reveals a rain storm in a middle tier of the sky. The desire for water keeps me from enjoying the splendour. What I'd give to taste rain on my lips. On my lips and over my eyelids, soothing sun-fried pupils.

Colbalt blue, his colour. A rainy highland hue, my own. The one clear and unequivocal, an easy read. The other shadow and suggestion, a pleasing con.

At which point the truck slows to turn onto a path. Dead Dog leaps; dead guy follows. A house of masoned brick and wood-framed windows sits in from the road. Passing through an entrance of beads, I discern low tables and stools for a kindergarten class. Plus a shrine: glass jars to hold joss sticks, a faded photo of a teenage Vadra Pani. A woman the top of whose skull comes to my chest awaits us. She wipes her hands against her apron, first the palms and then the backs, and issues a greeting. I remove my hat and wish her tashi delag. Her swimming gaze seeks only the dog. Her eyes are aquatic because her optic disks are damaged and her eyeballs have hardened. Coating them now is a milky film.

Cataracts. Easily correctable with surgery.

Nonetheless, Dead Dog raises his ugly puss to her. She appears to return the glance, meaningfully.

Before the shrine the woman removes matches from her apron. Feeling for the incense sticks, she flares a match and, lifting the bundle before her, bows to the photograph. Smoke spirals around her, as though she is herself an idol. She begins to talk. Though I cannot understand a word, and cannot be sure she is aware of my presence, I decide that her soft, cadenced speech, the tones gently aligned, the music in steady time, is a plea on my behalf for mercy and forgiveness, for the lamb of God who takes away the sins of the world.

The dog barks.

I can't help it, I explain. It's how I was raised.

It had little to do with money. I said it then—spring 1989—but no one believed me. Why would they have? Just twenty-nine, I already owned a house in Leaside and employed a Filipina maid. I wore suits the match of his, in fabric and cut, but double the price, thanks to their labels. My dress shirts were tailored, my ties were of silk. Equally, however, I still splashed with his everyman cologne and still slicked with his cheap gel. I still drank Macallan with ice. As for shoes, I had my own tastes, but kept a pair of Cole Haan loafers for family dinners at the house or one of the clubs. Though I accepted his hand-me-downs in college—both of us size eleven, high arch—by graduation I had begun to refuse offers, officially from Charlie but always via Gina, regardless, whether the leather was Italian, the coat cashmere. I didn't need his wardrobe any longer, except as a model for my own.

Which finds us standing back at roadside, watching the next possible lift—a truck burping exhaust—crawl up the valley rim.

And why shouldn't I be confused and afraid? I ask.

Death is real, the dog repeats. It comes—

You're one to talk, I interrupt. Like taking advice on gas prices from a burning monk.

The truck reaches level ground. My stomach drops at the khaki paint and red star emblazoned on the hood. I bury the computer under the cape and pull the hat down low. Dead Dog squats by my side. The army vehicle roars past, spitting gravel upon our worthless persons.

Shamos everywhere, huh—even in the underworld.

The dog grrs.

Sorry, I correct. The valley of death.

He grrs more loudly.

Okay. The passage between incarnations. The Gyatsian Book of the Dead.

Another wait brings another filthy truck. I stick out a thumb, but the vehicle shows no interest in slowing. The dog saunters onto the tarmac and fixes the windshield in its sightlines. Brake lights blink. Gears are shifted.

Mani? I ask the driver as we climb in. Is this the road to Mani?

He finds the question unworthy of response. Dead Dog, an armrest between us, receives pats on the head and mumbles of "nice doggie," presumably. When the driver lights up, a fecal-peppermint blend, he doesn't offer the pack. Gagging, I try to unroll the window. It is stuck.

Wilson Newspapers could go on owning stagnant small-to-medium market dailies and one sink-hole national magazine. Charlie Wilson, president and CEO, could insist on a tidy ten-year program of power transference with an eye to dignified retirement at seventy. If necessary, the Vicar might give over one of his titles to his grumpy bat man, Bill Coren, to assuage Coren's own late-career ambitions. All the heir apparent had to do was further learn the trade, and further wait.

Wait, even when a genuine media mogul, keen to expand his empire, made an unsolicited offer in June 1989 for the entire Wilson stable—daily, weekly, and monthly? An offer so generous, and so nicely timed—Coren and I had just about persuaded Charlie to issue a limited public share to generate badly needed capital funds—it seemed providential?

In the side mirror, the pale green of the valley has deepened. Up ahead, beyond a saddleback pass into the mountains, the day is wearing thin. Dead Dog instructs the driver where to stop, and then leads me past terraced fields to a settlement of a dozen flat-roofed stone houses at the base of an overhang.

Is this Mani? I ask him.

He has no comment.

Lavanya? I shout. Thomdup?

He selects the dwelling. It has one room, a partial roof, no door. A wooden crate is laid out like a dining room for children, or for a dog: a plate of dumplings stacked into a pyramid, a can of Heineken. Draped over the beer is a ceremonial scarf faintly scented of pine cones. Dried blood stains the cotton.

Lavanya! I call again in the lane. Are you out there? A few steps in either direction confirms it: the village is deserted. Is Thomdup okay? I ask. (Illogically. If they are here with me, with us, they are definitely not okay.) Can I help?

The wind moans. A swirl of choughs caw-caw. I watch an anvil of black rock sink into darkness. I observe the cloud traces below one peak absorb the pale orange of the expiring sun.

A blast of snow drives me back inside.

Dead Dog's snout is buried in the stack of dumplings. Shredded yak meat and flour casing fly, a blender with the lid left off. My gut wrenches. The beer helps calm the churning. It also momentarily quenches the thirst.

With Gina home from the hospital after a full hysterectomy, and the doctor declaring a cautious all-clear, and the under-used maid, Esther Ramos, that Catherine and I sponsored from Manila in anticipation of a baby she lost in the first trimester, volunteering to transfer down to the big house and act as nurse, Wilson *père et fils* resumed their dances of denial and deceit. The old man dismissed the mogul offer. He had no interest in hearing the terms. He couldn't care less if the deal represented a once-in-a-lifetime opportunity. I sulked at the rebuke for twelve hours and then began going behind his back. Bill Coren jumped at the chance to betray his friend. His job involved keeping at the Vicar in the faint hope that Charlie might eventually see the light and sign the documents. My jobs were both to negotiate those documents, in secret, and to plot the redirection of the company, using the funds that would soon be ours, into an on-line information provider, *the* break-out cyber industry that year. Naturally, I would get asked where Charlie Wilson stood. "He is against the deal at present," I would answer, picking and choosing when to be honest. "But we're working on him. And he's been distracted lately," I always made sure to add. "His wife, my mother, recently went through a bout of—"

She was readmitted into hospital in July.

Blowing air into my fists, I click on the Powerbook. What is cyberspace if not a place without time or, for that matter, space? And what is this? I am prepared for the voices, for "Hi Daddy" and "We love you" and "Now go to work!" I am prepared to blink back tears. What I am unprepared for is a boot-up mechanism of chirps and musical bytes, corporate logos and colour templates, but nothing else.

And a file titled C:wpwwin61\wpdocs\ocean.wpd. Opening onto a screen the white—how could this be?—of the Buddha's doctrine.

I shut the computer down.

Dead Dog, meanwhile, is chewing Pink Pig. I did not offer the stuffed animal. In fact, I had hoped to use it as a pillow. The dog gnaws on a cloth leg while simultaneously growling at me and, more impressive still, communicating displeasure.

I have to submit?

Growl.

I have to let go?

Growl.

But suppose I don't want to? Suppose I cherish the memories, even the bad ones?

Death comes unexpectedly. It cannot—

Suppose I know that but still—

Dropping the pig, he attacks. I am lying on my back, arms crossed, and offer no defence. My yelp is canine—his fangs pass through khaki to skin—and I shake him off my thigh. He returns to his spot, thumps his tail.

You didn't have to do that, I complain, rubbing the wound. I understand what is happening.

His beady eyes hold mine.

A gesture? I ask. A gesture that I am letting go?

So I am thinking this: A father minding his kids at a public beach. They splash and swim, two among two dozen; he relaxes in the sand. Direct sunlight and a missing pair of shades reduce the surface to glare, all light burnished, all swimmers anonymous. Though he hoods his brow, careful to track his children

232

through the bob and weave, he soon cannot be sure the girl in the pink suit is his own, the brown-haired boy out past the rope his beloved. He means to get up, to wander knee-high into the brine, to at least call their names and hear them reply. But he is snug on the beach, and sleepy, and his brutalized eyes wisely keep closing. A yell is what finally opens them. The scream of a girl treading water next to a body that floats face-down.

Is that better? I ask, rolling over so he can't read my expression.

The dog sighs.

You don't mind if I add a prayer, do you? Something a kid might say? Now I lay me down to sleep, I pray the Lord my soul to keep.

Another sigh, tapering into a growl.

Just kidding, I lie.

Chapter Two

The doorbell rings. It must be him, keys forgotten at the office. Forty-eight hours late; not a serious infraction. And the phone message he left on Monday morning, the one that has kept me from sleep two nights running? That had me sitting upright in bed, his face before my eyes, a backdrop of what—open sea? He will confess to a momentary loss of perspective. For this he will blame the elevation and the air, his own nagging doubts as to why he bothered with the trip, perhaps even why we are in Asia. I will scold him for scaring me and the kids, and will tell him it is his own fault we did not celebrate his birthday as a family. I will hint that it has to stop; that, as a man of forty, he has crossed a threshold, passed through a gate.

I will say this, then wrap my arms around his neck and, standing on tiptoe, kiss him hard on the mouth, the embrace of a hungry lover, not an angry wife. Only then, all things forgiven, some things better understood, will I share the news. Dominic, I will say, guess what—

I open the door.

A stranger.

"You must be Esther."

"Yes?"

His runs a hand through wet hair. "He told me to drop by the minute I arrived in Honkers. Visit the humble abode on Old Peak Road," he says, holding up a yellow sticky with our address written on it.

The handwriting is his.

"You know my husband?"

"I should have introduced myself. Patrick Chan. I met Dominic in Bon. We kind of hung out together."

"He isn't back yet."

"I know. May I come in?"

"You know?"

"I can be of some help," he says.

Patrick Chan is tall for a Cantonese. He also isn't built like a coat hanger. Even his walk—hips pinned and shoulders swaying—doesn't belong here. Though nice, his clothes are casual: a white dress shirt spotted with raindrops and a slim tie, khaki trousers and sandals. Short black hair, huge dark eyes. Too much movement around the mouth and dazzle in the smile.

"The apartment is pretty much as he described it," he says. He crosses the dining room to the sunken living area. "Classy address, for sure. Had to act sharp for the security fella downstairs."

"You are American?"

"Do I look American?"

"My husband," I say. "You saw him?"

"Two mornings ago."

"In Bon?"

"Where else? But listen, are the children still up? Dominic told me so much about them, and you. He is one proud husband and father," he says with another wide, winning grin.

"The children are in their rooms."

He feigns glancing at the newspaper on the table. I watch him, wonder what he is waiting for. Oddly, I get the impression he is doing the same with me. All I can think is to ask if he would like something.

"We'd all like something, wouldn't we?"

"Coffee? A cold drink?"

He grins again—clearly his best weapon. "Will you sit down, Esther? I've news for you."

I make for the couch, my legs rubber. He follows me with a gaze in equal parts curious and appraising.

"We had plenty of adventures, Dominic and myself," he says. "Met some remarkable people. Did some outrageous things. The reason he isn't home yet—"

The phone rings.

"You have to get that?"

I retreat to the stand by the door. What, a stranger gives me permission to take a call in my own home?

The voice in the receiver returns strength to my limbs. "Charlie," I say. "What time is it in Toronto?"

"Almost seven in the morning," my father-in-law replies.

"Shouldn't you still be in bed?"

"Have *you* slept well these last nights?"

I shake my head.

"You aren't by any chance shaking your head into the receiver, are you, Esther?"

"Can I call you back? I have a guest right now."

"Will you answer me one question?"

I already know it.

"Well?" he says. "*Have* you called the high commission? The police?"

"He is—"

"Missing for forty-eight hours."

"My guest, please..."

"I'll speak with you in the morning—Hong Kong time."

"Don't be angry, Charlie. I will get no sleep tonight if I think you are mad at me."

He is happy to reassure. I wish him good night, meaning good morning, and he signs off with an old man's sigh, more resigned than sad.

"Sorry," I say. "The call was from Canada."

"The Vicar?"

Hard to choose a response: indignation or disbelief. He wants me off-balance, I can tell.

"I don't mean to upset you," he says. "I'm just excited to finally be here."

Now it is the children who interrupt. They storm the stairs with false hopes for the call, or the voice in the living room. On seeing who sits on the far couch both stop dead, make shy. Mike would normally not recover from the sight of a stranger in our midst, and would retreat to his room. Gaby, being smart and nosy and a girl, would linger at a window or behind a chair, size up the visitor's face and clothes and even the melody of his speech, and then decide whether to apply her charms. With Patrick Chan, their reaction is different. He could be a magnet for how the kids are drawn to him.

"Gabriella, right? And this fine boy would be Michael?"

She nearly curtseys. He bites his lip, like his mom.

"I'm a friend of your dad's," he says, "and I am very pleased to meet you both." He digs into a leather satchel. "Small gifts, if Esther doesn't object?" His glance in my direction is cursory; he knows I have no choice; he is aware of the spell he is casting. "Sailor Moon stickers for Gaby. A Pokémon for Mike."

The awe in their eyes! As though he is a bishop offering first communion. Even I am momentarily stunned by his selections. Which is foolish: of course Dominic shared with him the latest raves of his daughter and son. What else would men having "plenty of adventures" talk about?

"Say thank you, children."

"And look, kids," he adds, "it seems I've even remembered a little gift for your mother."

A package of Thai incense undoes me. My husband told this person his wife loved to perfume the sterile apartment air? Possible. He added that during very specific periods incense helped block out the odours that assailed her, and that this happened to be one of those periods? Impossible. I am overcome by tears. To stop them, and hide their message, I shoo the children back upstairs, though not before Gaby can offer a "Bye-bye, Patrick," her tone stolen from the Cantonese farewell, and Mike, who appears unable *not* to stare, can wave. At the balcony window I gaze out at the mountain slope, the glass streaked by slanting rain.

"Still drizzling?" he asks.

"For many days now."

"Tail end of a typhoon, is it?"

He should know that typhoon season is in summer. "Just bad

weather," I answer, running a finger over the surface. "Just Hong Kong."

"They're fabulous kids."

I thank him.

"He described them to a tee."

"Mr. Chan. Have you—?"

"Patrick, please."

"Patrick," I repeat, my hands bunching into fists, "if you have news about my husband, about Dominic..."

He apologizes and relaxes into the couch. "Near the end of our time in Bon, Dominic got mixed up with... No, he came into contact with some locals who were in trouble with the authorities."

"Trouble?"

"He was trying to lend a hand."

"What kind of trouble?"

"I'm not sure," he replies quickly. He tugs on his right ear and then scratches it. His face is flawless, as smooth as a child's, except for a chain of spots, more cigarette burns than acne traces, imprinting the lobe of that ear. His nose, too, is bruised in one nostril. "All I know for sure is that two mornings ago he went to meet a Gyatsian couple who needed to get out of Bon. He was probably going to offer them cash. He was very generous with his money."

I decide to sit again.

"Are you all right?"

"He went to Bon for business trip," I say. "You were with him. You must know this."

"I was there, sure. But tell me—did he explain the nature of this business to you before he left?"

"I did not ask."

He is silent.

"Hong Kong is only about business," I say, hearing criticism in his quiet. "All talk is about money and power and nothing else. People's life conditions, their hopes and dreams, even their spiritual selves are not polite conversation here. Look in the newspapers. In the news digest columns, where unimportant local deaths and small tragedies are reported."

I flinch at my own words. He must think me crazy. And why, why in the world is he grinning, as if I have told a joke?

"Dominic warned me," he says. He waits, then adds: "He said you don't like Hong Kong much."

"What is to like?"

"There you go," Patrick Chan agrees.

There you go? American speech? He is working too hard to flatten his vowels and drawl his consonants.

I hint that the visit is over. He says he appreciates my taking a moment. His route to the door is wayward, with stops to examine the many nice objects in our apartment. Some of the stuff Dominic and I bought together in the shops along Hollywood Road: rugs and a teak armoire, calligraphy scrolls and an antique birdcage. Other things come courtesy of his travels. A cupboard from Bali whose wood cannot abide air-conditioning. Wayang puppets that the children asked to have removed from their rooms, on account of nightmares. A ceremonial sword from Japan. Korean theatre masks that *I* would like covered up, so grim are their faces. Patrick Chan seems especially fascinated by the wooden elephant, its trunk of glittering glass, from Thailand. Secretly, I am pleased that he halts at the tapestry of Burmese celestial dancers—my favourite. "Quite the collection of booty," he says. "The British museum might be interested."

"Booty?"

"Anything from the Philippines? Anything especially dear to you?"

What a question. "I am not feeling well this evening," I say. "Maybe you could—"

"Would you welcome another visit?"

Put so politely, I can hardly be mean. "You want to—you would like to have dinner, Patrick?"

"I'd be delighted."

"Not tomorrow evening," I say, deciding on the spot to make him—or is it me?—wait. "How about two nights from now? Six o'clock?"

"Dominic told me you cook a mean kare-kare."

"You like Filipino food?"

"Not especially."

"I make us some shrimps and rice," I say. Then I laugh in a manner that, were she present, would please Gabriella. Girlish. Almost a flirt. Shock at my own behaviour has me gripping the back of a chair.

"Maybe he'll be back by then, and can join us," Patrick says.

His first tactical mistake. He winces, as though at a needle jabbed into his arm, in acknowledgment. The cover-up grin does not deflect my attention.

"Did you see him again after he went off to help those people?"

He admits not.

"Then you do not know where he is?"

"I've some notions."

I wait.

"Gyatso is a strange place," he says on the landing. "It can mess with your head."

He presses the elevator button.

In the kitchen, the children back asleep and the dishwasher a sloshy beat, I light an incense stick and open a bar of Toblerone. Break the bar in half, then again. The rest is stored in the refrigerator.

Can a country mess with your head? I thought only you could do that to yourself. Even assuming Gyatso can manage such a feat, Dominic isn't a likely candidate for getting lost. Others, sure. Other Westerners, I mean: spiritual tourists and lazy Christians, genuine hungry souls. His sister, Franny, might lose herself in Gyatso, for the fun of it, and emerge from the experience the better. Chastened. Less flip, the way smart, privileged people can be. His mother, now that I think about it, were she still alive, would definitely go missing in the Himalayas. (His father wouldn't risk the journey at all.) Dominic similarly lacks grounding; he, too, has trouble making good choices. Still, a landscape of colossal mountains and a population of eccentric Buddhists won't lead him into temptation.

What might? Alcohol? Drinking only makes him first funnier, and then sleepier, than he is sober. Drugs? He has not used them since we married. His fingertip? He stopped obsessing over the injury years ago, after I chided him on how ridiculous were his concerns.

A woman?

I treat myself to more chocolate and cast a final eye over the *Morning Post*. Four articles of note for November 3, 1999. Two in the news digest, two short stand-alones. A paragraph on an old lady in Wah Fu estate who fell out the window while hanging laundry. A sentence on a thirty-one-year-old in North Point. Abandoned by her husband, she jumped off a balcony nineteen floors above King's Road. Three hundred words, and a head shot, for the businessman who lost all his money in the crash of '97, made it back, only to then become embroiled in a land deal in Shanghai. He showed Hong Kong courtesy by waiting until three in the morning to suicide onto the sidewalk in Shatin.

Finally, the single report worthy of inclusion in the shrine. Titled "No respect for Amahs," it relates the findings of a survey conducted by the sociology department of the University of Hong Kong. Students were asked to rank professions in terms of prestige and honour. Domestic workers were rated dead last, below street hawkers and prostitutes. Yet half the students surveyed were raised by amahs! Of those, more than eighty percent recalled the women fondly.

One article that I passed over before is now of interest, thanks to Patrick Chan.

Uncomfirmed Raid
Officials are denying reports of a raid on the Kata temple in
the Gyatsian capital of Bon. Separate eyewitness accounts
suggest that a small plain-clothed security force entered the
temple on the morning of November 1, later closing the Kata
to the public for several hours. Long the epicentre of Gyatsian
resistance, the Kata has been raided repeatedly by security
and army, most notably in March 1992, when two dozen
monks were killed or injured.

Reports of an explosion in Bon, and a separate fire that
same day, are also presently unconfirmed.

By a third rereading *I* am the one who is messed up. What
might Dominic have seen or done in Bon on November first?
Patrick Chan said he was helping people; he said he was generous. In his message he admitted himself that something had
happened, that he had become involved. He talked about a
child. He referred to a woman.

Crazy!

All he will come back from Gyatso with is one more statue or
scroll, an even uglier mask, a bigger sword. He is a businessman
who had to travel to a meeting. He runs a communications firm.
He is a husband, father to two small kids.

The phone rings on cue. I have no wish to talk with anyone,
except him, but still must pick up—in case it *is* him.

"Mrs. Wilson?"

I groan.

His name is Allan Wu and he met Mr. Wilson at a function in
early October. He works as a fundraiser for a project called
Train of Hope. The group is outfitting and financing train cars
to serve as in-field surgeries for—

I tell him I recognize the charity.

"We are grateful for your generous support," he says.

"People should always help other people."

His tone shifts at my pronunciation of "people": *peepul*. "Am I speaking to Mrs. Dominic Wilson, of WilCor Communications?"

Wrong fight with the wrong girl. "No," I answer, "I am family maid, pretending to be rich white lady."

"Please hand the phone to—"

"Dominic is not here right now," I interrupt. "But I remember the cheque that we wrote to your organization. Do you also remember the cheque? The signatures at the bottom—D. Wilson and E. Ramos-Wilson? You think Ramos is good Canadian name? Try Filipina. Our former president, Fidel Ramos, he was not construction worker or musician in hotel. First lady, Ming Ramos, she never worked as amah or topless dancer in bar. Okay, Mr. Wu? Understand the situation?"

Allan Wu sputters an apology. I detect sincerity, never natural for a Hong Konger, and his claim that my husband asked to be kept informed—"Mr. Wilson is a most kind man," he says—assuages my raw, mostly misdirected anger. I suggest he try us again in a few days.

The receiver jumps in my hand. I assume the fundraiser doesn't know what is good for him, and bark a hello. This caller barks back.

"*Sandali lang, Esther!* What side of bed you get up on this morning?"

"Sorry, Gloria."

"Or is just empty bed for you again?"

"Dirty mind."

"Different complaint now, girl? Every odour make you wobble? Most foods, too, just to look at them?"

What, she can smell incense through the phone? "How you know?"

"You tell me that, with Gaby and Mike, you ordered Dominic to shower before bed at night. His cologne, the gel for his hair— these made your stomach do somersaults."

"But I have not said anything."

She laughs, easy and at home. The sound is too big for her closet room behind the kitchen in a mansion in Repulse Bay.

Last summer Dominic and I attended a cocktail party in that mansion, with its holiday brochure views of raked sand and shark-netted beach, the outer islands glimmering at sunset. Gloria served sushi to guests. "Silly Japanese," she said in my ear, "keep forgetting to cook their fish!" Dominic, his hand on the small of my back, informed the hosts I had eaten something that didn't agree with me. Ten minutes I sat giggling in their fancy washroom, upper lip sweating, tears rolling off my chin. "Amahs use servant's toilet, girl," Gloria chided through the door.

"Come on, Esther," she says now. "Day after you make hot love with your hubby—silver cross on the table, too bad, buster—you know something has happened. You visit the doctor on Monday, right? What he say to you?"

"He say mind your own business, Gloria Ferrer," I reply, suddenly regretting that I told her about Dominic's request. "Doctor say, you tell the news to some nosy maid before your own husband?"

With Gloria, I let my laugh boom and my smile beam and my English—*hingesh*, I would pronounce it—slide. Filipina style.

"*Sa totoo lang*, Esther. Still not a word?"

"Only two days. One time, he had to sit twenty-fours in an airport in Jakarta. And in Tokyo he got caught in storm."

"Those times, he did not call?"

"Gyatso is poor country. No phones, maybe."

"Maybe," she says, not agreeing at all. "Maybe, too, Dominic—sorry, *cha*—he is just another man. Eye that goes up and down at the sight of every pretty woman. Zipper that stays down at the first—"

"Gloria! You are my friend?"

"Friends tell each other what is in their heart."

"Even if the heart is bitter?"

"How do hearts get this way?"

Six years apart from her family. Her husband, a bus driver in Manila who visits brothels. Her eldest son, in college thanks to her. Two hundred dollars a month she sends back.

"There is business to discuss?" I ask, sighing again.

"A woman in Happy Valley, Mindanao girl named Bibop, she is telling friends of problems with her employer. Maybe nothing. Still, we contact her, try to stop something bad from happening. We discuss this after mass, at regular meeting, okay? Listen, I have made you sad?"

"I am sad, Gloria."

"Scared, sister? You say scared?"

I confirm her instinct.

"God, he sees us," she says. "He cares."

"The Virgin Mary," I dutifully answer, "she understands our suffering."

All of which, I think once I have hung up, is so true. And so important. And such useless information tonight.

I sit on the bed in the shrine. *No Respect for Amahs* has found a spot along the far wall, next to *Filipino Dies in Fall* and *More Deaths at Airport Site*. Once, when Dominic said he would find the room less creepy if the objects belonged to a flesh-and-blood maid, I insisted that they did. Who lives in the Wilson staff quarters in apartment 203, 21 Old Peak Road? I asked. Let's study the résumé the agency sent to the Leaside couple who requested information. Girl from Santa Cruz, Manila. Not Tondo or Smoky Mountain; not Forbes Park or Das Marinas, either. Raised by her grandmother. Completed half an education degree at Philippine Normal. Named Ramos, Esther Mary, aged twenty-one. Black-and-white photograph included. Less than a beauty, but what can you expect? Bambi eyes and horse-sized teeth. Moles sprayed like paint from a brush. Good Catholic, needless to say. From a nation poor in every respect, except faith. And look, it says here that Esther loves children. Imagine it: a Filipina who likes kids!

How the colour drained from his face. How anger, clouded by hurt, lowered his gaze. I apologized at once.

For the past several nights I have slept in the shrine. Without

Dominic, our bedroom is a hotel whose staggering rate compels me to fold towels and straighten sheets in the morning. Here, at least, I eventually nod off, and dream of selling sampaguita laces in Intramuros and kneeling next to Corazon in Quiapo church, gazing at the statue of the black Nazarene. Yesterday Gabriella caught me tidying the bed at dawn. "I couldn't sleep," I said. Her eyes nearly rotated in her head, so great was her determination to finally get a peek at the clippings. I shooed her out, blaming her absent father, who forbids the children access as long as I use the walls as bulletin board. Gaby accused me of slipping downstairs to have a bed all my own. "Daddy always lets us sleep with him," she said. "Daddy never had you in his belly, girl," I answered back.

The shrine isn't air-conditioned—the central system fails to cool air much past the laundry area—and I retreat into the kitchen. The phone is once more ringing and I jump, both hands over my heart. It is nearly midnight; no good comes from calls at this hour.

Unless, that is, the caller is *still* confused about time zones, even after two years of dialling across the Pacific.

"Is it so late?" Charlie asks.

I assure him I am awake.

"So am I."

I don't tell him it is noon in Toronto.

"I'm thinking about my grandkids," he says.

I suspected as much. He asks if I am on the cordless. I reply that I can switch over to it.

"Could you, Esther?"

"You are a lovely man, Charlie Wilson."

"I am a tattered old coat upon a stick."

"We go up the stairs now," I say. "Three steps to landing. First door is Mike's room. I open it and there he is..." My voice drops to a whisper. "On his side, holding his... Funny! I thought maybe he clutched a G.I. Joe. But it is a machine gun."

He asks.

"From Halloween. Boy who lives on tenth floor, Gunter

Schmidt, he loans Mike a helmet and gun and even uniform."

"Of which army?"

"Just a green jacket."

"I see," my father-in-law says.

"I explain this already. Five o'clock on the thirty-first, no Dominic and no costumes for the kids. I make calls, find something for—"

The boy mumbles in his sleep. I cover the receiver with my hand.

"Was that him?"

"I find things for Mike from the Schmidts. Gaby is not so easy, but she has poster of Spice Girls in her room, and says she wants to go as Baby Spice."

"Baby Spice?"

"Chubby blond girl with finger in her mouth," I say. "Children are thrilled by costumes. Both know their father, he would not allow them to dress as soldier or sexy singer. I said, Why not—it is Halloween."

"Can I have a listen?"

I lower the receiver to the boy's face. He mumbles again for his grandfather. Shifting, Mike jams the barrel of the weapon into his cheek. What he murmurs next is comprehensible only to me: "Stop it! Stop it! Stop it!" he says in a single exhale.

"Did he speak?"

"In his sleep."

Charlie is silent.

"Should I slip into Gaby's room?"

"If you could indulge me a few moments longer."

The formal language suggests he is uneasy with his own behaviour, his own need. Such mild behaviour, too, such gentle needs. "Fancy words for a filipina girl," I say to reassure him.

Gabriella is cast in light filtered through a thin curtain. Less from the moon than street lamps along the hillside and the throb of a nearby building site, the light leaves her face radiant. Her eyelids are blue-red, her lashes like curled caterpillars. Pink lips, a tongue trapped between teeth.

247

I report that she sleeps clutching Miss Juice but not Pink Pig, who is also presently in Gyatso. He delights at her dainty snore and claims he can detect her faint scent of lemons and shampoo. Then, as I climb back down to the main floor, my father-in-law indulges his deep, if muted, emotionalism and, not even bothering to ask whether he has told this tale before—he has, repeatedly—goes on about his daughter Francesca's legendary Soft Baby. How Soft Baby, a cloth doll with a pompom hat, lay on her chest every night, the toddler winding her way to dreamland by weaving the pompom between her fingers, a pattern as distinct and unchanging as ocean tides. How Gina kept restitching the poor creature, without complaint or comment on its ugliness, compared with other members of the girl's collection. And how Franny has kept the doll these past thirty years, and even renamed it Inner Child, a reminder of a lovely, lingering childhood, of which she is in no hurry to be rid.

"But she's Franny, isn't she," he says.

"For sure, Charlie."

"As singular as her mother was, I am beginning to appreciate. Dommie and me, we're the normal ones."

The statement could be challenged. Instead I yawn into the receiver, only half meaning it.

"You've had a long day," he says. "And a visitor."

I am momentarily at a loss.

"When I called before..."

"Of course. A man came by. A friend of Dominic's," I add. There and then, I realize I need to think about Patrick Chan.

Charlie is also curious. I hear him readying to broach the subject from another slant. I picture him as well, in an armchair in the living room of his condo at St. Clair and Yonge, probably sporting a cardigan and a tie; as severely handsome now as when I first met him, and decided on the spot that he was *not* the fearsome patriarch that I had been warned about by Catherine and even—so disingenuous!—Dominic. Rather, here was a person who masked shyness with severity, vulnerability with impervious blue eyes. Quality suits to prop up self-image. A gold wedding band to assure himself his luck had been that good.

"Speaking of visitors," I say before he can, "when will we see you here in Hong Kong? When will my children be able to hug their grandfather?"

"Soon," he replies.

"If you have money enough for these phone calls..."

"Money is certainly not the problem. God knows, your husband arranged that my retirement would be of almost unconscionable financial ease."

Our conversation ends on that note—a sour one for Charlie Wilson. Don't ask me how retiring with a fat bank account can leave you bitter; another matter between father and son.

I open the balcony door. One in the morning and the heat remains suffocating. At dusk, when the rain teemed, halos hung off street lamps. Now a warm drizzle smears all artificial light lurid hues of yellow and orange. At the railing I run fingertips through pools of water and check the pots of orchids and lilies. I extend my face over the edge and let the rain ease my brow.

Cooking oil and exhaust still dominate the air. Mixed in now, to the relief of my overwrought senses, is a natural bouquet from the patches of cedar and wax trees and the undergrowth, mostly cassia and rhododendron, that blanket the Peak. Hong Kongers have always believed it cooler, and less polluted, above the harbour. The sleepy roar of cicadas is a five-star measure of luxury. The sing-song of magpies who cruise in and out of the brume that is forever climbing, or sliding off, the massif, is music only a Platinum card can buy.

Dominic actually apologized for failing to find an apartment with a view of Central. Why else live in Mid-Levels if not to glory every evening in the pillars of concrete and glass? Two years later he continues to gape at downtown Hong Kong, as though an incline of office towers packed so densely they blind each other with their glare, and mutually cancel out views and sightlines, is somehow the match of a God-made wonder: a sky of mountains, a range of clouds.

Our balcony delighted me. The illusion of being tucked into a slope among a few other buildings and winding roads, a tram pulling itself up the hill in the same manner as it did a century ago, otherwise only arcing birds and slinking mist; the view, or lack of it, was the apartment's finest feature. Within a few weeks I had a parakeet in a cage and pots on the railing. The orchids attract butterflies; kingfishers love lily nectar. Flowers grow riotously out here, too, fed by the near constant shade and the rains. The butterflies tend to appear at dawn, the kingfishers at sunset.

The parakeet stirs.

"Stop it! Stop it! Stop it!" Lucien mocks.

For once he speaks wisely. Fifty-odd hours late; not a serious infraction. He won't show up now without gifts. For the kids. For the wife. If he decides on flowers, they'll be different from those he flourished as apology once before. "Bauhinia," he said, unwrapping a pot containing a drooping pink flower with ugly leaves. "The national flower of Hong Kong."

"A hybrid, Dominic," I answered. "Sterile. Produces no seed."

I am hard on him sometimes.

Chapter Three

A guy walks into a bar with a dog. Who'll bet me twenty bucks I can't get this animal to talk? he says. A talking dog? a customer replies. No way. He slaps a bill on the counter. I'll take that action, too, the bartender adds. The guy antes up his own money and turns to his accomplice. Okay, he says. Name a book in the Old Testament. The dog tilts its head and paws the floor. Ruff! it answers. See, he tells the other men, he named the Book of Ruth. You owe me. The bartender clamps a fist over the twenties. Hold on a second. The mutt didn't talk—it barked. Ask it something else. Fine, the guy replies. Dog, what is...

Dead Dog? Are you listening?

A sigh, fluted through nostrils.

You've heard this one before?

A blink.

Anyway, I continue. Dog—what's that over my head? the guy asks, pointing to the ceiling. The dog follows with its eyes and thumps its tail. Ruff! it answers. There you go, he says, reaching for the money. He said roof. You trying to make jackasses out of us? the bartender asks. You and your manky, flea-bitten—

He grrs.

Just for colour, I explain. You and your manky, flea-bitten friend get one more chance, the customer warns. Try that again and— Okay, okay, he says. Dog, who was the greatest baseball player of all time? Think about your answer. Don't shout the first name that pops into your head. The dog stares at the ground. Its eyes roll up into their sockets; its sides heave. At last it swishes its tail. Ruff! it answers. See, the guy says, grabbing at the cash—Babe Ruth!

He winds up on the sidewalk. He's lying there, bruised and

broke, when the dog begins to lick his face. Who, the animal asks—Joe DiMaggio?

Maybe a puff of air. Maybe.

Tough room, I say sourly.

Take refuge in the Buddha. Take refuge in the Dharma. Take refuge in the Sangha.

Ruff, ruff, DiMaggio!

Take refuge in the—

Today's lesson in Gyatsian Buddhism, I interrupt. Something to chew on, to chant, while we make our way—wherever our way may be. I'm with you, Dead Dog. We're on the same frequency. Just not before breakfast, okay?

At which point I am noticing the fresh plate of dumplings on the crate and unopened can of beer. With the scarf gone. With the computer screen lit by a YOU'VE GOT MAIL notice. I run my hand along the back of the Powerbook, just in case. No phone line. No Internet. By touching Enter, the screen lands back on C:wpwin61/wpdocs/ocean.wpd—hardly an e-mail account. Text materializes before my eyes.

MANI ON FIRE. GET TO PADME!

But first a Heineken. My mouth is so dry my lips are pasted. I part them with suds, clear a path for a slow chug of half the can. Only for a second do I contemplate smashing the aluminum against my forehead. Fear of a cut, along with a sinking feeling that I am not—or was not—man enough, stops me. Dead Dog, in the meantime, slops his meal. The blender lid is off again and I am showered in dumpling shreds.

He never said it, not once. Who the hell do you think you are? To be playing with matches. To be putting the Wilson house at risk. He should have raged, aflame with indignation, fiery with wrath. It might even have worked, seeing him unsettled by passion and fear and—of his own quiet variety—ambition.

Scraping noises draw us to the doorway. A boy in a brown cloak halts in the frame. He is a busted Buddha, legs pretzelled into lotus but otherwise useless, arms doing the pulling.

Beneath a wool cap, a shaved head. On a face the hue of butter, an expression of serenity. Eyes of shore pebbles. A runny nose and mouth sores. And between the mouth and nose, a harelip.

Thump thump thump goes Dead Dog's tail.

Tashi delag, the boy seems to say.

I would like to intervene with a prayer. Take refuge from the occupation. Take refuge from any who say they can help your country. Take refuge from any who say they can fix your mouth, repair your legs.

Mother had the right, too, the right to ask, only she didn't have the reason. She knew exactly who I was and what the hell I was doing. And Francesca, who contained aspects of our parents in more equal measure than I did, despite her caramel skin and earthen eyes, and who accorded her brother the same bemused, faintly dismayed love she did her mother; Franny couldn't be bothered to level accusations as obvious, and lame, as those I kept waiting to hear. Instead, she would kiss me on both cheeks and taunt with a rhyme, its music from our childhoods: "Nicky-Nicky-Nine-Doors, has so much but still wants more!"

Dead Dog trots along a ridge that ends at the overhang. Painted on the rock are mandalas. The first is the familiar thin Buddha with the meaningfully crooked fingers. In his expression is placid self-abnegation. Off his shoulder is a saffron robe. The other mandala offers what I take, at first, to be an alternative version of the Enlightened One. But then daylight draws shadow from the granite. Who is this? Horns from the forehead and a trunk for a mouth. Sagging udders. Multiple arms and legs.

Over the second image float three smaller lamas. One points west, another east. Only the centre Buddha, outfitted in a conical hat with ear flaps, gestures downward in acknowledgment of the demon caged in half-circles of colour.

I'll take a crack at this, I say. Door #1 is retreat, the guy pointing back where we came from. Not an option, is it? Door #2, I bet, involves doing a dance with that beast there. No, thanks. Which leaves only door #3—farther east, into the mountains. Shambala and Dorondo. The one outstanding mystery.

The scent of incense turns me around. Juniper—still wet, judging from the smoke—burns in a stupa; a ceremonial scarf, now cleansed of blood, dangles from a line of prayer flags. I collect the scarf, then lead the dog to where the path descends to the floor of a valley emerging from the haze. So scrubbed and barren is the terrain that I look north, expecting to see the backside of a receding glacier.

They went thaddaway? I say playfully. Lavanya and Thomdup, they're headed up that valley, looking for Padme? And Padme is the pass into—?

A grr.

I'm not afraid, I add. I'm not confused.

A louder grr.

Okay, maybe I am afraid and confused. But I'm also serene and at peace. Will that do for now?

Dead Dog takes off down the slope.

"I'm so afraid, Nicky," she told me—and me alone, I was given to understand. "I have been invaded and am occupied. I am not who I was and who I cherished being. Is fleeing, getting out, so wrong?" I sat on the bed, her hand in mine. Always long and thin, more of a Florentine aristocrat than an Assisi peasant, Mother's hands now were brittle birds bound in translucent tissue. Her eyes, distended as though her body functioned in perpetual extremis—true, in a sense—told most of what she had lost, or perhaps abandoned, without much of a fight. Gone was their mischief and hunger for stimulation, for the giving, but mostly the getting, of pleasure. Gone was their desire.

No surprise, to me at least, that she had ordered a nurse to hang a towel over the washroom mirror. Nor that she had begun to discourage visitors, including her own husband, her private yardstick of integrity and self-discipline, a standard she had less hope of living up to now than before. No surprise, especially, that she would choose son over daughter as confessor. I would intuit in her words what she could not say aloud, even in extremis, the final hours, and would pronounce her heart given out without her having to tear open her chest and extract it, as she would with the old man, and say, Fool, look—it has already stopped!

And so I am walking along a valley floor. Beneath a crystalline sky. Below wheels of choughs. I am not looking back. I am not having second—or first, for that matter—thoughts. Ignoring the spindrift rasping my cheeks and the thirst choking my neck. What more can be asked of one poor pilgrim? Further letting go? Deeper forgetting?

But enough about me, Dead Dog. Let's talk about—

He bites.

How does it feel to get run over by a car? Shot up by a pellet gun? How does it feel to be missing a—?

Ouch!

"Is it cowardly?" she asked. "You know, not gritting my teeth and fighting it out. Battling like a brave soldier for a few more months. I'm sure it's a sin, Nicky, and a big one. I'm sure I'll rot in hell for eternity." I needed only a second to come up with the right answer. "You always loved the heat, Mom," I replied. "Aren't you terrible!" she said, thanking me with her gaze.

Mother, I would begin, let me introduce you to the children. Just two, like you and Dad. Here is Gabriella, who is six, and all your fire and light. And here is Michael, nearly five, who has the old man's ice and shade. Kids, this is your grandmother. Not Corazon in Manila (their great-grand, in fact)—your other grandma. Her name is Gina and she... What, why is her head shaven? And the sores on her skin? And her eyes, as cloudy as—

Stop it! Stop it! Stop it!

As Lucien the parakeet would say.

And Dead the Dog, I gather, would agree. Because he is chasing me, this prophet and sage, along a bumpy path buttressed by fortress walls. And I am running, one hand holding down the computer case, the other both hat and scarf, my skull being drilled by some sutra—Take refuge in the Buddha, the chart-topper this hour—and to my astonishment I am still managing to remember—

My father, entering the No Smoking lounge and seating himself in the chair across from mine. A grey linen suit and dark tie, shoes shined to high sheen. Still the presence of mind to shower and shave that morning. Still the control of his person, if not his life. The way he bowed his head slightly in greeting, unbuttoned his jacket and creased his pants; the manner in which he crossed his spider legs, levelled his shoulders and chin, and only then met my wobbly gaze; he was magnificent, Charlie Wilson, model parent and doting husband, church elder and stellar corporate citizen, and I, his son, Nicky-Nicky-Nine-Doors, was exactly what no one, aside from cryptic Franny and my own squeaky inner voice, would dare call me—a little shit.

"A word, son," he said, his tone no more Vicarish than usual. "Is it about the offer?" I asked. A blink sufficed as nod. "It's a sweet deal, Dad," I said. "You can't deny that. With the funds, we can redirect the company on our own terms. No public shares. No loans. Fiscal independence, even caution—just like you taught," I added with a mental cringe. I lit a cigarette and wished for a before-noon Scotch, to chase the buzz from my ears. He closed his hands into a steeple, the tower over his eyes. I admired the elegant fingers and impeccable nails, the gold wedding band.

Take refuge in the Dharma.

He is gaining on me, and I am forced once more to admit that a dog short a leg is still faster than a man with two lanky ones. That, or else I am running out of gas, sails dropping, white flag ready to be hoisted. The valley floor has narrowed to a pass no wider than a lane. A granite boulder slims the passage even further, and I barely make it through. On the far side I stagger before an abrupt increase in light. Odd, for it must be late afternoon, wane of day, not—

Now he stood as well. "Your mother is not ill, son," he corrected. "Do you understand that much?" His stare critiqued first the cigarette in my right hand and then—he must have been furious!—the hand buried in my pocket. "Sure I understand," I replied. "Do you understand," he said, "that what is happening here, to her, to us, is not an illness we will recover from. Not today. Not, perhaps, even tomorrow?"

Correctly interpreting my silence, he set off down the hall to her room without a word more.

Take refuge in the Sangha.

And in the dazzling white light.

For I am kneeling at the spot where the path terminates at a river now bisecting the pass, rendering it not a pass at all but a dead end. Only that isn't accurate, either. The river pours from a gap in the canyon wall, a gorge emitting light that is both smoky and diaphanous, clearly a reflection of some staggering source.

A glacier, I am suddenly convinced. Up through that gorge. Up onto the lines of the Buddha's forehead.

Padme, I say.

Winded by the chase, Dead Dog licks his chops. We slurp at stream's edge. My skin flushes and my throat, under the impression I am swallowing fire, closes. A cairn, hastily constructed and far from secure, hosts a shrine. I crawl over to it, drawn by the memorabilia. A crushed Heineken can and empty jar of Nescafé. A bar of chocolate and crumpled photograph. The snapshot shows a young couple, very much in love. Her gaze is clear and confident. He has no crow's-feet yet, no smoker's teeth.

I remove the scarf and lay it over the stones. To my dismay, the shrine collapses under the additional weight of cotton. My attempts to reassemble it only cause further ruination. Nor do I have matches to light joss and pay my respects.

It doesn't matter, I assure Dead Dog. I am serene. I am at peace.

At the funeral he quoted Oscar Wilde. The old man, quoting Wilde! "The mystery of love," Charlie Wilson told the assembled Gina-worshippers, "is greater than the mystery of death."

I am serene, I insist. That was a mistake, a slip.

He doesn't believe me. He is deciding whether I deserve a bite in the thigh, a nip to the groin.

For which very good reason I am conjuring this: A backyard pool in autumn. Leaves a skin over the surface, tendrils of algae beneath. Lawn chairs stacked. A table umbrella on its side. A girl wanders out the patio doors. She kicks leaves and runs a squirrel up a tree, behind which a father hides. Drawn to the water, she kneels before her blurred reflection. Sunlight catches her on the back, embracing and then holding her tight, denying resolved features and distinct eye colour. The girl pauses to wonder whether winter ice would also act as such a poor mirror.

Titanic! she shouts and jumps in. At once he is there, on hands and knees, brushing skin aside and peering into the thicket of leaves. Quickly the surface settles back, the skein resewn.

The dog sighs.

Names, I declare, the words entering my consciousness as I speak them, even of those most dear, most blessed, must be lost. Memories, regardless of how lovely and sustaining, need to be banished. Hopes and fears become irrelevant. The dance becomes the dancer, the dancer becomes the dance. The luminous continuity of existence! In the light, awareness. In the awareness, liberation...

Not bad, eh? I add. For a Catholic.

He sighs again.

Chapter Four

"Is Patrick here yet?" Gaby asks.

"Twenty minutes."

"And he's coming with us to see our grandpa?" Mike says.

"Not grandpa," I answer. "Your *great*-grandpa. And yes, he will come with us to the cemetery."

"He said he'd carry me on his shoulders."

"He said he'd carry *me* on his shoulders."

What, he is their uncle now? After one dinner?

"Go play in your rooms," I order. When they object, I give in. "Put on video, okay."

"Any video?"

"Not Spice Girls. Sorry I even bought that for you."

"It's a great movie, Mom," Gaby says with a smarty-pants grin. "Though Daddy won't like it one bit." She is loving the new house rules. Being his daughter, she is also pressuring me to expand those rules or, better still, abandon them entirely. More movies and television, unrestricted access to MTV Asia and Channel V; longer dance parties in pop star costumes. War games for Mike. Junk food and flexible sleep times and wee hour visits to an uncomplaining parent embarrassed back into her five-star bedroom cell.

"Is Patrick with our dad?"

"He was before, Mike."

"Now he's with us," his sister explains.

I shoo them from the kitchen.

Charlie Wilson is to blame for yesterday. First thing in the morning—evening for him in Toronto—he threatened his only daughter-in-law. If I honestly believed the best response to another twenty-four hours without news was feeble waiting and supplicant prayer, then he would have to disagree and act upon his disagreement. He knew people, he warned; he knew people who knew people. I didn't doubt him. I also didn't think the intervention of a man ten thousand miles away could be so swift. Within sixty minutes I was fielding phone calls from the Hong Kong police and the Canadian High Commission. A Detective Ko proved easy to throw off. He asked if I wished to file a missing persons report. I replied that my husband wasn't missing. His business in Gyatso had taken more time than expected. He couldn't just up and leave; to do so would be irresponsible, something Dominic Wilson could not abide in himself. How did I know all this? Detective Ko wished to know. He told me, I answered calmly. In a phone message left two—okay, three—days ago. (I declined to mention my other source of information.) On learning that Dominic had contacted us, the cop lost interest. He pretended to want to hear from me in forty-eight hours, should there be no developments. I pretended to write down his number.

The high commission, in contrast, would not be dissuaded. A woman called Lysianne Davaar-Lacombe—she gave her name as though it were a title—insisted on paying a visit. That very morning, if it would be convenient. I asked why the attention. Because I pronounced the word *attensheun*, Ms. Davaar-Lacombe decided to confirm that I was indeed the *wife* of the Canadian businessman Dominic Wilson. I held my tongue. "Your father-in-law has influence in important circles, Mrs. Wilson" is all she would say on the phone.

Feeling mischievous, I changed from slacks and a blouse into the cheap track suit I keep for when Sisters of Mary visit amahland on Sundays and must show the women we are truly their siblings, and not fancy ladies bestowing alms upon the poor. I dug flip-flops from the beach bag and tied my hair back with a scarf. Lysianne from the high commission kept a neutral face on greeting me, and escorted herself to a living-room couch. She declined coffee. She requested a glass of bottled water, no ice. In her black suit and shoes and severe glasses, she looked very serious, very career. No blood in her cheeks or flesh on her bones. Perfume so discreet it didn't flutter my tummy. A smile so flitting I mistook it for a twitch.

I fetched the water, making sure to flip my flops and walk like a duck. (Dominic says Filipina women walk this way.) She admired our apartment. Especially the high ceilings and sunken living room. Especially the staircase leading to three—three!— bedrooms, including an ensuite master. Even our view of the mountain, although a pity given how the building overlooked Central, impressed her. She and her husband, she volunteered, were paying 30K a month to stare at another balcony in another building off the escalator. Forty-two hundred U.S., she kindly translated, for two small bedrooms and low ceilings and zero view. Not even a decent residents' pool, she complained, craning her neck to examine the facility below. The last time her father, who, as it happened, was a retired member of parliament for a riding in Montreal, visited them, he declared Hong Kong even more exorbitant than Tokyo, where her brother worked as a banker. Her husband, she added in passing, sat on the Canadian Chamber of Commerce here, and they were concerned the city had become prohibitive for business interests. Except, obviously, for *my* husband's interests. An apartment on Old Peak Road. Offices in the Landmark. Lysianne Davaar-Lacombe's partner, matter of fact, knew Dominic socially. From chamber luncheons and the bar at the F.C.C.

"This morning," I said, "you talked first to my father-in-law and then to your own husband?"

I served her a glass of bottled water, no ice. In Mike's plastic cup. Pink, stencilled with the Hello Kitty logo.

"I did not speak with Mr. Wilson myself," she replied. "His conversation was with the high commissioner—the son of an old friend, apparently. The commissioner, in turn, asked me to call you."

Give the woman credit: she had trained well in diplomacy.

Except for her hazel eyes, which drained of the thimble of warmth they had held, she swallowed the cup insult. She even used a copy of *Asiaweek* as a coaster. No water rings on our rosewood table, also from Bali.

"And you asked your husband about Dominic?"

"I ran the name past him. He said that Dominic Wilson is a mystery figure in Hong Kong. WilCor's ventures are unconventional for a newly established Canadian company without—how to put it?—traditional connections to regional markets. Most businesses gravitate towards the exchanges and currency speculation. Plus the new technologies," she added. "If, that is, a non-traditional Canadian company is in Hong Kong *at all* in November 1999, if you catch my drift."

Her drift, no; her judgement, yes. "Dominic," I said, "he went to Gyatso on business."

She, too, scoffed at the notion. "Business" and "Gyatso" went together, her expression suggested, like "Hong Kong" with "personality."

I bit my lip.

"Esther," she said. "May I call you that?"

"You just did, Lysianne."

"Esther," she repeated, fixing me an immigration officer's stare, "I have a question about your husband. I'm sorry if it sounds hurtful. I don't mean it to be."

"I'm sure."

"It has been our experience, the experience of officials at Foreign Affairs, that when a husband goes missing in a country, the reasons can be, let's just say, complicated."

"Complicated?"

"Especially here. Western men are easily intoxicated by Asian women. Something about their exoticism. Clichés, I realize, but still, given how thin they all are, and the way they dress..."

Amazing: she had been looking right at me! (*Through* me, of course, at the lovely objects—the booty, Patrick Chan called it—surrounding my vague outline.) Finally, the light went on. Her features registered embarrassment, along with anger. For a second I couldn't figure the anger out. Then I got it. Lysianne Davaar-Lacombe was annoyed that I had caused her to make a fool of herself.

"I mean, Western men *think* the women here are—"

"Thai prostitutes, maybe?" I said. "Burmese teenagers working in brothels in Japan? Barrio girls in Manila whorehouses?"

"I did not—"

'Your husband, Lysianne—he has an eye for girls like me?"

She made for the door. The high commission would do some checking, she promised. In the meantime, she recommended I place personal ads in any regional publications that Dominic read. "Use simple, affecting language," she said. "Include some sort of word that would tip him off that it is you who is trying to make contact."

"Who else would it be?"

"One never knows."

My need to hope triumphed for a moment over my compulsion to snap at her. "I will write *tsinelas babae*," I told Lysianne Davaar-Lacombe. I even raised my foot. "Your flip-flop baby, in English."

Her smile rose and fell. "You are, I take it, from one of the islands in the Philippines."

"I live in Toronto," I said too hastily.

"We went for a holiday at a resort on Cebu last spring. Very nice, although the heat was unbearable."

"Very hot in the Philippines."

Be nice, Esther, he would whisper in my ear right about now.

Lysianne went to speak, thought better of it, then proceeded. "Tell me," she said. "Did you meet Dominic in Hong Kong? Many of the women one encounters in people's apartments, or sees in the parks on Sundays, are so lovely. We employ a girl from—"

My face gave her such a fright she almost raised a forearm in self-defence. Instead of slapping her, I marched to the bookshelf. "Our children," I said. "Here is school picture of Michael, who is four, which means he was born two years before we came to this place. Sunnybrook Hospital, Bayview Avenue and Lawrence. Maybe you know the facility? In any case, his eyes and nose, the dimples on his cheeks, mark him for certain as Tagalog kid. From one of the slums—Tondo or Sampaloc. Poor Mike, he winds up working in hotel, eh, or maybe gets job on cruise ship."

I returned the photograph to the shelf. But then, unable to control myself, I picked up the other portrait. "Now here," I said, running my fingers down the glass, "here is Gabriella. The girl is six, and went to junior kindergarten at a school maybe you know—St. Martins, in Leaside? But your people are from Montreal? Anyway, she is more lucky, Gaby, with that skin and those features. Ermita stock, pure Spanish. Daddy in the government, business deals on the side. Mummy a society shopper. Maryknoll College for girls and debutante balls at Manila Hilton. English spoken at home." Unlike with Mike, whose eyes and grin were too locked into childhood, I found I could mentally add a decade to my daughter's face, the pitch of her gaze and personality of her smile, and envision her a young woman. "Good marriage material," I added, the sentiments vicious even to me. "Better still, an important man's mistress."

Lysianne Davaar-Lacombe was showing herself out.

"You have children, Lysianne?"

"Not yet," she replied weakly.

"I have two wonderful children," I said. "Also a fine husband. He is away on business. Have a nice day."

Malate and Ermita, Intramuros and San Isidro, Santa Cruz and Binondo. Manila Cathedral and Rizal Park; Palacio del Gobernador and Plaza Roma; Fort Santiago and Basion de San Gabriel. These names alone should make me nostalgic? Long for two rooms in an alley, the bed my sister and I shared, the cot our grandmother slept on? How about Leaside and Don Mills, Hog's Hollow and North York, Danforth and the Beach. St. Michael's Cathedral and High Park; the squirrels in Queen's

Park and skating in Nathan Phillips Square; a baseball game in the SkyDome and a picnic on Centre Island. CN Tower, a needle to stitch the clouds!

Dogs trail us into the cemetery parking lot. Patrick flies out of the cab, swinging his jacket and shouting in a language that is neither English nor Cantonese. The dogs backpedal, snarling and yapping, until he pitches a rock. His toss is wild but the animals still flee, staking their ground by the road.

"Neato," Mike says. He tugs on my pant leg.

"That is how we mind the mutts of Bon," Patrick offers in a voice abruptly deepened, an accent less neutral. His face, too, struggles to stay mild. More strident qualities assert themselves.

"Thank you," I say.

He checks the grounds. The kids forget me and follow him. Issuing an all-clear, he repeats the information to Gabriella—aisle GG, plot 6—and she and her brother race ahead. Though the Chai Wan War Cemetery is perched above the eastern tip of the island, overlooking the curve of harbour and the old airport, today the site is swallowed in ground mist. Fog rolls down the slope, obscuring the memorial at the gate and dissolving the forty rows of white stones not immediately before us. When it briefly lifts, the shape of the cemetery is revealed: a ship, wide in the midsection and narrow at the bow, pitched forever forward into a swell. When the mist lifts higher, the harbour below looks as if it is on fire.

The fog swallows my children as well.

"Creepy," I say.

"Astonishing for it to be so foggy and yet so humid, so blazing hot," he says. "I'm still accustomed to damp mist and cold rain."

"In Hong Kong? The end of January, maybe. Not now."

Gaby and Mike kneel in golf-course grass before a stone, hands folded and heads bowed.

"Major Gordon Charles Wilson, 1906–1943, Royal Rifles," Patrick reads.

"Amen," Mike says.

"This isn't a church," his sister corrects.

"Is Daddy here?"

"Not your daddy," I answer. "Not your daddy's daddy, even. *Three* fathers ago, Michael. If you still cannot get this straight..."

His brow furrows at the rebuke.

"Your father, your dad, he told me all about his grandfather," Patrick says. He stands behind them now, a hand on each shoulder. Would only a shrew find the gesture presumptuous? "Major Wilson fought bravely for his country, you know. He couldn't stop the war, though, and so had to surrender, and live in a prisoner of war camp."

"They know already. Their grandfather lectured them this morning."

"He did? He's here?"

"On the phone. For twenty minutes Charlie tells the story of Major Wilson. Gaby on the cordless, Mike the receiver by our bed. Story that I already know in my sleep and that Dominic told us before, at this spot, like you just did." A point of detail in Charlie Wilson's version stands out. "Dominic's father," I say, "he even knew where the camp was located in Hong Kong. North Kowloon, off Cheung Sha Wan Road. Funny, don't you think?"

"He must have studied a map."

"Maybe."

"Can we still pray for Major Wilson, Mom?" Gabriella asks.

I shrug.

"Pray for the major, kids," Patrick says. "Your mother and I are going to take a walk around the grounds."

We are? He reaches for my arm. I pull away, shrewishly.

Leaving the children to be enveloped in cloud is like a scene from a dream. Their voices at least are calming. So is the silence, as though death can command the rudest city on the planet to hush up. In the quiet I almost *hear* mist dance in the air.

Twenty steps bring us to the ship's bow, the number of markers reduced to ten across, then five, then three. With the harbour lost again, we face back up the slope. A figure well above the kids also flits in, and then out, of sight.

"Do you see someone else?" I ask.

"Where?"

"Higher up—I thought I saw a—"

"Just us and the dogs, Esther."

I fix my gaze on the spot where I glimpsed the figure. "Dominic," I say, "he spoke to you about his grandfather?"

"He was fascinated by the congruences. Two generations of Wilsons in Asia, both in Hong Kong. He even made me call him major one night. He was well jarred, mind."

"Jarred?"

"Drunk. A local expression."

Local to where? "He rarely spoke of him to me. Only one time we visited this cemetery. I ask many questions, but he treated the subject of his grandfather as ancient history, not so interesting."

"Gyatso must have got him thinking."

There: an outline. Near the monument. I am almost certain of it. A man, alone, working his way down.

"Everything is so different in that country," Patrick says, "that you start acting differently as well. All bets are off in Bon. All clocks have stopped."

As though Gyatso teems with mystics casting spells over wayward Westerners. As though it is an invention of the movies, a fantasy in a book. But instead of arguing with him, I go along. "Clearly," I say.

"Yes?" he asks.

"Dominic is four days late returning!"

"Of course."

His smile is relaxed; he is under the impression he is no longer on trial. I am pleased he feels easy around us now. Normally, I would not read so much into an expression. Instead, I would concentrate on the eyes. But Patrick Chan, wherever he is from, has Asian eyes, their blurry wetness telling of nothing less or more than a long life of imposed hardship, a short night of dissolute pleasure. The usual enigma. The standard cover for the indulgence of desires.

"What," he finally says, "is that a dagger you see before you?"

"A dagger?"

"The way you're looking at me."

"I was just thinking..."

"Aye, and why do I suspect I'm better off not inquiring as to the exact contents of your thoughts?" he says with another smile.

"I am thinking I do not know where local is for you, Patrick. Where jarred means drunk."

He nods, not like an American, at the query. "My passport declares me a native of Northern Ireland."

I wait.

"You're not smirking in disbelief?"

"I am Filipina. We also travel the world to find work."

"Haven't lived in Belfast for years, truth be told. Not since my parents passed away. No reason to visit there even."

"To see the house you grew up in?"

I have no idea why I said that. His profile confirms the question is unwelcome; perhaps the reason I asked it.

"A flat above the family business is all I ever knew as home," he says softly. "It burned, along with the take-away we owned, nearly a decade ago."

"A bomb?"

"Grease fire."

"And your parents?"

"Turning the tables, are we?" He grins, waits for me to give in and confess my strategy. When I don't, he shrugs. "My father died in the fire. Ma and I were out on the sidewalk, but he insisted on going back in to fetch something. The roof collapsed while he was inside," he adds, scratching his ear with abrupt ferocity, like a dog with fleas. A trickle of blood pools at his lobe. "Which meant, of course, that I never had a chance to ask him what could be so effing important, pardon my French. But I had my suspicions. Two paintings on the wall. Paintings he couldn't quite live with, couldn't quite live without."

"Tragedy."

"Farce is more like it."

"Patrick," I say. "Your ear."

I notice the man again. Now I understand why I've had trouble tracking him in the mist. He is descending through the cemetery row by row, as though to train his sight on every stone, every name. At this rate, he won't reach aisle GG for a few minutes. Gaby and Mike, meanwhile, are engrossed in a make-believe. From the snippets of conversation that carry to us, and their gestures whenever they float into sight—deep bows and signs of the cross, arms raised to beseech the heavens—I conclude that my angels are committing blasphemy by imitating a priest offering a mass.

"You see him?"

"Who?"

"Maybe fifty yards above the children."

He squints. "If you say so."

"Keep your eyes wide open."

"Aye, aye, captain."

Now he hopes to joke his way out of saying any more. "And your mother?" I ask.

"She moved back to London, where she had people. Died of lung cancer last year, if you can believe it, a kiss from the grave from my da. All of fifty-six. Terrible young age to pass, don't you think?"

He claims my gaze. The assertion is so unexpected I let him communicate in this intimate manner, show me his sorrow and unresolved rage. As though we are brother and sister. As though we are—

My daughter is calling for her dad. Twice she calls to him. I have to stop myself—shame, Esther!—from correcting her.

Blocking the path is an unfurling wave of mist so brilliant with light that I half-expect the resurrected Jesus, as depicted in children's catechisms, to step from the radiance. I crash into it and am momentarily blinded. Crying out in fear—or is it long-ing?—I allow a hand to take my own. We pass through, he and I, and emerge baptized, born again.

A man stands across from the kids, wagging a finger at them.

Ironically, it is Patrick who releases me. He alters his appear-ance as surely as I changed clothes for my meeting with the woman from the high commission. His pupils dim. His mouth purses. His body language shifts as well: shoulders more mili-tary and arms limp, hands fisted.

He slides between headstones, coming up behind Gaby and Mike. He smiles, kind of, at the finger-wagger.

The man has slits for eyes and dirt for a beard. Dressed in baggy pants and a smeared T-shirt, he could be anywhere from thirty to sixty and could be a homeless person on the streets of any city I have lived in. He emits a slide of guttural Cantonese. The scream below his words is piercing, and I focus on the walking stick in his grasp.

"It's okay, kids," Patrick says. Only now does he position himself as a shield. The children accept his protection with gratitude. "This poor fella is upset about something."

"Were we being bad?"

"It has nothing to do with you. He's just—"

The stranger raises the stick. Patrick is suddenly in his face, menacing in his language, pressuring a retreat. Wet grass cuts the legs out from under the man and he is dumped on his rear. His gaze up at Patrick Chan—the last thing I observe while shepherding the kids to safety—is muddled by fear, as to be expected, but also clarified by respect.

Which is a surprise.

Not as much of a surprise, though, as my response. At the prospect of him threatening my children, even of simply disrupting their sleep in the nights to come, my impulse is to break that walking stick over his skull.

Patrick rejoins us.

"What did he want?" I ask.

"He thought Gaby and Mike were Japanese, believe it or not.

Claimed Japanese tourists have been sneaking into war cemeteries around the city and defacing the gravestones."

"He thought they were—?"

"The guy is touched, Esther. He said he lost most of his family in the war and that he can't forgive or forget what happened."

"He scared me," Gabriella says.

"Bad guy," Mike adds.

Patrick asks Michael if he wants to ride on his shoulders. He raises him up with ease but not skill; he is new to this fatherly task.

"Thank you again," I say.

"He's a shouter, is all. Wouldn't have laid a hand on them."

But I would have cracked his skull?

At the monument I turn for a last look. Thirty-two aisles below, the man, having taken Patrick's order not to move literally, sits legs-sprawled next to a tombstone, ground mist slowly swallowing him. The cemetery remains in low cloud, but the world beneath it is about to be revealed with the drama of a sheet pulled off a statue. A vertical suburb of apartment towers is so close I could reach out and unpeg balcony laundry. The harbour feels a high dive away.

A helicopter whizzes by. Jackhammers, the city's outdoor Muzak, resume playing inside a building splinted in bamboo scaffolding. The air, briefly fresh, is once again choking.

The taxi has waited for an hour with its engine running. I am the last to re-enter the deep freeze. As usual, needles prick at my brain. I tug on my shirt to let the sweat coarse freely down my chest.

In the front seat Patrick rolls his sleeves. He alerts the driver to where three mangy dogs, still smarting from their earlier humiliation, block the exit. "Remember to drive like hell through the dogs," he says.

The joke, judging from his grin, is private.

How often, and to how many people, am I apologizing these days? My trigger temper. My obscure allusions to the trials of motherhood. I should be nicer with Lysianne Davaar-Lacombe. I should be grateful to my father-in-law. And if my children want to keep me company in the raft-wide master bed, kick and slap and mutter song lyrics in their sleep, I should awaken with kisses for their foreheads and smiles for their eyes.

Patrick must instruct the driver to return to Mid-Levels along the south side of the island. The route takes longer, but is more pleasing, especially on days when the narrow road isn't bumper to bumper with Mercedes-Benzes or slick with rain. Today is such a day, and the cab crosses the TaiTan reservoir well above the last remaining isolated coves and beaches. Even a passing glimpse of this landscape soothes my spirit. Sun, sea, and burnished light; shore, sand, and burnt scrub. Smells of seawrack and decay. Perfume of mangrove and shell ginger, bamboo orchid and garcinia. And the sky? Outside of typhoon season, the Asian sky I so love—and trust, even—is a protecting dome.

The car slows at the hairpin curve beyond the exit to Stanley, a stream trickling across the lanes to reconnect with a gulley below, and then climbs and descends, climbs and descends, in the direction of Repulse Bay.

Gaby rarely makes it out to Stanley for mass without her stomach executing gymnastic routines. Today I am the car-sick passenger.

"The man in the cemetery," I finally say. "Nothing like that has happened to us before. Someone showing their emotions here. Acting out of passion. Maybe..."

"Maybe what?"

"Maybe there is more spirit to Hong Kong than I realize."

"What, a loopy old one is the city's conscience?"

I shrug.

"More likely this," he says. "It's all my doing. I'm the fire starter. Wherever I go, stuff happens. An Irishman abroad, wha." His smile is unattractive.

"Is that what Dominic found out in Bon?"

The kids perk up at the mention of their dad.

"Which reminds me," Patrick answers, the smile frozen. "Did you have a chance to look at the *Post* this morning?"

I shake my head.

"Good thing I saved this for you. It's not unrelated to what we're talking about."

He passes me the front section of the *Morning Post*, twice folded, a headline blaring. Then he engages Gabriella in a purposeful discussion about Boyzone, her latest teenybop idols.

Terrorists Arrested in Gyatsian Capital

Xinhua, the official news agency, is reporting the arrest of two individuals believed responsible for a series of bombs in the troubled autonomous region, including a recent explosion that resulted in a woman's death. Thomdup Norbu, 30, and Lavanya Kamala, 28, were arrested in an unspecified location outside Bon. Officials are dubbing the couple the "masterminds" of an unnamed dissident group, and have taken the unusual step of confirming that Norbu was suffering injuries when detained. Norbu and Kamala are also suspected of setting a fire in the Gyatsian Quarter of the city on November 1, in which several historic homes were destroyed.

Not for a second do I presume he isn't watching my face, deciding what to say and do next. He is still speaking to my daughter when I rudely interrupt, knowing he will drop the pretense.

"You saw him in this temple you mentioned? Four mornings ago, you watched him walk down a lane and open a door?"

He nods.

"But you did not follow him?"

"There was a commotion."

I wait.

"A disturbance in the Kata," he says. "I had to get out of there myself. I wasn't wearing the same racial insulation as your husband. I could have gotten roughed up or worse. The plan was to—"

"And the people he was going to help? This couple?" I point to the article.

"I think so."

"You *think*, Patrick?"

"It was them."

"Are you guys talking about Dad?" Gaby asks.

I tell her to be quiet.

"Your mother is just having a bad day," he explains.

I bite my lip. He is going too far. He is presuming too much. Another headline jumps at me:

Amah Survives Plunge

A Happy Valley domestic worker, Bibop Cruz, 33, survived a fall of six storeys from the apartment in Sing Woo Road where she was employed. The Filipina landed on a canopy outside the building, which broke her impact. She still suffered life-threatening injuries and was taken to nearby St. Paul's Hospital. Ms. Cruz was alone in the flat at the time of the accident.

Bibop: the name Gloria Ferrer mentioned on the phone the other night. The woman in trouble, whom Sisters of Mary were planning to contact, offer to intervene. I was supposed to call Gloria back.

"Mom, are you crying?"

"Stop the car."

The cabbie frowns.

"Patrick! Tell him to stop!"

He and the driver exchange words. When the car does not slow—though reeling, I can tell we've swooped down on

Repulse Bay and are racing through the village, the road shaded by apartment towers—I punch open the sick bag I keep in my purse.

At last, the driver pulls into a parking lot. I slide out and stagger over to a shrub—an incense tree, another beautiful local plant—and vomit. A magpie shoots from the bush, its tail blood-red. My torso quivers, like a fish on a cutting block, and my head is too heavy to hold upright.

"What is going on?" I ask, sensing him behind me.

"Easy now."

"Just a week! Not a year. Not five decades. Where is Dominic?"

"In Gyatso. He's—"

A security guard in a ridiculous uniform, complete with frilly epaulets and a sea captain's hat, scolds me for choosing his building for this latest act of self-humiliation. For the third time today Patrick serves as protector, barking with such menace the guard retreats into the lobby, no less cowed than the dogs.

I straighten with difficulty. First I call to the open door of the cab, assuring the children I am okay. Then I wipe my mouth with my sleeve, too undone to worry how it looks. "Who are you, Patrick Chan?"

"I love the way you say my name—*Paterhik*."

I repeat the question.

"A friend."

I repeat it again.

He narrows his eyes into the sun, sweat beads racing each other to the cliff edge of his chin. The blood on his ear has dried. "A journalist, if that is what you're asking," he answers. "Over here on assignment for a magazine."

"Not what I am asking," I say, though the information is interesting.

"You're in a tough spot. No one should be expected to manage all this alone. And I want to help."

"Stop saying that."

"Why?"

"Because…" Why, Esther? Why should he stop saying it? "Because you've already done so much."

"Then let me do more."

"How?"

"Ask."

"Pardon?"

"Ask me. I'll do it. Anything, Esther. Just ask."

Chapter Five

I come to with a fright. And a thought—a problematic one, no doubt.

I have a name, you know, I announce.

The dog, head in paws, grrs.

Well, I do. You haven't acknowledged it, and there's no one else around to confirm who I am, or was. But that doesn't mean—

He directs me to the Powerbook. The screen is upright and lit. Have I got more mail? An address with a name would be nice: DEAR SO-AND-SO... But all the file shows is a murmur, an exhale.

Hummmmmm, offers the computer.

Dead Dog takes off for the gorge. I climb to my feet, scouring the ruined cairn for beer and dumplings. (I would fight him now for the food.) No alms for the pilgrims this morning. Nor the leisure to gather meagre belongings. Near the entrance is a standing rock that I noticed last night. What the twilight hid is a man-sized mandala—painted in lieu, perhaps, of an actual gatehouse guard—on the side of the rock. The mandala shows a single figure, all beast, no Buddha. Four mini-skulls on sticks, eyes popping and grins sinister, poking from its head; a sumo body boasting polar bear paws and stiletto nails. Unlike the beast at Mani, this representation does not dwell in a cage of halos. He is at large. He is here and now.

A demon, I say, echoing the teachings. Manifestation of a consciousness that clings to a past life, that refuses to let go. Hope we don't run into him.

But my guide has already scrambled to where the trail enters the gorge. He hobbles into a mist of descending light, along with steam rising eerily from the river, which runs at no more than a couple of degrees above freezing—hardly a Himalayan hot spring. I wait until Dead Dog has vanished into a slit in the canyon wall before thinking a thought I am confident he would not approve of.

I miss my wife and kids.

I want another chance. I want to go home.

So I am entering the portal, noting at once how a glaze of ice not yet melted by a sun that probably never penetrates the cavity is rendering the path treacherous, remarking as well on the state of the walkway, floor crumbly and wall damp, drop-off abrupt and into darkness, the river raging below; I am entering the pass, intending simply to do as told, to not make trouble, despite my clinging, refuses-to-let-go thoughts—and what really can you do about your thoughts?—when an errant step causes a cave-in and a leg, finding no foothold, slides off.

Esther!

Terror pins me to my stomach. I check back to confirm it: the path is gone, a gap of several feet. The sound and smell of dog have me redirecting my vision. He is upon me, his growls intended to menace, his breath unaccountably meaty.

You going to bite again?

His response is emphatic. He snaps at my cheek, teeth clacking. Something bizarre happens—his snout swells like a fire-hose—and I am up and climbing, the triumph of one fear over another.

And I might be okay, I might cooperate, let him do his job, lead me on; I might even allow the hummmmmm that is flooding the gorge to flood my senses until they drown, were it not for the grotto I spot across the canyon.

A statue on the shelf of a rock. A figure with eyes also lowered and palms also turned out. The robe and veil and queenly crown, the soft features and delicate limbs; it is her, the Hail Mary, full of grace, the Holy Mary Mother of God. There she is, and here I am, dropping to my knees to beg her forgiveness, her mercy, and though I am unable to pray, exactly, I can hold my head in my hands and weep, because I am confused and terrified and I take no more refuge in the Buddha, the Dharma, or the Sangha than I do in the Curly, the Larry, or the Moe, and I honestly haven't the faintest idea what THE JEWEL IN THE HEART OF THE LOTUS means. Why would I, Dead Dog? I am husband to Esther, she of the map of moles and delicious nape, and father to Gaby and Mike, they of rosewater and talcum, and I am son to Charlie and Gina and brother to Francesca, and, by the by, I do have a name, Mr. Death Guide, and that name is—

He sinks his chops into my ankle. I roll onto my backside and begin kicking with my other foot. He takes several heels to the snout before deciding to regroup. Thinking fast, I smother him in the cloak. For a second Dead Dog is hamstrung and gagged. A single bout tumbles him backwards to the edge, where he slides, still body-bagged, thump, thump, splash.

I am in pain! I shout after him. I am in torment!

With each sob—the sorrow comes from deep in my abdomen—the growls register more urgently. My eyes are webbed in fingers but I still puzzle over the phlegmy wetness to the warnings. On my feet, ready to absorb his airborne assault, I cry out at the beast blocking the path.

You try disappointing someone like that, I say to the demon. You try living with the consequences. A third step back sets off another rock slide and I teeter on the brink, arms windmills. I correct my balance and, feeling the earth dissolve beneath me, run straight into its embrace. At which point, of course, it vanishes.

The gorge throws back my laughter, along with a new word—dukkha. Meaning suffering. Meaning thirsting, quenching, thirsting more. Since I need a name, can it also serve that function? Why not.

What man betrays his own father?

Dukkha.

What man wants to sleep with virtually every woman he meets?

Dukkha.

What man abandons his family to purge his sins?
Dukkha.

At a zigzag, the path finally levelling as the gorge widens and the stream it is funnelling emerges beneath, I am stopped in my tracks by visions of such ferocity that they achieve where dead dogs and demons failed. The first is of a boy. He looks about twelve and is dressed in a shirt and school tie. A belt holds two clips: a cell phone and a Discman, a cord running to the head-set in his ears. Acne spots his nose and peach fuzz moustaches his lip. His hair is combed, maybe gelled, and his skin is scrubbed. That skin remains milk-coffee brown, a distinctly mid-Pacific hue. His eyes, too, defy pigeon-holing, both their shape and their colour. I see more of her in him than of me, but mostly I see my father, especially the erect posture and high forehead. Michael, I say, though I realize it is pointless. Son. Such a handsome young man. So turned out. But do you really need a cell phone? And why no smile?

Up ahead, equally still, equally unaware of my presence, is a girl of fourteen. In her kneesocks and tartan dress, her white blouse, she is stunning: a half-foot taller than her mother, most of it leg, with hardly any hips and still only the hint of breasts. Glimmering blue-black hair falls to her waist—I knew she would insist on growing it—and marble eyes dare anyone, man or woman, not to quarry them. Her face is more round, more Filipina (surprise!) than I expected, and the mole on her cheek, the dimples when she smiles, are Esther's. The arch of her brows, however, even the curve of those eyes, belong neither to Ramos nor Wilson. They are Ponti. Gina, her loveli-ness—and much of her spirit, I bet—two generations later. Gabriella, I say, my God, you are beautiful. I hope your mother is keeping watch—

She raises her arms over her head. At once her gaze glazes and her face shuts down. She begins to swivel her hips, then to thrust them, in out, back forward, tossing her head and allow-ing hair to cloak her sight. Her dance is recognizable from a thousand music videos, from bars in Manila to New York.

When I reach out to retie the hair, she all of a sudden turns to me, a knee-knocking shock. Her mouth reshaped in a way I could not have foreseen, my daughter drops a loose arm onto my shoulder and runs a hand up through my hair. She pulls me into her. She kisses me, hard. Her tongue, hot and sticky, pries open my—

I throw myself off the path.

HUMMMMMM roars the river. HUMMMMMM murmurs the radiance.

He is revived by saliva being lathered over his cheeks and chin. Dead Dog is the field medic, and he sheds a tear at the sorry sight of him. Rising to his elbows, he inspects the top of his skull, certain he has cracked bone and created an opening. Then he surveys the surroundings: a rocky river bed, a slope imprinted with skid marks. Aware that he is squinting, he turns to the source of the tenfold increase in light.

A valley between three ranges. To the south, a ridge of serrations, their upper tiers under snow. To the north, the same anvil peak part smothered in cloud. Directly ahead, a glacier. Terminal moraines of snow patches at the forefront, near vertical ice fields in the distance. A steep incline of ice, frost-sparkled and glinting.

Chenla glacier, he announces. We've made it.

The dog fords the river, now a shallow stream, using a bridge of stones. He follows, slipping twice. On the far bank, visible through flurries, is a free-standing structure. It could be a stupa, large enough to house the remains of a reincarnated Buddha. It could be a crypt in a cemetery, room for generations of a prosperous clan. It could even be, he thinks, an author's imagination, as infinite as a mountain range, as contained as a short story with walls, ceiling, and a door.

As they near it, the building's roof lifts off: a flock of wide-winged birds, not choughs. Scraw! scraw! these birds complain.

He pauses before the low doorway. The stone structure is rectangular, its wooden roof an inverted V. The shape is unmistakable—a miniature chapel, the kind a Portuguese missionary in Gyatso, or a French Jesuit among the Huron in Ontario, might hastily construct—but his consciousness, busy fleeing his head (so it feels), can't make the leap. He has to crouch through the entrance, the dog already within, and observe how light slants onto the floor via a cruciform window, to understand the connection.

Amazingly, around his neck is a crucifix. Of all the possessions lost—passport and clothes, computer and wallet—why should this borrowed artifact have clung to him so determinedly? He sinks to his knees.

You got me here, he says, patting the animal's flank. Well done.

Thump. The first bird lands back on the roof.

The chapel walls are decorated. He notices red swastikas, painted backwards. He identifies a Latin inscription over the door: INTROIBO AS ALTARE DEI, along with a sequence of Roman numerals: MDCLXX or maybe LXV. Finally, he discerns a pattern of ideograms, one, then two and two, then one again.

OM—MA NI—PAD ME—HUM.

THE JEWEL IN THE HEART OF THE LOTUS!

Ahh, he says, sliding to the earth. Of course. No paradise. No kingdom. Begin again, begin again, begin again.

Thump. Thump. More birds.

Your final thoughts determine your next incarnation.

And then the dog is gone. Slipped into a doorway of light so luminous it cannot be viewed, except by the dead, the awakened.

His final thoughts?

Not a dream. Not a fantasy.

If only she would say his name.

Chapter Six

He commands me to sit in the living room. He is lucky, for I am in a funny mood, with no interest in a fight. A hospital visit with Bibop Cruz, the Mindanao woman who tried taking her own life three weeks ago, has left my hair wet and my eyes sore. The trip has rumpled my thinking as well. Thoughts float like ground mist through a cemetery. I cannot be mad at Patrick Chan this morning. I cannot be furious with Hong Kong. In my heart is sadness for the suffering of all creatures and compassion for the living and the dead.

Sweet, these emotions. Sweet and warm and ineffectual.

Besides, the answering machine is blinking and I still jump at the prospect of a message. I cross to the couches and tidy the newspapers sprawled over the table between them. Patrick, whose T-shirt is also stained with rain, asks me to stop fussing. I swallow this impertinence, too. He raises his arm dramatically and unfurls a scroll.

"Found this in the art gallery gift shop," he says, draping the scroll across the table. "The original is up in the Ming dynasty room, on the third floor." He drops onto the couch beside me, expelling cigarette stink. "Seeing the painting in the flesh just about blew the top off my head. All these years I've taken the meaning of the act, the nature of the nature, so to speak, at face value. Today, this morning—boom! A staggering new insight."

My confusion must be plain.

"It's a painting by the guy I'm doing my thesis on," he explains. "Among the last great exponents of a school of nature art dating back nearly two thousand years."

"You're doing a thesis?"

"PhD. Trinity College, Dublin."

"But you are a journalist," I say. Matter of fact, I have a question about his journalism. A question about his journal, which he writes in every morning and evening and unwisely leaves open on his bed, the door ajar, the flowers needing their daily watering.

There is no guile in his eyes. His face is set, and he looks at me as might a bright child, unhindered by complexities. It is a mask, one of several. I am getting good at distinguishing them.

"You are journalist, you are student," I say. "You come from Ireland, you come from here. Not easy to follow, Patrick."

"Don't I know it."

"Do you?"

"Can I tell you what I discovered this morning. Please?"

The warm feeling is dissipating.

"The painting depicts what is called a dream journey. Those craggy mountains and clinging trees, the wee folk shuffling from pagoda to pagoda, the misty earth and high, clear sky—it's all a vision. A philosophy, more exactly. You see such scenes everywhere. In airport lounges and hotel lobbies. In restaurants and—"

"I recognize the landscape."

"There was even one in the reception area in the hotel in Bon where..." He reconsiders the detail. From his back pocket he removes a flattened pack of Marlboros—same brand as Dominic's. What, now he is going to smoke in the apartment? "In any case, what exploded my brain was the revelation that the unifying emotion here, if you want, is death. The preparation for it. The longing, even."

I am speechless.

"Don't jump on me just yet," he says. "Dream journeys are invitations to shift perception from the real to the visionary, the body to the soul. By design, the paintings allow the viewer to experience bliss. What I'm suggesting is that the invitation is equally to prepare for another kind of forgetfulness. How could people living such pleasant lives in such a dreamy place be thinking about death? Only if they *are* already dead, and this is their—"

I stand up. "Crazy," I say.

"You're hearing me wrong. I'm not talking about him."

"Of course you aren't," I snap. Compassion, for this man? A slap across the face is more my inclination now.

"I need a cigarette."

"You know where to go."

He crosses to the balcony. "If you'd known I was a smoker, would you have invited me to stay?" he asks with his irresistible grin.

I scowl. He reads the expression correctly—I am forgiving him, once more—and is happy.

At my request, he leaves the door open. On the balcony he squats to commune with the parakeet. The way he bends, heels flat and toes out, buttocks nearly brushing the ground, is unmistakable: the coolie squat, I once heard it called. His shirt is pulled tight, the sleeves tugged into his armpits. Over the course of the past two weeks my houseguest has revealed himself to be—or to dress like, at any rate—a tough guy: laced boots and jeans, T-shirts that flatter arms corded with muscles and veins. This morning I notice nicks in the skin below his neck. Cuts, long ago healed, now scars.

The sky is a showerhead with a broken faucet. Sheets of rain roll off the platform above, soaking the flower pots and darkening the back of his shirt. Normally I can keep the flowers on the railing year round, except for monsoon. One more hour of this, the plants will drown.

He stands and fires a match. "See what I mean about the dream journey?" he says, holding the matchbox out for my inspection. It is decorated with a painting like the one on the scroll. "Picked this up at the Island-Shangri-la hotel when I stopped in there for some smokes."

He extinguishes the match with one, two, three strokes.

Lucien does his car alarm imitation: "*Wooh-wooh-wup!*"

Patrick laughs. "Brilliant,"

I shrug.

"Tell me the story again, will you?"

I retreat back inside the frame. I had thought I wanted to be cooled by contact with real Hong Kong air, however ripe. My body, though, is saying otherwise.

"Mike," I say, "he was wild boy when we first came. Always touching things, always knocking them over. I bought the bird for company—Dominic, he worked at the office until nine or ten every evening, to make calls to Canada—and put his cage out here. Seems that parakeets, they memorize the first sounds they hear, and then not much after. Every morning and night, Lucien listens to security systems being activated in parking lot below. Wooh-wooh-wup!"

"And his other specialty?" he asks, cupping the cigarette like a sailor on the bridge of a ship.

The bird sings on cue: "*Stop it! Stop it! Stop it!*" It hops over to my side of the cage, cocking its blue-helmeted head to inquire: *Do I sound like you?*

Patrick clutches his stomach in amusement.

"I am scolding the boy so often, when he knocks Thai carving off the table or breaks the vase that Dominic has brought from Japan, the parakeet learns to copy my words. Stupid bird," I say, cocking my head back at it: *No you don't!*

We watch the rain.

"Tough, being on your own again," he finally says, his broad back to me.

"There is still no body," I answer. "The police said as much. No body, no proof that he is—"

"Nearly a month now, Esther."

"How could there be no body? A Western man, in a place like that? Tell me how it could not be noticed? And remember what the woman at the high commission told me last week? He never used the return ticket. Never went through customs in Bon or at Chek Lap Kok. Like you said when we first met—he's still in Gyatso."

"Or else Gyatso is still in him," Patrick replies.

I wait.

He blows a smoke ring at the water. The smoke is rebuffed

and curls back around his head. "Hate to say it, but what's happened feels like something out of 'Ocean.'"

It takes me a second.

"The short story, of course," he adds.

"I think he mentioned this in his phone message."

Patrick turns to me. For an instant he can find no mask to put on and his face shows genuine astonishment. "You haven't read 'Ocean'?"

I admit not.

"You need to read it. Fast."

"You have a copy?"

There is the slightest pause. "I looked at the story on his computer," he says. "He must have left the book here."

"I don't think so," I say. Right away, I know the book he is talking about, and recall the evening Dominic read the story, and how he reacted to it, and the sequence of events his reaction set off. Where is "Ocean" now? I think I know that as well.

I tell Patrick I must lie down.

Back inside, he collects the painting on the table. Instead of rolling it up, he carries it like a banner to a space of wall currently occupied by a piece of calligraphy. "Do you mind?" he asks. Not waiting for a reply, he removes one scroll and hangs another. "By rights the painting should be viewed crossway, not up and down. Still, you get the general idea."

"Are you—?"

"It's a gift, aye. For your hospitality."

"Thank you."

"Would you like me to pack my bag and go?"

I would. I wouldn't. My expression says as much.

"Then you'll need to do two things," he says. "First, find 'Ocean' and read it, so we can have a proper discussion about Dominic and Gyatso. Second, tell me the news. Tell me the news, which I already know, and then tell the kids, who don't know but are aware there are many changes afoot in their lives. And maybe then your family in Canada."

"How dare you."

"I dare," he answers. "You know how. You know why, too."

I repeat my desire to lie down.

He heads into the kitchen and his room at the far end of it. "Have a look at the *Post* once you've rested," Patrick says. "A couple of clippings for the walls of shame. Also an article, something else we might want to talk about."

I check the phone message. Another call from Jimmy Chu, office manager at WilCor. Chu says four weeks of inactivity in Hong Kong are like a year of suspended operations in Toronto. Deals are falling apart; money is being lost. He begs me to step in and make business decisions on my husband's behalf.

Which would be funny, if only it weren't.

I tried to be him after my first conversation with Jimmy Chu. Before the closet mirror in our room. A dark green linen jacket, one of his favourites, and a gold silk tie. Cuffs burying my wrists and fabric to my knees. The hairs on my arms on end. Sweat pooling in my nape. I flipped open his cell phone and pretended to dial. I pulled a business card from the breast pocket and held it out with both hands and a slight bow. *Dominic Wilson, President, WilCor Communications, 32A Tower 2, Landmark Building. Central. Hong Kong.*

Then I collapsed onto the bed, a forearm across my eyes.

E not holding up well, I read in Patrick's journal yesterday. *She sobs every night and has no appetite, except for sweets. Swelling in the face and wrists. How much longer before she admits it has happened? How much longer—* But then the toilet flushed in the water closet next to the shrine, and I slipped out. To examine myself in another mirror, and stare at a puffy old woman, abandoned by her man.

"You are staying with friends?" I asked him. We sat drinking iced tea at the kitchen table that afternoon, the cemetery visit behind us, my breakdown in the taxi still stinging.

"Worse," he replied. "Distant relatives over in Tuen Mun. The older ones speak some Pearl delta dialect. Can hardly make out what they're saying."

I invited him to use the spare bedroom. Until that moment, I hadn't been sure I liked Patrick Chan and wouldn't have acknowledged that we *had* a spare bedroom. But we did, a cot and end table and vase of flowers, sink and toilet in the adjacent cubicle. So long as the guest didn't mind the heat, or the decorations.

He smiled. "Bedtime material. No bother with some book or magazine. Just roll over and start reading."

The tone was for my benefit. To let *me* off the hook about the clippings. To spare *my* feelings about someone else's natural shock at this private gallery. He could be courteous.

And I did like him.

And he was the last person to see my husband alive.

In the bedroom I make two brief calls. First to Gloria, to report on Bibop Cruz. The insurance will cover the hospital bills, I tell her, but not the ticket—one way: her life here is finished—home to the Philippines. Gloria says maybe Sisters of Mary could canvass the women in Statue Square on Sunday. A few dollars from each might be enough. I say I will write a cheque instead. For the ticket, and enough money to allow Bibop to recover among her people. When Gloria Ferrer, who has not seen her husband or children in eleven months, claims that I am kind, I disagree. "Today I feel only compassion," I say. "Today I feel only sadness."

The second call, to Betty at WilCor, is brief. The book I am asking about, an edition of short stories, has been sitting on Dominic's desk for four weeks. She will send it over by courier. Three hours or less, she promises. "And Mrs. Wilson," Betty adds—I cannot convince her to call me Esther—"we all so sorry about Dominic. He was a good boss."

"Since I'm sleeping in the amah shrine," Patrick said, "I figure it's time I was given a tour of amahland. Who better for a guide than a card-carrying Sister of Mary?"

An odd request. Still, could I refuse?

Sunday morning he joined our bus trek out to Stanley. He chased Mike up the stairs to the upper deck. He howled with Gaby whenever a branch leaning over the road smacked the window. In the village he walked us to the door of St. Anne's and then met us there ninety minutes later, mass and meeting both complete. That kind of man, I could tell: anxious to show he could be reliable, eager to demonstrate character. (Meaning, Dominic would say—thinking about himself, I always assumed—that he questioned his own character and reliability.) The same bus dropped the four of us outside city hall on Connaught Road.

Of the Hong Kong amahlands, the one in Central was the epicentre. Fifty thousand women squatted from dawn until past dusk, rain or shine, blistering heat or unseasonable cold, along the outer walls and near the terminal entrance, the tunnel linking the Star Ferry with Statue Square. They read newspapers and wrote letters, dining al fresco on stews and pieces of fish. They formed choir groups and study sessions and cheered each other up enough to get through the next six days. These were the rented mothers and surrogate housewives who allowed the city to maintain its manic schedule. They, not the bankers and stock brokers, ensured those office towers could blaze all night; they, not the merchants and market vendors, guaranteed tourists round-the-clock shopping. As far as I was concerned, the amah sprawl in various parks on the island and in Kowloon constituted a silent protest, a good-humoured sit in. These ladies might even have been threatening their masters. If they could keep Hong Kong going, they could also make it stop. If they could do this on Sunday, why not in mid-week?

That afternoon, I squirmed walking through Statue Square with Patrick and the kids. Usually I would change my clothes before coming here, put on a cheap watch, slip my wedding ring into my purse. Today I felt like some society lady caught in a mob without a hankie to press to her nose. My body kept wanting to hurry along, as though I was in danger of being heckled, stoned with jars of shrimp paste and yam jam.

Some of the women knew me from the group. I responded to their greetings with such excitement they probably thought I had sipped too much communion wine. Some knew my story, or at least as it would have been told before October 31. I had never resented them the pleasure of their benign gossip. And the story of Esther Ramos-Wilson since Halloween? With certain amahs who avoided my gaze, I sensed in my stomach the rise in cadence as *that* gossip got spread. Those words, hushed and bitten in part by guilt, in part to heighten the intrigue, were not so benign. *Poor girl, her husband taken off... Another woman, they say... No word, not even to the kids... Once a maid, always a maid, eh?*

Gabriella and Michael helped. Filipino eyes, even those fatigued from minding other people's kids, followed them in open admiration. Smiles fanned out at their features and manners, how they spoke. A *"komusta po"* from Gaby would earn laughs and touches of her hair and arms; if Mike managed a *"mobuti po"* or, better, offered a proper blessing upon any woman I designated his auntie—grasping her right hand and pressing it to his forehead—the amahs would sigh with satisfaction and pride. I had such lovely *chillderen*. Yes I did. I thanked the Lord every day for this blessing? Every day and every night.

We were about to cross Queen's Road when a woman I had once assisted with a visa problem called to me. She draped a sampaguita lace around my neck. "Because even you need help from your sisters sometimes, Esther," the woman said in Taga-log. I hugged her and wept, stumbling over her name.

Patrick watched all this without comment. He laboured up the slope, releasing the kids to pump his thighs with his hands. The vertebrae in his spine showed through his shirt and his face seemed almost bruised by the heat. He insisted on buying ice cream in a fast-food restaurant in Lan Kwai Feng, pinching fabric in relief at the frigid air.

"Edith Aguilar," I finally said.

He frowned.

"The woman who gave me the sampaguita," I explained, running the flowers between my fingers. "What a hard life she has had."

"Why exactly are you involved with Sisters of Mary, anyway?"

I did not answer.

"You must be the only woman in the group who isn't, you know, one of them," Patrick said, feeding a cigarette from a pack straight into his mouth.

"One of them?"

"You're not a resident of amahland, Esther. You're not stuck in some humiliating job for five years. Not a thousand miles from your family. Not—"

"Poor?"

"On a domestic worker's visa."

What, he could read my mind? Then another explanation presented itself. "Dominic," I said, "he thinks I shouldn't be part of Sisters of Mary? That I should do more rich people things? Join yacht club? Attend chamber of commerce luncheons and ladies' group?"

"Nothing of the sort. He's in awe of your character and strength. You're his moral compass."

"Then why you ask?" I said, guiding the kids back through the doors.

"Just curious."

A few steps farther along the hill and Patrick was once more wheezing. It made no sense; smoking aside, he was a fit young man. And if ascending a sidewalk in Mid-Levels wore him out, how had he fared in Gyatso?

I am upstairs, not resting; he is downstairs, writing about me in his journal. When the phone rings, I pick it up at once.

"Esther?"

"Lysianne."

"You recognized my voice?"

"Your lilting French accent."

Lysianne Davaar-Lacombe from the Canadian High Commission pauses to decide if I am intending to insult her. "Are you seated?" she asks.

"No, are you?"

"I have some news."

"Your husband, he has left you for silky Hong Kong girl?"

"I simply do not understand your hostility," she says. Her tone is authentic, almost one human being to another. I would happily register a hint of apology there, and quit baiting her. But her diction is too clipped, like she really doesn't have a spare moment to ponder my hostility. She remains, in other words, a busy woman. Daughter of a politician. Half a power couple. Someone people who want to know people want to know.

"Too bad," I answer, behaving terribly. "Because I *do* understand your condescension."

The silence is long. I am seated, of course, on the bed, and flop backwards and stare at the ceiling.

"As you know," she finally begins, "the high commission took the extraordinary measure of contacting embassies in the region about your husband. They, in turn, made overtures to the authorities at the various passport control offices, which is how, for instance, we found out—and relayed the information to you, as a courtesy—that Dominic Wilson never exited Gyatso or attempted to re-enter Hong Kong. Last evening we received a communication from our embassy in New Delhi. The information is confidential, and I am not supposed to be sharing it with you..." She lets the guilt soak in. I feel some, but not enough to give her what she wants. "Authorities in Sikkim, a province in the northeast corner of India, are reporting that someone named Dominic Gordon Wilson passed through border customs the third week of November."

I swing my legs over the side of the bed. "Dominic, he is in India?"

"The information is—"

"Someone saw him?"

"An official entered his passport into a computer."

"Was he sick? Was he—?"

"Esther," Lysianne Davaar-Lacombe says, "we received no eyewitness confirmation. All we have is evidence that he crossed into India."

"He did, or his passport?"

"That is one possibility."

"I only want to know he is all right," I say.

She sighs, as though sorry for me, my plight. "I do have one more piece of information, which I hadn't intended to relay... I mean, this is *totally* unconfirmed... If your father-in-law calls my supervisor to say that one of the high commission's officers told him..."

"Our secret, Lysianne. Promise."

"It's such a wild report."

"Even a rumour would be okay."

"The official in Sikkim, in reply to the query about Dominic Gordon Wilson, thought he recalled the said individual being, well, Asian."

"Asian?"

"Canadian passports are rare in that province. Even the mountaineering teams tend to pass through Nepal. The official claimed he stamped only one Canadian document that week and it belonged to an Asian man travelling with a small child."

I can summon no words.

"He was obviously confused. Your children have their own passports, don't they?"

"Gabriella, yes. With Michael, we did not have chance in Canada to arrange this. He is listed on Dominic's..."

"Even so," she says, "the report is preposterous. Dominic Wilson, I take it, would not likely be confused for Asian, would he, Esther? Esther?"

My tone infers respect, I hope, along with a faint suggestion of my own regret. "Thank you, Ms. Davaar-Lacombe," I say, and hang up.

As usual, the phone rings again almost immediately. In my distraction I decide it sounds three short rings, a fax, although no paper emerges. An Asian man? Travelling with a small child? Someone else's story, surely. Someone else's flight.

The first time I caught him jotting in his diary, fresh from a conversation in the kitchen, he claimed to be noting an idea. "Can't believe I didn't think of it sooner," he said, backing me out of the shrine. "Have you tried e-mailing him?"

I made a face.

"I'm serious. He brought his laptop to Gyatso. If I know the man, he'll find an Internet hook-up before he finds a phone. It's worth a go, isn't it?"

We kept the home computer in our bedroom. The kids had just been put to bed, obliging Patrick and me to slip past their rooms, stealthy as teenage lovers anxious not to alert the parents. Mike now insisted his door be left open. Hall light angled to the foot of his bed. "Daddy?" the boy called from within a shallow sleep. Gaby slumbered through our climb, but I still closed the door behind us. Patrick made for the desk, though not before halting at the closet and wondering whether this was where Dominic's "Armani army" was stored. Stunned—I had *not* shared my cross-dressing experience with him—I busied myself straightening pillows.

Within a few seconds Patrick had the monitor jumping with

colour and logos and columns of information. "No chattering children in this boot-up," he said. Seated at the terminal, posture perfect, keys flying over the fingerboard while his gaze locked onto the screen, he looked more natural—more like who he probably was—than ever before. "I know the two security codes," he continued. "ESTHER and GINA. Now it's a question of guessing the password for his e-mail account. He didn't by any chance tell you?"

I folded my arms defensively.

Keys click-clacked. Patrick glanced up, down, then up again. He hit a key hard. "There! Easy call. It was you again, Esther."

"Me?"

Whatever the suddenly crowded screen showed, it jarred him. My eyes hardly knew where to settle—lists of numbers and addresses, even flashing ads for products—but I did locate one striking phrase: 217 NEW MESSAGES.

"So many?"

"Mostly junk," he answered. His voice, though, told otherwise.

"Can you tell when—?" I cut myself off. Beside the first line highlighted by a red arrow was the date October 23, 1999.

"I'll set you up to compose an e-mail to the home address. That's a kind of letter being written, in effect, to yourself, although anyone with access to the account can read it. Meaning Dominic, we hope."

"Or you."

"Why would I read it?"

"Maybe this is not such a good idea."

"It's a great one," Patrick said.

We switched positions. "Out, please," I told him.

The screen glowed white, a vertical bar at the top corner. Typing had never been a skill of mine—at York University I wrote essays by hand and paid to have them typed—and I hated mistakes. But bad spellings and typos might help assure Dominic it was me keying in the message; my clumsiness would crinkle his eyes in amusement.

DOMINIC—

You know I type badly. You know I cannot think this way.
Patrick your friend (?) from Bon, he says maybe you will read
this. Gaby sleeps most nights, lucky child, but Mike, he has
monsters in his closet and vampires behind curtins. Halle-
ween scared the boy. He whimpers until I bring him into my,
sorry, OUR, bed, which I really do not mind. I rub his back
and smell his hair and skin.

But I want you in OUR bed instead. Talking about news,
the news, great news I have for us both, and then not talking.
NOT talking for a while. I will try not to be such damn good
girl. I will keep the cross on.

Charlie calls every day. Franny calls every other. Even
Cathrine has called twice from Montreal. Your father, he
forgves everything. He even forgets some of it. He wants you
back, wants us back, his grandkids, in Toronto, where we
belong, where we live. Not here. Where is here?

I will keep the cross on.

And I pray. Patrick—you know him, yes? You told him
stuff about us? Told him to visit? He says Gyatso has your
soul. He says you are living inside some story. My prayers
can fight a country, a book? Crazy.

Do you know what we have made? Do you, love?
Esther

"Telephone!"

I force myself to sit up, despite the fish hook being yanked in
my tummy. *An Asian man? Travelling with a small child?*

"Esther?" Patrick calls from the bottom of the landing. "Can
you talk to your father-in-law?"

I lurch to the door. He is climbing the stairs with the cordless.

"The phone rang?"

"Twice. I assumed you were asleep both times. Charlie,
though, is demanding I get you."

I snatch the receiver. Sensing what is good for him—he calls Charlie Wilson by his first name only?—he vanishes. I slump onto the top step.

"Charlie," I say, curling hair behind my ears.

"How dare you, Esther."

"It's three in the afternoon here. That makes it, what, four in the morning?"

"Franny woke me up. And you had no right to keep such a secret from us," he says. "Your own family. I had to hear it—"

"Stop!" Slowly, the fog in my head lifts. "What secret am I keeping?" I ask. "Please tell me." About all I can think of is Francesca's lifestyle. But surely he is aware of her preferences.

"A baby changes the picture. Even with him still missing, even with only a month gone by, a baby *definitely* changes the picture."

"You... you know about this?"

"My daughter just informed me."

"Franny knows?"

"I believe," he says, groaning in apology for his methods, "I believe her source was your houseguest. Your rather *mysterious* houseguest, if you ask my opinion. Which you won't, clearly."

I hear the front door click below.

Six steps and I'm in the living room. I check the balcony as well, ignoring a *wooh-wooh-wah!* from the parakeet. The kitchen and shrine are also deserted. His notebook lies open on the cot, inviting a snoop.

While I hunt for my betrayer, Charlie Wilson outlines his night in Toronto. Franny, it seems, called here an hour ago, hoping to share with her sister-in-law a dream that had startled her. She wound up chatting for ten minutes with this guy Patrick, who claimed I was resting, and who in the end divulged his deep concern for how I was handling the stress of both a missing husband and an early-term pregnancy.

Satisfied that Patrick has fled, I sink into a chair at the kitchen table.

"I was waiting—" I say.

"Time to stop waiting."

"What, Charlie, you have bought a plane ticket to Hong Kong?"

"Don't get smart."

"Me, smart? Never a chance of that."

"I have a ticket booked, in point of fact," he says. "The dates are in my planner. I realize I owe you an explanation, Esther. I am hardly being consistent here."

"You owe me nothing." Worried that might sound wrong, I add: "You have given me everything already."

"Fathers who go away, they sometimes never come back. I learned that when I was a boy. Took the lesson too much to heart, I suppose."

"He is coming back."

"I wasn't talking about him."

"He is."

"Then leave him a note on the door!" he roars. As usual, I sink to my knees before the authority of the Vicar. Dominic and I used to laugh at how differently Charlie Wilson's taskmaster voice affected us. Vicar mode always made Dominic want to react, to do something to infuriate his parent, pour gasoline on the fire. The voice always sat me down, like my grandmother's raised hand, like my one memory of my own father, on a porch, his arms around me. He died when I was four.

"Charlie!"

"We're past talking about a simple resolution to a simple problem. Past Dominic just reappearing and resuming where he left off. This whole Asian scheme..." He shifts in bed, or in his chair. "Can you explain his thinking, Esther? Why he did what he did?"

"I am poor Filipina girl."

"You belong here," he says, his words now slurred by fatigue. "In Toronto. Not in a month. Not in two weeks. Today."

"No one belongs in any one place anymore."

"Of course they do. The Wilsons have lived in the mid-town for almost a century. This is our home and community. This is *your* home and community as well." He draws a shuddery breath. "You are my beloved daughter-in-law, mother to my two astonishing grandchildren. And now I find out that you are carrying a third child?"

"And your only son, Dominic?"

"He has made his choice," Charlie Wilson says.

I am silent.

That is going too far, and he knows it. "He'll figure out where to find you, won't he?" he asks quietly.

"You are so angry with him!"

"Should I not be? Should *you* not be, too?"

He is probably right. But for some reason I once again feel only sadness and compassion. A pointless state. Of even less utility than prayer.

The doorbell rings.

"I've said too much."

"We can talk again soon, okay, Charlie?"

I dab my eyes with my sleeve.

"The mystery of love, Esther, is far greater than the mystery of death."

Gina, I think to myself, recalling the funeral, and his eulogy. *Always about Gina with these men.*

"You," my father-in-law adds, reading my bitter thoughts.

"Okay," I say in a small voice.

"*Only* you."

"Okay," I say again.

Before I can turn the handle the door flies open. In burst the children.

"The school bus!" I say, covering my mouth.

"I thought you might have forgotten," Patrick offers, trailing behind. "I met them at the gate downstairs. We ran into a delivery guy coming off the elevator." He hands me a package.

"We must talk."

"I'd like that, only I promised the kids a snack. And your

sister-in-law, Franny, she'll be ringing back any minute."

Mike asks Patrick if he'll play G.I. Joe. Gaby insists they have a date for Spice Girls dance, whatever that might be.

"I need to speak with Patrick first," I tell them.

My children glower at their mother.

"What's in the package?" he asks.

A book. From WilCor Communications.

"Are you writing about us, Patrick?"

He is pouring glasses of juice, and smiles.

"In your journal, you are making notes about us, about me?"

"You read my journal?"

"Don't bother being outraged. You wanted me to."

"Are you two fighting?"

"Quiet, Gabriella."

"We might want to leave that business until later, Esther."

"I don't think so. I think we want to talk right now."

He has crossed to his room, slipped in and out, and now returned to the table. "Have a look at this first," he says.

Today's *Morning Post,* again. Folded open to an article.

"Friends do not make notes about friends," I say, pushing the newspaper back at him. "Journalists do. What, are we going to become a magazine story?"

"I like stories," Mike says.

"I already have one of those," Patrick replies. "Right here in the paper. A beginning, middle, and now an end. Reported, by me and my assistant, but not yet written up."

He leaves the *Morning Post* on the table and commands the children to lead him to their rooms. They do, naturally—he is their best friend and pal, their action hero and MTV pin-up. What a role model Patrick Chan is: skin and eyes the same as everyone else's in Hong Kong, but a demeanour, if not exactly an accent, belonging to Toronto. Like them, in effect. Half East, half West.

I read the article. Twice, the second time frantically.

Crackdown Intensifies

State officials have confirmed the arrest of more than twenty Gyatsians associated with a dissident group believed responsible for a series of bombings in Bon. Reports that several monks, and at least one minor, are among the arrested are being denied, but sources within the Gyatsian capital claim a 12-year-old youth was picked up in the crackdown that followed an explosion on November 1 at the offices of Bon Tourism.

Another report, that the husband of the woman killed in the incident is now suspected of involvement in the group and has fled Gyatso, is also unconfirmed. No names are being given.

In a related news release, officials have announced that the trials of the two leading suspects, Lavanya Kamala, 28, and Thomdup Norbu, 30, took place in an undisclosed location. Kamala received twenty years for "subversive activities" and "crimes against the state." Norbu, found guilty in the bombing of Bon Tourism, was given the death penalty. His sentence was carried out according to the law.

I sit on the couch, hands folded and spine straight, studying Patrick's dream journey on the wall. The scene depicted in the painting certainly looks peaceful. Gazing upon the images does encourage serenity and forgetfulness; who knows, perhaps the subject is—must be, in the end—death. I feel pity for the figures depicted by the artist, men and women scurrying through the mist, out of the rain, helpless before the careless might of nature and the cruel randomness of fate. Are the colours of death really gold and brown and eggshell blue? Strange. I would have thought white and only white.

The phone rings, and I listen as my sister-in-law first advises me to ignore whatever the old man said before, then offers congratulations on the new baby, and finally asks, in passing, if that nice guy Patrick she spoke with earlier is maybe gay. Three separate issues blithely dispensed with, as only she can, Franny gets down to her real business. "The dream I had, the one that made me call you in the first place?" she says. "It was about Gina. Leo, here in the bed beside me, she doesn't think I should tell you it... Well, that's what you *said*, Leo, not five minutes ago..." I hear Leonora's voice in the background. "Oh, yes, Leo blows kisses to you and the lovelies... In any case, the dream is about Mother. She's at a party in this huge ballroom and is looking fabulous in a red silk gown. Très Gina, in her prime, though you didn't know her then. I'm standing beside her. 'You should see how they dance, Franny!' she is saying. Also, 'These are all the people you'd ever want to meet.' Then her escort steps into the frame. He's in a tuxedo. His hair is slicked like Jay Gatsby's and I can smell the Old Spice on him, even though Leo is certain... You said so twice, Leo!... she is certain dreams don't have smells. Anyway, guess what tall, handsome Wilson male is escorting Mother to the ball? Nicky-Nicky-Nine-Doors! 'Big brother,' I say to him, 'so *this* is where you've been for the last month!'"

Later that evening, Patrick reads "Ocean" aloud to me. I have switched off the ground-floor air-conditioning. Aside from a lamp near where he sits, the apartment is dark, the air glinting the smothered light of a moon mostly behind banks of running cloud. I wear an undershirt and track pants, flip-flops showing ruby-red nails. My hair tied with a scarf. The cross around my neck. From my spot in the balcony doorway, watching for the Peak tram, the heat is a plunge into uniquely Asian waters, where I have been swimming for much of my life.

He reads softly and slowly, in no hurry. The surprise in his voice early on, the growing bafflement and impatience, are hard to figure, given that he knows the story already. An hour must pass. Lucien stirs at my presence, but soon falls back into a trance. The squeal of car brakes and whoosh of a helicopter, the ships calling out in the harbour, are all that emerge from the toneless roar of nocturnal Hong Kong. Patrick's accent is openly

Irish tonight and the cadences of his speech are lulling. While listening to him I float over the room and gaze down at a man on a couch, head in a book, and a woman by the door, arms crossed. I drop briefly into Franny's dream, my mother-in-law in a gown, a dashing escort by her side. I even flit to a hospital ward in Happy Valley and observe a Filipina woman sleeping through the pain, casts on both her arms. Finally, I visit the porch of a beach house in southern Luzon and snuggle in the lap of a man whose rheumy eyes and collapsed cheeks confirm that he is not well, but who still holds me and still loves me, and so must be—now and forever—my father. Vincente Ramos, a gentle man of no consequence, unlike the father in "Ocean." Husband to Delia, the mother I never really met but who still would be dismayed, I think, at the direction I am taking.

"Esther?"

"Hmm? Is it finished already?"

"Don't tell me you want more." He stands up. "Too weird for me, to be frank. Too far gone."

"There is a paragraph near the end I would like you to read again. When the writer decides he must save his characters from the fates he has assigned them. He says he cannot fail."

"I remember." He flips through the book, drops of his sweat staining the pages. "Dominic mentioned that scene as well. Of all the notions—an author meeting his own characters! Boffo, really. And you want to know the truth? I can't begin to see how this story would have sent him racing off to Gyatso to meet the guy who wrote it. It's hardly that astonishing."

The *guy* who wrote it? "Ocean," I am convinced, belongs to a woman. A woman who despairs of understanding men. A woman gripped by scattershot anger—this I recognize!—at the ways of the world. "Have you found the paragraph?"

He reads. "'To correct my mistake I had to bring Anitya and Songsten back in.' Is this what you're after?"

I nod.

"'The literary stakes were high. If my lovers could not be saved, neither could I. If a deeper liberty continued to elude them, I would have no choice but to withdraw into the same ruined monastery, the same burnt-out temple.'"

Like a beam thrown upon an area of darkness, a vision crosses behind my eyes. A chapel in a snowstorm; blackbirds landing on a roof; a forgotten burial chamber. I stagger to the couch, brushing past him.

"You look terrible, Esther."

He isn't coming back, I think. Or do I say it?

"And can we please fire up the air? I'm melting here."

"You're in Asia now."

"Maybe so, but I'm also in a palatial flat on Old Peak Road. Suffice to say you can expect all the mod cons for the rent you're—" He stops. "What you just said there. You think so because of 'Ocean'?"

"All my fault," I say. "All my responsibility."

His mouth falls open. "You're serious? You can't be. Those are some words on a fucking page! Not even a newspaper article or a confirmed report."

Now I am the one who has information on Dominic Wilson, who knows the real story. Without ever stepping foot in Gyatso, either, let alone trading in nonsense about thin-air deliriums and elusive paradises. To explain myself, I ask Patrick to sit across from me. "I am Esther Ramos from Manila," I say. "Former domestic worker, now mother and housewife. I am Filipina and Catholic. Nice to make your acquaintance."

I expect him to pretend not to follow. Instead, he does me the honour of keeping his guard down. "Lucky you, Esther Ramos," he answers softly.

I wait.

He strikes a match, the flame a prayer candle in a side-altar, and lights a cigarette. "In Ireland, you see, I was a freak. As a child in Belfast, in this take-away my parents ran, and later at college in Dublin, among the Micks and Liams and Bridgets and Marys. To have tried playing the freedom fighter, the hard man, well, they'd have laughed me right out of town. 'Good one, wee yellow guy.' 'Give us a cod 'n' chip, Chinky boy.' In these parts, at least, as an honorary member of the Pearl River Chan clan, it is *conceivable* I might be a terrorist or a spy or a scholar or, why not, a journalist on the sly. Home, surely, is where they don't think of you as a pet. *And* where they have to take you in," he adds with a wistful smile.

He blows smoke upwards. That, too, reminds me of a church; a snuffer lowered onto a flame to allow a new candle to be lit, a newly departed soul to be commemorated. He is goading me, of course—even Dominic never dared indulge his habit in the apartment—but I swallow the fumes without comment. "Home is where your family live, Patrick," I answer. "Or where you make a family, if that is what you must do. A country cannot be a family. A race cannot be a house."

"Jesus," he says, pinching his tongue, "am I hearing this from you, of all people? A girl, like you said yourself, from the barrios of Manila? Member of the largest underclass on the planet? Skin is skin, Esther. It *is* the nationality in your passport. It *is* your address and postmark."

I recite to myself our Toronto address and telephone number. The phone rings.

"Leave it, for God's sake."

"It could be him."

"You just bloody well said it could *not* be—"

Allan Wu, from the surgery train charity. He has been penitent indeed; his unfortunate last call seems a year ago now. "Dominic?" I reply to his query. "No, I am afraid he is still away. But *we* think the project is excellent, and wish to show support for it."

He asks if I might be ready to contribute again.

"Let me think," I say.

Patrick has crossed to the door, seeking cool air from the landing. With a single motion he washes his face from chin to forehead and then applies the moisture to his hair. The cigarette, I note, has disappeared, most likely over the balcony railing.

I am still pondering how much to offer when a figure—a

stunning figure—pops into my head with the same certainty as our street name in Toronto. "How about fifty thousand Hong Kong dollars."

Allan Wu pauses and then translates the amount into American currency, in case I am still confused by the exchange. "Fifty K," I repeat with equal patience. "I know how much it is."

Next, he asks if I wish to dedicate the donation. That requires reflection as well. Ignoring Patrick, I examine our parquet floor. Then it happens again: the right words are on my lips, certain as prayers.

"You have a pen, Mr. Wu?"

He does.

"Write this: For Gina, of Assisi."

He needs help with the spelling.

"A-S-S-I-S-I, I think. A town in Italy."

Allan Wu thanks me, thanks us; he praises me, praises Dominic; he says he hopes we meet some day; he wishes me good night.

How many seconds before Patrick asks?

"His mother?" he says on the second count.

"Maybe I need to rest now for a few minutes."

"Her memory is so important to you right now?"

"Not to me," I answer.

He unfolds his arms and cups them before his crotch, a child sent to the principal's office for punishment. "Esther," he says, "here's a question even you won't have anticipated. No disrespect intended, understand. No insult, least of all. But I'm wondering, needing to know for my own plans and so forth, if, once this is all settled, I might, you know, stand a chance?"

"I cannot read minds."

"We're closer to each other in age, right? Also in background. And tell me you won't be needing a pair of hands around the house—wherever that house ends up being. With a baby on the way..."

Secretly, I want to hug him. Poor boy. Poor man. "Time for you to leave," I say instead.

He retreats into the landing.

"Please don't be angry with me," he says, both palms out.

His eyes are round and dark and more than wet; they are barrels of oil. Because he is about to weep or because he cannot, now or ever, weep? The usual enigma. The standard cover for the indulgence of desires.

A force, an energy, draws me through the kitchen to the shrine. The air is stifling, but the dark is shot through with light and even colour—gold and blue and the yellow-red of a pollution sunset. The same energy sits me on the cot, instructing that I close and put away Patrick's diary, and never again confuse a lost boy with a grown man. This is not a coffin, I think to myself. Nor a confessional. It is a cubicle in a "special" Manila hotel, where men drunk on beer bring the women they have nowhere else to take. Where lovers grunt and moan in a manner that is more than faintly mournful, a sort of keen.

The shrine is that place this evening. And here I am, alert and ready. No longer at the mercy of morning sickness, I cross back to the main washroom at the base of the stairs. I spray his cologne over my neck and breasts and brush a glob of his gel into my hair. Though my stomach flips once, the scents are electrifying and I stumble to my sex cubicle. He is there now, naked and erect, and he treats me with gruff tenderness, instructing that I change positions and please him in certain ways. He enfolds me from behind and, while we move, he charts a path of kisses from the curve of my shoulder to my collarbone, each one lingering, explosive. Thirsty, he tongues my nape. Starving, he takes the cross in his mouth.

How that night in October went:

Dominic suggested five thousand dollars. Nearly a thousand Canadian: twice our standard donation. I wondered if we could afford to give Allan Wu's project more—10K, say. I asked not because the charity was especially worthy but on account of how the train surgery so obviously, and so sweetly, affected him. The humility in his voice and recognition in his eyes.

Ten thousand dollars would be no problem, he agreed. We co-signed the cheque.

And then went to bed. And finally talked about our anxieties, some of our fears.

Not a dream? Not a fantasy?

He asked me to say his name.

Dominhic! Dominhic!

But then the energy dissipates and she sits abandoned. Flicking on the lamp, she makes a brief raid of all four walls of graffiti: Bereaved Parents Hang Themselves. Amah Dead From Plunge. Filipino Killed in Accident. Domestic Worker Accused. *She claws at the clippings less in rage than in panic, littering the cot with shreds of yesterday's mess and last week's sob story, some small tragedy from a month ago. She is making noise, apparently—when she wipes her face with her undershirt it comes back tear-stained—for soon she is joined by a wailing daughter and a son whose deer-caught-in-headlights expression is so lovely she smiles.*

She holds them too tight, and they complain. She kisses them too sloppily, and they say, "Stop, Mommy, please!" Their skin, rosewater. Their hair, talcum.

"You smell like Daddy," Gaby says.

"And you look like him," she replies. "Both of you."

She decides they are lucky to have come through the peril. Having thanked God for this, she declares the airless cubicle the only secure spot in Hong Kong. Outside, she now believes, is a reckless sky; outside is no shelter, no ceiling. They should never leave the shrine. Sleep cosy and comfortable in the narrow bed. Buy a hot-plate to cook noodles and eggs.

Knock, knock.

"Who's there?" she says, happy to play an innocent game.

Gabriella stares at her in puzzlement.

"Well, who's there, Gaby?"

Knock, knock.

"Aren't you going to get it?" Mike asks.

"Get what?"

"You're funny, Mom."

Knock, knock.

It sinks in. Why not ring the bell? Why at this hour? "Stay here," she orders them. "Until I return for you."

"But it's boiling!"

"Stay here," she repeats, "and I'll tell you a wonderful secret when I get back."

"Hurry," her daughter says.

She crosses the kitchen into the dining room. Her legs know the route, otherwise she could not manage it. A hand settles over her stomach. Her eyes swim.

She answers the knock.

Acknowledgments

In 1989, while living in Beijing, I read a short story by a young Tibetan writer. The story was called "A Soul in Bondage" and the author went by the pen name Tashi Dawa. A year later I spent an hour with Tashi Dawa in a room in Lhasa. He offered coffee. He owned a collie that seemed much friendlier than most dogs in the capital. Congruences between fact and fiction pretty much end there, but the encounter eventually sparked *House on Fire*.

For their help and encouragement, I am grateful to Mark Abley, Annie Beer, David Manicom, Larissa Sangmo, Mark Kingwell, and Ian Jamieson. For efforts well beyond the call of duty and friendship, special thanks to Iris Tupholme, Jan Whitford, Mary Ladky, and Guy Lawson.